PENGUIN BOOKS

The Lark

E. Nesbit was born in Surrey in 1858. A world-famous children's author, her works include *The Railway Children* and *Five Children and It*. She also wrote several works of fiction for adults. With her husband, Hubert Bland, she was one of the founding members of the socialist Fabian Society; their household became a centre of the socialist and literary circles of the times. She died in 1924.

Penelope Lively is the author of many prize-winning novels and short-story collections for both adults and children. She has twice been shortlisted for the Booker Prize for her novels *The Road to Lichfield* and *According to Mark*. She later won the 1987 Booker Prize for her highly acclaimed novel *Moon Tiger*. Her other books include *Oleander, Jacaranda*, a memoir of her childhood in Egypt, *Heat Wave*, *A House Unlocked*, *The Photograph*, *Making It Up*, *Consequences*, *Family Album*, which was shortlisted for the 2009 Costa Novel Award, and *How It All Began*. She was appointed CBE in the 2001 New Year's Honours List, and DBE in 2012. Penelope Lively lives in London.

The Lark

With an introduction by Penelope Lively

E. NESBIT

PENGUIN BOOKS

Random House UK

First published in 1922 by Hutchinson & Co.
First published with a new introduction in Great Britain by Penguin Books 2018
001

Introduction copyright © Penelope Lively, 2018

The moral right of the copyright holders has been asserted

Set in 11/13 pt Bembo Book MT Std
Typeset by Jouve (UK), Milton Keynes
Printed in Great Britain by Clays Ltd, St Ives plc

A CIP catalogue record for this book is available from the British Library

ISBN: 978-0-241-98348-5

www.greenpenguin.co.uk

MIX
Paper from
responsible sources
FSC® C018179

FSC
www.fsc.org

Penguin Random House is committed to a
sustainable future for our business, our readers
and our planet. This book is made from Forest
Stewardship Council® certified paper.

'Oh, Pallas, take your owl away,
And let us have a lark instead!'

Thomas Hood

Introduction

Edith Nesbit is known today only for her children's books. *The Lark* is one of her eleven novels for adults; to read it is to recognize at once the Nesbit voice – her humour, her turn of phrase – slightly adjusted for an adult readership. It is an engaging period piece, replete with all the attitudes and assumptions of the day, and shot through with the light-hearted Nesbit touch.

That inherent gaiety seems valiant; her life was far from easy. Married to a philandering husband, she had five children, one of whom died at fifteen, and accepted into the family two more of her husband's by a mistress who was also absorbed as housekeeper and secretary. Alongside his infidelity, Hubert Bland was also apparently incapable of earning a living, which accounts in part for Nesbit's vast working output: forty books for children, eleven adult novels and thirteen collections of short stories, a great deal of poetry. She *had* to write. Maybe we should be obliquely grateful to Hubert Bland for the joys of *The Wouldbegoods, Five Children and It, The Phoenix and the Carpet*, and all the rest. She and Bland were both followers of William Morris and members of the Fabian Society. Nesbit wrote and lectured on socialism in the 1880s: they entertained lavishly and casually; their home was seen as a bohemian retreat.

So she was out of step in many ways with the ethos of the day. That said, *The Lark*, published in 1922, reflects absolutely the social mores of that time. The nineteen-year-old girls Jane and Lucilla, who are at the centre of the story, have a problem because they are living alone together and carrying on a business without a chaperone, class distinctions are richly manifest, the various working-class characters, sympathetically portrayed, have an element of stereotype in both speech and attitudes, and there is a fine contempt for those perceived as *nouveau riche*. The language of the girls and their associates is nicely peppered with contemporary jargon: people make asses of themselves, rag each other, are duffers or bricks, have a ripping time. Reading *The Lark*, you are plunged back into the early twentieth century.

The crux of the story is itself something of a period set piece: genteel young women deprived of their inheritance and obliged to set up in business. But then Nesbit has fun with the situation: the girls try flower-selling, fail at that and take in paying guests, who are perfect fodder for a series of well-paced scenes of farce. Person after person turns out not to be what or who they had seemed to be, and of course eventually all is nicely resolved and the girls rewarded for their pluck and determination. Throughout, there has been emphasis on the virtue of picking yourself up, making the best of things, treating adverse circumstances as 'a lark': hence the title. It is impossible not to see a reflection of what must have been Nesbit's own attitudes towards the challenges of her life. That alone, apart from its intrinsic merit as a charming and brilliantly entertaining novel, makes *The Lark* a significant work amid her prolific output.

Penelope Lively

Chapter I

'You wouldn't dare!'

'Wouldn't I? That's all you know!'

'You mustn't dare her,' said a third voice anxiously from the top of the library steps; 'if you dare her she'll do it as sure as Fate.'

The one who must not be dared looked up and laughed. The golden light of midsummer afternoon falling through the tall library windows embroidered new patterns on the mellow Persian carpets, and touched to a dusky splendour the shelves on shelves of old calf and morocco, where here and there gilded lettering shone like rows of little sparks. It touched also the hair of the girl who must not be dared; she sat cross-legged on the floor among a heap of books, nursing a fat quarto volume with onyx-inlaid clasps and bosses, and touched the hair into glory, turning it from plain brown, which was its everyday colour, to a red gold halo which became her small white face very well.

'Fate, indeed!' she said. 'Why, the whole thing's Fate. Emmeline asks us here — good old Emmy! — because we'd nowhere to go when everybody got mumps. I shall always respect mumps for getting us this extra month's holiday. I wish it had a prettier name — Mompessa, or something like that; we have the time of our lives amid all this ancestral splendour.' She indicated the great beams and tall windows of the library with a gesture full of appreciation. 'No, don't interrupt. I'm telling the story. Angel Emmeline protects us from the footman and doesn't let the butler trample on us. She's given us the run of the baronial halls, and the stately ballroom, and the bed where Queen Elizabeth slept, and the library that came over with the Conqueror. We grub about and we find *this*, and because this isn't the first library I've been in I happen to be able to read it.' She thumped the book on her lap. 'Don't tell me it's not Fate. Fate arranged it all. Fate meant me to try the spell. And I mean to. And as for not daring – pooh, my darling Emmeline, pooh! . . . Likewise pshaw!' she added pensively.

Emmeline smiled with calm indulgence. She was stout, squarely-made, plain-faced, kind-eyed, with a long, thick, mouse-coloured pigtail and small, white, well-kept hands. She began to pick up her books one by one and to put them back in their proper places on the shelves.

'It's all very well to say "pooh!"' she said.

'*And* "pshaw!"' the not-to-be-dared interpolated.

'My Aunt Emmeline tried it. *A* spell – and I expect it was that very one; at least, she set out to try it, but she lost her way in the wood. The night was very dark, and she gave it up, and came back, and when she got to the garden gate she couldn't open it and couldn't find the handle. And then the moon came out, and she found it was the door of the mausoleum in the park she was trying to get in at.'

'Shut up!' said the girl on the top of the steps, a long-legged, long-armed, long-nosed, long-chinned girl rather like a well-bred filly. 'Jane, do say you won't do it. Not after that, will you?'

'It's a perfectly horrid story,' said Jane, unmoved, 'but you can't frighten me in that way, Emmeline. However, it decides me to have lights. Those fairy lights and Chinese lanterns you had for what you called the "little" dance – I suppose they're somewhere about. Do you know where, exactly?' She urged the question with a firm hand-grasp.

'Don't pinch,' said Emmeline, disengaging her ankle. 'You can have the lights. But we shouldn't be allowed to do it.'

'Who's going to be asked to allow anything?' Jane said innocently. 'Hasn't Fate arranged it all? Aren't all the grown-ups going to the Duchess's grand fête and gala – fireworks and refreshments free?'

'They're going to Lady Hendon's garden-party and dance, if that's what you mean,' said Emmeline, rather coldly.

'That's right – stand by your class. Ah, these old aristocrats!' said Jane.

'Lord Hendon was beer, wasn't he?' Lucilla asked from the steps. 'Or was it bacon? He looks rather like a ham himself.'

'Well, anyhow, beer or bacon or ham, all the grown-ups will be out of the way. We're too young for these frantic dissipations. By the way' – her straight forehead puckered itself anxiously – 'I'm not too young to try *that*, am I? It says nothing about age in the book. It just says "any young maid or young bachelor". I was fifteen last June.'

'In James the First's time, when this book was born, girls were married at fifteen,' Lucilla reassured her, 'but I do hope you won't let that encourage you.'

'I don't need encouragement. I'm just going to. I'll try that spell or I'll know the reason why. Don't be surly, Emmy; let's go down and arrange the lanterns now while the sun's shining, and get the candles and matches and have it all ready. Then we'll have that nice little quiet dinner your dear mother's ordered for us, and go to bed early just as she said. And then get up again. And then . . .'

'Don't,' said Lucilla.

'But I shall,' said Jane.

'Very well,' said Lucilla with an air of finality, coming down the steps; 'we have told you not to in at least seven different ways, because it was our duty, but if you really mean to – well, do, then! And I think it will be no end of a spree – if you don't walk into the mausoleum and begin to scream and bring the retainers down on us, or do anything else silly that'll get Emmy into rows.'

'She won't do that,' said Emmeline. 'We shan't go beyond the park. Nobody minds anything if we don't go outside. Besides, no one will know, if Jane manages it as well as she mostly does manage things.'

'Miss Jane Quested's Meretricious Magic. Manager, or General, Jane,' said Jane, displaying herself as she rose with the square book under her arm. 'I'm going to take this up to my room and learn the spell off by heart. It wouldn't do to have any mistakes, would it? I may take it?'

'You may take anything – but only on one condition,' said Emmeline firmly.

3

'Conditions? How cautious and sordid! What condition?'

'That if you do see anything you'll tell us exactly what it was like. You never can tell what it will be that you see. Sometimes you see a shroud, or skeleton, or a coffin, I believe, if you're to die a maid.'

Jane laughed.

'What a merry companion you are, Emmy; not a dull moment when you're about! Pity it's alone or not at all. I should have loved to have you with me to-night to keep my spirits up with your cheery chatter. But, alas! it can't be. Don't look so glum.

> '"Come, Pallas, take your owl away,
> And let us have a lark instead!"'

'If you call this a lark,' said Emmeline, 'I don't.'

'Now look here, Em,' said Jane firmly; 'if you don't want me to do it, really I won't. You've been such a brick to us. Say the word and I'll chuck it. I really will. Don't look so glum. I'm not wholly lost to all gratitude and proper feeling.'

'Oh, don't chuck it *now*!' pleaded Lucilla, 'just when Emmy and I have reconciled our yeasty consciences to the idea.'

'Shall I chuck it, Emmy?' Jane persisted. 'Shall I?'

'No,' said Emmeline. 'And stop talking about gratitude. And I won't have your old owls thrown in my face for the rest of my life. Let's have the lark.'

If Jane, Lucilla, and Emmeline had not been debarred by their fifteen, fourteen, and sixteen years from the enjoyment of Lady Hendon's hospitality they would have had the pleasure of meeting — or at least, for it was a very big garden-party, they might have had the pleasure of meeting — the young man whom it is now my privilege to introduce to you.

John Rochester was young and, I am sorry to say, handsome. Sorry, because handsome men are, as a rule, so very stupid and so very vain. Still, there must be some exceptions to every rule. John Rochester was one of these exceptions: he was neither vain nor stupid. In fact he was more than rather clever, especially at his own game, which was engineering. Brains and beauty were not his only advantages. He had brains, beauty, and brawn – an almost irresistible combination. That is the bright side of the shield. The black side is this: he was not so tall, by three inches, as he could have wished to be, he had very big ambitions, very little money, very much less parsimony, and a temper.

He also had a mother who powdered too much, rouged rather too brightly, and appeared to govern almost her whole life by the consideration of 'what people would say'. She was quite a good mother in other respects, and John Rochester was quite fond of her. It was she who dragged him to this garden-party – that is to say, it was she who suggested it as an agreeable way of occupying the last day of the short holiday which he was spending with her. The young man himself would have preferred to loaf about in flannels and make himself useful by attacking the green-fly on the roses in his mother's garden with clouds of that smoke so hopefully supposed to be fatal to aphides. But Mrs Rochester thought otherwise.

'You ought to go,' she said at breakfast. 'The Hendons may be very useful to you in your career.'

'I wish these pork-butchers wouldn't use English place-names,' he said, taking more honey. 'Why can't they stick to their age-old family names? I shouldn't mind Lord Isaacs, or Lord Smith, or Lord – what was this chap's name? – oh yes, Lord Hoggenheimer – but Lord Hendon! Yes, thank you, half a cup. This is a very jolly little place you've got here. Have you taken it for the whole of the summer?'

'Yes, dear, you know I have, so don't try to turn the subject. Even if his name were still Hoggenheimer, Lord Hendon might be useful to you. He's something very important in the city.'

'Perhaps I shall meet him some other time, when he'll be able to realise my existence and be attracted by my interesting personality. He couldn't do that at a crowded garden-party, you know.'

'You don't know Lord Hendon,' she told him; 'he could do

anything anywhere. Why, he once bought a gold-mine from a man he met quite casually in the fish department of the Army and Navy Stores.'

'Still keeps his old villa-dwelling habits? Brings home a little bit of fish to placate the missus when he's going to be late home. Now I respect him for that – most men bring flowers or diamonds.'

'Don't be silly,' said his mother serenely. 'I want you to meet him, and that ought to be enough. Besides, I've got a new frock on purpose; crêpe-de-chine in about six shades of heliotrope and pink and blue.'

'Oh,' said John, 'of course that settles it.'

And indeed, he felt it did.

'And a new hat,' she went on. 'It really is a dream. So you *will* go?'

'All right, dear,' he said, 'I'll go, since you've set your heart and your frock and your hat on it. I must catch a train to-night, though, so I'll send my traps to the station, and then I can go straight from Lord Hoggenheimer's. I know you won't want to leave as long as there's a note left in the band.'

'Yes, that will be best,' she agreed; 'and now that's settled comfortably, I want to have a little quiet talk with you.'

'May I smoke?' he asked, at once plunged in dejection. He knew his mother's little quiet talks.

'Of course you may smoke, if it doesn't distract your attention, because what I've got to say is very serious indeed. I've been thinking things over for a long time; you mustn't suppose this is a new idea. You know, my darling boy, my little income dies with me. Yes, I know you are getting on very nicely in your profession, but it only advances you financially, and that very slowly. There's no *social* advancement in it.'

'I shall invent something some of these days, and then you can have all the social and financial advancement you want,' he said rather bitterly.

'That's another point. You have no *time* for your inventions – I'm sure you've often told me so. You want time, and you want money, and if you don't want social advancement your poor old mother wants it for you.'

'Well?' he said, now very much on his guard.

'Think what it would be like,' she went on, 'never to have to work for money — just to have that workshop you've so often talked about, and just look in and do a little inventing there whenever you felt inclined. No bothers, no interruptions — entirely your own master. And all the steel things you want always handy.'

'A lovely and accurate picture of an inventor's life!' he laughed.

'It's nothing to laugh about,' she said; 'because I have an idea. Why shouldn't you marry? Some nice girl whom you really like and who has money.'

'When I marry,' he said, getting up and standing with his back to the ferns in the fireplace, 'it won't be to live on my wife.'

'Of *course* not,' she agreed; 'that would be dreadfully shocking. I quite see that, darling. But just to begin with — till you bring off your first great invention — so that your mind could be quite free for wheels and cogs and springs and strains and levers and things. Then afterwards, when your royalties begin to come in, you could repay her a thousandfold for any little help she'd been able to give you.'

'You've thought it all out very thoroughly, and you put it very convincingly,' he said, and laughed again. 'But when I marry, my dear mother, I think it would be more interesting to be in love with my wife.'

'Then I'm afraid you'll never marry,' she said very gravely. 'You're twenty-five, and you've never been in love yet.'

'You can't possibly know that,' he said quickly. And still more quickly she answered:

'You can't possibly deny it.'

He could not, it was true. There seemed to be nothing to do but to laugh again. So he laughed. Then he said:

'Then the time must soon come when I shall.'

'I don't think so,' said his mother, speaking as one who knows. 'Your dear father once told me he had never been in love in his life. Of course, he led me to believe otherwise when we first became engaged, and it is true that he was in one of his tempers when he said it. But it was true for all that. I knew it was true before he said it, if you understand, only until he said it I didn't know I knew it.'

She got up rather hurriedly and walked to the window, and stood swinging the little ivory acorn that held the knob of the blind-cord. 'You see, dear, I could always tell when he was telling the truth. He didn't always, I am sorry to say. No, you needn't say, "Poor mother". We were quite as happy as most people. Marriages aren't really unhappy when one of the people is kind and the other is loving. And I was quite fond of him. And in the marriage I hope you'll make there'll be plenty of love on one side at least.'

'Mother, don't.'

'I'm quite sure of what I say.' She turned and faced him, and her face showed sharp and old under her powder. 'You're exactly like your father. Your face, your voice, your foot-step, your temper — even that aggravating way you have of tilting your chair . . .'

The chair went down with a bang.

'There are some men who never fall in love. But they need companionship and a home. And here's a really good nice girl who worships the ground you walk on.'

'Nonsense!' he put in, and almost felt as though he were blushing.

'Well, judge for yourself. Now I've told you, you *can* judge. You can make this nice girl happy and make yourself comfortable for life. Now don't say anything. All I want you to promise me is that you'll think it over. No, don't say anything. Don't speak. Think. Think hard. You'll never find a wife more suited to you in every way than Hilda Antrobus.'

'Hilda Antrobus! —' he was beginning, but she came swiftly to him and put her hand over his mouth. A soft little hand, adequately ringed and scented with lavender.

'Not a word; just promise me you'll think it over. And when you see her, notice. She'll be there to-day.'

'Oh Lord!' said John Rochester, looking towards the door.

'Say you'll think it over.'

'You haven't said anything to *her* about it?'

'My darling boy! As if I should! Now just promise to think it over.'

'Oh, very well, I'll think it over all right,' he said. 'And now let's drop it, shall we?'

'By all means – not another word!' she answered. 'You're a dear, good, clever boy, and you deserve to be happy, if ever a boy did, and if you and that nice Hilda . . .'

But he had escaped.

He did not mean to think it over. But he found that he could think of nothing else; and when on the lawn at Hendon Towers among the moving kaleidoscope of strangers he suddenly met Miss Antrobus, and saw the quite pretty blush and smile that lighted the quite plain face of Miss Antrobus as she greeted him, he felt that he had never really seen the girl before. Suppose he actually were like his father, in that respect as in others? Suppose he were the sort of man who cannot ever fall in love, and who yet wanted a home, companionship – leisure too (that thought would slip in)? Supposing Hilda really cared? . . . Why then . . . why then . . .

Supposing she really cared? The thought touched him oddly. He had never been in love with any woman, but he had been, for long enough, in love with love. He knew well enough what love must be; and if this girl cared . . . why, then, he could make her happy, make his mother happy, and set free that caged bird in him that year in and year out beat its wings against the constraining bars of an enforced activity that was not the activity he longed for, but one enforced by circumstances and the will of others. If only the inventive genius that he felt penned in him could take free flight! Marrying for money had not a pleasant sound, but this would be marrying for freedom and happiness – his freedom, her happiness, and, perhaps in the end, his own. To this her money would be a means. It would never be an end in itself. That was where baseness would have been.

Under the influence of these sentiments he found himself smiling kindly at Miss Antrobus in her simple, expensive dress of unbecoming blue silk, and saying, 'How jolly to meet you here!'

It was the tenderest speech he had ever made to her; and, having made it, he could think of nothing else to say. A fleeting wonder crossed his mind: what would it be like to sit at table for half a lifetime, opposite a woman to whom one could think of nothing to say? But she herself was speaking.

'It *is* nice to see you,' she said; 'and what a beautiful day, too!'

The naïveté of her words touched him again.

'Come,' he said, 'let's get away from the crowd and explore. Do you know your way about?'

'I'm staying here,' she said. 'Come and see the ruins. Oh, they're not real ruins, but Lord Hendon thought they'd look pretty. And they do. I shouldn't like antiquarians and people like that to hear me say so; but they do, especially now the ivy's growing so nicely. Come and look.'

They moved off. It was the happiest moment she had ever known.

Later in the day Miss Antrobus and Mrs Rochester found themselves together on the slope of the beech wood. There is a wooden seat here from which you look out across the Kentish valley to the blue of the hills beyond. Away to the right was the house, its lawns gay with the many-coloured patchwork of the guests.

'Well, dear?' said the elder woman; her voice was both very gentle and very alert.

'Well?' said the girl awkwardly.

'He's been paying you a good deal of attention, hasn't he? You seem to have been a good deal together.'

'He has been very kind,' said Miss Antrobus, and put her gloved fingers to her burning cheeks. 'Dear Mrs Rochester – I feel so ashamed. I wish you'd never found it out.'

'Why should you be ashamed?' purred Mrs Rochester suavely. '*I* can only be proud that you care for my boy. And I know he likes you very much. And he has never cared for anyone else.'

'You haven't said anything to him about it?' the heiress asked with quick suspicion.

'My darling girl! As if I should,' the mother answered earnestly.

'He's very . . . well, not exactly shy – and modest isn't exactly the word either. I mean he's not vain – he's not the sort of man who would think he could carry all before him; not one of our conquerors, you know. He'll need encouraging. No – I don't mean exactly that, but I don't think you ought to disguise from him that you *like* him.'

'I don't, really I don't,' said Miss Antrobus, not knowing at all how truly she spoke.

'That's right; and don't let me see tears in those pretty eyes – there's nothing to be sad about. Life's just beginning for you, and I'm certain it will be a beautiful life, full of love and happiness.'

'You *are* good to me,' said the girl, and her tears brimmed over. She pulled out her handkerchief.

'*Dab* your eyes, dearest,' said Mrs Rochester hastily, 'don't rub. It makes them red. If you gently dab, those tears will only make them brighter.'

'You *are* good to me,' said Miss Antrobus, dabbing obediently at her red-rimmed wet pale blue eyes. And for the rest of the day his mother's words rang in her ears: 'Your pretty eyes. Your pretty eyes.'

John Rochester walked from Hendon Towers to the station. He walked through the woods, partly because the way was shorter and partly because it was quieter. Motors hooted and stank along the high road, and he had no fancy for being pursued by goggled acquaintances offering lifts. The way through the wood was shorter, but it was also sinuous. He missed his way, and, as a direct consequence, missed his train. He saw it coming, ran, saw it retreat, and arrived at the station with just enough breath left to say 'Damn!'

The porters were sympathetic. Yes, that was the last train. And the Lechmere Arms was quite handy. Very good beds, they believed. Oh, the gentleman wanted to be in London early in the morning? Well, there was a goods train at 3.15, if the gentleman didn't mind travelling in the guard's van? The gentleman did not? Good; that would be all right then, and thank you very much sir, they were sure.

Rochester walked out of the station. He had no intention of

returning to his mother's house. Miss Antrobus, who that morning had been little more than a name and a face to him, was now a person whom he did not want to discuss with his mother or anyone else. He was beginning to like her; he felt that some day he might begin to feel affection for her. She was a straightforward, simple little soul. Not at all a bad sort.

And he knew now that she did care; which gave one quite a different feeling for her. He had felt nothing but a sort of awkwardness when his mother had told him this. But now that Miss Antrobus had told him with her own face and voice, and the light that shone in them at his presence, things were quite otherwise.

He would go back into the woods and think, perhaps rest on that thick moss under the big beech trees. The woods would be very beautiful under this rising moon. The night was hot, the roads dusty; the woods would be sweet and fresh. He got over the stile and passed under the arch of hazel and sweet chestnuts. The moonlight dappled the grassy ride ahead of him. The cool, fresh leaves brushed now and then against his hands. He did not sit down; he walked on thinking, thinking. And all his thoughts were of the ingenuous heiress to whom till now he had never given a thought. Yes, one might grow quite fond of her; he was sure of it. And the conviction seemed to wash him clean of sordid soil which the idea of 'marrying for money' does beyond doubt bring with it. Supposing one grew to be honestly fond? He walked on, bareheaded, through the dew and the moonlight, keeping now to the straight rides and essaying no by-paths.

How still the wood was; how dark in its shadows; how greenly silver where the moonbeams touched it! Peace wrapped him like a cloak; perhaps love ought to be like that – quiet, unchanging affection, a community of interests, mutual kindness . . . none of that wild unrest, that passion of longing, that triumph of possession which men call love . . . but just mutual kindness – peace. He seemed to be learning much.

'Everything seems to be deciding itself here,' he said, sinking deeper into the peace of those silent, moonlit woods.

And then suddenly he saw a light that was not moonlight — a mellow, yellow light deepening to orange. It was not the light from any house windows, it was too diffused. It was not the light of the festal illuminations at the Towers, it was too near. What we call idle curiosity turned his feet towards it. It gleamed through the leaves, almost vanished, reappeared. He made straight for it through the wood; briars tore at him, hazel switches stung hands and face; he pressed on, only to be checked at last by an oak fence. He vaulted it; and now were no more brambles, but smooth green sward under his feet; and no close-clinging woods, but space, set with trees and bushes in groups. He went towards the light, but cautiously, for he perceived that he was not now in a place where any and every one had a right to be. Under cover of a clump of huge rhododendron he drew quite near to the light, parted very carefully and silently the resilient boughs and peered through.

He saw a glade, ringed round with rhododendrons and azaleas, their big heads of bloom glistening in the wan light cast from the Japanese lanterns that hung like golden incandescent fruit from the branches of the fir-trees. In the middle of the glade a ring of fairy lights shining like giant glow-worms were set out upon the turf.

In the middle of the ring stood a girl, slender, still, silent. Her gown was white and straight and reached to her feet; her white, elfish face was set with stern resolution. On her dark hair shone a crown of starry golden flowers. On her faintly moulded breast lay a kindred blossom; two more golden star-flowers she held in her hands. She stood there, silent. There was no one else. Among the trees under the moon he and she were alone together.

He held his breath. A dull, heavy, resonant, metallic sound startled his heart to a quick fluttering. The repetition of the sound reassured him. It was the clock of Lechmere Church beating out the hour — midnight.

The sound had startled the girl-child within the ring of fairy lights. The resolution of her face broke up into fear that rippled quickly into something like the shadow of a smile. Then she stood listening, and, as the echo of the last bell-beat died away, she began to speak. Plain and distinct, her words came to him in the clearest, finest, most charming voice in the world.

> 'O, good Saint John, now condescend
> For to be a maiden's friend.
> On your feast a maid stands here
> With your weed in breast and hair.
> Good Saint John, now to me show
> Portents plain of weal or woe.
> If I am to die a maid,
> Let white flowers be round me spread;
> But if I a bride shall be,
> Let me now my true love see.'

The voice ceased, and then, 'Oh!' it said, with an indescribable inflection. Fear, surprise, pride, joy, and something else mingled in it. Then there was silence. She stood like a young fawn at gaze. And her eyes met his. For, as she had spoken her spell, he, in listening, had forgotten caution and had let his face pass the guard of the shining leaves and blossoms. So that now they stood looking at each other across the green sward and the little green lights. Her eyes were wide with wonder, and beautiful with the light of dreams come true. Still as a statue she stood, in her white robe and her golden garland. It was he who moved first. Slowly he drew back, slowly the leaves closed between his face and hers. Yet he could still see her, but she could no longer see him.

And when she could no longer see him the charm broke that had held her moveless. She put her hands to her head, drew a long breath, and called aloud:

'Emmy, Emmy, quick!'

And at that there was a sound of running footsteps, and almost at once two other girls came flying down the hill into the glade and ran to her. She clung to them without words.

'There,' said one, with soothing voice and gentle pattings, 'you've frightened yourself to death – I knew you would.'

But the other said, 'She has seen something.'

Then said the first, 'You promised to tell.'

'I will tell,' said the girl with the starry flowers and the starry eyes, and freed herself. 'I've seen *him*,' she said in a strange little clear voice.

'You haven't! What was he like?'

'Like a . . . I don't know . . . not like anyone real. Like a Greek god . . .' said the child with the gold-flower crown.

And at that Rochester drew back and fled very quickly and quietly across the dewy turf.

He had meant to disclose himself, to beg pardon for his involuntary trespass, to scatter the mists of magic and bring everything back to the nice, sensible, commonplace that frightens no one — but he could not do it now. No man could. What man could walk out of a clump of rhododendrons at midnight into a magic circle of little green lamps and say, in cold blood, to a group of schoolgirls: 'I am the Greek god to whom this lady has referred'? It was impossible. The only thing he could do was to go away as quietly and as quickly as might be. He crept along the fence till he found a narrow swing gate and squeezed through it. Then he looked back. The golden lights were gone. All was moonlight and silence. The whole thing might well have been a dream. To all intents and purposes it was a dream. He did not know who the girl was into whose eyes he had gazed — who had gazed into his and thought him a god. He probably would never know, would never see her again.

'Certainly I shall never see her again,' he said. He also said: 'But I will never marry Miss Antrobus.'

Chapter II

Jane Quested was a schoolgirl when the war began, and she was a schoolgirl when it ended. So was her cousin Lucilla. Explanations are tiresome, but inevitable. Even on the stage people draw their chairs together, and one tells the other – for your benefit – what both of them must know perfectly well, beginning, probably: 'It was just such a stormy night as this, twenty years ago, my dear wife, when that mysterious stranger . . .' or 'I often think of the secret marriage of the Duchess, when you and I – I her butler and you her maid – were sworn by Her Grace to eternal secrecy. The circumstances, you will remember, are these . . .' And then he tells you all about it. As I will now tell you. So let us face the explanations, which are really short and simple.

Jane Quested's father, who was also Lucilla's uncle, was in India. He had nothing but his pay, which he found insufficient. A great-aunt had left Jane quite a pleasant little fortune – nothing dazzling, but enough to keep the wolf from the door of a reasonably prosperous home. This little fortune, in charge of a trustee, a solicitor, was tied up and secured by all those arts and crafts which lawyers could devise and execute to protect it from impecunious fathers. It was to be Jane's when she reached the age of reason as defined by law. To Lucilla the same relative had left the same competence.

When war broke out the cousins were at school in Devonshire, and to both father and trustee it seemed desirable that they should stay there for the duration of the war. The father had no wish that his daughter should undertake a long and perilous journey merely to embarrass him in his Eastern housekeeping – and, to the trustee, school seemed, for a thousand reasons, the best place for Lucilla and Jane. So at school they had stayed, and knitted socks and sweaters for the army and navy, and heard selections from the papers read aloud by careful governesses, seeing and hearing as little of the war as any English-speaking young women in the world. Of course they thrilled at our disasters, triumphed in our successes, pitied and prayed for the poor soldiers and sailors, execrated our enemies, and idealised our Allies. But it was all to them very far away; it hardly came near them, never touched them, till Jane's father died like a hero in Mesopotamia, leaving her his heroism to glorify her sorrow. Even then it was only as though an echo of the thunder of the waves of war had somehow reached the quiet, ordered house in Devonshire.

When the war ended Jane was nineteen. She felt incredibly grown up. For two years she and Lucilla had devoted the whole of their fortnightly letters to their trustee – now their guardian – to entreaties to be allowed to leave school.

'And he never takes the least notice,' Jane said to Lucilla on the first day of the summer holidays; 'he just sends boxes of chocs., and bottles of scent, and embroidered handkerchiefs, and books and things, and tells us to be good girls and complete our studies and fit ourselves for the battle of life. Not much battle, thank goodness! I heard the Head once asking Miss Graves, in that "life is real, life is earnest" voice of hers, what she thought was the most beautiful thing in the world. And Gravy said, "The most beautiful thing in the world? A small but settled income, I think. And no work." The Head was sick.'

'I don't mind work so much,' said Lucilla, going on with her knitting, 'so long as you don't have to do the sort of work other people say you must. If I *had* to do this I should hate it.' She heaved up the lumpish grey mass on her lap. 'As it is, I like it.'

'I don't like anything here,' said Jane; 'we're wasting our youth – our precious, golden, unreturning youth. I want to do things and see the world.'

'Please, miss,' said a maid at the door, 'the post is in, and you're both to go and see *Her*. I hope it ain't bad trouble,' she added sympathetically; 'and afterwards, if there's anything I can do . . . There's something up, miss. There was a letter for you, and she kep' it back at breakfast – and one for you, miss, too. It isn't safe to let 'em write by post, it really isn't.'

'To let who write, Gladys?'

'The young men as you walks out with,' Gladys explained kindly. 'At least, of course you young ladies don't walk out, being kept alive in a cage, so to speak, but I expect it's the same at heart. I gets the confectioner's girl to take in *my* letters,' she added with simple pride. 'It's best to be on the safe side in a house full of old cats like this here. Is he dark or fair, miss – yours I mean?' she suddenly asked Jane.

'My what?'

'Your young man.'

'I don't know,' said Jane. 'I haven't got a young man yet.'

'Then the letter can't be from him,' said Gladys, with irresistible logic.

'No, it certainly can't. But it might be from somebody else. In fact it must. I wonder how long she means to keep us in suspense? When are we to go and see her? After dinner?'

'*Oh no.* She is looking forward to the blow-up she's getting ready for you to give her an appetite for dinner. Do you know, miss, I shouldn't wonder if it was a nonny-mous letter from a true friend, or "one who has only seen you in church but wants to know you better", or "a respectable admirer who picked up your umbrella". Thursday week as you got off the tram. Oh, *I* saw him, miss. It was my afternoon out.'

'I always enjoy your conversation, Gladys,' said Lucilla gravely, 'but have you no work to do this morning?'

'Oh, very well'; the round, pink face of Gladys clouded over, and she tossed her head. 'Just as *you* please, miss, I'm sure. I can take a hint as well as anybody. I never intrude and I never say a word more than needful. If my room's preferred to my company I never linger. But oh, I say, miss, have either of you noticed the new baker's boy? He's just like a picture, blue eyes and golden curls, six feet high and four medals, and he can talk French. He says lots of it. I don't know exactly what it means, but he has such expressing eyes.'

'Gladys, begone!' cried Jane; 'but before you go just tell us *when* we're to go to the Head.'

'I've told you a dozen times, if once,' said Gladys reproachfully, 'that you're not to lose a moment. I shouldn't even wait to comb my hair or powder my nose if I was you, miss. She's waiting for you in her own room, and I was to tell you to go down at once. And my advice is, you go and get it over. Because why . . .'

They found the Headmistress in her sitting-room — the room so well adapted to the beguiling of parents, the room so tasteful and yet so learned-looking — books, flowers, autotypes from Watts and Burne-Jones, busts of Mozart and Socrates; 'all kinds of culti-vated tastes catered for,' as Jane used to say.

The Head was not looking pleased. She held in her hand three letters, and said, 'Be seated,' without looking at her pupils. Then she tapped one of the letters, the open one, on the neat fumed-oak writing-table before her, looked out of her window, and asked:

'Had you any idea of this?'

'What?' Jane asked.

'*Of* what,' corrected the Head mechanically. 'Perhaps you had better read your letters.' She handed a square, hand-made envelope to each. There was the sound of torn and rustling paper. The canary in the window rustled sympathetically among his sand and groundsel.

'Well?' said the Head. 'I suppose your letter contains the same news as mine?'

'I suppose so, Miss James,' said Jane. 'Mine — but you'd better read it, perhaps.'

Miss James read it, aloud.

'Dear Jane,

'Please take the 12 o'clock train to London on Wednesday. You will be met at Paddington. I have made all arrangements for you and enclose notes for expenses.

'I am writing to Miss James, and no doubt she will be willing to accept a term's fees instead of a term's notice. Bring all your luggage. You will not return to school.

'Yours very truly,
'Arthur Panton.'

'Mine's the same,' said Lucilla.

'And you had no idea of this?'

'No,' said both the girls.

'It is very sudden,' said the Head. 'I feel it very much.'

'Cheap!' said the canary.

'We should have had to leave some time,' said Lucilla.

'You are now,' began Miss James, leaning back comfortably, 'going out into the world. You will no longer have the guiding hand, the mature mind, the affectionate heart of your teachers to rely on. You will be free . . .'

'Sweet, sweet, sweet!' said the canary.

'. . . from all the restraints of school. Let it be your care . . .' Miss James went on. And we need not follow her further. Every girl who has left school knows exactly what she said. The last words were all that mattered.

'The matron will pack your boxes to-day. You had better assist her. And never forget in the rush of the battle of life that you are St Olave's girls. Let that thought be your shield and your banner. Be proud of the school, and let all your actions be such as shall make the school proud of you.'

'Yes, Miss James,' said the two girls meekly.

Outside her door they fell into each other's arms, breathless with whispered ecstasies.

'How quite too perfectly ripping!' said Jane.

'To-morrow!' said Lucilla. 'It's like something in a book – a bolt from the blue.'

'A bolt from the blue-stockings,' said Jane. 'Come away, or she'll catch us.'

'I feel as if someone had left me a fortune . . .'

'I feel as if I were going to elope.'

It was not till most of their books and work and little possessions had been collected and set ready for the packing that they were sufficiently sobered to question the future.

'I wonder where we're going to live, though?' Lucilla said over the pile of books she was carrying.

'What does that matter,' said Jane, 'so long as it's not here? When persons escape from the Bastille they never ask where they're going to live. With him, perhaps. Keep his house and entertain his clients. I say, Lucilla, let's keep a salon, and make dear Guardian's invitations the most sought after in London.'

'I don't think!' said Lucilla. 'I expect he's engaged a tabby to chaperone us. I hope she's an engaging tabby.'

'Oh, don't let's bother,' said Jane, turning a drawer full of ribbons and gloves on to the floor. 'Help me to sort these. I nearly cried yesterday when all the other girls kept going away in cab after cab — to say nothing of the motors — and we left behind, and dear Emmie in Norway on her wedding tour and nobody to lend us a helping hand. And now ours very truly, Arthur Panton, has turned up trumps. May the choicest blessings — Look out, those chocs. are sticky. Don't let them loose among my collars!'

Glad as wild birds released from their cage, the cousins parted from Miss James. Their faces were serious and respectful, but each heart danced like the sea on a breezy sunny morning. The world was before them: school was behind. They were travelling to London alone — no chaperone; they were no longer schoolgirls, they were young women. The matron saw them off at the station — a kind, stupid woman, but not stupid enough for it to be necessary for them to maintain the serious and respectful mask before her.

'I wish we'd seen Gladys to say good-bye,' they said. 'You might give her this for us.' They pressed half-crowns on the matron. 'Poor old Gladys, she —'

They were getting into the train, when a clatter of clumsy feet made them turn. It was Gladys, but panting and almost in tears.

'Thought I'd missed it,' she exclaimed, thrusting a large box into the carriage. 'It's a parting present, miss. For both of you.'

'We shall prize it for ever, whatever it is,' said Lucilla.

'I got it from me brother,' said Gladys, 'that's why I'm so late. It's just like him to live the other end of the town. I do wish you wasn't going! I don't know whatever I shall do now you've gone. For of all the old —'

'Shish!' said Jane.

'Oh, I beg your pardon, Miss Blake — I didn't see you were there. Oh, good-bye, Miss Jane dear, and you too, Miss Lucy, I'm sure! Good-bye!'

Miss Blake pulled her back. A porter banged the door and the train moved off.

They waved hands from the window till the station was out of sight. Then, withdrawing their heads from the window, they stumbled over Gladys's present.

'Let's see what it is,' said Jane.

It was a fine black rabbit in a home-made hutch, not new.

'Well, perhaps it's lucky,' said Jane; 'like black cats, you know. We'll call it Othello. Poor old Gladys!'

It was a delicious journey. The wildest speculations concerning their future brightened every mile of it. At Paddington they were met by a sour-looking man who announced himself as Mr Panton's head clerk.

'But how do you know it's us?' Jane asked.

'I've been shown your photos,' he said. 'This way to the car.'

It was a beautiful car. Behind it stood a taxi for their luggage.

'I feel like a duchess,' said Jane in the car.

'Your hat's all on one side,' said Lucilla beside her.

'That will be all then?' said the clerk at the window. 'This is the address,' and he thrust a paper at them. 'The man knows where to go. And this,' he said finally, dropping something cold into Lucilla's hand, 'is the key. Drive on!'

And the car slid out of the station.

'The key! Whatever of?' Lucilla asked.

'Heaven alone knows. Perhaps we are being kidnapped. Oh, Lucy, how frightfully exciting.'

'But what's it the key *of*?'

'A house. Unless it's the key of a mausoleum, like Emmeline's great aunt battered at the door of.'

'But why a key? Oh, Jane, suppose that dusty person at the station didn't really recognise us? Suppose he thought we were somebody else, and this is somebody else's key? Or suppose we're really being kidnapped? Held for ransom, you know, till our guardian shells out. The key – it's so heavy; it might be the key of a church.'

'Whatever else it is, it's the key of our future. Don't let's get fluttered, Lucy, like two silly schoolgirls. Where's the paper with the address on it?'

They found it on the floor among their rugs and bags and umbrellas. Lucilla unfolded it.

'What does it say?' Jane asked.

It said 'Hope Cottage', adding the names of a road and a suburb.

'There,' said Jane, 'that's all serene. It's Guardy's handwriting right enough. It's not a bad hand. Curious we've never seen him. He had very good taste in chocs. and books. I daresay he's quite a decent sort. I wonder if he'll let us travel by ourselves? Abroad, I mean?'

'Italy,' said Lucilla.

'Egypt,' said Jane.

'Greece.'

'Mexico.'

'Spain.'

'Samoa.'

'But about this key!' Lucilla began again, but Jane stopped her with a squeak of triumph.

'I know! This car is for us, and this is the key of the garage. How unspeakably splendid! Our guardian is one in a million! I wonder how much money Aunt Lucilla *did* leave us? It must be an awful lot if it runs to a car like this.'

And all the time the car was worming its swift, gliding way through strange crowded streets, between unfamiliar rows of gloomy houses and brilliant shops. It crossed the Thames, and the roads became sordid. It left the sordidness behind and passed among villas whose gardens grew larger as they slipped past. Then came trees – fields – more villas.

'It's almost real country,' said Lucilla. 'I hope Hope Cottage is bowered in roses and jasmine. It must be a big cottage to have a garage.'

'I should like it thatched,' said Jane, 'but I suppose that's too much to expect.'

More big gardens – a road that was almost a lane, with fields on one side and cabbage-fields on the other – some half-built houses – some trees – another cabbage-field – and then suddenly the motor stopped, purring, before a little yellow brick house as square as the rabbit-hutch itself and almost as small.

The chauffeur got down and opened the door. He had quite a nice face, Lucilla thought.

'This is Hope Cottage,' he said. And, indeed, a black description on its white gate said so in plain capitals.

They gathered their belongings together and got out. The chauffeur unlatched the gate for them, and they passed up a tiled path to a narrow green door.

'Oh, Jane, this can't be right!' Lucilla whispered.

'Where's the key?' said Jane.

A large key-hole invited it. It turned easily, and the door opening showed a vision of a narrow carpeted passage and steeply-rising stairs.

'Good afternoon, miss,' said the chauffeur; 'the taxi is paid for.'

'But here – I say, stop a minute!' said Lucilla.

'Sorry – another appointment,' he said. 'You'll find it's quite all right. This is Hope Cottage,' and he turned to his machine still pulsing loudly.

'No, you don't!' cried Jane, and, springing to the gate, caught him by the arm. A look of positive terror came over his face.

'My dear young lady,' he said, 'surely you won't detain me by force?'

'Yes, I will,' said Jane. 'You can't go off and leave us like this.'

'Mr Panton told me to bring you here, miss. I assure you it's all quite as he arranged. You need be under no apprehension.'

'I'm not,' she said shortly. 'But I'm not going to let you go till you've helped to get the boxes in. How on earth do you suppose that taxi man's going to get all those boxes up these stairs? Or do you expect *us* to do it?'

'I beg your pardon,' he said. 'I never thought of that. Of course I will,' and he turned to the waiting taxi and began to haul at a suit-case.

'You must take them all upstairs. There's no room in this passage for luggage.'

'Certainly,' said the chauffeur; 'please don't worry. I'll manage everything.'

He did. When motor and taxi had died away into silence Jane said:

'That chauffeur was a gentleman. Did you notice his voice? And towards the end he quite forgot to call us "miss". I thought he had an awfully nice face, didn't you?'

'We've got something to think of besides chauffeurs' faces,' said Lucilla. 'There are no shops for miles, I expect, and I'm absolutely starving.'

'Perhaps there's something to eat in the house.'

'Not likely,' said Lucilla.

'Well, let's look over the house. It's no use standing in the passage all night saying how hungry you are,' said Jane impatiently.

There were two little sitting-rooms, one on each side of the front door. The first was furnished primly in Middle-Victorian walnut and faded satin. It had a piano with a fluted yellow silk front, and glass lustres to the mantelpiece. A vase of roses stood on a table in the window.

'Nothing to eat here!' said Lucilla bitterly.

But Jane had opened the door of the other room.

'Oh, Lucy!' she called. 'Come here!'

The second room was a little dining-room, with mahogany chiffonier and maple-framed engravings of the Monarch of the Glen, the Maid of Saragossa, and Bolton Abbey in the olden time. In the middle of the room stood a table — almost it seemed to beckon, with its white cloth, its gleams of silver and glass.

'Cold chicken!' said Lucilla. 'Salad – raspberries – tea-things – milk – bread, butter, jam – everything! Oh, and cream! Oh, Jane!'

'Here's a letter,' said Jane. It wasn't really a letter just a slip of paper in the well-known handwriting of Mr Arthur Panton.

'Unavoidably called away. Please make yourselves completely at home. – A. P.

'P.S. – Kettle and spirit-stove in the kitchen. Tea in caddy chiffonier.'

The two girls looked at each other.

'Well!' they said simultaneously, and Lucilla added, 'Never mind about tea. Can you carve a chicken?'

'I can try.'

'Try, then, in the name of the Prophet!' said Lucilla. 'I can cut bread. If you can't carve, chop; our lives are saved. I prefer the liver wing. I've never had one, but the important people in books always have the liver wing. You can have all the legs. Oh, our guardian is really a gem. Isn't it the loveliest supper? He must be a man of perfect taste and sensibility. Pass the salad, please. This doesn't look like a wing, it looks all bone; give me some off the top – yes, that white part. No, I don't want to wash my hands first, I don't want to do anything but eat for quite a long time.'

When they had eaten, they went all over the little house and found a tiny kitchen and scullery, and upstairs three small bedrooms choked with their luggage. From the windows they saw a large garden, painted with many bright flowers and rich with the promise of fruit trees.

'It's rather a dear little bandbox,' said Lucilla. 'I wonder if our mysterious guardian will come to-night or to-morrow?'

When they had explored every hole and corner and shed and cupboard, and had tried the piano and gone all over the garden, they sat down to wait.

'We won't go to bed till twelve,' said Jane, 'in case he comes. And if he doesn't, it will be rather a lark to sit up till twelve anyway.'

But by twelve o'clock he had not come, so they went to bed. They were roused at eight o'clock by a knocking at the door, which repeated itself as they hastily dressed after shouting 'Coming!' through the window. Through the glass of the hall door they saw a manly figure.

'Here he is!' they both said. And so he was. But it was only the postman. He had one letter — a very large, registered one. It was addressed to Miss Jane Quested and Miss Lucilla Craye, and they both signed the green receipt form.

'It's his writing,' said Lucilla, as the postman stumped away. 'You open it.'

The stout envelope yielded several long, legal-looking papers and a bank pass book. Also a letter.

'Dear Jane and Lucilla,

'Enclosed with other papers of less interest are the title-deeds of Hope Cottage, which is the property of Lucilla. Also a bank-book for Jane. I have paid £500 into Jane's account at Barclay's Bank.

'This, my dear Jane and my dear Lucilla, is, I very much fear, all that you will ever see of the fortune bequeathed to you by your late aunt. I have been unfortunate in speculation, and I have decided, rather than face the bankruptcy and other courts, to fly the scene.

'I am leaving you the house, which I cannot take with me, and £500, which I hope may enable you to start in some business that will keep you. A dressmaking business? Horticulture? A bonnet-shop? Duchesses do it, you know, nowadays.

'I can ill spare the £500, but I cannot bear to leave you penniless. And I feel that I am the most unfortunate of men in having to leave you at all. But I have no alternative.

'You have often begged me to take you away from school. Well, now I have done it. And to let you lead your own lives. Well — lead them.

'And accept the warmest wishes for your success in every department of life, from your unfortunate and absolutely dished and done-for trustee,

'Arthur Panton.'

The girls looked at each other.

'Whatever shall we do?' said Lucilla breathlessly.

'Well, first of all,' said Jane, very pale but steady, 'I think we ought to do what we ought to have done last night.'

'What's that?'

'Feed that rabbit. There's no reason why *he* should starve.'

Chapter III

When Fortune suddenly upsets the coach and tumbles you on to the hard, dusty road, you can, of course, sit where you are and weep. If you do, something will certainly run over you and your distress will be increased. Or you can move to the side of the road and sit down and cry here in comparative safety. Or you can go your way afoot, cursing the coach and the driver and your own beggarly luck. Or you can pick yourself up with a laugh, protesting that you are not at all hurt and that walking is much better fun than riding. The last is, on every count, the course to be recommended, but it is not everyone who has the qualities needed for such a snapping of the fingers at Fate. To do the thing convincingly you must have courage, a light heart, and, above all, presence of mind. The gesture of 'I don't care' must not come as a second thought. You must not cry out and then protest that you are not hurt. The laugh must follow the smash without an instant's pause, to be followed as quickly by insistence on the charms of walking – so much superior to carriage exercise. Afterwards you can talk things over with your fellow-victims, if you have any, and decide how fast you shall walk and how far, what shoes are best for walking, and which road you shall walk on.

Jane, spilled out of the quite luxurious carriage of comfortable income, had at least the presence of mind to laugh and to feed the rabbit.

'And now,' she said firmly, turning away from his green munchings. 'Then there's nothing to do but to go for a walk. Come along in and put on thick boots, Lucy. We're going to walk miles.'

'All right,' said Lucilla shortly. And they went in.

'And look here,' said Jane, 'don't let's talk.'

'I'm not the one who usually wants to talk,' said Lucilla, busy with bootlaces.

'No. I know. It's me. But not this time. This time I want to think. Really to think. I'm not sure, but I don't believe I ever have really thought yet. I've only dreamed and imagined and planned. Now I'm going to try to think. Come on – how horribly narrow these stairs are! Latch the gate; it looks tidier. Now we'll step out. Which way? It doesn't matter a bit. What was I saying? Oh, that I meant to try to think. And you try to, too. It won't be easy, because I don't believe you've ever done it before either. And when we get home we'll tell each other what we think. If we begin to talk about everything now we shall only get confused. We want to see it clearly and see it whole, and –'

'I thought we weren't going to talk?' Lucilla put in.

'No more we are. I'll shut up like a knife in a minute. I want to say one thing, though.'

'So do I,' said Lucilla. 'I want to say I think it's a beastly shame.'

'No, no!' said Jane eagerly. 'Don't start your thinking with that, or you'll never get anywhere. It isn't a shame and it isn't beastly. I'll tell you what it is, Lucy. And that's where we must start our thinking from. Everything that's happening to us – yes, everything – is to be regarded as a lark. See? This is my last word. This. Is. Going. To. Be. A. Lark.'

'*Is* it?' said Lucilla. 'And that's *my* last word.'

They walked on in silence. The houses grew fewer. There were fields instead of market-gardens. Trees; hedges. A lonely, tumble-down cottage. A big deserted house, with windows boarded up, standing in a walled garden. A lane; a stile; more trees, and a long stretch of white grass-bordered road – real country. They walked sturdily along the dusty road. The sun was warm and grew warmer. The road rose and fell in gentle undulations. Still in perfect silence the girls walked on. But their pace was not so good as at first – one might almost indeed have said that their footsteps lagged.

A turn of the road brought to view a village green, a duck-pond, a pleasant-looking inn. In front of this Lucilla stopped.

'Look here, Jane,' she said.

'We said we wouldn't talk,' said Jane rather faintly.

'Who wants to talk?' Lucilla asked. 'What I want isn't talk, it's something to eat. Do you realise that you dragged me out without breakfast?'

'It was silly,' said Jane; 'very. At the same time, I'm quite sure we couldn't have eaten a proper breakfast just after reading that letter.'

'Perhaps not,' Lucilla admitted, 'but I want my breakfast, and I'm going to have it here – in these tea-gardens at the side of the inn.'

'I'm hungry too,' said Jane; 'at least, I feel as if I'd been for hours in a swing-boat. I suppose that's what people mean when they say they feel faint for want of food. But oh, Lucy, I'm so sorry. I didn't bring any money!'

'*I* did,' said Lucilla grimly, and led the way to the green-latticed tea-gardens.

In a tumble-down arbour, with faded blue seats and a faded blue, warped table, breakfast was presently served to them.

'Oh, Lucilla, you are It!' Jane admitted. 'Doesn't the bacon smell lovely? And the coffee? Sweeter than roses in their prime . . . And real toast in a proper toast-rack! . . .'

'Don't talk,' said Lucilla; 'eat.'

After a silence full of emotion Jane spoke again.

'I never had breakfast out of doors before – and all by our two selves, too . . . Surely even you will admit that *this* is a lark?'

'It would be,' said Lucilla, 'if –'

'No ifs,' said Jane. 'It is a lark, unconditionally and without qualification. And I've been thinking – at least I haven't really till this moment, but I'm thinking now. Bacon is an admirable brain tonic. Don't speak for a minute. I am evolving what they call a philosophy of life.'

'More coffee, please,' said Lucilla.

'Well,' said Jane, putting in far too much milk, 'it's like this. If we're going to worry all the time about the past and the future we shan't have any time at all. We must take everything as it comes and enjoy everything that is – well, that is enjoyable; like this very lovely breakfast. Live for the moment – and do all you can to make the next moment jolly too, as Carlyle says, or is it Emerson?'

'It may be Plato or Aristotle,' said Lucilla, cutting more bread, 'but I think not.'

'It's common sense,' insisted Jane. 'We've got to try to make our livings somehow. We'll try all sorts of things, and we'll get fun out of them if we don't worry and grouse. But we shall never do anything if we think of ourselves as two genteel spinsters who have seen better days. We must think of ourselves as adventurers with the whole world before us. Frightfully interesting.'

'There's something in what you say,' said Lucilla.

'There's much more in what I am going to say,' Jane rejoined; 'it's wonderful how bacon clears the mind. Have you ever thought seriously about marriage?'

'Don't be silly,' said Lucilla.

'There – that's exactly what I mean,' said Jane cryptically. 'Now I have thought about marriage – a good deal; and I believe that one reason why so many married people don't get on together – well, you know they *don't*, don't you? – is that they're not polite to each other. They think they know each other well enough to say, "Don't be silly," and things like that. No, of course I'm not offended. It was all right to rag each other when we were just cousins with nothing to do but play the fool. But now we're partners, my dear; almost as much as if we were a married couple. And don't you think it would be a good scheme to try to be polite, and drop ragging each other?'

'You can't,' said Lucilla.

'Well, anyhow, I think we shall have to try; at any rate, not to say, "Don't be silly" before we know what the other one's going to say.'

'I apologise,' said Lucilla, 'and leave the omnibus.'

'Nonsense,' said Jane. 'I didn't mean that; it might just as well have been me. And now I'm going to tell you something.'

'I beg your pardon,' said a voice, 'but can you tell me how far it is to Leabridge?'

They turned, to find at Lucilla's elbow a young man in

knee-breeches. He held in one hand a panama hat and in the other a glass of ginger-beer.

'Oh!' said Lucilla, with what was almost a cry.

'I am sorry if I startled you,' he said.

'Not at all,' said Lucilla; 'at least, you did rather, but it doesn't matter – and we don't know anything about Leabridge. I'm sorry. But they'd know in the inn, wouldn't they?'

'I suppose they would,' said the young man, as though this were a completely new idea. 'They're sensible people, I suppose?'

'I don't know,' said Lucilla; 'we aren't staying here. We just came to have breakfast' – she indicated the greasy plates and sloppy cups. 'But they'll be *sure* to know, of course.'

'Yes. Thank you so much,' said the stranger. 'You see, I've been in the Red Sea for over four years, and I don't seem to know where anything is. It's wonderful how different Kent is to the Red Sea.'

'It must be,' said Lucilla, rather stiffly. 'I'm sorry we can't help you.'

'Not at all,' said he vaguely. 'Thank you so much.' And with that he retreated to the furthest of the green tables.

'We'd better go,' said Jane. 'Whatever did you want to snub him so for?'

'He didn't really want to know about Leabridge. He just wanted to talk to us.'

'I should think he did! After four years of the Red Sea anybody would want to talk to anybody. But that wasn't it. Don't you see, he came into the garden just when I was saying I was going to tell you something. He had to let us know he was there. I think it was very, very nice of him. Now, Lucy, you must bow as we go by.'

'We won't go by,' said Lucilla; 'we'll go round the other way, and turn our backs on him at once.'

They did. And it was rather a pity, because if the young man had seen more of Jane than a large hat and a chin, and if Jane had seen the young man distinctly, either or both might have been moved to oppose Lucilla's severe and severing tactics. I don't quite see what either could have done – but I incline to think that the situation would have been changed.

As it was, Jane and Lucilla paid their bill and John Rochester was left to drink ginger-beer in the sun and wonder why he couldn't be allowed to talk for half an hour to two ladies just because no one had mumbled their names to him and his to them. He was thirsty for the companionship of women – any decent women. So that presently he carried his glass into the bar and tried to talk to the barmaid; he found a nice, respectable woman with very little conversation. Then he rode on to lunch with a wealthy uncle who had expressed a wish to see him. Later he would go down to his mother's. He had not seen her yet. The uncle had been imperative. He wondered whether Miss Antrobus was married, and then he thought of the gold-crowned child in the moonlit wood, and wondered . . .

Little did he think – as our good old standard authors would say . . . But volumes could be ineffectually filled by the recital of what Mr Rochester didn't think. The point for us is that he had seen the child again, and that she had seen him. He did not recognise her now that she wore a straw hat and the charm of nineteen instead of a crown and fifteen's wild woodland grace. And she did not recognise the face that had come in answer to her invocation, because four years in the Red Sea set their mark upon a man, even without that scar that he got when his ship was torpedoed. They have not recognised each other, but they are in the same county; more, they are in the same district: she anchored to a house called Hope Cottage, he less closely attached, but still attached, to a resident uncle. If there is anything in these old charms the two will meet again quite soon. If there isn't anything – well, still they will probably meet. Of course he may fall in love with Lucilla – it was she who spoke to him. If he does, we shall know that charms on St John's Eve are worse than useless.

Anyhow, he is now definitely out of the picture, which concerns itself only with the desperate efforts of two inexperienced girls to establish, on the spur of the moment, a going concern that shall be at once agreeable and remunerative.

They talked it over. The forethought of the defaulting guardian in providing an intelligent, drab-haired woman to come in and do for them left them free to talk. And talk they did. Presently talk crystallised into little lists of possibilities. As thus:

Be milliners. Be dressmakers. Market-gardening. Keeping rabbits ('We've got one to begin with, anyhow,' said Lucilla). Keeping fowls. Taking paying guests. Writing novels. Going out as governesses ('Not if I know it,' said Jane. 'Think of Agnes Gray'). Selling the house and furniture and going to Canada ('Too cold,' said Lucilla. 'Besides, they have no old buildings,' said Jane. 'Your mind would be cold there as well as your body'). Wood-carving. Going about as strolling minstrels.

It was not an unhappy time. Freedom was theirs. They might be unlucky, but there was no one to tell them whose fault it was. The house, though small, was very comfortable, as houses are that have been lived in for years and had all that houses need gradually added, a little at a time – not crammed down their throats in one heavy, dusty meal, by a universal provider or a hire-system firm.

The garden was full of flowers – daffodils, tulips, wallflowers, forget-me-nots, pansies, oxlips, primroses – and on the walls of the house cherry-coloured Japanese quince. The buds of iris and peonies were already fat with promise, and roses were in leaf and tiny bud.

Twice a day a long procession of workmen passed the house, on their way to and from the new estate that was being (developed). The girls got quite used to the admiration which their garden excited in these men. As they passed every eye was turned to it. One day Jane was cutting the pyrus japonica for the house when the procession began.

'You might spare us a buttonhole,' said a fat, jolly man with a carpenter's bag.

'All right,' said Jane handsomely, and handed him a little sprig of red blossom.

'Thank you, I'm sure,' said the workman.

'But what about me?' said the man behind him.

'Me, too,' said another. 'Give us a bit too, lady.'

'I'm awful fond of flowers.'

And next moment there was a crowd of men and boys holding on to the green railings of Hope Cottage, and all clamouring for just one flower. The group blocked the pathway, and newcomers stopped to see what was going on, and the crowd grew and grew.

Jane came to the fence and raised her voice. She had learned to do that in the school plays.

'Look here,' she said, 'I'm awfully sorry, but I can't give flowers to all of you.'

'Never mind, miss,' said one, 'we know your heart's good.'

'No need to give,' said a black-bearded, serious-looking man. 'I'll pay for mine.'

'So'll I,' said a dozen voices.

'I was first, miss.'

'Me next.'

'How much?'

'How much ought I to say?' Jane lowered her voice to ask her first friend, who had pinned her gift to his buttonhole.

'Twopence a bit,' he answered.

Jane broke off her cherry-coloured blossom into sprays and handed them over the railings, receiving many pennies in return.

'You ought to sell bokays, miss,' said one of the men. 'Lots of the chaps would like to take home a bunch to the missus of a Saturday. You put up a board and say, "Flowers for sale here." Not but what it would be a pity to rob the garden.'

'Oh, but we want to sell the flowers,' said Jane. 'Thank you so much. I'll get a board ready.'

'I'll bring you along a bit o' board,' said the man with the carpenter's bag, 'all ready painted white – and you can do the letters on it yourself with Brunswick black. All saves expense.'

When the little crowd had dispersed, Jane was left rather breathless, with blackened hands and apron-pockets weighed down with what the police call bronze.

She heaved it all out onto the kitchen-table, where Lucilla sat busy as usual with pencil and paper. The coins rattled and rang and spun on the smooth scrubbed deal; a couple of adventurous sixpences and a rollicking halfpenny escaped to the floor, and at least three pence rolled under the dresser.

'What on earth's all this?' Lucilla asked, as well she might.

'Your destiny, my destiny,' Jane told her. 'It's the finger of Fate. Drop those everlasting lists. Away with them! We're in trade!'

'But where did you get all this money?' Lucilla asked, beginning to arrange the pennies in piles of twelve.

'In the garden,' said Jane dramatically; 'buried treasure – first instalment, to be continued in our next. No, don't look vacant, Luce darling. I'm not insane, and I will tell the truth as soon as I get my breath. Put away that pencil, burn that paper. No more lists! I got that money by selling flowers out of the garden. We will get our living by selling flowers out of the garden. Ourselves. To people who go by and admire. No sending our flowers to market to be sold all crushed and bruised and disheartened. "Fresh flowers sold here" – that's what's going on the board. No, "Fresh cut flowers sold here." I shall paint the board tomorrow. Why, the board for the gate, of course, to show the world what we sell. Let's count the money. I make it fifteen and eightpence.'

'It is fifteen and ninepence halfpenny,' said Lucilla, and added slowly, 'it's quite a good idea, Jane.'

'Out with it,' said Jane, adjusting the little silver tower of her eleven sixpences. 'What's the dreadful drawback?'

'I hate to throw cold water,' said Lucilla, 'but how long will the flowers in our garden last if we sell them like this? You'll be "sold out", as the shops say, before the paint's dry on your board.'

'But more flowers will come out.'

'Not fast enough.'

'We could buy flowers at Covent Garden and sell those.'

'Then they wouldn't precisely be fresh-cut, would they?'

'True. How right you always are!'

'The fact is,' Lucilla went on, 'you make fun of my lists – but I've learned one thing by making them. I see that every plan we can make for making money here is made impossible by one thing. The house is too small.'

'Then we must get another house.'

'That's so easy, isn't it, with all the papers we bought at the station full of the housing problem? There aren't any other houses. You know there aren't.'

'I don't know anything so absurd. There must be houses with bigger gardens than ours. People might want to exchange.'

'You think we might advertise: "People who don't want to be bothered with large gardens can have small one in exchange"? It's our only chance. We can never do anything with Hope Cottage except live in it – and that we can't do on the interest of your five hundred pounds – or else let it. Now, if we let it furnished, we could partly live somewhere else on the money.'

'I don't want to "partly" live anywhere,' said Jane. 'I wish to warm both hands before the fire of life.'

'Well, you'll never warm them here,' said Lucilla.

'The worst of it is that you're so often right,' said Jane, tying the money up in a clean blue-checked duster and hiding it in the plate-warmer. 'No burglar will ever think of looking for it there. Now let's go out and look for a house.'

When they had locked the front door behind them Lucilla stood on the step surveying the front garden.

'What's-his-name and the ruins of Carthage,' said Jane, flippant, but a little uneasy too.

Lucilla walked to the corner of the house and looked round it.

'Why,' she said, 'there's not a flower in sight!'

'Fifteen and eightpence,' said Jane – 'I mean ninepence, and a good deal of that was ivy.'

'I shouldn't put up the board here,' said Lucilla, 'it's hardly worth while.'

'If we can't get another house I shall plant flowers here.'

'Flowers take time to grow.'

'Annuals don't – at least, not much. Let's go and buy a gardening book and find a house.'

They did not find a house, but they bought a gardening book – and spent the evening over it. In the kitchen. You tend to sit in the kitchen when it is very light and clean, bright with gay-coloured crockery and sparkling with silvery tinsmith's work; and when you have it to yourselves; and when, anyhow, you have to get your own supper, and you may as well eat it where you cook it. It saves carrying trays in and out, and you get it hotter – and afterwards, why bother to move? Especially when the kitchen window looks out on the back garden, where the fruit trees are near blossom, and the parlours both look out on the front garden, the whole of whose floral splendour has just been sold for fifteen shillings and ninepence.

A very happy evening they spent over the gardening book. Lucilla made a list of the seeds that would be wanted to carry out what was really a quite brilliant scheme for a year's flower-growing.

'Perhaps you're right,' she owned; 'something might be done with this garden. And then there'll be all the soft fruit coming on in the summer.'

'*Soft fruit?* Yes, that's right, it says so in the book. Currants and raspberries and gooseberries – all the squashy kinds. Hard fruit's the sort on trees – apples and pears. We might make jam, put "*Home Made Jam*" on the board.'

'And "*New Laid Eggs*" if we only had fowls.'

'And "*New Milk*" if we had a cow.'

'And "*Home Cured Bacon*" if we had a pig.'

'And everything that people do sell if only we'd got room to grow it – if this were a decent-sized house instead of a chocolate-box.'

'It's the perfect house for an old maid,' said Jane. 'A place for everything is easy, but everything you ought to have in the place where it ought to be – that's rare, Lucy, rare as black swans. That ought to mean money. Somewhere or other there is the real right tenant gaping open-mouthed for just this bait.'

'Bed gapes for me,' said Lucilla, 'and it's mutual.'

'I suppose being in trade *does* make you vulgar.' Jane seemed to ponder. 'Even the little bit of trade *we've* had.'

Chapter IV

The house stood large and lonely among a wilderness of little streets, brickfields, cabbage-fields, ruined meadows where broken hedges and a few old thorn trees lingered to remind the world of the green lanes and meadows of long ago. Long red walls, buttressed in days when the eighth Henry was king, enclosed a garden that even then had been a garden for uncounted years. The orchard and paddock, too, were ringed with the same high, heavy brickwork, but in front of the house the wall gave place to a tall railing wrought in iron of a very beautiful and graceful design, and at each end of this a double carriage gate, also of wrought iron, flanked by square brick pillars with stone coping and stone balls. A much more magnificent entourage than seemed demanded by the house itself, a dwelling comparatively modern. It could not have seen two hundred summers, and had obviously been built on the site of a much older and more magnificent mansion. Its light Italian structure showed strangely among cedars that had grown up beside the solid splendours of a Tudor dwelling. The long, low, white front of it faced the road, and the queer, squat, round tower at one corner rose against a background of yew hedges that must have been already tall when the house began to rise from its foundations.

Though the house looked deserted it did not look decayed. There were no loose copings on the wall, and the iron screens and gates had not been suffered to rust. The weather had not yet destroyed the stucco complexion of the house, and though ivy rioted over half the green-grey of its roof, every slate was in its place.

The wall and iron palings were strong and practically boy-proof, but the house was near enough to the road to be assailable by the skilled catapultist or the unskilled brick-bit thrower. For this, or for some other reason, all the windows on the front of the house were shuttered fast, or, in the upper storey where shutters were not, frankly boarded up with rough deal. The untrimmed lawn before the house was sprinkled with daffodils and hyacinths, and beyond, through and over thick shrubberies, were glimpses of blossoming almond and thorn, and the brown haze of fruit trees covered with the gauzy veil of little buds that spring throws over wood and orchard.

'The house was made for us,' said Jane, when they had ranged up and down the iron grating and tried both the iron gates.

'Too big,' said Lucilla. 'Besides, look at the board.'

'That only shows that the owner's weak-minded. We'll apply to the Court of Chancery, or whatever it is. The Lord Chancellor will say, "Certainly, dears," or whatever Lord Chancellors *do* say. And we shall have the house.'

The board, whatever weakness it stood for, was strong enough in its statements. It said in large white letters on its black self:

THIS HOUSE
IS <u>NOT</u>
TO LET.
Apply to:
Messrs. P. Tutch & Co.,
207, High Street.

But the '*Apply to*' had been painted over by the same unskilled hand, apparently, as had painted in the wavering *IS NOT*.

'I don't care what you say.' Jane addressed not Lucilla but the board. 'I shall apply to Messrs. Tutch and Go – and I shall do it now. Come on.'

'It's much too big,' said Lucilla, but yielding.

'Not for P.G.'s,' said Jane.

'We couldn't furnish it.'

'Hire purchase,' Jane reminded her. 'I saw *that* in the paper too.

You pay out of your income so that it doesn't cost you anything. No, I don't exactly see how – but there it is. We can't expect to understand everything.'

'We should want an army of gardeners.'

'Men who've fought in the war and got pensions too small. They can come and garden and share the profits.'

'But when the board distinctly says that the house *isn't* to let . . .'

'Bother the board!' said Jane. 'I expect we shall find it doesn't know its own wooden mind.'

But apparently it did. Messrs. Tutch and Co., represented by a small inky boy who ate something secret out of a paper-bag throughout the interview, held out no hopes. The house was not to let. Nothing would induce the owner to let it. Yes, it had been let, but the party that had had it did something they oughtn't – blest if he knew what – and the old gent it belonged to said no more lets for him.

'So he went and disfigured of our board, and pays our firm so much a year to let the board stay there looking silly. No, miss, we ain't got no other houses to let – what do *you* think? Could sell you one – a nice semi with bay windows, five rooms and scullery. No bath. Twelve hundred. Like to go over it?'

'Not to-day, thank you,' said Jane, quailing, 'but we'd like to go over the big house. Couldn't we do that? What is the house called?'

'Cedar Court. No, that you couldn't . . .'

'Not even if . . .' said Jane, her fingers busy with the silver meshes of her bag – one of the Guardian's latest gifts.

'Not if it was a hundred thousand down,' said the boy, filling his mouth. 'You see,' he added with frank regret, 'we ain't got the keys at the office.'

'Who has got the keys?'

'Him. Himself. The old gent,' said the boy. 'He don't let them out of his 'ands except to the charlady as cleans up a bit sometimes. He's close, he is.'

'And what's his name?' asked Jane insinuatingly.

42

'Oh, go along, miss, do,' said the boy. 'I ain't going to get into trouble along of gells – coming round me like spinxes. I see your game. Worm his name and address out of a chap and then go and badger him same as you're doing me now. Lose me my job as like as not. Good morning, miss.'

'So that's no good,' said Lucilla, as they walked away. 'I don't think he meant sphinxes. He meant sirens. It's rather nice to be sirens, don't you think?'

'Not when Ulysses is eating out of paper-bags.'

'I wish we'd asked the charlady's name.'

'Perhaps our charlady would know?'

Their charlady knew a little. She knew why the house was so definitely not to be let, and told them as she compounded a plum cake.

'The gentleman as owns it,' she told the girls, 'he don't live in it 'cause it's too big, him being a single man. And he's rolling in money; he just only let it to keep it from the damp, so to speak. The last tenant, he didn't mean no harm. He thought the old gentleman would be only too pleased – he did it all at his own expense and looked for thanks, instead of which explosions and Catherine wheels and no renewing the lease. "Out you go, my lord," and double quick it was. The tenant, he was here to-day and gone tomorrow as the saying is. The old gentleman must have been a holy terror – it takes something to get anybody out of a house, doesn't it? But he went like a lamb, explaining to the last, with the very cab at the door, that he had only done it to oblige and meant it all for the best. Don't take the stoned ones, if it's all the same to you, miss. I shall have to weigh up again.'

'Sorry,' said Lucilla, and left off eating raisins. 'But what did he *do*? What was it he meant all for the best?'

'The paint, miss,' said Mrs Doveton, beating eggs. 'He'd painted the woodwork first rate, three coats.'

'Three coats, and everything handsome about him,' murmured Jane.

'Yes, miss, two flat and one round – and the house needed it, I tell you. Never a bit of paint since it was built, and most of the rooms lined with wood right up – same as doors; black as your hat they was, and he painted them nice bright colours – pink and blue, and a good gas green and a canary yellow; and how was he to know the old gentleman liked 'em all black and crocked? He hated paint, he did – same as you and me might hate dirt. Well, it was no use talking. There it was, and there it is. And that's why he won't let the house no more.'

When they were back in the little sitting-room with the lustres and the beaded fire-screen, Lucilla said:

'I don't want to be mingy, but do you think we ought to have cake – with all those raisins and so many eggs? I hate to say it, but oughtn't we to economise?'

'No,' said Jane firmly, 'that's the one thing we won't do. You can't have a lark of any sort if you're always counting the half-pence. We won't spend more than we're obliged – that's not economy – it's just common sense. And we'll make as much money as we can. That's the way to get on in life. Not by saving, but by making. Let's get some oranges and make some marmalade, and when people come for flowers and we haven't got any we'll sell them marmalade instead. There are heaps of jampots on the top shelf in the china cupboard.'

They made fifty-six pounds. It was hot work, but printing the labels with pretty letters was fun. And, sure enough, they sold every pot. And could have sold them twice over.

'Do you think we sold it too cheap?' they asked Mrs Doveton.

'Lord love you, no!' she said. 'It's good marmalade, and besides, there's the novelty; the boys enjoy buying it off you two sweet young ladies with no hats and their hair blowing in their eyes. Why wouldn't they buy it? Lucky to get it, I say.'

'But we can't live on what we make out of the marmalade, and there aren't half enough flowers,' Lucilla would say. And Jane would say:

'Oh, if we only could have the House! I say – let's go and look at it.'

And then they would go and look and look and long and love it through its iron railings, and desire passionately the right to gather and sell the flowers that budded and bloomed and withered before their eyes out of reach – out of reach.

'If we were born fortunate,' said Lucilla, 'we should catch the charlady here on one of her cleaning days, and bribe her, and then . . .'

'We *are* born fortunate,' Jane insisted. 'That's what you don't seem to see. We *are*. Our star would make Napoleon's look small. When did two girls of our age have such a chance as we've got – to have a lark entirely on our own? No chaperone, no rules, no . . .'

'No present income or future prospects,' said Lucilla.

'No slavery!' cried Jane.

Every day they went down to the House. And ('We were born fortunate, I told you so!' whispered Jane) at last came the day when a change in lines and angles smote their eyes. One of the big gates was ajar. Going down the road was a retreating figure, stout, char-lady like, bearing a basket and a jug.

'We can get into the garden,' breathed Lucilla, and on the tip-toes of conspirators, with the haste of hunted rabbits, they stole through the iron gates and up the weedy drive.

'We can get into the house,' said Jane, catching Lucilla's hand. And indeed, beyond the wide, moss-green semi-circle of the front door steps the front door showed two dark inches beyond itself.

Jane ran up the steps and pushed the heavy, sombre Georgian door, which swung back, revealing a dark hall – marble-floored. Tall portraits loomed from the walls. The dusky distance gave hints of shallow stairs and broad wooden balustrade. Close by the door stood pail and scrubbing-brush. And most of the floor was clean and damp.

'Oh, Jane – don't, she'll be back directly!'

'She won't be back for half an hour. And if she does come back she can't kill us. Come in – come in, I tell you! You outside and the door open are enough to give us away to the whole neighbour-hood. Come in and don't upset the pail. Now close the door. I say, it's jolly dark! Where are you?'

45

'Of course it's dark, all the shutters are shut!' said Lucilla impatiently.

'Hold on, there's a crack of light there!'

There was. Jane pushed a door and the crack broadened to a parallelogram of soft yellow light. It came, they saw, from a candle burning on the long table of a noble kitchen, oak raftered, wide hearthed.

'What a dream of a place!' said Jane. 'Come on, let's explore.'

'Better not,' said Lucilla. 'This will land us in trouble. I feel it in my bones.'

'It's the adventure of our lives,' said Jane. 'Come on,' and she caught at the candle.

'I should only like to know,' Lucilla protested, 'whether it's burglary or just housebreaking.'

'It's neither,' Jane told her, throwing open a door at the other end of the hall. 'It's what they call a youthful indiscretion. This is the drawing-room – it's at the back; let's open the shutters and have a peep.'

The shutters creaked back and the spring sunshine flooded the room. The furniture was mellowed and faded in a perfect harmony, but its walls were a vivid, heartless pink.

'Like cheap sweets,' Lucilla gasped. 'Shut it up again, do.'

They found the dining-room, and perceived it to be furnished, but one could not see the furniture for the walls. Their colour was a fierce full blue.

'Poor old gentleman, I really don't blame him. But he might have got the walls scraped. Now let's get out before she comes back. You see it's miles too big for us – we couldn't afford it even if he'd let it. Oh, Jane, don't be an ass – do let's get out of it!'

'Not till I've seen all over it'; and Jane led the way up the dark, shallow stairs. 'There must be any number of rooms up here.'

There were – and all were furnished and all were dark; not a window but was close shuttered or boarded up. The two girls saw as much of the house as a candle carried hastily through room after darkened room can show.

'I love it, I love it!' Jane said at each new hint of curtain or panel. 'I love it all.'

'Hopelessly,' said Lucilla. 'I never thought you'd be one to love in vain. But we haven't seen the yellow-painted room yet.'

They found it — a round room, opening out of the drawing-room — and its yellow was even as the yellow of mustard.

'But look at the shape of it,' said Jane; 'the lovely little book-cases rounded to the shape of the room — no books though, Luce. I'm going to put on my very nicest hat and go and call on that old gentleman.'

'*Vous en serez pour vos frais,*' said Lucilla.

'What? Oh, I know, French idiotisms. How it brings it all back! Like yesterday. Whereas it is really to-day. All right, we'll go now.'

They carried the candle down and replaced it on the kitchen table and moved to the front door. Jane opened it cautiously, and instantly, with desperate caution, closed it again.

'There's a man coming up the drive!' she said, and at once the instinct of flight caught at them both. Noiseless flying feet skimmed the stairs; they clung together on the landing. Then Lucilla pulled her friend into a dark cupboard.

'Hush!' she whispered, quite unnecessarily. 'It's a man — he'll think we're burglars. Be quiet.'

'Be quiet yourself,' said Jane intensely. And they held their breath, listening.

Firm footsteps sounded below — of feet that said at every step, 'Why should I go quietly? I have every right to be here.' 'How different!' thought Jane, comparing his footsteps with their own light, terror-stricken escalade.

Then there were voices. A woman's voice. A man's voice. One excusing, the other reproaching. The clink of a pail's handle against a pail. More words, but undistinguishable. 'Let me go — I want to listen; he's scolding her for leaving the door open,' said Jane, struggling in Lucilla's grasp.

'No, no, no, no!' said Lucilla fervently. 'He'll come up here to see that no burglars have got in.'

'Better be found on the landing than hiding in a cupboard. I won't be made a fool of – let go!'

But Lucilla did not let go.

'Oh, don't!' she said. 'It would be hateful if we were sent to prison – if he thought we were thieves.'

'It would be trying, certainly,' Jane answered. 'Listen!'

They listened. All was silent. And then, suddenly, echoing through the great empty house came the heavy bang of a door. The front door. Footsteps on gravel. Silence.

'There,' said Jane, 'now you've done it! What absolute asses we are! . . .'

'Well, thank goodness *you* haven't,' said Lucilla. 'We're not branded as burglars, anyhow.'

'A was an absolute ass, B was a branded burglar,' said Jane, pushing open the cupboard door. 'And now we've to get out somehow.'

'Does it occur to you,' said Lucilla sweetly, 'that their going away may be a *ruse*? They may be watching the house.'

'My hat!' said Jane briefly. And stood stock still.

'I think we ought to wait a little, don't you?'

'We ought to *get out of it*,' Jane insisted. 'If we're caught in the garden it's nothing to being caught in the house. There must be a window somewhere that we can get out by.'

Holding each other, still in nervous tenseness, they stole out into the gallery – dark, dark, very dark. But at the long gallery's end green light showed, a small square window, almost covered with ivy, but not shuttered.

'Let's,' said Jane. 'Oh, what was that?'

'That' was a sound in the house below, very faint but very distinct. The creaking of a board that is trodden on.

'It's the stairs,' whispered Jane. 'Fly – under that window. It's always darkest under the lamp.'

'I can't fly,' said Lucilla. 'I put my bag down on the shelf of that cupboard. You fly. I'll get it.'

Jane fled – and Lucilla, returning as in a flash with the bag, was just in time to hear a scrambling clatter-crash, and to see Jane's head, a moment ago clear between her and the window, disappear suddenly. She was also just in time to save herself from the black treachery of the stairs down which Jane had fallen.

She felt her way down the stairs to meet a small whisper.

'Don't walk on me – I can't move.'

She reached down and touched a shoulder. Jane was lying in a crumpled bunch at the foot of the stairs. Lucilla got past her and crouched by her side.

'Are you much hurt? Have you broken anything?'

'You said it would land us! You felt it in your bones. Well – I've landed! And I feel it in mine! I didn't scream, did I?'

'You might just as well have done. You made a noise like a factory chimney coming down.'

'Well, anyhow,' said Jane, 'it shows that creaking board was only rats or mice or owls or something. Anything human would have been on to us like a shot. Look here, old angel. I don't want to make a fuss – but I think I've broken my leg. And I don't quite see how we're going to get out of this.'

'If we only had a light!' moaned Lucilla.

'Just so,' said Jane. 'You'll have to go and get the candle. There are matches in the candlestick. Feel your way carefully. It's perfectly straight from the top of these hateful stairs to the top of the other ones. Then the kitchen's the first door on the left. And the table's right before you.'

'All right,' said Lucilla. 'Can't I do anything before I go? To make you more comfortable, I mean – lift you, or anything?'

'For pity's sake don't try to lift me,' said Jane; 'that really would be the last straw. At least, I mean I feel safer where I am. There may be another flight of stairs, or a well, or an oubliette.'

'Oh, Jane – this is awful!'

'Nonsense!' said Jane bravely. 'It's an adventure; but I can't really enjoy it till we get a light. Does my leg hurt? Yes – it hurts *damnably*.'

'Oh, Jane!' said Lucilla.

'Damn damnably,' said Jane with firmness. 'Oh, go and get that

49

candle, do. I wish you'd fallen down instead of me. *I* should have gone straight for the candle. At least, of course, I don't wish it was you – but go, go, go!'

Lucilla went. And Jane, alone in the darkness, set her teeth and cautiously felt her ankle; she could not find any pointed bits sticking through her stocking, which was, she supposed, the attitude a broken bone would take up. But she could find pain, pain, and more pain, at every touch of her finger-tips.

What a very long time it did take some people to go up one flight of stairs and down another and come back with a candle! She leaned her head back against the wall at the stair-foot and strained her eyes at the dark cavity of the staircase above her. No light – only the faint, false, green gleam of the ivy-masked window that had betrayed her. No light – no sound of returning footsteps. Only darkness and silence.

Then suddenly, cutting the darkness like a knife, a wild shriek echoed through the hollow emptiness of that closed house. Then silence again. Silence and darkness.

Chapter V

It is pleasant to be able to record that Jane, alone in the dark with a wildly painful ankle at the foot of the stairs down which she had just pitched head first, on hearing that scream and knowing all too well the accents of Lucilla in terror, did, in spite of the pain and the ankle and the darkness, hoist herself on hands and one knee, the other foot dragging red-hot behind her, to the top of the stairs. Just so, and not otherwise, had Lucilla screamed one night at school when Daisy Simmons, the school's incomparable ninny, had put a sheet over her head and pretended to be a ghost, gliding up to a sponge-and-towel-laden Lucilla coming all glowing and fearless from the bathroom. After that Lucilla had fainted. Suppose she fainted now – alone in that dark house? The thought was enough to nerve our Jane to effort. But at the top of the stairs the most extraordinary sensation caught her. A curious feeling like flying – a creeping sensation at the back of the neck – a fancy that the ivy-green window was going round slowly but indubitably – these warned her. She sat down on the top step and shut her eyes.

'If you think,' she spoke silently to the universe, 'if you think that I'm going to faint, I'm not. I must find out what has happened to Lucy. I shall shut my eyes and go on in a minute.' So she shut her eyes. But she did not go on.

What had happened to Lucilla is soon told. With her heart, as they say, in her mouth, she climbed the steep stairs, went along the corridor, and, feeling her way, went more slowly, though she did not mean to go more slowly, down the wide, shallow steps of the front staircase.

'The first door to the left,' she kept saying to herself. 'The *first* door to the left.'

And so reached the lowest step, turned to the left, felt for the door and pushed it open. And, even as she did so, something leaped at her. Before she knew whether she was assailed by the claws of a wild beast, or merely by the iron arm of the law, she found her two wrists clasped. By hands, not by fangs, she noted, after she had sent that one wild scream echoing through the house.

She felt her left wrist transferred to the same strong fingers that held her right, and a low voice said: 'Don't scream – it's no use. Come along,' and she was being urged, quite gently, towards the front door.

With his free right hand her captor opened the door, and the bright spring sunshine struck at her eyes, blindingly. She closed them – and before she could open them again she felt that her wrists were released. She opened her eyes and found herself on the moss-greened door-step, leaning against the heavy door-post, trembling, shivering, decontrolled, and facing her, very deeply and obviously discountenanced, a young man – a handsome young man – the very exactly and beyond any doubt same young man who had thrust himself among the remnants of their arbour breakfast to ask the way to Leabridge.

'Well,' he said slowly, 'I'm . . .'

'I know you are,' said Lucilla breathlessly. 'Of course you would be, but we're not burglars. We're just . . . well, you remember we had breakfast at the Rose and Crown?'

'Yes,' said he, and as she seemed to advance, so he seemed to accept, this certificate of respectability.

'But why? . . .' he asked. 'How? . . . Are you,' he added, breathing more freely in the clear air of a sudden enlightenment, 'a party with an order to view?'

Lucilla hesitated. 'No,' she said, 'how could we, with that insane board? It doesn't let you have orders to view.'

The young man threw his head back and laughed.

'Come!' he said, 'what have you been up to? Tell me all about it.'

'Well,' said Lucilla, who had slowly been recovering her wind and her *sang-froid*, 'the first thing to tell you is that my friend has pitched head first down your treacherous back-stairs and broken her leg.'

'Good Lord!' said the young man. 'And you're standing here talking to me about boards!'

'I'm only just recovering from your catching hold of me like a ghost,' said Lucilla. 'And before we go any further, do you mind defining the situation?'

'Defining? . . .'

'Yes. Are you arresting us for burglars, or –'

'Oh, don't be silly!' said the young man, with a lamentable want of polish.

'Well, then,' said Lucilla, coldly and carefully explanatory, 'my friend has fallen down the back-stairs of this hateful house. She thinks she's broken her leg. Will you help me?'

'What do you take me for?' he said. 'Where is she? Come on!'

'You won't send us to prison?' Lucilla insisted.

'Don't be so extremely silly,' said the young man. ('No manners,' said Lucilla to herself.) 'Where is she? Come on.'

So it happened that Jane in that shivery strange borderland that lies between you as you are and you as you are in mad dreams, heard footsteps coming near, and voices.

'Look out,' said Lucilla, 'you'll tread on her!'

'But you said she was at the bottom of the stairs.'

'I heard . . . you . . . scream . . . and . . . I . . . came . . . as . . . far . . . as . . . I . . . could,' said Jane very carefully, not opening her eyes.

'Help me to get hold of her – that's right,' said the young man. 'Now cut along down and open the shutters in the dining-room. No, the kitchen will be best. Yes – you can take the candle.'

He had Jane in his arms by now – quite easily, for Jane was thin and slight.

It was no fine figure of a woman that he laid on the long kitchen table, but a small, slender, brown-haired person with a white, sharp-chinned, elfish face, which she instantly covered with an arm.

The young man took off his coat and rolled it up and laid it under her head.

Then, very matter of fact, 'Which foot?' he said.

'The other one,' said Jane, kicking slightly with the uninjured leg.

He took off her shoe and felt the ankle. 'Oh, don't!' said Jane. But he took no notice. Presently he said:

'No bones broken, thank goodness. Now look here,' he went on; 'there's a copper full of hot water in here – the char was char-ing. Get a basin or something on this chair, and bathe her foot – as hot as you can bear your hands in it. Keep on with that, and don't let the water get cold. I'll go and get some brandy and a carriage.'

'I'm all right,' said Jane. 'I don't want brandy – I hate brandy.'

'Go ahead with the hot water,' he said to Lucilla. 'Yes, that's the scullery in there. But I've just thought . . .' He pulled a bunch of keys from his pocket. 'There might be something in the cellar – it's just worth trying.'

'Anyhow, *we* haven't stolen anything,' Lucilla comforted her-self as she lifted pails and jugs and copper-lids. 'If he steals things out of the cellar he can't have the face to give us up to justice.'

She had set a clean pail of hot water on a chair augmented by a hassock, had got Jane's stocking off and was bathing the swollen ankle before he came back – the keys clinking against a bottle.

'Where,' he asked sternly, 'where do people keep corkscrews – kitchen corkscrews?'

'*I* don't know,' said Lucilla. 'I never have corkscrews to keep anywhere. Is that brandy?'

'No – old port; well, there are more ways of killing a cat than choking it with butter.'

He retreated to the scullery, and they heard the tinkle of broken glass. He came back with the beheaded bottle and two tea-cups.

'Here,' he said to Lucilla, 'you first. Oh, *don't* be silly. Think what a shock you've had.'

'I thought you were a ghost – or pretending to be; it's just as bad. I don't like wine.'

'Well, drink this, or I shall think it's a ghost I'm seeing. I'm sure you're white enough. That's right. Now lift her head and I'll hold the cup. I hope *she* isn't going to make a fuss.'

54

'No, I'm not,' said Jane shortly, raised her head and drank steadily. 'Thank you. That'll do me lots of good. But really, I'm all right, you know.'

'Yes, you look all right,' said he, and for the first time his eyes dwelt on Jane's face. Lucilla, who happened to be looking at him, remarked an extraordinary flash of something. It couldn't be recognition, because he had not seen Jane at all on the morning of the inn breakfast. It could not be admiration, for poor old Jane was looking like a cross, sick kid. But there was something. No doubt of that. Whatever it was, there it was, Lucilla told herself. Then she looked at Jane to see if Jane had noticed – and there was something about Jane's face too, something odd.

The young man was moving about the kitchen, picking things up and putting them down quite aimlessly. Embarrassed by a dish-cover, he walked to the window and absently set the cover down on a chair. Then he tapped a copper warming-pan as though it had been a barometer.

Lucilla continued her splashing ministrations.

'I'm much better now, thank you,' said Jane suddenly. 'I believe I could walk home.'

'I will go now for that carriage,' said he. 'And I'll get some bandages. You stick to the hot water.'

'I say,' said Jane feebly.

'Well? . . .'

'Don't tell anybody, will you? Not till we've had a chance to explain. We're not really so black as – as your fancy painted us. If you let people know, we shall have to fly the neighbourhood. You won't, will you?'

'By Jove,' he said, 'you *are* better?'

'I told you I was,' said Jane impatiently. 'You won't tell, will you?'

'Silent as the grave,' said he. 'You can trust me. The secret shall be buried with me.'

And he went.

The moment the sound of his footsteps had died away on the

gravel outside Jane sat up and swung herself round so that both feet hung from the table.

'Lucy,' she said, 'let's go. Let's get out of it. I can't face him and tell him what fools we were.'

'*I* wasn't,' said Lucilla.

'Thank you, dear,' said Jane. 'What a fool *I* was, then. If I lean on you we could get away and be gone when he comes back with the carriage.'

'We should meet him,' said Lucilla, stolidly bathing the ankle, 'half way home, and then we *should* look like fools, both of us. What do you want to run away for? He's very nice. I like him very much. I think he's got a very nice face.'

'You think all young men have such nice faces — even chauffeurs,' said Jane.

'Well, he has. And look here, Jane. What was he doing here, anyhow? What right had *he* to send the charwoman off? How did he come by the keys of the cellar? How did he know how big the kitchen table was? You mark my words. He's the owner . . .'

'But he's not old,' said Jane, feebly resisting the flood of Lucilla's eloquence.

'He's thirty, I daresay — and boys think everybody's old.'

'But Mrs Doveton?'

'Oh, hers was only hearsay. You mark my words . . .'

'You said that before.'

'And I'll keep on saying it. You mark my words. He's the owner, and if we play our cards well he'll let us the house.'

'But you said it's too big, and we couldn't afford the rent and the army of gardeners and —'

'I don't care what I said — that was before I'd seen him. He's the owner. I feel it in my bones. Jane, do be decent to him — I feel this is a turning-point in our careers. I feel that this house is going to be the making of us.'

'It's very nearly been the unmaking of me,' said Jane, raised on her elbow to discuss the question more actively.

'I feel as though I'd had about enough of the house. No, don't tell me to mark your words – I can't bear it. If you say that again I shall scream. Let me get off this table, anyhow, and be right side up before your nice young friend comes back. Look here, if that ankle's to be bandaged at all it ought to be *now*. I feel it in my bones, as you're so fond of saying. Can't you find something – a roller towel?'

Lucilla found one and split it into bandages with a carving-knife.

'If he takes wine we may take towels,' she said, and bandaged the red, swollen ankle.

'Now get my stocking on before he comes back. What a blessing we wear sensible, opaque stockings. I don't think there's anything in the world more loathsome than red legs showing through the thin black of imitation silk stockings. Now shut the shutters. Give me that broom – it'll make a lovely crutch.'

'Where are you off to?' Lucilla followed the clump, clump of the broom.

'To where there's a looking-glass,' said Jane. 'I don't agree with you about his nice, kind face, but if he was a criminal insane South Sea Islander I shouldn't like to show myself to him, upright, with my head like a bird's nest and my face wet with your tears. Oh yes, I felt you crying over me when he'd gone for the wine.'

'I didn't,' said Lucilla indignantly.

'Dear old thing,' said Jane, 'I enjoyed it. You're not half a bad old thing, are you, Lucy?'

It was some time before the young man returned with the mouldering relics of a landau, drawn by something which must once, as he said, have been a horse. The blue cloth lining of the carriage had turned to a livid green, and the cushions were, as he did not fail to point out, fossilised by the centuries. But, he humbly confessed, it was the best he could do.

'Where shall I tell him to go?' he asked, when Jane had been made comfortable, with Lucilla beside her. 'Or would you rather' – he lowered his voice beyond the hearing of the tottering relic enthroned on the box – 'would you rather I told him to drive along and you'll tell him later?'

'Thank you,' said Jane; but Lucilla said, '*No*, of course not! Tell him Hope Cottage. And thank you ever so. And . . .'

'Good-bye,' said Jane.

'But look here,' said he. 'I must know how the ankle goes on. May I call – this evening – to-morrow? I can't just say goodbye in this heartless way, and not know whether our first aid was successful.'

'Of course not,' said Lucilla heartily; 'besides, we owe you a roller towel. No, I can't explain now. But will you come to-morrow and . . .'

'What time?' said he.

'Oh – er – I don't know. Tea-time, I suppose,' said Lucilla.

'Tell him to drive on, please,' said Jane coldly.

The decayed remains of a carriage were set in motion, and the young man was left planted there, as the French say, on the door-step of Cedar Court.

'Well,' he said, as he turned to lock the big dark door. 'Well – I really am! Completely and without any nonsense about it, I *am*!'

The parlour was made very pretty with flowers. ('Not too many, Lucy; we don't want to look like the florists we are. Keep out the professional touch if you can,' said Jane.) And Jane, her foot hardly hurting at all, lay on the narrow Empire sofa, covered with the Paisley shawl that Lucilla had most opportunely found that very day in a previously unexplored hair-trunk in the attic.

'And there are all sorts of other things there too,' she told her friend: 'silk gowns and scarves, and fans and parasols – but I wouldn't really explore till you could too. I just took the shawl. It was on the top – it seemed like the hand of Providence. And there were satin shoes and lace petticoats, and satin ones. They'd be gor-geous, those things, for dressing up or charades. And another thing: we can cut them up and make dresses for ourselves. That's the best of those old dresses six yards round.'

'You seem very jolly to-day,' said Jane, almost morosely, from her nest of Paisley and holland-coloured silk – tussore they call it, I believe.

'Well, you see, our first tea-party is just going to happen. And you . . .'

'Don't tell me to mark your words,' said Jane, 'because I can't bear it.'

'I won't,' said Lucilla, stopping short in her final touches to the already almost over-arranged room. 'I'll say something quite different. Where did you see him before?'

'*What?*' said Jane, sitting bolt upright.

'Well, you have seen him before, haven't you?'

'Who?' said Jane uselessly.

'Him. The man that you won't let me tell you to mark my words about. You have seen him before, haven't you?'

'I don't think so . . . I . . . I really don't exactly know. No . . . of course I haven't.'

'Well!' said the exasperated Lucilla, and then the doorbell rang.

'Why,' said Jane, 'it's hardly half-past three! He must be simply longing for his tea.'

'It's all right,' said Lucilla. 'Thank goodness we're perfectly tidy!'

'Too tidy,' murmured Jane. 'He'll know we can't always live like this. Nobody could.'

And then Mrs Doveton flung back the door. And:

'The gentleman you was expecting,' she announced sympathetically.

Jane looked stony, but Lucilla turned with a kind and welcoming smile. But the smile was, as old novelists say, frozen on her lips, when she confronted, not the young man with the nice, kind face, but a tall, gaunt, grizzled old man, with bushy eyebrows and uncompromising side-whiskers.

'Er . . .' said Lucilla.

'Quite so,' said the old man; 'allow me to introduce myself. I am the master of Cedar Court, which you yesterday did me the honour to explore.'

'Er . . .' said Lucilla, fluttering hopelessly.

But Jane said, 'How do you do?' and held out a warm, welcoming hand. 'How very good of you to come,' she went on. 'I can't get up because I sprained my ankle on your dark stairs yesterday. That's the most comfortable chair. Do sit down and let us tell you all about everything.'

'Humph,' said the master of Cedar Court. But he sat down.

Chapter VI

And then with the most graceful self-possession, lying pale and interesting under the Paisley shawl, Jane told the master of Cedar Court all about it, Lucilla uttering timid confirmatory noises.

'So you see,' Jane wound up, 'if we'd had the least idea that you were — at all like you are, we should have come and asked you . . .'

'Butter,' said the old gentleman shortly.

'It's the *best* butter,' quoted Jane. 'I mean that it's quite true; and I wish we *had* asked you.'

'You mean to tell me, then,' he said, looking very straight at her, 'that you crept into that house and explored it by candlelight merely because you thought it a suitable residence for two young ladies who wish to sell flowers?'

'Well,' said Jane handsomely, 'of course there were other reasons, but I've given you the best ones. The others aren't so respectable. Of course there was curiosity, and the-soul-of-romance feeling that there is about old houses; and . . . and . . . well, I suppose the sort of idea that we weren't going to let a silly old board keep us out if we wanted to get in.'

'I admire your candour,' said the visitor, and he quite evidently did; 'but suppose the house had been locked up for some really romantic reason — because someone had lived there so dear that no one else was good enough to live there after her?'

'We never would have,' said Jane indignantly. 'Of course we wouldn't. You see, we knew it was only temper . . . distemper, I mean . . . I mean paint . . .'

The visitor laughed. Jane, cold with excitement and rigid to the ends of her fingers and feet with the stress of the struggle, relaxed a little.

'And what does the other young lady say?' He turned to the still inarticulate Lucilla.

'I say what Jane says,' she answered, still fluttered.

'Do you always?'

'No, of course she doesn't,' Jane put in, 'but she can't say anything true without blaming me, because the whole thing was entirely my fault.'

'And you're paying for it, eh?'

He glanced at the hump that her bandaged foot made under the shawl.

'Well, a little, perhaps,' said Jane. And Lucilla said, 'It was really my fault quite as much. I wanted to, just as badly, only I shouldn't have had the pluck. Jane's so brave.'

'Yes,' he said musingly, 'so it appears. And your relations, how do they regard these heroic exploits?'

'We haven't any relations,' said Lucilla, and explained their position.

He listened, and when she had done, said: 'That guardian ought to be shot. And you're left like that, with only a few hundred pounds and this little house between you and destitution?'

'It's a dear little house,' said Lucilla, gaining courage, 'but you see it *is* so little. We can't grow enough flowers to sell; and all the flowers in your garden . . . We couldn't help gloating over them and wishing we could sell them. We've sold quite a lot even here. And we absolutely *must* do something before all our money is gone. You see, Jane might be an artist, or I might go on the stage, but we should have to learn how – and that takes time; and you have to have meals every day, don't you? So you see we must begin to earn money at once. If it wasn't for that, how lovely to live in this dear little house and learn how to paint and act!'

'I am glad you appreciate the house,' he said; 'it is a lady's house. The lady from whom you inherited it was one of my very oldest friends.'

'You knew my Aunt Lucy?' cried Lucilla. 'How splendid!'

'Yes. I have often been in this house – when I was a boy your aunt and her mother lived here. Your great aunt, she must have been, by the way. I am pleased to see that you haven't altered anything.'

'Oh no,' said Jane; 'how could we, when everything's so absolutely right?'

'That's true, and I compliment you on your clear sight in perceiving it. Now, Miss – Jane, you've told your tale admirably. And Miss Lucy has come up well in support. What do you expect me to do?'

'I hope you'll forgive us.'

'Butter, butter, butter!' he said warningly – 'and not the best either. It isn't my forgiveness you covet. It's my forget-me-nots. Now I tell you candidly, I'm not going to play the part of the benevolent uncle and hand over Cedar Court to you to play the fool with.'

'No, I suppose not,' said Jane regretfully.

'But I'll tell you what I *will* do.'

Jane clasped her hands and sat bolt upright on the sofa. 'Oh, what?' she cried. 'Tell us what you will do!'

'I will let you use the garden and cut the flowers. You may even employ a gardener if you like. *I* shall be the gainer by that.'

'And we can cut all the flowers we like and bring them home here and sell them? Oh, thank you, thank you! How perfectly glorious!' Both girls took part in this spirited reception of the old gentleman's offer.

'Very glorious,' he said drily, 'having to buy a hand-cart or a barrow and lugging the flowers here in all weathers, dragging your petticoats through the rain, and spoiling the blooms. And nowhere to display them when you've got them here; besides destroying the whole atmosphere of Hope Cottage. No, I'll do better than that, young ladies. You shall have the run of the gardens and you shall have the key of the garden room. That's the room you tumbled into,' he explained, turning to Jane, 'only of course you didn't see it. It's painted gas-green. Perhaps it will show off the flowers. You can put a board up at the gate: "The

Misses Jane and Lucy, Florists." By the way, what are your full names?'

'Jane Quested – Lucilla Craye,' they told him.

'Well, as a matter of fact, I shouldn't put up your names if I were you. Just put "Cut Flowers, Fresh Vegetables and Fruit". Oh yes, there'll be vegetables if you employ a gardener. And there'll be fruit in any case. The garden room is at the end of that wing that comes nearly to the gate, so it will be quite convenient for all purposes.'

'You *are* good!' said Lucilla. 'Oh, you are! And I *was* so frightened of you!'

But Jane said, 'It is very, very good of you. And what rent are we to pay?'

He looked at her curiously.

'I hadn't thought about that,' he said. 'Suppose we say ten per cent on your sales?'

'How much exactly is that?' she asked. 'I mean, if we sold a pound's worth of flowers, what would the rent be?'

'Two shillings,' he told her, smiling.

'Then thank you,' said Jane; 'that seems quite fair, because, of course, we shall have to pay the gardener and to spend most of our time there if we're to make anything out of it.'

'I think you will make something out of it,' he said. 'You seem to me to have some aptitude for business. Well, my name is Rochester – James Rochester. I'll send you the keys of the gate and the garden room, and a letter giving you formal permission to sell the garden produce. I am just off to Madrid. There is a book in the library there which I have to consult. And now I'll wish you good afternoon, and good luck!'

'We've had that,' said Jane, beaming at him. And again he said, 'Butter!' But he said it quite gently.

When he was gone the two girls fell into each other's arms.

'Who says we weren't born under a lucky star?' said Lucilla, rocking to and fro with her head on Jane's lean shoulder.

'Yes; but,' said Jane, 'it's all turned out very well as it happens, but what about your young man with the nice face? Treacherous dog! He must have gone straight away and told the old gentleman.'

'He didn't look as if he would,' said Lucilla. 'Perhaps he found out in some other way.'

'That's so likely, isn't it? Put not your trust in young men with nice, kind faces, Lucy. Well, I'm only thankful that we found him out in time.'

'In time?'

'Yes. Mr James Rochester might have called later on, after we'd received that nice, kind-faced young viper and given him tea and cake and gratitude and cream sandwiches. Whereas now! . . . Just tell Mrs Doveton we're not at home to anyone, will you, Luce?'

'But surely you'll give him an opportunity to . . .'

'To what? To tell us that he deceived us? Give him the chance to do it again? Not much. If you like to see him and listen to his lies, do. I'll go to my room.'

She moved on the sofa as if to get up.

'Oh, don't!' said Lucilla. 'Of course I'll do as you like. But I don't care what you say – I believe it's somehow not his fault.'

'If it's any comfort to you to believe it, go on believing by all means. Meantime tell Mrs Doveton. Death to all traitors. If you can't behead them you can at least cut them dead.'

Thus it happened that the helpful young man with the nice, kind face, coming to call on two ladies from whom he had parted on quite friendly terms, was met at the door by a neat, drab-haired woman who entirely filled the doorway and said stolidly:

'Not at home, sir.'

'But,' he said, 'I am expected.'

'Not at home, sir,' was the reply.

'I was to call at five.'

'Not at home,' said Mrs Doveton monotonously, faithful to her trust.

'Oh, very well,' said the young man, and went down the white steps of Hope Cottage.

'He does look furious,' Lucilla said, peeping round the yellow damask curtains; 'and well he may! Oh!' she added, drawing back hastily.

'What's the matter?' said Jane.

'He turned round,' said Lucilla.

'And saw you, of course. Well, you've done it thoroughly this time, Lucy.'

'Done it?' said Lucilla, bewildered.

'Yes – we can never make it up with him now, whatever explanations he gives.'

'But you don't want to make it up with him. You said he couldn't have any explanations,' Lucilla urged.

'Still, there's such a thing as manners. Saying not at home is one thing, but looking out of the window and putting out your tongue at him is another.'

'I didn't.'

'Well, the principle's the same. Don't let's weep over him. We shall never see him again, or know how he came to have the keys, or why he isn't the owner, or how he dared to burgle the cellar for that port wine – or any single thing.'

'But you don't want to know.'

'Of course I don't. He's dead and done with. But Cedar Court, Lucy – Cedar Court. Don't let's talk of silly young men with kind faces and black, false, knavish hearts. Let's talk about Cedar Court. Our Cedar Court. Aren't I tactful? Don't I always do the right thing? How extraordinarily clever it was of me to fall down those stairs, wasn't it? If I hadn't done that, Mr James Rochester would never have come to see us, and we should never have got our heart's desire. Our Cedar Court.'

'It isn't ours,' said Lucilla – 'only the garden and one room.'

'Ah – but that garden and that room – don't you see what that is? It's the thin end of the wedge, my dear. And not such a very thin wedge either. And on second thoughts we won't talk about Cedar Court, because I want you to slip on your bonnet and pop up street, as cook used to say at school. What a long time ago that seems, doesn't it?'

'What do you want "up street"?'

'Why, a bath-chair, of course,' said Jane. 'You don't suppose I can keep away from Cedar Court? And a carriage couldn't go all over the place. And a bath-chair can. And you can push it, can't you? We won't have any wheezy old pug of a bath-chair man spying on us. We'll take possession of Cedar Court all by ourselves — just us two.'

They did. The key and the note from Mr Rochester were duly brought that very evening by a sober-faced man-servant. The bath-chair was found, with some difficulty. It was the only one in the district, Lucilla was assured — and the chickens had unfortunately taken to roosting on it, in the outhouse where it had spent its later years. But it should be well cleaned, miss, you might be sure, and brought round to Hope Cottage at ten to the minute. And it was.

It was, as Jane said, a moment worth living for, when, the big key having unlocked the wrought-iron gate, Jane and Lucilla and the bath-chair passed through.

'Lock the gate,' said Jane. 'We'll not leave it open till we've got our board up. We'll paint that to-night. What a lovely lot of things we've got to do.'

'Garden first?' Lucilla asked, pushing the wicker bath-chair up the mossy drive.

'Rather — we'll keep the gas-green room for the last. Oh, look at the hyacinths! And the daffodils! And the narcissus! And the forget-me-nots just coming out!'

They had turned the corner of the house and, passing close to the yew hedge, now rough and, as it were, hairy, instead of close-shaved, as yew hedges should be, came upon a lawn surrounded by trees and shrubs.

At the end of the lawn two tall cedars stood like king and queen. On each side a weeping ash, its long branches trained over iron hoops, stood, as Jane said, like crinolined ladies-in-waiting. Round the lawn were grouped the courtiers — all in court mourning for last summer, but with the promise of new green suits already displayed. Lilac, broom, gueldre-rose, American currant, and almond trees like pretty girls in their coming-out dresses. And all among the grass and along the edges of the shrubberies were flowers, and flowers, and more flowers again.

'It's like the field of the Cloth of Gold,' said Jane. 'Why, what's the matter, Lucy?'

'It's all too perfect,' said Lucilla, sniffing. 'Look at the trees and the grass and the quiet. What on earth can we have done to deserve this?'

'Nothing,' said Jane. 'Let's hope we shall do something to deserve it before we die.'

Chapter VII

Hot water, the ballet-dancer's remedy for a sprain, does indeed work wonders. Doctors have been known to recommend cold water for this ailment. Charles Reade points out that the interest of the ballet-dancer is to expedite the cure, whereas the doctor's interest . . . But let us have no scandal about doctors. All we are at present concerned with is Jane's ankle, which cured itself 'a perfect miracle,' as Mrs Doveton said, so that by the time the board was painted and dry, and the giver of the board notified of the new store of flowers that would be purchasable at Cedar Court, Jane was able to hobble to the gate to receive his congratulations.

'I never would 'a beleft it,' said Mr Simmons – did I say before that his name was Simmons? Anyhow, it was. 'Never, I wouldn't. All the talk is as the old cove's loony, and now for him to do a sensible thing like that. It don't seem natural, do it?'

Mr Simmons was very sympathetic about the sprained ankle. 'You ain't 'ad a doctor?' he said. 'No, and that's where you're wise. But you want something to cheer it up like, after all that hot sopping. Got any rosemary in either of your gardens? Nor rue either? You don't know? Well, well! I'll bring you a bit to-morrow. You mash it up well in boiling water, and strain off the liquor, and wet a rag with it and put on that foot o' yours. You'll be as right as ninepence in a couple of days.'

They showed him the board and he admired and approved it. 'I was afraid, being young ladies, you might have drawed it a bit too fancy,' he said. 'But no. Plain and clear. That's the style. Have you thought how you'll fix it up?'

'We thought we'd nail it on the post under the board that says "This House is Not to Let".'

'Better let me clip it on the railings for you,' said he, 'with a

69

couple of nuts and bolts. It'll be more noticeable, and the boys won't nick it. I'll bring them herbs along to-night, and you'll see, day after to-morrow, you'll be able to walk down to the Court. That'll be Saturday, and I'll be there.'

'How did you come to know so much about herbs?' Lucilla asked.

'I *do* know a bit,' he said. 'I learned it off my granny. She was a great one for herbs. Ay, and spells too. She'd allus got a rhyme to say when you took the herb tea or whatever it was.'

'Oh, do tell us what to say when you use the rosemary.'

'I can't remember,' he said; 'but the rue one, it goes like this:

> '"Rue, rue, fair, kind and true.
> Do as I would have thee do;
> In a night, in a day,
> Take my pains and griefs away."'

'How lovely!' said Jane. 'Say it again! I shall say it when I put the rue on my foot. And "griefs" too? It's a cure for heartache.'

'I understand from the book,' said Simmons, 'that in those old times when that book was written they just mean pains when they said griefs. It says rue will cure all ache and grief in the bones.'

'Have you got the book?' the girls asked together and eagerly.

'That I have – I'll show it you some day,' said Simmons. 'Funny old book it is, with a picture at the beginning of a gentleman being ill in a four-poster and a doctor with a ham-frill round his neck holding a knife and a basin. Thank you, miss, I *should* like a few violets for a buttonhole if it's not troubling you too much.'

So Lucilla gathered them and Jane pinned them in and Mr Simmons went on his way.

'What a nice world it is,' said Lucilla; 'how nice everybody is!'

'Not everybody,' said Jane sternly. 'But I do think Mr Simmons is a dear. Fancy his knowing that old rhyme. What a lot of friends we're making – Mr Simmons, old Mr Rochester, Mrs Doveton . . . and all the men who buy flowers of us that we don't know the names of. We'll open our shop on Saturday, Luce. What do you think we'd better wear?'

'Whatever does it matter?'

'It's most important,' said Jane, 'to produce a good impression. We want something that looks at once attractive and business-like. Come indoors now, this minute, and let us go through our things and see if we can't find frocks that will be at once elegant and sensible. Yes – I know it's not usual.'

They went in; in the hall Lucilla stopped to say solemnly, 'Jane, we ought to have overalls. Something different from any overalls that anyone has ever had before. Do you think it would be wrong to cut up those dark Indian cotton bedspreads in the servant's bed-room? They're very lovely – rich and rare and crimson and blue. And there are two of them.'

'Angel!' said Jane. 'Let's cut out the overalls now, and make them ourselves.'

'But we don't know how.'

'We'll cut them like those blue Chinese coats our kind guardian sent us – make them a bit longer. They'll be all right, you'll see. What a lark it will be to sell flowers in radiant Eastern garments! Your aunt's little sewing-machine. We can use that and do the hems and necks by hand. Do you think we ought to wear caps? Or coloured handkerchiefs knotted round our heads?'

'Certainly not,' said Lucilla; 'we don't want to look like actresses. I'll go and get the bedspreads.'

The bath-chair was very useful in conveying not only Jane – who did not desire to risk the journey on the restored ankle – but the finished overalls and complete tea equipage, scissors, bast, the oil-cloth from the kitchen table, and various other desired objects. It made several journeys – the last with a number of glass jampots and a few pretty china vases.

Lucilla hung the board provisionally from the top of the rail-ings by a cord, as pictures are hung. Then she took the ever-useful bath-chair and the bread-knife and went into the garden to cut the flowers.

Jane remained in the garden room. It was a panelled room, small and rather high, with a curious domed ceiling. An unusually wide French window opened on the drive, and on each side of this were casements, so that almost all that side of the room was of clear glass. The room was at the end of the left wing of the house, which, so to speak, balanced the round tower on the right side of the building. Another window, also unusually large, opened on the lawn where the cedars stood. In the corner was a door leading to the stairs down which Jane had tumbled, but this door was now locked. Opposite the cedar window was the fireplace, of carved wood, an elegant Adam design. A corner cupboard charmingly panelled stood between fireplace and French window. There were also cupboards on each side of the cedar window – these set in the thickness of the wall. The floor was of black and white stone, laid diamond-wise.

For furniture there were two low chairs with curved, carved backs and soft red and green coloured tapestry seats of the shape associated with the name of the Empress Eugenie; two or three polished beechwood chairs, ladder-backed, rush-bottomed; a large long table and a little round table. A polished pierced brass fender and a dark rug before it completed the furnishing. It would have been a quaint and elegant room but for its colour – the walls, cupboards, mantelpiece, all were painted a clear gas-green.

'But it's not such a bad background for flowers,' Jane told herself, as she opened one of the cupboards to stow away the tea-things. 'Hullo!' she added thoughtfully.

For the cupboard, which had been empty at their last visit, now held a tray of Japanese lacquer, delicate blue-and-white Chinese tea-cups, other blue-and-white china, and the most delightful collection of jugs and mugs and pots and vases that Jane had ever seen.

Green Bruges pottery, Welsh lustre, Grès de Flanders, old pewter. Jane looked at the jampots huddled on the floor and laughed.

She sat down to laugh more at her ease, and was still sitting and still laughing when Lucilla returned wheeling a bath-chair full of daffodils, forget-me-nots, and big budding boughs.

'If ever there was a fairy godmother,' she said, 'it's Mr James Rochester. Look in that cupboard! There's forethought for you! There's delicacy! There's taste! Every kind of possible pot to put flowers in, and not an inch of water for them! We shall have to carry every drop of water for our flowers from Hope Cottage. He might have trusted us with the key of the scullery!'

'He's done better,' said Lucilla, carefully laying the flowers on the long table where Jane had spread the kitchen oilcloth. 'Come here.' She led the way to the window; just at the side, where it could conveniently be reached from the stone doorstep, was a tap, perfectly new, as its own brightness and the bluish bloom of its lead pipes alike testified.

'Is he an angel, or isn't he?' demanded Lucilla. 'You get these flowers in water and I'll get some more. Let's set up pots on those wide window-ledges each side of the door, and we'll put the little table outside to make a show. I'll go and get some more flowers. And let's put our pinafores on. And put away our hats and coats — they spoil the look of the room. There's nothing in the other cupboard, I suppose?'

'This door's jolly heavy. You want too much,' said Jane. 'You've almost got it too,' she said, falling back a little from the open door.

For in the cupboard was a jug and wash-basin, painted with large roses and peonies and gaily-feathered birds, and to the inside of the door was fixed a long looking-glass.

'Replete,' said Jane thoughtfully, 'with *every* modern convenience.'

'It's very wonderful,' said Lucilla. 'I mean *he* must be very wonderful. I can imagine a *young* person taking all this trouble — but an *old* man . . .'

'All old people don't forget what it felt like to be young,' said Jane, voicing a great and rarely recognised truth. 'Get all the flowers you can. When Mr Simmons comes we'll get him to help lift out the big table. This is going to look more attractive than any bazaar stall, Lucy. But I don't like the oilcloth – those little lilac spots . . . And yet, I don't know – it's cottagey. Oh, hurry up! This is going to be what Gladys calls a fair treat.'

It was, though, as Jane pointed out, they would never know *how* fair a treat it would have been, because the board attracted the notice of every passer-by and people came in to buy flowers long before the 'shop,' as they called it, was arranged, and, of course, the more flowers they sold the fewer they had to make the shop pretty with. Still, in spite of this drawback, it was very pretty. Table and window-ledges were golden with daffodils in green pots. Lucilla found a small garden bench, dragged it from its place, and set it up on the drive a couple of yards from the French window. On this was a double row of low pots running over with the blue of forget-me-nots, behind which rose-coloured tulips stood up like little lanterns. On the round table they put a great Flanders jug filled with tall boughs all leaf and blossom, and round it more forget-me-nots.

'Heaven bless good old Mr Rochester for this!' said Jane, washing her hands in the bird-painted basin. 'And a towel and soap! I suppose he must be the best man who ever lived.'

There was no doubt about the success of the shop. Every woman who passed, and who had a few pence to spare, came in, drawn by irresistible curiosity, through the open gates that had so long been closed. And when the dark stream of workmen came down the road it diverted its course through those same gates, and before Mr Simmons had finished the adjustment of his clips and bolts and nuts to the board and the railings, the shopkeepers were hugging each other behind the screen of the open cupboard door and repeating to each other in ecstasy the words: 'Sold out, my dear, sold out!'

'Sold out, Mr Simmons!' they cried in chorus as he came up to the window to announce the completion of his clipping and bolting and nutting; 'and we've got a whole bag of money, and thank you a thousand times for being such a friend.'

'Sold out, have you?' said he, looking a little wistfully at the bare, water-splashed tables and bench on which stood the empty vases. 'I wish I'd 'a thought to ask you to save me a few.'

'Oh, but we *have*,' said Jane, 'only we hid them because people did bother us so to let them have them. And, Mr Simmons, this isn't business. It's a presentation bouquet.'

She took from the cupboard a bouquet of tulips and narcissus; a white paper stuck out stiffly from among the flowers. He read the paper slowly:

'To Mr Simmons on the occasion of the opening of the Cedar Court shop. From his friends Jane Quested and Lucilla Craye.'

'Well,' he said, 'I do take this kind. I never expected anything of the sort. I meant to —'

'We know you did. But we like it best this way,' said Jane; 'and now we're going to have some tea, and you'll have a cup with us and tell us some more about the herb book.'

It was not a merry tea-party, because Mr Simmons was not yet wholly at his ease with his new friends, but it was a pleasant one, and when it was over Lucilla volunteered to show their guest round the garden.

'I don't know,' he said, 'as I like anything better than what I do a bit of garden.'

Jane, left alone, put as much order as she could into the room, and was just beginning to think that the others were a long time gone when a shadow darkened the doorway. She looked up, expecting Mr Simmons and Lucilla. But it was not Lucilla and Mr Simmons. It was the 'kind-faced viper', as Jane had called him. It was the young man who had carried her down when her foot was hurt and had got wine and a carriage for her, had promised secrecy and had then betrayed her trust.

'Good afternoon,' he said. 'I hope your foot is quite well again.' Just like that — as though nothing had happened and he and she were the best of friends.

There was a very small silence. Jane, very white and with thunder on her brow, stood looking at him. Then she spoke.

'I wish you to understand,' she said, 'that we wish to have nothing more whatever to do with you. We decline the honour of your acquaintance,' she insisted, so that there should be no doubt about the matter. And her pointed chin went up as she said it.

He stood looking at her, overwhelmed.

'Oh, I say!' were the only words he found ready for use.

And before either of them could speak again Lucilla and Simmons were standing beside him on the mossy path, and the young man and Simmons were shaking hands with violence, and Simmons was saying, 'Oh, sir, to think of meeting you like this, sir! Oh, miss – oh, young ladies! What a day to be sure! This gentleman's my boss, that I was all through the war with – Suez and Aden and Jeddah and all. You'll excuse me, miss, but may I ask him in for a few minutes while the other young lady sees if she can't find him a few flowers? There's a one or two here and there in the garden. These young ladies as keeps the shop is friends of mine, sir, and I know I may take the liberty to ask you in.'

'May I come in?' the young man gravely asked Jane.

And Jane said, with as little ice in her voice as she could manage, because of Simmons glowing in the joy of re-union, 'Certainly, come in by all means.'

So here they were!

Chapter VIII

When you have just declined the honour of a gentleman's acquaint-ance and have reason to believe that your declination will be accepted as closing the incident, it is more than disconcerting to have a great strong, thick spoke put in your wheel by an enthusi-astic friend who recognises in your rejected fellow-creature his adored hero, and, planting that hero then and there on one of your chairs, stands looking from one of you to the other with a face beaming with joy at the happy coincidence.

'And if the other young lady can't find you enough flowers, sir,' said Simmons, 'I'll let you 'ave my own bouquet – if the lady will excuse me. It isn't the honour or the kindness I shall be giving away, miss,' he added acutely, 'only the beautiful flowers.'

And with a flourish he produced his pink and green and white bouquet, thrusting the written paper proudly under the nose of the newcomer.

'I couldn't think of it,' said the young man strongly; 'if I may be excused, I will follow the lady into the garden and explain what it is that I really want.'

'But . . .' said Jane.

'Quite so. I understand perfectly,' said the young man. 'Forgive me if I seem to hurry, won't you? I don't want your friend to take unnecessary trouble.'

Jane and Simmons were now left. And instantly Jane had a sudden and piercing conviction that Simmons must be got rid of. It seemed to her that almost everything depended on Simmons' not being there when Lucilla and the stranger should return. With that innocent-serpent wisdom which is the amazing hall-mark of the girl we all kneel to, she said in a voice that would have melted a Judge Jeffreys:

'Mr Simmons.'

He answered alertly. 'Yes, miss?'

'I wonder if you would . . . it's getting late and we've such a lot to get home. Would you take the bath-chair up to Hope Cottage, with these jampots, and then bring it back? Oh no, you won't miss your friend – your boss, you said, didn't you? I'll keep him till you come back.'

'Why, of course,' said Simmons, with ready acquiescence. 'I'll load up and set sail this instant minute.'

He did. And the moment he was out of sight Jane limped out through the glass door and round by the Portugal laurels to the cedar lawn. It seemed to be extraordinarily important that this strange young man should not have an opportunity of beguiling Lucilla with, no doubt, untrustworthy excuses.

'Lucy would believe anything,' she told herself, as she stumped quickly along the weedy path towards the distant beacon of Lucilla's brilliant pinafore. When she reached that bright object its wearer was leaning undecidedly against the sundial, and the young man, whose back was towards the approaching Jane, was actually stamping his foot and saying:

'But what on earth was I to *do*? What else could I have done?'

'What *did* you do?' Jane found herself saying, almost in his ear.

He executed a *volte face* of unusual celerity.

'Oh!' he said.

'Yes,' said Jane.

'He says,' said Lucilla, very superfluously, 'that he couldn't have done anything else.'

'What – did – you – do?' Jane repeated very slowly, and distinctly. 'After you had broken your promise and betrayed us to Mr Rochester, what was there left for you to do?'

'Oh, thank you very much!' said the young man unexpectedly. 'That's very kind and candid of you. Now we can get on. There's nothing like straightforwardness. Your friend wouldn't say anything except that you were disappointed in me.'

'*I* wasn't,' said Jane. 'I didn't expect anything but disappointment.'

'I have Irish blood in me, too,' he said, and for an instant the conversation lapsed. Then the young man began to speak, very quickly:

'I didn't betray you. At least, not more than I was obliged to do.'

'Obliged!' said Jane.

'Yes – obliged,' said he; 'and do sit down. The steps of the sun-dial are quite dry, and your ankle . . .'

'Thank you,' said Jane; 'my ankle is my own affair.'

'Quite so,' he said, 'but . . . Well – what happened was this. After you'd gone away in the cab I went back to the house to – to tidy up – the pail and the towels and candles and so on, and before I'd done a single thing the owner of the house came in. There was the pail, there was the towel, the bottle of port with its neck knocked off. There was I, holding a perfectly unexplainable hand-kerchief and an absolutely speaking pink scarf. And he had seen the carriage drive away from the door! What was I to do? Short of pretending to be dumb and deaf, what could I do?'

There was certainly something in that, Lucilla's anxious glance at her friend seemed to plead. And Jane acknowledged that there certainly was by suddenly sitting down on the steps of the sundial and saying, 'Well?'

'Well,' repeated the young man, much encouraged, 'I told him the exact truth. If anything inexact would have been of the slight-est use I would gladly have perjured myself for you. But I couldn't make up a better story than the truth,' he urged shamelessly. 'I told him everything – or almost. But when he asked me who you were, I told him I didn't know. And when he wanted to know where you lived, I didn't know that either.'

'But he did know; he came to see us.'

'He didn't know from me. There is only one livery stable here. Of course he went and asked the cabman. Now, honestly, if you'd been in my place, what else could you have done?'

'Nothing,' said Jane handsomely. 'I'm sorry. But it did look black, didn't it?'

'Black as night,' said the young man; 'and yet, as you see, it wasn't, really. Will you allow me to forgive your terrible and unjust suspicions, and in return will you forgive what I really, you know, couldn't possibly help?'

'Oh yes,' said Lucilla, but Jane said: 'Yes – but I *should* like to know what you were doing in the house at all, and why you had the keys and knew where the wine was, and the towels and everything.'

'Oh,' said he, 'didn't I tell you? I'm his nephew – Mr James Rochester's, I mean. He sent me down because he suspected his charwoman of being drawn from her duties by beer. And he was quite right. I'm staying at his house while he's away. And now, I won't insist on forgiving you if you don't like it. But you will forgive me, won't you?'

'Let's wipe it all off the slate,' said Jane briskly. 'I'm awfully glad you haven't turned out a traitor. I do hate people not to turn out as – respectable as you thought they were going to be, don't you?'

'Yes,' said he, 'but they very seldom do. If you expect people to be decent they almost always are. Will you let me give you my arm?'

Jane let him give her his arm and they went back to the garden room, Lucilla following with five daffodils, two tulips, a hyacinth, and a handful of forget-me-nots.

'Where's Mr Simmons?' she said as they neared the house.

'I sent him home with the jampots,' said Jane, and was intensely annoyed to feel a slow, hot flush spread over face and neck, and even to her very ears. However, if you are a little lame it is an excuse for stooping, and she kept her face turned downwards.

Mr Simmons and the bath-chair reappeared almost at once, and the garden house was locked up, its Persian shutters adjusted and padlocked and the iron gates secured. Mr Simmons and his 'boss' made an appointment for another meeting, and it was John Rochester who wheeled the bath-chair to Hope Cottage, at whose gate Lucilla said:

'What about another tea? At least, have you had yours?'

Mr Rochester hadn't. So he came in, and there was tea, and old china, and Queen Anne spoons, and thin bread-and-butter – but everything was stiff and lacking in charm.

'There had been too much forgiving, and too lately, for any of us to be really comfortable,' said Jane when he had gone. 'What on earth made you ask the man in, Lucy?'

'I thought you'd like me to,' said Lucilla, with quite monumental tactlessness.

'You never made a greater mistake,' said Jane; 'my one wish was to be rid of him and try not to remember the perfectly awful things I said to him when he first turned up.'

'What *did* you say?' Lucilla asked, with a perhaps justifiable curiosity.

'I quite forget,' said Jane briskly. 'However, I'm glad it's all straightened out. I hate muddles.' She stretched herself luxuriously on the narrow Empire couch. 'What a day it's been! The best day of my life, Lucy!'

'It has been nice,' said Lucilla, still thickly entangled in an unwonted tactlessness; 'it *is* nice to have things straightened out with nice people.'

'Oh – *that*!' said Jane slightingly. 'I meant because we'd made so much money! Look here, Luce, you fetch the papier-mâché tray out of the dining-room – the one with the mother-of-pearl roses on it – and we'll pour out all the money on it, and count it, and gloat over it; and then we'll make three lovely satin bags to keep it in – one for copper and one for silver and one for gold.'

'You mean notes,' said Lucilla, and went to fetch the tray.

Meanwhile Mr John Rochester went on his way with a good deal to think about. He felt, emotionally, rather battered: forgiving and being forgiven is exhausting work. Also he had to write to his mother – not the ordinary duty-letter, all affection and *petites nouvelles*, but a serious answer, too long delayed, to a serious letter of hers.

When he reached the small brick-built house where every room save those where folk slept was covered from ceiling to floor with bookshelves and pigeon-holes, he sat down at a large littered writing-table and pulled out a letter, it was a long one, several sheets of pale blue linenish-looking paper. Among many words he read:

81

'Your dear father once told me that he had never been in love in his life. Of course he told me differently when he proposed, or I should never have accepted him. But I am sure what he said later was true. You are so like him, dear Jack, in face and voice and everything, I think, as I have so often told you, that you are very likely like him in this too. But it is quite possible to be happily married without being what is called in love. You are twenty-eight, dear, and if you had been the sort of boy who falls in love you would have done it before now, don't you think? It's no use waiting for what will most likely never happen. I assure you, if *one* of the two parties loved the other, marriage is quite easy and pleasant. And your whole future depends on your having money to pursue your experiments and inventions and things. Now, dearest, do let me warn you not to build *any* hopes on your great-uncle James. He let your father think he was going to do something for him, and then he never did. He is very eccentric, and you never know. He is always running about – now to Italy, now to India or China. Though he is an old man, he might marry a Contadina or a Ranee or a Geisha at any moment and have troops of children. Now, darling, remember what I've always told you about Hilda Antrobus. She has simply heaps of money – not tied up at all. Her solicitor is a great friend of your Uncle Philip and told him this *in confidence*. She has not changed at all in all these years. She has practically owned to me that she would accept you – at least, of course, not in so many words, but she has owned to me as plainly as a modest girl can that she *likes* you. She has refused *dozens* of offers. She simply won't look at anyone else. Now, my own treasure, I am asking her for the twenty-seventh, and I want you to come too. I am sure when you see her again you will think she has greatly improved in looks. And she has a really lovable nature, so noble and unselfish. The man who gets her will be very lucky. It isn't as if you were *likely* to fall in love, my precious treasure; and esteem and respect and affection are really better for getting married on than this wild love we hear so much about. Especially when joined to a handsome income, so that no sordid worries can interfere with your happiness. Write to me at once and tell me that *for once* you'll be guided by my advice. I don't want you to promise anything. Just come and meet her. That's all I ask.

'Your affectionate mother,
'Estelle Rochester.'

John Rochester read the letter twice before he took up his pen. But, once started, that pen travelled smoothly over several pages of his uncle's special hand-made paper with the little coat-of-arms in the corner. The pen dealt with the weather, with the writer's health, with Uncle James's health, with Uncle James's journey to Spain, with the object of that journey; and so to the obligation which the writer was under to occupy Uncle James's house till Uncle James's return. On the last page, which was the sixth, the pen was driven to say:

'I have thought over all you say about my future. I am not so very sure that you are right about my being so like my father. And perhaps he was not exactly like what you always say of him. Perhaps he said what you say when he was in a temper. People do say the oddest things at such times, don't they?

'Please remember me most kindly to Miss Antrobus. I am so sorry that I shall not have the pleasure of meeting her again this spring, but I have promised my uncle to guard his books and curios as with my life, so, of course, I am planted here till he returns. I trust Miss Antrobus will have a very pleasant visit – but of course she will, with you, best of mothers.

'You have often talked to me of Cedar Court. I went all over it the other day. It is a most delightful place, just as you said, and my visit was full of interest. The furniture, the garden – everything – quite different from anything I have ever seen before. I hope to go there again and again. These old houses well repay repeated visits. With fondest love, I am, dear mother, your loving son,

'John.'

Chapter IX

'And six is seventy-nine,' observed Lucilla; 'seventy-nine pence – how many shillings, and what pence?'

Jane told her, and waited patiently till the agony of the shillings column had given place to the easy sparseness of the pounds. It was Saturday night, and they were 'making up the books'.

'I make it three pounds seventeen and fivepence,' Lucilla announced at last. 'See what *you* make it.' Jane made it four pounds two and a penny. So then they added it all up again, the two of them together, and the total was four pounds three shillings and fourpence.

'This is too much!' said Jane desperately.

'Yes,' said Lucilla, 'much too much!'

'I mean it's too silly. Here we've been a thousand years at school, and you took an arithmetic prize when you were nine . . .'

('"Sundays at Encombe,"' put in Lucilla).

'. . . And yet we can't add up six little sums of pounds, shillings, and pence and then add the totals together and get them right.'

'We don't know that we haven't got them right. One of the answers may be right for anything we know. It's so different doing it with real money,' said Lucilla, fingering the little piles of coin on the table of the garden room, where, with two candles in brass candlesticks to light them, they were seeking to find some relation between the coins – so easily counted – and the figures referring to these same coins which all through the week they had laboriously pencilled in an exercise-book.

'I think it's the garden distracts us,' said Jane, looking towards the open window, beyond which lay lawn and cedars bathed in moonlight and soft spring air.

'Let's shut the shutters or else take everything home,' Lucilla suggested. 'It's awfully late, and I'm very, very hungry.'

'Nonsense — stick to it! Not a bite or sup do you get till our figures agree. Oh, I say — we spent ninepence on chocs. — *that* came out of the shop money. And that gipsy who had the wallflowers, she didn't pay, you remember — that makes a difference of twopence. And did you put down the half-crown we paid the man who swept up the path and tied back the creeper?'

And so the maddening work of the amateur accountants began all over again.

'They ought to have taught us all about this at school,' said Lucilla; 'there's something called "striking a balance".'

'I shouldn't mind — I feel quite violent enough. I'd strike it fast enough if I could find it. It means when everything adds up to the same as everything else, I think,' Jane added instructively. 'Don't giggle, Lucilla, it wasn't really funny. You're faint and hysterical from want of food. Look here — this looks more like it.'

It did, much more like it — so much so that a mere difference of ninepence-halfpenny might have been allowed to assume the disguise of 'sundries' so useful in these emergencies. But then Lucilla suddenly remembered that she had put a Bradbury in the first volume of Browning for safety. That made the balance wobble again horribly, and go down on the other side with a surplus of nineteen and twopence-halfpenny.

'Oh, *stop* it!' said Lucilla, pushing her hands through her hair. 'Let's get home, and do it after supper. Our brains are reeling with famine. Don't you know when you're hungry all your blood rushes to your stomach and your brain's left high and dry? At least, I think that's it. What's that?'

'That' was a footstep on the gravel outside.

'Idiots!' said Jane, and flung a duster over the money. 'If it's a burglar,' she whispered — 'well, we've been asking for it, sitting here with candles, making a show of our money and our unprotectedness.'

'It's out in the road,' said Lucilla in the same low voice.

'It isn't,' said Jane. And it wasn't. For the next moment the footstep was heard, not on gravel, but on granite, and the figure of a man blotted out the picture of the moonlit lawn. Jane stood up between the door and the duster-covered table, and said, 'What do you want?' rather sharply, and, 'Oh, it's you!' in tones that were a little flat. She sat down suddenly.

'I thought you were a burglar,' she said. 'Yes – I know we thoroughly deserve that you should be.'

'Well,' said young Mr Rochester, 'I thought that myself the prospect might be tempting to a not thoroughly high-principled passer-by. So I thought you wouldn't mind my coming in – in the character of watch-dog. May I help you with the shutters? I suppose you're going to close the shop soon?'

'We have a vow in heaven,' said Jane, 'not to close the shop till the accounts come right.'

'And they never will, you know,' said Lucilla in gentle desperation; 'unless . . .' she added, with a sudden ray of hope, 'unless you can do sums?'

He could; he did. He brought the sundries to the irreducible minimum of elevenpence. He made the books *look* balanced, at any rate, and announced the takings for the week at four pounds, six and twopence, a total which had for the young accountants the double charm of comparative magnitude and complete novelty.

Then he helped them to put up the shutters and to lock door and gate. And that was the beginning of Mr John Rochester's activities as accountant to the flower business.

'You see,' he pointed out when the girls protested politely, 'it's a positive charity to give me something to come out for. I'm stuck at my uncle's place till he gets back from Madrid. I'm trying to invent a thing that's never been invented before – a much more difficult job than you'd think – and I've absolutely no one to talk to and nowhere to go. If you wouldn't mind my looking round now and then to see if I can lend a hand in anything? Please don't thank me – the thanks will be all the other way if you'll let me.'

So it was understood that they gratefully would let him. And he saw them and their bag of money to their own door.

'How nice he was this evening,' said Lucilla, as the two friends sat over their cocoa and bananas and bread-and-butter. They took it in turns to keep house. This was Lucilla's week, and this was an economical day. 'So much nicer than the first time.'

'He's not bad,' Jane admitted.

'He's awfully nice,' said Lucilla. 'I do think –'

'Don't say you think he has such a kind face,' said Jane quickly, 'because I won't bear it. He's all right, and quite nice and friendly and all that. And I hope he'll keep so. We've got our livings to make, and we don't want young men hanging round, paying attentions and addresses and sighing and dying and upsetting everything. If he likes to be a good chum I don't mind, but the minute I see any signs of philandering, the least flicker of a sheep's eye, we'll drop Mr Rochester, if you don't mind.'

'Well,' said Lucilla with firmness, taking a third banana, 'I do think you're horrid. Can't a young man be civil to us but you must begin to think things? Why can't you let things be? It would be time enough to talk like that if he'd shown the faintest signs of anything of the sort. Girls oughtn't always to be on the look-out for addresses and attentions and so on.'

'Yes, they ought,' Jane insisted; 'just as you ought to be always on the look-out for snakes in the grass – I mean if you live in snaky sort of countries. We've – got – to – earn – our – living. And when we've done that it'll be time to think about playing at Romeo and Juliet and all that. We're business girls – and I hope your young man will see that we are.'

'He's not my young man,' Lucilla retorted placidly; 'and the poor dear hasn't shown the faintest sign of Romeoishness, anyhow.'

'He'd better not,' said Jane fiercely.

'What would you do?' Lucilla asked, her pretty eyes shining with a mild curiosity above her fourth banana.

'He'd soon see what I'd do,' Jane retorted. 'But there – perhaps I do but wrong the lad. I daresay it's only in books that a young man can never do a friendly act for a young woman without its meaning some silly nonsense or other. Perhaps really young men are just as sensible and reasonable as girls are.'

'I shouldn't wonder,' said Lucilla. 'You see, we know very little about them except from books. And in books they *have* to be lov-erish, and so do the girls, because they're all heroes and heroines, of course. But I've sometimes thought that real life is most likely quite different from books.'

'You bet it is,' said Jane – 'from some books, anyway. Don't look so pleading, Luce – I'll promise not to bite his head off if he behaves like a real person. But business girls have to be on their guard against behaving like heroines or allowing other people to behave like heroes. Let's get to bed. I'm dog-tired and there's no more cocoa.'

'No more there is,' said Lucilla, looking into the jug with one eye. 'Come on then.'

And they went.

Business was very slack on Monday, and still slack, though brightening, on Tuesday. There were not very many flowers in the garden, and cutting and arranging these occupied but a small part of the day. The girls read and talked and sewed and wrote letters during the long intervals between customers. And the gas-green walls, which on Saturday had made a tolerable background for the masses of flowers and the brisk sale for them, formed a poor setting for an almost domestic scene.

'I wish we could get it off,' Lucilla said. 'I can't think how any-one *could* paint old oak such a colour – or any colour for that matter. Look how lovely the insides of the cupboard doors are. I wish we could get it off. What *do* you get paint off with?'

They asked Mrs Doveton, and she answered with unexpected cynicism that the stuff they sell to clean it generally does the trick. 'In time,' she added, as one desiring to be fair to an enemy. 'If you wanted it off sudden I should soak in soda and scrape.'

There are difficulties about soaking four walls still occupying a vertical position. But our young enthusiasts bought some soda and a paint-brush and painted the door of the corner cupboard with a strong solution of soda. Then they scraped with Lucilla's palette-knife, and the paint came off – some of it. Some of it, on the other hand, did not come off. The effect was speckled and streaked, the old oak showing through the half-vanquished paint like brown mould under thinly-sown new grass.

'How perfectly awful!' said Lucilla. 'I do wish we hadn't.'

'Never regret, never apologise, never explain,' Jane quoted.

'Who said that?'

'I said it. But someone else said it first. Napoleon or Socrates or Machiavelli or someone. It does look pretty ghastly,' she owned; 'unless we can do something to get the rest of it off we shall have to paint it again.'

'Suppose our landlord comes back from his castle in Spain while it's looking like that? He'll turn us out as sure as fate.'

'Paint it with soda again,' said Jane, 'and we'll try again to-morrow.'

This was on the Wednesday, and in the afternoon Mr Simmons called 'to see if the board was holding up'.

'Whatever you been after with that cupboard door?' he asked.

'Trying to get the paint off,' said Jane shortly.

'Don't you like the colour, miss? I thought it looked so nice and refined myself.'

'We don't want to be refined,' said Lucilla; 'we want to see the colour of the wood.'

'What you tried?'

'Soda – and it's not taken off half the paint, but all the skin's off our hands!'

The girls displayed four scarlet paws.

'Dear, dear!' said Simmons, deeply concerned. 'Why-ever didn't you ask me? My boss, him that was here the other day, he knows all about chemistry and dyes and engines and dynamite and all sorts. I lay I can get him to give me something to eat off that green paint as if it was caterpillars on a cabbage-plot. You put some honey and lily leaves on them poor hands of yours, and I'll come along Saturday and see what I can do to the paint. I've got a day off then.'

'You *are* good, Mr Simmons,' said the two girls in absolute unison.

'Granted,' said Mr Simmons absently. 'Though I can't see what you wanted to touch it for, myself. But there's no accounting to be placed on tastes, is there? Good afternoon, I'm sure.'

When the girls reached the shop on Saturday morning they found the shutters down, the glass doors open, and two figures in blue boiler-suits busy with a pail and a step-ladder. The door of the cupboard was a smooth grey-brown. Not a streak of paint remained on it.

'How splendid!' said Jane to Simmons, whose face beamed above the first suit of blue overalls. 'Why, it's you again!' she said, not very graciously, to the wearer of the second suit.

'Yes,' answered Mr Rochester. 'I thought I might as well lend a hand. Try to disguise your annoyance, won't you? I know I'm only an amateur, but I mean well.'

'There's no reason why you should,' said Jane.

'On the other hand, there's no reason why I shouldn't,' said he. 'Don't be so stony. Only those who have spent lonely weeks waiting for an uncle who fails to return from Madrid can begin to estimate all the possibilities of boredom which life has to offer. Don't be so bristly, Miss Quested.'

'There's no reason why you should do this for us, or anything else for that matter,' said Jane. Lucilla had gone out into the garden, and Mr Simmons was whistlingly at work in the room's farthest corner.

'I am not doing it for you, if I may say so,' Mr Rochester said coolly. 'I am doing it for Mr Simmons, whose faith in my omnipotence you surely would not have me lightly shatter. Besides, this is the day for balancing the books. I thought I ought to be here in good time.'

'It's nine o'clock in the morning,' said Jane. 'We balance the books when we've shut the shop. At seven to-night.'

'Well, then, I *am* in good time. I thought I was.'

'You're talking nonsense!' said Jane.

'How you read me! Concealment is at an end. I am talking nonsense. Is that forbidden in the Temple of the Muses?'

'We aren't Muses,' said Jane.

'I know you aren't. But if I said the Graces you'd have been cross.'

'I'm cross now,' said Jane. 'For goodness' sake go home and do your inventing and let Mr Simmons do the paint scraping.'

'You're not really cross,' he said; 'you only think you are. It's much too fine a day to be really cross on. You're not cross. You're disappointed.'

'Disappointed?'

'Yes. You are the princess setting out to seek her fortune, and you want to kill all the giants and ogres yourself – with your own hand and your own trusty sword. Do let me help Simmons to kill this very little green dragon for you – it isn't really a dragon, it's only a baby drakeling. And besides . . .'

Jane had not enough experience to enable her to perceive that he only paused there so that she might ask, 'Besides what?' She asked it.

'Besides – I deserve some slight concession.' He added something which she could only just hear. She would have liked to ask, 'What was that you said?' but experience comes quickly and she did not ask it. And really she was almost sure that what he had said was, 'I have kept away from you for a week.'

She stood silent.

'Well,' he said, 'does the princess relent? May I go on scraping the paint off?'

'Oh, do as you like!' said Jane, and went out into the garden. Again she was not quite sure of his answering words. They certainly sounded like: 'I wish I could!'

Chapter X

'Look here,' said Jane one morning as they sat in their shop, now almost wholly oak and bearing but few gas-green streaks on its furthest wall, 'we've been at it now for over three weeks and we haven't had a single holiday. Here we are, in London, or as good as, and we haven't seen a picture gallery or a museum. We haven't seen Madame Tussauds or the Thames, except just crossing the bridge that first evening; we haven't seen the Tower or Westminster Abbey or the Houses of Parliament; we haven't been to a theatre.'

'We couldn't do *that*, anyhow, without a chaperone.' You see how very old-fashioned Lucilla was.

'Yes, we could – matinées,' said Jane, who was old-fashioned too. 'They're quite respectable. The only difficulty is the shop. Really business people never leave the shop.'

'I've sometimes thought,' said Lucilla, 'that perhaps there's something almost slavish about our opening the shop on Mondays. We took ninepence last Monday and one-and-a-penny the Monday before, and the Monday before that we took nothing, and I lost my green bag coming down with two shillings and a pair of perfectly good gloves in it.'

'You're quite right,' said Jane, 'we mustn't make an idol of the shop. That's bowing down to Mammon, and you end in frock-coats and top-hats, and buying up the country seats of impoverished county families, and being road-hogs, and getting titles if you bow down long enough. Business is a good servant but a bad master. I'm sure I've read that somewhere. Look here, we'll take a holiday next Monday – at least, a half-holiday. We took that one-and-ninepence in the morning. We'll open the shop from nine to twelve, and then we'll go to London and see life.'

'Where shall we go?'

'We'll write all the places we want to go to on bits of paper and put them in a hat and shut our eyes and draw fair.'

They did – only instead of putting the papers in a hat they put them in a Lowestoft bowl, and each drew a paper.

'Mine's the National Gallery,' said Jane, in rather a disappointed voice; 'and I wrote it myself, too. Serves me right.'

'Mine's Madame Tussauds,' said Lucilla.

'Oh, well,' said Jane, cheering up, 'we'll go there first. I've never seen any waxworks and I've always wanted to most frightfully, ever since we read "The Power of Darkness". You remember about the young man who betted he would spend a night alone with the waxworks, and when it was dark one of the wax things moved or came alive or something? Oh – horrible!'

'We'd certainly better go there first,' said Lucilla. 'I don't think I should like those things at night – the guillotines, and Marie Antoinette's head, and Marat in his bath, and all the murderers. Do you remember that catalogue Kate Somers had? And she used to read bits out of it and make up stories to fit, till the little ones were afraid to go to bed. There was one horrible tale, do you remember, about poor little Madame Tussaud having to make wax models of the heads of kings and queens and people – just the heads – loose – no bodies you know – just as they came fresh from the guillotine? It must have been a nasty business – all the blood.'

'Shut up!' said Jane firmly, 'or you'll be afraid to go to bed. I know you! I'm not at all sure that I shall allow you to see the Chamber of Horrors at all.'

'I'm not sure that I want to,' Lucilla retorted.

But when they stood on the brink of the Chamber of Horrors she felt otherwise.

After a most interesting ride on the top of a tram, a luncheon consisting almost entirely of cream buns, éclairs, ices and tea, and a really exciting journey by Tubes, on which neither had ever travelled before, they came to the big building in Baker Street, and made a leisurely progress through the Halls of Fame, where

Byron and Bottomley, Dan Leno and Father Bernard Vaughan, Voltaire, Mrs Siddons, and Lady Jane Grey compete for the notice of the visitor with those waxen faces that would be exactly lifelike if they were not so exactly like death. They saw Luther and Mary Queen of Scots next-door neighbours, and Burns not too proud to be next door but one to Sir Thomas Lipton. They saw the Grand Hall and the Hall of Kings, which Jane said was like a very nice history lesson. It was when they paused at last before the Coronation Robes of Napoleon and Josephine that Jane said: 'I've had enough. Let's get out. I'm beginning to feel as if these people were alive and just going to speak to us.'

'We'd better see the Chamber of Horrors now we *are* here,' said Lucilla.

'Well, don't blame me!' said Jane elliptically, and they went forward with new vigour. But when they came out of the Chamber of Horrors even Jane was pale, and Lucilla said:

'It's very much more horrible than you'd think it possibly could be. They're only wood and wax and cloth, and their eyes that seem to look at you are only glass eyes. At least . . . well, if I were to stay in there long I shouldn't be sure of that or anything else. They're uncanny; there's a sort of horrible magic about them.'

'That's your highly-strung nature, my child. They're really only wax and glass and wood and clothes and stuffing – just dolls with murderous faces. Well, I don't like the heads myself. But I'll tell you what I think is really much more horrible, in a way.'

'Oh, what?' said Lucilla, almost in a whisper.

'Well, *I* think,' said Jane, 'that the most horrible thing is the ordinary people, standing and sitting about – they really *are* life-like; some of the others are rather too like life to be quite lifelike and rather too dead for you to want to be alone with them in the dark. But the other ones – I don't really like them, even in broad daylight. Look at that one on the seat there – just a hard-up, tired boy – shabby clothes, worn shoes – all complete – just like life, and yet it's much more like . . . Oh, I don't know!'

'That's not wax,' said Lucilla, 'that's real.'

'It does almost look like it,' Jane confessed, 'but you can tell by the hands. That sort of waxy pale yellow – that's what gives it away. Come close and look if you don't believe me.'

They went close to the figure on the red velvet bench, which certainly represented with extraordinary fidelity a tired youth asleep, head dropped on the breast, arms folded, waxen white hands on the sleeves of a very shabby coat.

'There's one mistake though,' Jane pointed out. 'If he was real and as shabby as that, his hands and nails wouldn't be so beautifully clean.'

She sat down on the bench by the figure with Lucilla on her other side.

'I believe it is real,' Lucilla persisted, 'and I don't like it. I mean I don't like its being so like real if it's only wax. It *is* real, Jane – come away!'

'It isn't,' said Jane, 'look here!' and she caught in her hand the arm of the wax figure.

Of course you are prepared to hear that the figure sprang to its feet, and that it was not wax, but neither you nor anyone else could have been prepared for the shriek with which the wax figure leapt up, nor the answering shriek which Jane contributed when the wax figure came to life, so to speak, in her hands.

The man who had been wax, and the girl who had been so sure that he was nothing else, stood staring at each other.

'What was it? Did I call out?' he asked.

'Ye – ye – yes,' said Lucilla.

And then a custodian was upon them asking questions, and a vista opened up of possible unpleasantness for everybody.

'What's the matter, miss?' he asked, as one who has a right to know. 'This young man been annoying you?'

'Certainly not,' said Jane, with an almost convulsive but successful clutch at her self-possession. 'We were only laughing.'

'Funny sort of laugh,' said the custodian sourly.

'It does sound so to strangers,' Jane explained; 'all our family laugh like that,' she added a little wildly.

'You know the young man then?' said the custodian grudgingly.

'Of course I do,' said Jane. 'He's my brother, and he fell asleep
and I woke him up and then we all laughed. It's nothing to make
a fuss about. Come along, Bill, or we shall be late for tea and Aunt
Emma will be furious.'

She actually, as she wondered afterwards to remember, took the
arm of the stranger and led him away from the 'house of the pale-
fronted images'. The three moved in a stricken silence, the young
man walking as in a dream, and it was not till they were a couple
of hundred yards down the road that he spoke, and his voice was a
very pleasant one.

'How splendid of you! How you carried it off!'

'I appear to be carrying *you* off,' said Jane, 'but it seemed the
only way. That man had prison and fines and all sorts of things in
his eye. I don't know what they can do to you for screaming in
public buildings, but, whatever it is, that man would have seen to
it that they did it.'

'Such presence of mind,' said the youth — he was hardly
more — 'and so very, very decent of you to rescue me. I don't
deserve it, after frightening you like that with my yells. But I was
dreaming, and something woke me up suddenly.'

'I did,' said Jane, 'and then I yelled. We'd been frightening ourselves with the Chamber of Horrors — and then . . . Well, you see,
it was like this . . .'

'You can't stand here explaining things on the pavement —
everybody's staring at us. Let's go and have some tea — yes, now,'
said Lucilla strongly, though her voice trembled, 'and you can
explain sitting down.'

'Yes, let's.' Jane welcomed the suggestion, for the arm she held
was actually trembling and her own heart was still beating wildly.
'I'm sure we all need something to revive us after the shock of
being screamed at by each other.'

'*I* didn't scream,' Lucilla reminded her.

'No,' said Jane, 'but you said, "Ye-ye-ye-yes-s," and nearly gave the show away. Besides, *you'd* nothing to scream about. We had. There must be thousands of tea-shops about here. You will come and have tea with us and let us explain?' she urged her captive, who murmured, 'If you'll let me. You're too good. I don't want to be a nuisance . . .' and yielded.

'And of course,' said Jane, ending her explanation with her elbows on the marble-topped table among the tea-cups, 'if we hadn't been frightening ourselves with murderers, and Marat in his bath, and guillotined heads, and muddling ourselves with whether things were wax or weren't, I shouldn't have grabbed you like that and you wouldn't have yelled, and then I shouldn't have yelled either. And anyhow, I can't think how I could have been so silly.'

'If you come to that, what makes people so silly as to go to waxworks when they know they're going to be frightened?' Lucilla asked.

'I went because my landlady gave me a ticket,' said their new friend, 'and it seemed a good place to rest in. I didn't mean to be frightened.'

'We went because we drew it out of a hat,' said Lucilla; 'and we didn't exactly mean to be frightened either – we came out expressly on a pleasure hunt.'

'I've been hunting too – but mine's for work,' said the young man; 'and I was so unsuccessful and so weary that I felt I must sit down or die. And as I had the ticket I postponed my decease. And then sleep came over me,' he went on absently, 'and I dreamed I was in prison again – and when you caught my arm I thought you were . . . Oh, it was really too overwhelming.'

'Have another cup of tea,' said Jane, with sudden and not too overwhelming tact. She felt that she must speak before her own silence and Lucilla's had time to become embarrassing. 'And those little fat cakes are quite good, do try one.' To herself she was saying: 'This is what comes of making friends with strangers. How awful! But how frightfully thrilling too! Prison! Just out of it, I expect! That's why he can't get work. How dreadful for him!'

She looked across the table at the thin face of the young man, at his fair hair, with the one long lock that *would* drop over his blue eyes – at his thin, delicate mouth and finely-cut chin. How dreadful it was that a young man – such a young man – should have every gate closed to him, should be unable to get back into honesty, just because he had been in prison – perhaps not for anything very bad. She was sure that with that face he had not done anything very bad. She must say something, or he would see that he had let out about his having been in prison, and then he would get up and go, and they would never be able to help him. And Jane felt that they must help him. Fate had thrown him and them together in such a very marked manner; it was as if Fate meant them to help him. And they would. She must think of a way. But also she must speak again, for the young man had only said, 'Thank you,' for the cup of tea, and Lucilla's silence was becoming monumental.

'What sort of work were you looking for?' Jane asked gently.

'Anything,' he said, 'but I'd rather not go into an office. I feel as though I could not endure the confinement after –'

'I understand,' Jane interrupted, 'but what would you *like* to do, if you had your choice – what do you think you do best?'

He laughed and put back that lock of hair.

'*I* think I write verses best,' he said, 'and sometimes I even think I don't do them badly, but the world is not of my opinion – yet. As to what I would *like* to do – well, one has one's dreams, of course . . .'

'I beg your pardon,' said Jane, stiffening, 'I didn't mean to be inquisitive.'

'You aren't. You couldn't be. It's only too gracious of you to take the faintest interest. All I meant was that my dreams would waste too much of your time if I let myself begin to bore you with them. Besides, I must not dream any more for a long time. I must work. And I would rather work out of doors.'

Lucilla was still saying nothing so carefully that Jane, without looking at her, knew that she was in an agony of anxiety as to how they should get rid of this new and shockingly undesirable acquaintance. This inexplicably deepened her own resolve not to get rid of him, but to stand by him in his trouble as one human being should stand by another.

'Out of doors?' she repeated. 'Do you mean farm work or . . .' She smiled encouragingly at him. (Poor fellow, who knew how long it was since anyone had smiled at him? she thought.)

'I was really thinking of gardening,' he said, smiling back at her. 'I would be contented with quite small wages. I want to be out of doors. I want to get strong again after . . . I was brought up in Kent. My people had a farm. I know a good bit about gardens. I suppose you don't know anyone who wants a gardener?'

'Yes,' said Jane resolutely, 'we do!'

Then Lucilla spoke.

'Oh, Jane,' she said, 'how *can* you!'

'I beg your pardon?' said Jane, with frigid politeness.

'I mean,' Lucilla tried to explain, 'we hadn't really decided on a gardener, had we? And I don't know that we can afford it.'

'You see' — Jane turned to the self-confessed jail-bird with a smile nicely calculated to efface anything that might have been unpleasing in Lucilla's words — 'my friend is determined not to make a stranger of you. I assure you it isn't everyone she'd talk to about our poverty.'

The silky smooth tone and the sweet smile should have warned Lucilla; long experience at school might have taught her to recognise the symptoms of Jane at bay — or, rather, Jane with the bit between her teeth. But Lucilla was not quite her acutest self. The waxworks had set her nerves tingling and twittering, and she said:

'I didn't mean to talk about our poverty or anything of the sort.'

'I know,' said Jane, affecting sympathy, 'but one gets led away into these sort of confidences, doesn't one, with congenial people? I feel just the same myself. Now *I* was going to suggest that Mr —?' She turned to him with raised, interrogative eyebrows.

'Dix,' said he.

'Thank you. My name is Quested and my friend's is Craye. I was going to suggest that Mr Dix should give us his address and we should write to him; then we should have quietly talked over our means between ourselves, you know, Luce dear, and decided what we could or couldn't afford. But since you've taken Mr Dix into our confidence so fully, dear Luce, concealment is at an end, and Mr Dix may as well come and talk it over with us. Could you come to tea, Mr Dix? Next Sunday? Cedar Court, Leabridge, S.E.'

'Please don't worry about the gardening idea,' said Mr Dix, looking from Jane to Lucilla. 'Of course I should be enchanted to be allowed to come to tea, but are you sure . . . I don't want to be a bore.'

'Reassure Mr Dix, Lucy darling,' said Jane. 'Tell him how pleased we shall be.'

Lucilla found it impossible to avoid saying how pleased she would be – but she eyed Jane like a basilisk.

'And now,' said Jane, carrying off the situation with graceful aplomb, 'we must go and catch trains. And we expect you on Sunday. I think Destiny's certainly meant you to be friends with us. One doesn't exchange yells with perfect strangers every day, does one?'

'Such happy fortune as mine certainly doesn't happen every day,' said the youth, with a kind of formal gallantry not at all unpleasing. 'Thank you a thousand times for your goodness,' he said, taking the hand Jane offered. 'And you,' he said, offering his to Lucilla – and there was a gleam in his blue eyes that looked not exactly malicious, but a little elfish. Jane perceived that he had done full justice to Lucilla's reluctance.

Chapter XI

You cannot quarrel comfortably in the street, nor in the Tube, but a third-class railway carriage, if you have it to yourselves, offers every facility for recriminations.

Jane replied with chill venom to Lucilla's intense reproaches and assured her that she had only herself to thank.

'It is entirely owing to you,' she said several times, 'that this youthful jail-bird is coming to peck at our seedcake. *I* should only have written to him, as I said. But I was obliged to make up for your — forgive me if I say rudeness.'

'I believe you go out of your mind sometimes,' Lucilla repeated more than once; 'the things you do — the things you say!'

Jane replied.

Lucilla retorted.

And so on. You know the sort of thing?

But between London Bridge and New Cross, Jane suddenly laughed.

'Let's stop,' she said. 'I'm sorry I lost my temper. Let's kiss and be friends.'

'And now you can laugh!' Lucilla complained.

'I can't help it. You know I can't help it. I never could keep on quarrelling — on and on, I mean. My temper's all you say it is, but it doesn't *last*, and then suddenly I can't help seeing how silly it all is, and then I laugh and say I'm sorry.'

'You go on being hateful just as long as you like,' said Lucilla hotly, 'and when you're tired of it you expect the other person to be tired of it at exactly the same minute, and to kiss and be friends the moment you say so, just as if nothing had happened.'

'I know I do! And it's not fair! But she *is* going to forgive me and kiss and be friends all the same, isn't she? I am a little beast, Luce.'

'Don't be so superior. You go into these rages and then you make a merit of apologising for them. You positively wallow and revel in apologies.'

'I know,' said Jane again. 'It's the very least I can do. It's very aggravating for *you*, but it's the only really satisfying thing for *me*. If you weren't an angel, Luce, you'd never stand me for a day.'

'That's right,' said Lucilla, 'now try flattery!'

'No – but look here!' said Jane earnestly. 'Do let's make it up. Because we've got such lots to talk over. And really, it *is* rather awful about that boy coming on Sunday to tea. I didn't at all mean to ask him, but I lost my temper and I lost my head – no, I'm not wallowing – and I simply couldn't stop myself. I wish I hadn't.'

'And whatever made you ask him to Cedar Court?'

'I thought it seemed less intimate. I *do* wish I hadn't.'

'Couldn't we get out of it? Write and put him off?'

'We haven't his address. No, events must take their course. We needn't have him for a gardener. But perhaps we really can help him. Perhaps he'll tell us more about himself. Do you remember, Lucy, the first day we went to Cedar Court – not the dark day, but when we first saw the garden, and you said what have we done to deserve this? Perhaps we shall deserve it a little bit if we help the wretched Dix.'

'If we're going in for philanthropy,' Lucilla said, 'I think it would be better to begin with ugly old women – not with handsome young men.'

'So you did think him handsome?'

'I thought he had a –'

'Not a nice, kind face! No –'

'No. I was going to say an almost classic profile. It's very romantic and all that to put out helping hands to people with classic profiles and lazy blue eyes, but –'

'But you think it's more meritorious to help old washerwomen who squint? Well, if it had been a squinting washerwoman I'd exchanged yells with, and she'd told me she was looking for work, I do think I should have felt inclined to send the washing to her. It isn't my fault that the waxwork turned into a live, classic profile. Oh, Luce, what a shock it was! I think we ought to be thankful it wasn't worse. Suppose one of the murderers had come alive!'

It was next morning at breakfast that Jane said: 'I have thought it all over, and I have done with dissipation and the life of pleasure.'

'Dear me!' said Lucilla across the tea-pot.

'Yes, it's – what was it old Gravy used to call it? – "morally disintegrating". Look at us. We spend week after week in humble toil – not a breath of dissension; my will's your pleasure, and your pleasure's my law. We might have been doves or seraphs or dormice. That's the influence of honest labour, my child. Then we go out gallivanting – become mere pleasure-seekers – and at once we fly at each other's throats like sharks or alligators. Influence of dissipation.'

'That wasn't dissipation; it was the young man.'

'It always is, I believe,' Jane admitted; 'but then, dissipation so often turns out to be the young man – at least, in books he is never quite out of it. The scenes of dazzling worldliness would be incomplete without him. Come on, let's get down to the shop.'

'We shall probably find a young man there too,' said Lucilla drily.

'Oh, well – *he* doesn't count,' Jane said. 'He's all on the side of honest toil. Besides, he's got an uncle: a rich uncle. If the miserable Dix had had an uncle he might be in a very different position to-day. Come on, I say. Down with dissipation! Long live the shop!'

The shop was indeed becoming very engrossing. As more and more flowers budded and bloomed in the lovely, neglected garden of Cedar Court, business became more and more brisk, and the bag of money that had to be carried home nightly was heavier and heavier.

The peonies were out now – great balls of splendid crimson – and the white balls of the gueldre-rose, sheaves of violet and purple flags, the wide graceful arches of Solomon's seal, armfuls of lilac sweet as Spring herself, tall tulips rosy and white and gold, the yellow stars of the leopard's bane – oxslips, cowslips, and always forget-me-nots; the garden room was a bower of beauty, and behind the changing glory of the spring flowers the old-panelled walls were changing bit by bit – a little at a time they were gradually regaining their ancient beauty of grey oak, as the meretricious gas-green veil was slowly scraped away. By Jane and Lucilla? Well, not altogether.

Mr Simmons's faith in his old boss had not been wholly justified. Science has not yet found a solvent which will remove paint instantaneously without injuring the surface of the wood below. There is no royal road to the hidden oak, and even the most accomplished chemist will be driven to fall back on plain old-fashioned scrubbing and careful scraping. Scrubbing and scraping is hard work for ladies. Mr John Rochester liked hard work; he said so, more than once.

Do not suppose that he was always in the garden room during shop hours. Far from it. Many a scrub and scrape did he administer in the late evenings when he whistled at his lonely work and enjoyed the solitude as your real worker does enjoy it. Many a morning's sun from a sky flushed with rose and gold peeped through the branches of the cedars and lighted Mr Rochester at his task. Still, there were times when his scrubbings and scrapings coincided with the selling of the flowers, and while the two girls arranged their beautiful stock-in-trade, made and sold their bouquets, and struggled with their day-book and their cash, he honourably kept himself to himself and scraped away in the background exactly like a real workman. If you think that two ladies ought not to have allowed a comparative stranger (Mr Dix was now the positive one) to do so much for them, I can only remind you that it is difficult to repel a determined assistant – unless you wish to quarrel with it; also that Mr John Rochester, as the nephew of their landlord, had a certain natural footing, as it were, in Cedar Court; further, that the presence of one to whom sums had no terrors was really a boon to the business, that they really did want to get rid of the gas-green paint, and that soda did take the skin off

their hands. But why seek to labour the point? The girls often gave
each other dozens of good reasons why it was so right and natural
for Mr Rochester to be so often in the garden room – any one of
which would be sufficient to convince any young person. Anyhow, there he very often was.

As the week matured, and still more as it declined, the immi-
nent visit of Mr Dix loomed larger and larger and less and less
desirable in the eyes of his prospective hostesses. Jane, in particular, found herself on Saturday contemplating with positive dismay
this terrible tea-party. She hesitated to express her sentiments to
Lucilla – she had no desire to revive the discussion that had raged
on the train coming home last Monday.

That Saturday was a very special day, for on it, at last, the traces
of the gas-green paint vanished, and the garden room was again as
it had once been – soft-coloured wood from floor to ceiling. Mr
Rochester had brought most interesting cakes to celebrate the
completion of the great work. It was as they ate these companion-
ably, admiring the oak-panelling and now and then breaking off
to attend to customers, that Jane yielded to an unexplained
impulse, and said suddenly:

'We're going to have tea here to-morrow as well. A Mr Dix is
coming. Won't you come too?'

'It would be very nice,' Lucilla put in before he could answer,
'but as Mr Dix is coming to talk about business, I am afraid Mr
Rochester would find it rather dull.'

On which more than hint Mr Rochester acted instantly, and
lied obligingly about an unfortunate engagement with an old
friend to play tennis.

'At Wimbledon,' he added, remembering just in time how he
had told the girls he had no friends at Leabridge.

'You're lucky,' said Jane, telling herself that she admired his
readiness to be snubbed. 'I wish we could get tennis. Yes, I know
there's a local club, but we mustn't go making acquaintances. They
only eat up your time.'

'There's a tennis-lawn here, you know,' said Mr Rochester. 'We could get it in order again, but you'd want a man with a scythe before you could put the mowing-machine over it. By the way, this garden does want a gardener – or gardeners.'

Lucilla trembled, but Jane let the opening pass.

'Yes, it does,' she said smoothly. 'We shall have to think about it. But I've never seen any tennis-lawn. Whereabouts is it?'

'Behind the stables.'

'But we've never seen any stables!' said Lucilla.

'Beyond the cottages.'

'But there aren't any cottages!'

'Ladies, ladies,' said Mr Rochester, 'you haven't half explored your domain. Did you never open the big double door in the garden wall?'

'It's locked.'

'Where did you think it led?'

'To the road, I suppose. We never thought about it. Oh, let's go and explore now this minute.'

'You can't leave the shop,' Lucilla reminded her.

'Besides, the key isn't here; but I'll bring it to-morrow – I mean on Monday.'

'Could you perhaps bring it to-morrow,' suggested Lucilla, 'after you get back from – Wimbledon?'

'About seven? Certainly.'

So it was settled.

And now it was Sunday afternoon. The garden room, all traces of the shop removed, showed itself as a charming parlour elegantly prepared for the reception of the felonious Dix.

One of Aunt Lucy's prettiest tea-cloths embroidered in soft blues and pinks lay between Aunt Lucy's Sheraton tea-tray and the round table. Aunt Lucy's silver tea-service glittered upon it among the blue and white of the Chinese cups and saucers. There were flowers, in studied moderation: a few rosy tulips, half a dozen flags among Solomon's seal, and some purple lilac – but you cannot be moderate with lilac.

Both girls were a little *endimanchées*: when you wear opaque pinafores all the week you desire on Sundays the delicate silky-diaphanous.

It was five o'clock, and the kettle had boiled on the spirit-lamp and had been suppressed because the visitor had not arrived, and it was no use making tea yet. There had been rain in the morning, and every leaf and bud of the garden was newly washed and sparkling in the sun.

Lucilla was conscious of a sudden relenting.

'Do you know,' she said, 'I'm almost glad you did ask him. Think what it will be to him to see a garden like this after prison.'

'Or even after London,' said Jane. 'Hush, here he is!'

But it was not Mr Dix. It was a much older man. He came in at the open door, and he did not say, 'How do you do?' or 'How are you?' or 'Good afternoon,' or any of the things that Mr Dix might have been expected to say. He looked at the flowers, looked at the tea-table, and he looked at the walls – and then he said in a voice (as Jane remarked later) exactly like the voice of the biggest of the three bears in the story:

'Who's been messing about with the panelling?'

And he had every right to ask, for he was their landlord, Mr James Rochester, unexpectedly returned from Spain. And at any moment the footstep of the prison bird Dix might sound on the gravel.

'Who did this?' repeated Mr James Rochester, more like the bear than ever.

Chapter XII

For once Jane was speechless. It was Lucilla who rose instantly and went towards the old landlord, with both hands outstretched, delighted recognition in her eyes, and on her lips – words of wonder, indeed, but also of welcome.

'You?' she said. 'How wonderful! We thought you were at the Alhambra or Bilbao or somewhere, and here you are! It *is* nice.'

By this time Jane was almost herself again, ready to offer her hand and then to push forward the easiest chair.

'It seems rather a cheek to offer you tea in your own house,' she said, 'but it would be worse still not to, seeing that we're here and the tea's here and you're here.'

'I am sorry if I am inopportune,' said the landlord, quite without cordiality. But he took the chair. And again he looked round him.

'You seem to have made yourselves thoroughly at home,' he said, and he said it grudgingly.

'Yes,' said Jane, preoccupied with the kettle and spirit-lamp. 'And you're not a bit inopportune. In fact it's very much nicer for you to come when we're all tidy, though perhaps you'd rather have come on a working day, and found us up to our ears in wet ferns and flower-stalks, and as likely as not no tea ready – at least, it wouldn't have been such a nice tea as this, and certainly not the best cups.'

'I'm glad to hear *that*, at any rate,' he said grimly.

'Oh, of course we wouldn't use those lovely cups every day,' said Lucilla, one ear for him and one for the step of the jail-bird on the gravel. Jane's ears were also doing a double, or, rather, a divided, duty. Both girls were desperately searching for something to say – something to delay the moment when old Mr Rochester should repeat his first big-bear question. Both felt that the longer that could be delayed the better – if they could only get him comfortable, get him interested, give him a really good cup of tea and some of the fat, home-made cakes before having to explain about the panelling.

'The garden,' Jane began, and, 'The flowers,' said Lucilla, at exactly the same moment, and both stopped.

Then:

'The board,' they said simultaneously, and again stopped short.

'Why not speak one at a time,' suggested Mr Rochester, 'and explain to me . . .'

'I was just trying to,' said Jane very quickly, and got in before Lucilla that time. 'I do hope you don't mind the board? We couldn't have sold anything to speak of without a board – and we left the original label . . .'

'Label?'

'"This house is *not* to let." I do think that's lovely,' said Jane, with an air of the completest candour. 'Do you know, Mr Rochester, I knew you were nice. The very minute I saw that notice I knew it. And when they told me you were . . .'

'They told you I was what?'

'We knew it was only that they didn't understand you,' Lucilla put in.

'They didn't say anything really dreadful, you know,' said Jane; 'only that they didn't think you would let anyone have the house.'

'Was that all?'

'Well,' Jane acknowledged, 'one person did say you were a grampus, but I don't think he could have been serious.'

Mr Rochester gave a short, sharp bark of a laugh.

('Come, that's something!' Jane told herself. 'If we can only make him laugh!')

'Do you take milk and sugar?' she asked hastily, and acted on his reply.

'Do have a cake. They aren't bought ones. Our Mrs Doveton made them herself, out of one of Aunt Lucilla's receipt-books.'

Lucilla was keeping her end up. 'It's such a darling book, bound in violet morocco with gold ferns on it, and the pages are different colours – like girls' albums – and there are bits of poetry and little pictures stuck in all among the recipes. Dear little pencil sketches of ruined abbeys and thatched cottages, and little paintings of auriculas and tulips and Spanish dancers with fans and white stockings, and valentines with silver loves and cupids and the loveliest verses.'

'It must be a very interesting book,' said Mr Rochester. 'And does your Mrs Doveton find her way easily among the poetry and the paintings and the recipes?'

'Oh *no*!' said Lucilla, shocked. 'The book's never been in the kitchen. *We* copy out what she's to make, on the kitchen slate. We tried buying cakes – but they aren't really nice in the shops here. I can't think they're made of real eggs and butter, and they all taste of essence of lemon. Besides, the shop-people call them pastries, and that does sound so dreadful, doesn't it?'

'It does,' said he, with the first glance of approval that they dared to recognise. 'And I am very glad that you perceive it. The vulgarism is getting itself accepted, somehow. "Pastries"! We shall have people talking of "grouses" next, and "deers" and "snipes". Already the *Daily Yell*, I understand, allows its American contributors to write of billiards-rooms, to say "around" when they mean "round", and to use the expression, "he made himself scarce", in a serious narrative. One of the saddest things in this machine-made century,' he added, 'is the neglect, the decay, the corruption, of the English language.'

'*I* saw billiards-rooms myself, the day we bought a lot of newspapers,' said Jane helpfully, 'and I thought it looked horrid, but then I thought it must be a mistake of the printers.'

'Not at all,' said Mr Rochester, 'it is intentional. So is that revolting and unnatural plural "pastries"; so is . . .'

He was launched. Jane and Lucilla found means to exchange glances of congratulations. But still ears were pricked – as far as young ladies' ears can be pricked – for the sound of the feet of jail-birds on the gravel. And still none came.

It seemed to Jane that she and Lucilla had quite enough on their hands in this sudden necessity for soothing Mr Rochester and compelling him to refrain from the subject of the panels till he could contemplate it through a haze of shortcake, without having to introduce to him such an acquaintance as Mr Dix, a young man who had not only been in prison – that, Jane felt, might happen by accident to any of us – but was actually not ashamed of it.

'. . . The degradation of the language,' Mr Rochester was saying. 'The depraved Cockney accent of half-educated teachers replacing the sturdy local dialects . . .'

The girls leaned forward, attitude and expression alike designed to convey the impression of rapt attention. 'If he'll only keep on till he's had his second cup,' Jane told herself, 'it won't be so bad.' He finished the first and accepted the second. There was a pause, which both girls were afraid to break.

'What,' he asked suddenly, 'do you call the article of food which is baked in an earthenware dish, rather deep and usually of an oval form, though sometimes round or oblong: outside is pastry, within are apples, cloves and sugar? What do you call it?'

'Is it a riddle?' Jane asked.

'No, no,' he said impatiently; 'a perfectly plain question. You recognise the thing from my description? Well, what do you call it?'

'An apple-pie, of course,' said Lucilla and Jane almost together.

'Good,' said Mr Rochester, actually rubbing his hands, 'but, believe me, there are young women – yes, and women old enough to know better – who think that they show refinement by calling an apple-pie an apple-tart. Why don't they consult their dictionaries? A tart is an open piece of pastry with jam, apple, or what-not *on* it. In the pie the apple or other adjunct is covered.'

'Of course it is.'

'Of course it is,' repeated Mr Rochester; 'and now,' he went on, putting down his cup and speaking quite mildly, 'perhaps you will tell me . . .'

They looked at each other and felt that the hour had struck. They must tell the truth about the panelling.

'. . . Tell me,' he ended unexpectedly, 'how you managed to get into the house again?'

'But we didn't,' said Jane. 'You said we weren't to and we didn't. Of course we didn't.'

'Then how did you get these things out?'

'?'

'The chairs and tables – the tea-things – the flower-vases – the Belgian pottery?'

Again, and now really startled, they looked at each other. Was it possible that their benefactor could be insane?

'You put them here for us – don't you remember?' said Jane gently.

'It won't do, my dear,' he answered with almost equal gentleness. 'I may be absent-minded – in fact I am. I may be forgetful – of trifles – but I am not so silly as you suppose. Come – why deny it, when here the things are? Own up! How did you get into the house?'

'We didn't,' said Jane with extreme coldness. 'Please don't doubt our word. We shouldn't have dreamed of doing anything so dishonourable.'

'We found the things here, you know,' Lucilla explained quietly. 'Don't you think you must have given orders for the place to be made nice for us, and then forgotten about it? We found it all ready for us, and the looking-glass and the jug and basin' – she swung open the door of the further cupboard as she spoke – 'and all the beautiful jugs and vases.' The other cupboard opened at her touch, confirming her words. 'And the new tap by the front door – all so convenient and so lovely. And we did think it so frightfully nice of you; and we have been so grateful and thought about you such a lot – and wished you luck, and that you might find whatever you were looking for in Spain. You *are* absent-minded, you know. You *must* have ordered it, and forgotten, Do try to remember. And don't be so cross,' she added, with a sudden inspiration of courage, 'because we really haven't done anything to deserve it.'

'I apologise for having doubted a lady's word,' said Mr

Rochester with blighting courtesy, 'but my position is a difficult one. The age of miracles is past. And I know that I did not give any such order as you suggest, because I remember perfectly a sudden sense of remissness which overcame me between Tours and Bordeaux, just because I had not given such an order. I wondered how you would get on, and whether you would have to disarrange Hope Cottage in order to make the garden room possible even as a living-room for part of the day.'

All the while, through his talking and their own, they had been listening for the footfall of Mr Dix. And now at last it sounded on the gravel. They were almost grateful. They felt that they could trust Mr Rochester not to scold them before Mr Dix. And if only Mr Dix would not talk about his prison life . . .

'I'm rather early, I'm afraid,' said the newcomer apologetically, 'but – Hullo, uncle!'

Again it was not Mr Dix. It was the younger Mr Rochester.

'You are just in time to solve a trifling mystery for us,' said his uncle, when the little bustle of greetings had died down. 'Can you suggest any way in which the chairs and tables and tea-cups out of the house can have transferred themselves into the garden room?'

Men should not blush, but Mr Rochester did it; he tried, however, to conceal the blush by instant speech.

'I did, uncle, of course. I knew you'd wish it. I felt certain you'd have done it yourself, or given orders about it, if you hadn't left in such a hurry. I hope you approve my choice,' he added, taking up a tea-cup and putting it down again.

'So the miracle's explained,' said old Mr Rochester; 'and the explanation's like that of all miracles, quite simple when you know it.'

'I knew it, of course,' said Lucilla, 'directly you said it wasn't you who put the things here.'

'Oh, you did, did you?' said the old gentleman.

'Why, of course,' said Jane; 'but we couldn't give Mr Rochester away, could we? We didn't know whether you would approve his choice,' she added, looking up at the old gentleman under her eyelashes in a way which the young gentleman thought might have charmed the most savage breast. 'But you do, don't you? You said you thought of it between Tours and Bordeaux, and wished you had.'

'So I did. You were quite right, my boy. Thank you.'

'And now *we* may thank you,' said Lucilla. 'It wouldn't have done for us to thank you until we were quite sure that your uncle approved, would it?' she turned on the uncle a glance half timid, half arch.

'We do thank you – both of you, as much as ever you'll let us,' said Jane. 'I didn't think there were such kind people in the world – people who aren't your relations or anything, I mean. I think it's wonderful. And, dear Mr Rochester, it was our fault that the paint was scraped off the panelling; we thought you'd like it, and Lucy and I tried to do it ourselves, and then Mr Rochester – your nephew I mean – came and helped, and Mr Simmons helped, and it really does seem as if everybody is ready to help us, and if you're not pleased I really don't know what we shall do. We did so very much want to please you. You are pleased, aren't you? It does look nice, doesn't it?'

'I'm more pleased than I can say,' said old Mr Rochester most unexpectedly. 'I can't imagine why you thought I wasn't pleased.'

'Why, the way you asked who'd been messing about with the panelling.'

'Oh, that was before I'd seen what had happened. Coming in out of the sun, in the half light, I thought someone had repainted everything brown. But when I saw the grain of the wood – why, I was delighted.'

'Oh,' said Lucilla, 'I do wish you'd said so! We've been so afraid you were cross! And now it's all right.'

And Jane was saying to herself: 'Yes – it's all right. Everything turns out lucky for us. I believe we are born lucky. Mr Dix can come when he likes! Who's afraid? Let him come!'

But Mr Dix did not come.

Chapter XIII

When the new brew of tea had been made for young Mr Rochester, when he had drunk three cups and had helped to wash up the tea-things and put them away in the cupboard, when the garden room and the gate had been fastened up for the night, and the girls had parted from the always friendly nephew and the now completely placated uncle, they had leisure, as they walked back to Hope Cottage in the golden-rayed evening, to exchange conjectures as to what had become of Mr Dix.

'Lost the address, I suppose,' said Jane.

'More likely he didn't want to come,' said Lucilla. 'I expect he thought we were insane – inviting him to tea in that sudden way and promising to engage him without a character.'

'Perhaps he's a clairvoyant, a thought-reader; perhaps he felt how much we didn't want him to come while old Mr Rochester was there.'

'Yes – wasn't it awful! I kept wondering what Uncle James would do when Mr Dix said how nice Cedar Court was after the horrors of prison life. It's just what Mr Dix would have done, you know – as soon as look at him. It's certainly all for the best that Mr Dix didn't come – whatever his reasons were.'

'I don't feel happy about him, all the same,' said Jane. 'I can't get him out of my head. Did you notice his right boot?'

'His right boot? No – why?'

'Well, *I did*. It was cracked right across. I believe that young man's at his last penny. Why on earth didn't we make him give us his address? Perhaps he's starving. He may die – and we shall never know – and we might have helped him. No, Lucy, it's no comfort to me to think that I can find a suffering charwoman and help *her*. I wanted to help Mr Dix.'

'Yes, I know, dear,' said Lucilla meaningly.

'Cat!' said Jane, but without malice. 'It isn't because he's a good-looking young man. At least,' she added, with one of her flashes of candour, 'if it is, I can't help it. Perhaps it's natural for us to be more interested in good-looking young men than in plain old charwomen. Yes, I'm sure it's natural. It would be, if you come to think of it. I'm not ashamed of it. And people can be interested in good-looking young men without any Romeo nonsense too. I know they can. Because I am.'

'Yes,' said Lucilla drily. 'I see you are. Yes.'

'Yes — and so are you, Luce, so don't pretend! Only you're ashamed of it and I'm not! I can't exactly express . . . but I will . . . Let me see. It's like this. This is why I'm so annoyed at our losing Mr Dix. It's as if we'd lost a stray dog. No — not that exactly. But you see you can't take a tremendous interest in a young man just because he is a young man. Look at the organist at school — and all the awful young men that Gladys used to go out with. But when he's nice, and a gentleman, and when you've frightened each other into screams, and when he wants to be a gardener and you've got a garden that wants to be gardened — well, it all seems so heaven-sent — so expressly arranged by Fate, so that you *shall* be interested — and then — down comes the curtain — it's all over.'

'Oh well,' said Lucilla, 'if you put it like that . . .' and, basket-laden, they reached the gate of Hope Cottage.

It was not till ten o'clock that they found out that they had left the silver tea-pot and milk-jug and sugar-basin and spoons and sugar-tongs in the cupboard with the other tea-things in the garden room at the Cedars. To continue to leave them there was unthinkable — though the fine rain which had followed the golden sunset made the rescue party anything but a party of pleasure.

'We must change our shoes and put on mackers,' said Jane. 'Bother! I thought of course you'd got them. And you thought *I* had. But we can't leave them there. Cedar Court's just the place to be burgled. I'm sure I wonder it hasn't been ten times over. Come on.'

Cedar Court and its trees loomed dark through the rain. The one gas-lamp nearly opposite its gate gave light for the fitting of the key to the padlock. But no key was needed. The padlock was undone.

'I thought you fastened it,' said Jane.

'No – don't you remember? Old Mr Rochester did it: at least, I hope he didn't do it. I hope it's only that, and not a burglar who has opened it with a skeleton key.'

'Don't talk about skeletons,' said Jane. 'It's quite bad enough as it is.'

'You're not frightened?' Lucilla asked, in a voice that was not quite steady.

'No – and I don't want to be,' Jane answered firmly 'Come on.'

The door of the garden room was well and truly fastened. But when they had undone it and crossed the threshold Jane suddenly shut the door and bolted it.

'Draw the curtains,' she said, 'before we strike a light.'

Lucilla obeyed. Then by the irresolute glimmer of a newly-lighted candle they looked round the room.

It was empty of any human presence except their own.

'So *that's* all right,' said Jane.

'Oh, Jane,' said Lucy, 'suppose there *had* been a burglar in here, and we'd locked ourselves in with him! How frightful!'

'Yes, dear,' said Jane. '*I* thought of that, the minute I'd bolted the door. However, it's all right, so far.' She opened the cupboard, held the candle to its dark depths and closed the door again quickly.

'The silver's there all right. Now, look here. Do you really believe the padlock was left undone? Suppose it wasn't. Suppose someone opened it, and we disturbed them before they could get in here? If we go out carrying the silver they might attack us – to get it.'

'They wouldn't know we'd got it. We could put it under our mackers.'

'We should look lumpy. Yes, I know it's dark – but they may have electric torches and flash them at us. We mustn't take the silver away – we must hide it.'

'Where?'

'Up the chimney, of course. It's the only place. I've been

thinking. Put the candle down on the floor behind the table. Now then – hand me the things. No – one at a time. Don't let them chink.'

She reached her hand up the chimney, holding the silver teapot. 'Talk about chinking!' exclaimed Lucilla, not without some reason, for, with a devastating clatter, the teapot, which Jane imagined herself to be placing on a safe ledge in the obscurity of the chimney, escaped from her hand and fell into the hollow depths behind the iron grate.

'Well,' said Jane, forcing a laugh, 'it's safe now, anyway. We shall have to have the fireplace taken out to get it back. It's in a perfectly burglar-proof spot.'

'It'll be awfully dented, I'm afraid,' said Lucilla anxiously.

'All the same, I'm going to send the other things after it,' said Jane. 'It'll be no more trouble to get out the lot than the one.'

'Well, wrap them in dusters, then, or they'll be dented to pieces.'

The milk-jug and sugar-basin followed the tea-pot with what is sometimes called a sickening thud.

'And now,' said Jane, standing up and rubbing her sooty hands on a third duster, 'let's get out of it as quick as we can. Let's talk and laugh all the way to the gate, so that if there *are* burglars in hiding in the shrubbery they may not think we're frightened.'

So they locked up the garden room, and went through the rain to the gate, beginning their progress by a very artistically-tuned laugh from Lucilla, and another, not nearly so good, from Jane.

'It is absurd,' said Lucilla, very distinctly, 'to have come at this hour of the night to fetch the work-bag. But with all that sewing to do before breakfast, it was much better to come now.'

'Much – ha-ha!' laughed Jane, unconvincingly.

'It'll be quite a funny adventure to write to Miss Graves about,' said Lucilla.

'Yes, won't it?' Jane agreed with enthusiasm, and laughed mechanically.

'The dear old thing will think it quite recklessly amusing,' said Lucilla, laughing again. Really, anyone in the bushes would have been quite sure that the speaker, who had now reached the gate, was wholly free from fear or care and very much amused. 'It will fill up our weekly letter beautifully . . . Oh!' she ended, fumbling with the padlock.

'What's up?'

'It's locked. It is, really.'

'Nonsense,' said Jane, 'let me.' She pushed away Lucilla's fingers, and something fell, rattling against the iron of the gate and resounding on stone.

'It is, though,' said Jane. 'What was that you dropped?'

'Only the key of the garden room. I'll pick it up directly. The padlock *is* locked, though, isn't it?'

It was – beyond a doubt.

'Did you leave the key in it?'

'Of course not. You know it wasn't locked.'

'Then where *is* the key?'

'I must have put it down inside,' said Lucilla. 'Let's find the other key and go back and get it.'

But they could not find the other key, though they felt all about along the wet gravel – and all the time the rain came down, more and more earnestly and searchingly.

'Oh, bother!' said Jane. 'And it's no good trying to strike a match in this waterfall.'

'Jane,' said Lucilla, pointing, 'what's that?'

'What?'

'Out there on the footpath.'

'It's a key,' said Jane. 'It's *the* key.'

It was.

In falling from Lucilla's hand it must have struck the horizontal iron of the gate and rebounded out towards the road – well beyond their reach.

'We're locked in,' said Lucilla.

'And we're locked out,' said Jane.

'If we'd only got an umbrella!' sighed Lucilla.

'Someone else's, then, with a crook handle. Ours are both knobs, you know.'

'Couldn't we cut a crooked stick in the shrubbery?'

'Nothing easier,' said Jane bitterly, 'if we had a knife.'

'Couldn't we break one off?'

'If we knew where to find the kind of stick we want, and could find it in this pitch-dark Niagara.'

'We must wait; perhaps someone will go by and we can ask them to pick it up for us.'

'We may wait,' said Jane. 'It must be past midnight – everyone about here goes to bed at nine, I believe. Let me think.'

Lucilla was obediently silent. There was no sound but the patter-patter of the rain on stone and gravel and dripping leaves and mackintoshes. The lost key lay before them glistening in the light of the lonely gas-lamp – perfectly visible, wholly unattainable. At last Lucilla giggled softly but naturally.

'You say everything's a lark,' she said. 'What about this? Not much lark about this, Jane?'

'Yes, there is!' said Jane instantly. 'It's a tremendous lark really – a real adventure – something to talk about for years. It'll make a lovely story – a splendid joke, and at our own expense too, as the best jokes always are. And there's one thing to the good. *The burglars are gone* – if there were any. Whoever it was that unlocked the padlock has locked it again and gone. So we're just out in the rain in our own garden, and all we've got to do is to wait till morning – and it gets light about four or five . . .'

'We shall be locked up all the same even if it's light,' said Lucilla.

'Yes, but you won't be frightened when it's light – all right, I mean me as well; besides, we can get hold of a stick then and scratch the garden-room key back, and get in there and get our own key and get home.'

'I *can't* stand here in the rain for four hours,' said Lucilla, 'and I won't. I shall go and sit on the doorstep – the porch will keep off some of the rain.'

'We can do better than that. What about the summer-house. *That's* not locked, and there are wicker-chairs.'

'Oh yes!' said Lucilla. 'And I don't really mind the dark now we're sure there's no one but ourselves in the garden. Come on.'

The summer-house was beyond the lawn where the cedars were – a largish, rustic, hexagonal building with three blind sides, two windows, and a door. The girls felt their way along the paths guided by the overgrown hedge of dripping shrubs.

'You're sure the burglars *have* gone?' Lucilla murmured as they neared their goal.

'If they *were* burglars. Why, not even a burglar would care to be out on a night like this. It's a night to make the boldest burglar bolt home to his burrow like any old rabbit. I say, Lucy, this really is a lark.'

'Ye– yes,' said Lucilla, her hand on the latch of the summer-house door. It yielded to her touch and they were in, closing the door behind them.

'Thank goodness!' said Jane. 'It's dry here, anyhow. Get your macker off.'

A silent struggle with wet buttons occupied them for a few moments. Then:

'I say,' said Lucilla, 'you might strike a light. Of course I know there's no one here but us; only – suppose the burglar hadn't bolted home to his burrow? Suppose he'd just taken shelter here like us?'

'Don't be silly,' said Jane, but she felt in her pocket for the matches. 'Don't be silly,' she repeated; 'and I haven't got the matches, you had them.'

'I didn't,' said Lucilla. 'Oh, Jane – *I heard something move* over here at the back! I'm certain there's something here – no, don't stop me. I'm going out again; I don't care *how* it rains –'

'Don't be a duffer,' said Jane, holding her. 'There's no one here but us.'

'Don't hold me!' repeated Lucilla, struggling. 'I *will* go!'

And then, in the black darkness at the far side of the summer-house, something moved – and out of the black silence something shuffled. A wicker-chair squeaked.

'I told you so!' cried Lucilla. 'There *is* someone there!'

And there was.

Chapter XIV

'Don't be frightened,' said a voice in the deep dark of the summer-house. 'I'm not a burglar. I'll strike a light.'

There was the scratch and spurt of a match, by whose light the girls saw vaguely the figure of a man rising from one of the wicker-chairs.

'But if you're not burglars what are you doing here?' It was Jane who spoke.

'Sheltering from the rain. I am so very sorry if I startled you,' said the intruder, striking another match.

'But why here?'

'It seemed convenient. I see now I had no right, but who could have thought that you would come here through the wild night and the rain?'

'But who *are* you?' Jane persisted.

Suddenly Lucilla said, 'Why, of course, it's Mr Dix!'

'Yes,' said the stranger, 'I am that wretched outcast.'

'Of course you are,' said Jane. And then she and Lucilla first became aware that ever since the first squeak of the basket-chair they had been clinging to each other, as people do in romances, clutching each other's arms and keeping very close together. Their clasp now relaxed.

'But how –' Lucilla was beginning, but Jane stopped her.

'Not here,' she said. 'Mr Dix can probably climb the wall some-where and pick up our key. He can explain all about everything afterwards.'

'Where is your key?' asked the voice in the dark. And Jane, in a few simple words, explained where their key was.

'And of course you can get over the wall and get the key and give it to us through the gate, and then we can go and get the garden padlock-key. It's quite easy to climb up one of the but-tresses inside and drop down outside, but then you can't get back again. I should have gone myself but I didn't like leaving my friend alone in the garden, because, you see, it might really have been burglars.'

'But,' said he, 'I have a key on my bunch that opens that padlock — that's how I got in. Padlocks are all alike. And then I thought it wasn't safe to leave it unlocked, so I went back and locked it.' And he struck another match.

'How simple everything is when you understand it,' said Jane; 'and do stop striking matches. It only makes it darker afterwards. Go along and get that key, please. It's lying on the path outside the gate. We'll meet you at the garden-house door. It's quite near the gate.'

'I must strike another match,' he said apologetically, 'or I shall go barging into you as I go out.'

He struck one, sidled past them, and was gone.

'What shall we do?' Lucilla whispered.

'Go home, of course. He can stay in the summer-house if he likes. I daresay it'll seem luxury after his prison life.'

'No,' said Lucilla, 'don't let's. I can't bear not to know *why* he came at night instead of to tea, and whether he's really a gentle-man burglar and came down just to burgle us, or whether . . .'

'All right,' said Jane recklessly. 'Come on. There's only one thing certain. We asked him to tea and he hasn't had that tea. Let's light up in the garden room and have tea again — again and again, until we extort his full confession. I'm very wet and very cold. We'll have a fire. Thank goodness we collected those sticks and fir-cones! If he *is* a burglar the fire will camouflage the teapot and things.'

When the candles were lighted in the garden room the three looked at each other — wet, draggled, streaked with green and brown from the caresses of the old shrubs, blinking with dazzled eyes in the candlelight; they looked at each other — doubtfully — anxiously. Then suddenly Jane laughed, Lucilla laughed; Mr Dix laughed too, but only a very little — as became an outcast.

'Who says life isn't a lark?' said Jane.

'Not I, certainly,' said Mr Dix, 'but I implore you to let me explain —'

'Not yet,' said Jane; 'better light the fire — there's wood in that cupboard. And we'll boil the kettle; whatever happens, Mr Dix, you *shall* have that tea that we invited you to.'

'I ought to insist on explaining myself and then go away at once,' said Mr Dix, dealing expertly with wood and paper, 'but no human being could resist your kindness.'

After that he said no more till the table was set out with tea-things and what remained of the afternoon's cakes. The tea was brewing in the second best brown tea-pot, and Lucilla was beginning to apologise because they had drunk all the milk in the afternoon, when she stopped short at: 'I'm so sorry . . .'

She had seen his boots. At least, she had seen one of them. The other was only half a boot. The sole was gone. This was all too plainly to be seen as he knelt to put more wood on the fire. There was quite an appreciable interval before she went on '. . . that we drank all the milk this afternoon. But there's lemon.'

'And now,' said Jane, very brisk and business-like, handing his third cup of tea to Mr Dix, 'first we'll tell you how we came to be taking refuge in the summer-house in the middle of the night, and then you shall tell us how *you* did.'

Their story was quickly told. 'So you see,' said Jane. 'Now for your adventures.'

'My simple story,' said Mr Dix, almost placidly, 'is this. I started to walk from London, and it was further than I expected. My boots are not what once they were; and it came on to rain, and having come so far I thought I would at least go on, and mark down your house, so to speak, so that I should find it more easily when I came to explain, if I ever could, why I hadn't turned up at the proper time. When I got here I found that I could not possibly walk home again to-night. The sole of my right boot had deserted in the mud. I saw the angle of your summer-house roof. I saw that the house was locked up, and I burgled your garden. I had a key that fitted. That's the worst of those cheap padlocks – there is always a key that fits them. And if you ask me why I didn't go back by tram or train, I can only confess that it was because I had no money. And now let me thank you once again for your angel kindness, and say goodbye.'

'Oh *no*!' said both the girls. And Jane said: 'We can't possibly let you go like this. You've told us a little – won't you tell us all about everything, and why you haven't any money, and what you're going to do?'

'I'll tell you anything you're good enough to want to know. I was a clerk in an insurance office. I enlisted in 1914. They promised to keep my job for me – they didn't. My people went to New Zealand just before the war. I hope and expect to get work. I get employment benefit, as they call it. It's a pound a week. Affluence, of course. But I spent most of last week's on advertisements – that's why things are worse than usual. Of course I ought to have told some lie – said I was engaged for Sunday – but I couldn't. It's such a long time since I've talked to anyone. I wanted so much to see you both again. And I've behaved like a fool and frightened you in that wretched summer-house, and I don't know how to look you in the face.'

He stood up, looking from one kind, puzzled face to the other. 'Don't you worry about me – I'm not worth it. I shall be all right.'

'You *shall*,' said Jane firmly. 'Anyway, come and be our gardener for a bit and see how things go. Will you?'

'It doesn't seem fair – you don't know anything about me.'

'But you'll tell us all about yourself – all the rest, I mean,' said Jane; 'but not to-night. There's only one thing. But first, will you be our gardener?'

'I should just think I would. And you'll see. I do know something about gardening. And the "one thing"?'

'Don't be angry with us for asking, will you?'

'Of course not,' he answered, a faint surprise in his voice. 'Anything . . .'

'You won't be offended and rush off?'

'Of course not.'

'Then,' said Jane firmly, 'you are going to be our gardener, and we should like to know what it was that you went to prison for.'

'I was taken prisoner in 1918 – had over a year of it. At Recklinghausen. And I had shell-shock. The hospital I was in – it was all very horrible. I don't a bit mind your asking, but I don't want to talk about it.'

'You were a war prisoner? In Germany?'

'Yes.' Then their silence and the shame in their eyes struck at him the knowledge of how different an answer it was that they had expected to hear.

'My God!' he said, almost in a whisper. 'You thought I'd been in an English prison – that I was a criminal? My God!'

He sat down heavily on the chair from which he had just risen, put his elbows on the table and buried his face in his hands.

The girls looked at each other miserably, questioning with their eyes. What could they do? What could they say?

'What *have* I done?' Jane's eyes signalled.

And Lucilla's replied with sympathy, rather deeply tinged with reproach: 'Yes, indeed, what *have* you?'

By the pleasant light of fire and candle they could see the shoulders of the man shaken a little, as though by laughter; but they knew that no laughter could have followed that cry – the cry wrung from him by an overpowering emotion: 'My God!'

Lucilla's eyes signalled to Jane.

'This is your doing,' they said. 'You have blundered us all into this. Now get us out of it. Say something. Do something. It's *your* business, not mine.'

'All right, I will,' Jane's eyes signalled back defiantly. With the least little shrug of the shoulders she rose and went and stood beside Mr Dix.

'Don't,' she said; 'please, please don't! We didn't know. We don't know anything, really. We're only silly schoolgirls. Do try to forgive us, won't you?'

At that he screwed his knuckles into his eyes like a schoolboy, pushed his chair back and stood up.

'Forgive you?' he said. 'You must forgive *me* for behaving like a baby – but no, there's no excuse for me – but it came on me so suddenly. That you should have believed that I was a criminal and yet treated me as you have done – why – you must have believed *that*, even when you first asked me to come and see you and to be your gardener! That you should have thought *that*, and yet been so good to me! Why, I didn't believe there was so much goodness in the world. That sort of thing is enough to bowl a man over. Forgive me for having made such an ass of myself – and –'

'Oh, stop!' said Jane in fluttered distress. 'It's nothing. I mean it's most awful for us, don't you see – to have thought . . . Oh, don't let's say any more about anything. You're tired out, and no wonder – and so are we. Let's shake hands and be friends and not talk any more nonsense. Look here – we must get home. It must be about a thousand o'clock. Now you aren't going to be silly about this; here's some money – part of the wages, you know.' She pressed two notes on him, rejoicing that she happened to have them with her, 'Yes, yes, yes, yes! You'll want breakfast tomorrow, and you'll want boots. I hope that's enough, because it's all we've got with us, and you can stay here to-night and we shall be round about ten. There's a tap just outside the door when you want to wash – and that big chair's quite comfortable. Where's my hat? – oh, here! Where are my gloves? – oh, there! Lucy, help me with my macker. No, please don't talk any more. Good-night, Mr Dix. Sleep well, and don't worry. We were born lucky –'

'*I* was,' he interjected.

'Of course you were. Not another word. Good-night.' She talked without ceasing till they had got away. The gate was padlocked behind them and his good-night came to them through the bars. Jane clutched Lucilla's arm as they hurried home in a silence broken only by the sound of their feet splashing through puddles and by Jane's sniffs. Presently Lucilla sniffed too. And then Jane stopped to fumble for her handkerchief.

'Don't *you* start snivelling!' she told Lucilla sharply. 'You haven't anything to cry about. *You* haven't done anything. You haven't made a perfectly abject idiot of yourself – and insulted one of our own soldiers who fought for us and was hurt and imprisoned and . . .' She stamped on the pavement. 'Cry? What's the good? I could kick myself! Always blundering in where anyone with the least sense would at least have held her tongue. Why didn't you stop me?'

'You know it's as easy to stop a steam-roller as it is to stop you when you've got the bit between your teeth,' said Lucilla with some truth. 'And I wasn't crying. I've caught a cold. And really, I don't think you need worry. He thinks you're an angel.'

'What does it matter what he thinks? What's the good of his thinking us angels when I know we're fools – at least, I mean me? Goodness, how wet I am! Look here – let's run. I expect we've both caught the colds of our lives!'

Jane's last words that night were: 'What a day! But it has been a sort of lark too . . . all but that one awful bit.'

In the garden room Mr Dix, having taken off what remained of his boots, sat warm by the fire, watching the steam rise from his wet jacket, now hanging from a chair-back before the blaze.

'The dears!' he said. 'The splendid, brave, impetuous, quixotic dears! Beautiful, beautiful, beautiful! And to think that only this morning I was asking myself if it was really worth while to go on with life. And all the time there was all this in the world. Beautiful!'

Chapter XV

The great days of our lives seldom bear their names on their foreheads. We get up and come down to our featureless breakfast, read our dullish paper, and tap the barometer and wonder whether it would not be safer, after all, to take an umbrella, remarking that it is certainly colder (or warmer) than it was yesterday, though not nearly so cold (or warm) as it was the day before. Or, not being men and breadwinners, we do not concern ourselves with umbrellas or barometers, but, instead, wonder whether we had better spring-clean the spare room this week or next, and wish that we could think of a perfectly new breakfast dish. But in either case we feel no least suspicion that this is not going to be just another day like all the other days. And we go about our business warmed by no transfiguring hope, frozen by no devastating fear. And then, as life goes running smoothly, or perhaps a little unevenly, but still in its accustomed grooves, suddenly the great thing is upon us – the thing that is to change for good or ill the whole course of our Fate. The loved one who went out with a smile and a careless, gay goodbye is brought home white and still, never to smile here any more; the brother we thought dead comes back to us from the ends of the earth; we lose all our money – or inherit all someone else's money; our sweetheart jilts us – or we see for the first time the eyes that are to be the light of life for us. And we never guessed that this was not to be a day like other days.

So, when Jane and Lucilla walked down to Cedar Court on the morning after the affair of the Strange Man and the Summerhouse, they felt no premonition of anything more wonderful than the sale of a few flowers and the adjustment of Mr Dix to his new situation. The affair of Mr Dix was interesting, certainly, but it was not epoch-making.

Jane was in a somewhat chastened mood; one cannot recover all in a moment, as she explained to Lucilla, from the crowning imbecility of a lifetime; the dark stain of ignominy takes some time to clean off.

'Tears ought to lay the dust, anyhow,' said Lucilla.

'Don't let's throw up tears at each other,' said Jane.

'No,' said the other, with laboured conciliation, 'but I really mean it. And besides, look how the rain last night has washed the world clean and bright as a new pin. I do think when you've done anything wrong or silly, and been really and truly sorry, you ought to try and forget it. Wipe it out.'

'Ah,' said Jane, 'you got that from Miss Whatever-was-her-name; you know, that used to read Ibsen to us and talk about sickly consciences. She wore aesthetic gowns till Jamesie stopped it and put her into a blouse and skirt. I liked her – and I don't mean to have a sickly conscience. But don't you think one ought to dwell a little on one's croppers, so as not to do the same thing again?'

'Miss Prynne – yes, that's her name – used to say that you shouldn't look back, but look forward. Don't go on regretting what you've done that's bad, but try to cancel it out by doing something good. Cheer up, old Jane; don't forget that life is a lark!'

'I know it is,' said Jane, 'but it's a lot of other things too. I some-times think life isn't so simple as they make out at school. For instance, do you think Mr Rochester and Mr Dix will like each other? Because I don't.'

'Does it matter?'

'*Doesn't* it? How can we have any peace and quiet, let alone joy, in life if our kind friend and protector, Mr John Rochester, growls at the thought of our protecting a stray dog. You know how I hate tact . . .'

'Yes,' said Lucilla, with emphasis.

'. . . But I've always been told that it's useful sometimes, and I almost think that this is one of the times. Only I've had so little practice in being tactful – I don't know how to begin.'

'You did pretty well with Uncle James. Don't be mock modest.'

'Exactly. Uncle James. He may turn up again this morning – In fact I'm certain he *will* – and I have a sort of feeling that Uncle James's ideal young ladies would never have got themselves mixed up with young men in dark summer-houses and midnight tea-parties.'

Lucilla pointed out that they needn't, after all, tell Uncle James.

'No, but Mr Dix will. That fatal frankness of his – do you know, I rather like him for that. Suppose we hurry and find spades and forks for him, and rakes and hoes; it will be easier to explain a gardener in the act of gardening than an unoccupied young man who has never been introduced to us.'

'I wonder why Gravy always made out that it was so *awful* to talk to young men that weren't introduced to you? It doesn't feel awful, does it? It feels perfectly natural.'

The gardens at Cedar Court looked lovelier than ever. The morning sunlight glittered on the wet leaves, and against a blue sky trimmed with rolling white clouds the trees stood up in their green-rounded perfection – all the leaves new and not yet a leaf fallen. The chestnut tree by the gate towered against the blue, its pointed white cones standing up like fat candles on a Christmas-tree for some fortunate and giant child. All the roads and paths were clear and bright.

'The world really does look like a little girl that means to be good now, please, and has had her face washed and her curls combed out,' said Jane as they went up to the door of the garden house.

'With a green frock embroidered with daisies,' said Lucilla. And with that they came to the door. And even then, seeing Mr Dix come to meet them and trying not to look at his new boots seemed to be the chief event of the day.

'I've sold eighteenpenny-worth of flowers,' he announced joyously. 'A woman who was going to a hospital. I couldn't leave the place, so I let her have the flowers out of the vase here – was that right?'

'Splendid!' said Jane. 'Why, we hardly ever take anything on Monday – it's a glorious beginning!'

'You didn't either of you catch cold last night?' he hoped.

'More likely you,' said Jane. 'I'm afraid you were awfully uncomfortable here. No, don't be polite about it – because, of course, the truth's the truth. Have you been into the garden yet – by daylight, I mean?'

'Rather! It's a beautiful place – but . . . well . . . the sooner I get to work the better. Is there a scythe? Nothing short of that will make any sort of successful attack on your armies of docks and nettles.'

'Those sort of things are in the toolshed among the lilacs beyond the summer-house. Of course, there might be a scythe there, but I've never seen one.'

'Yes,' he said, but still he lingered.

'Look here,' he said quickly, looking out of the window over the cedar lawn, 'you must just let me say "thank you" *once* – I won't keep on saying it. I've been in London for months – all grey and black and grimy – everything greasy with being rubbed up against by the bent shoulders of unhappy people. And all the faces – anxious, worried, sad. And the noises – the screaming machines rushing about. The motor-vans begin at three in the morning. This morning the birds woke me. I was out in the garden by five. I'd almost forgotten what dawn was like in a green place.'

He went out abruptly without looking at them. And they very carefully avoided looking at each other.

The morning seemed unusually long; there were no more sales. When they had swept and dusted the garden room there was nothing more to do but to wonder whether their landlord would come again to-day, to-morrow, every day, every other day.

'You know,' said Jane, 'if dear Uncle James is going to live next door, so to speak, and if we're liable to be dropped down on at any hour of the day or night –'

'He didn't drop down exactly,' said Lucilla.

'Oh, didn't he? Liable to be dropped *in* on, then – we shall never feel safe. I do like him, too – but he's so sudden.' And it was then that she explained how exactly the elder Mr Rochester had resembled the eldest of the three bears.

To Mr Dix, sweltering in mid-day sunshine, amid swathes of

mown grass and groundsel, dock and comfrey, nettles and thistle and willow herb, came a bright vision of basket-bearing maidens in flowered gowns, all pink and green and blue and purple.

'Dinner,' said one of them.

And, 'You'll want to wash,' said the other; 'lock up the garden room when you've done, won't you? And when you come you might bring the plates and glasses off the table – and the jug of lemonade.'

They spread the cloth by the fishpond – dry now and overgrown with the thorny arrogance of rambler roses all thick with the promise of countless little pointed buds.

It was a very nice dinner – the cold lamb from yesterday, and what was left of the gooseberry-pie, and lettuces and radishes, and what sounds so nice when you call it (fair white bread). The sun shone, the green leaves flickered and shivered in the soft airs of May. The peonies shone like crimson cannon-balls, and the flags stood up like spears; the birds sang, and three very contented people ate and talked and laughed together. It is idle to pretend that three is not sometimes a much better number than two. Jane realised this.

'So long as it's not four,' she told herself, and ever and again her eye scanned the shadowy shrubbery beyond which lay the gates by which, if at all, the fourth must come. And the more she liked Mr Dix – and she did go on liking him more and more – the more certain she felt that the fourth, if that fourth should be Mr John Rochester, would not like Mr Dix so much as she did.

There was a breathless feeling of being on the edge of things.

They made conversation:

'I wish Shelley hadn't said that about the lamb that looks you in the face,' said Lucilla. And that kept them going for a while.

Then: 'This gooseberry-pie ought to have cream with it,' said Jane; 'but the cream here doesn't seem real somehow. Let's write to Gladys to post us some from Mutton's, shall we? Gladys was one of the maids at school.'

Then they told Mr Dix about Gladys.

They all laughed a great deal and ate up everything that there was to eat.

When the meal was over, Lucilla produced with an air of conscious pride a crumpled packet of cigarettes.

'You'd like to smoke?' she said, offering also matches.

The cigarette which Mr Dix extracted from the packet was bent but not broken. He straightened it and lit it. Not for worlds would he have produced the new crisp cigarettes that he had bought that morning. Something about that timeworn little packet of Lucilla's convinced him that neither of the ladies smoked. Still, he put the question.

'But you?' he asked. 'What am I thinking of?' and he proffered the broken-backed case.

'We don't,' said Jane. 'I believe everyone else does, so we tried. But we don't like it.'

'Gladys smokes,' said Lucilla. 'It was Gladys who got us the cigarettes to try; we only tried one each. They didn't make us ill . . . Gladys said they did some people – but they don't really taste nice, and we couldn't smell the flowers or the wet grass or pine-woods nearly so well afterwards. So we didn't go on with it.'

'You don't dislike my smoking? Doesn't it poison the air for you?' he asked, laying down the cigarette.

'Oh no!' said both together.

'It smells all right here,' Lucilla explained, and Jane added:

'It makes you feel that this is the great world: so different from school. Do go on.' And he did.

'It was jolly clever of you to think of those cigarettes,' Jane said later; 'it was a score to you. But I expect he'd really bought some already. No, I don't really – don't look so dismal; it was a splendid thought. If he'd been the snub-nosed charwoman you couldn't have made him happy with cigarettes. I say, Luce, we never offered Uncle James his share of the money.'

'No more we did. Now we shall have to calculate what ten per cent of all our shop money comes to. What a way to spend a bright day in May!'

'You'd rather spend it sitting by the edge of the fishpond watching our gardener smoke.'

'Yes – and so would you! Instead of which we'll mind the shop – and let Uncle James jolly well find us minding it if he drops down – I mean in – on us this afternoon.'

But it was Mr John Rochester who dropped in.

'I thought perhaps you would,' said Lucilla, rather out of politeness than as a statement of fact, 'because of the stables, you know.'

'Ah – the stables!' said Mr John Rochester. 'I kept the stables dark yesterday because I didn't know exactly how we stood with Uncle. I wasn't sure that there mightn't be a recurrence of grumpiness on the part of Uncle. About the crocks and the sticks, you know.'

'And was there?'

'No – on the contrary. I have never known him so amiable. Our noble work in cleaning off the gas-green paint has gone straight to his heart. He could talk of very little else.'

'We were just wondering how to find out how much ten per cent of all our shop money would come to. You know that was what we settled to pay your uncle – as rent for the garden room, you know.'

'I didn't know,' said Mr Rochester, 'but I don't think you need bother about that. He's changed his mind.'

The girls looked at each other in dumb horror. Mr Rochester was getting some keys out of his pocket, and did not see their faces. The keys of the stable, no doubt. But what did stable or cottages or tennis-lawn matter if their landlord changed his mind? Somehow they had never thought of his doing that.

Jane was the first to find words.

'He doesn't want us to go on with the garden and the garden room? He doesn't want us to go on as we are?'

'No,' answered John Rochester absently, and still busy with the keys. 'He doesn't want you to go on as you are. You see, he's decided not to keep the house empty any longer.'

An end, then, to everything!

I think it is to the credit of my Jane and Lucilla that the first thought of each as they caught breath under the assault of this wave of misfortune was:

'And we've just engaged a gardener! Oh, poor Mr Dix!'

Chapter XVI

'I think,' said Jane, in a small, flat voice, 'that I would rather go before he comes.'

'Before who comes?' Mr Rochester was laying the keys out on the table, one by one, in a row.

'Your uncle.'

'But he isn't coming,' said Mr Rochester, still intent on the keys. 'Why can't people use key-rings? These were on a cord, and it's broken. They were all in a certain order. Only two labelled A and B – the rest *en suite*. A silly game. No – he's not coming. He's gone to Thibet. There's a Buddhist manuscript there that he must see, or perish. So he's gone to see it. But I've got a letter for you from him.'

'You can post it to us,' said Lucilla, in a voice smaller and flatter than Jane's.

'No need for that – I'll give it you in half a minute. I'm only trying to remember how these things go. My dear girl,' he ended, in a quite changed voice, 'whatever is the matter?'

'Oh, nothing,' said Jane, now sufficiently recovered to bristle defensively. 'Everything's for the best in the best of all possible worlds, as Marcus Aurelius said, didn't he? Only those unexpected things do rather take your breath away. I daresay our new gardener can take down the board. I don't mind in the least,' she went on, and she was now, indeed, a little breathless; 'but I must say I think it would have been better to have let us alone, and not let us begin to work here and hope and plan things, and then spring this on us.' She walked to the window and stood looking out at the cedars, which looked, to her eyes, twisted and rainbow-rimmed.

'Springing what?' asked Rochester in complete bewilderment. 'Tell me – what?' But Jane could find no voice to tell him what.

'Springing *what*?' he asked again.

'What you told us,' said Lucilla, in a sort of faint, timid growl, and then she too became speechless, and turned to the other window and gazed out at the gates and the board, also, to her, prismatically coloured.

'But I haven't told you anything yet,' Rochester protested. Four eyes bright with unconcealable tears turned on him astonished reproach.

The bewildered young man was quite overcome. He gazed from Lucilla to Jane; his heart experienced a twinge at the sight of Lucilla's brimming eyes, but when he saw the dejected droop of Jane's head he lost his own.

'Ah, don't!' he said, in a voice of extreme tenderness, and he took two steps and put his hand over Jane's hand, which lay on the window-ledge. 'Please, please don't. I must have been incredibly stupid – I don't know what I've done, but . . .'

Will it be believed that Mr Dix chose this exact moment to appear at the glass door and ask cheerfully where the wheelbarrow was kept? He looked very handsome though; his classic brow was dotted with beads of sweat, and his blue shirt, open at the neck and rolled up as to the sleeves, accentuated the blue of his eyes. He spoke with perfect respect, of course, but it was the respect of the young man to the woman who is his social equal, not the respect of the gardener to his employer.

'I can't find the wheelbarrow anywhere,' he said.

'We hid it behind the laurels,' said Lucilla, 'in case of burglars. We couldn't get it into the shed. I'll show you,' and felt herself being tactful. The spectacle of Mr Rochester laying his hand on Jane's, and Jane not whisking her hand abruptly from this unusual contact until Mr Dix's voice was heard at the door, made Lucilla extremely anxious to get away, somehow, from the garden room. But Jane also appeared anxious for flight.

'No – I'll go,' she said, and was out of the door like a flash.

'Who's that?' asked Mr Rochester, when she was gone.

'Mr Dix. He was going to be our gardener.'

'Oh,' said Mr Rochester coldly; 'why only "was"?'

'Well – we don't need a gardener at Hope Cottage, and since we're not going to go on here . . .'

'Oh,' said Mr Rochester slowly, 'I begin to see. Well, it's no use my trying to remember what I said – something more than usually idiotic, I suppose – but what I came down to say was this: my uncle is so charmed with the panelling, and the tea, and you, and Miss Quested, and everything, that he's changed his mind completely; he says you can have the whole of Cedar Court to do exactly as you like with – no restrictions. Only in return he wants to have Hope Cottage kept exactly as it is – not let – but kept as it is.'

'Just as it is? No one to live in it? Like a museum?'

'More like a sacred relic of the past.'

'I don't understand,' said Lucilla; 'but then I don't understand anything this morning. Let me go and tell Jane.'

'Just a minute,' said Mr Rochester. 'Who is this Mr Dix?'

'A friend of ours,' said Lucilla cautiously.

'Known him long?' asked Mr Rochester – 'though, of course, I've no earthly right to ask.'

'No,' said Lucilla, with some spirit, 'I don't think you have – any earthly.'

And a gloomy silence fell between them. The young man broke it by a laugh that was not very merry.

'Why,' he said, 'this is like a nightmare! I couldn't sleep last night – literally and actually I couldn't sleep – for thinking how frightfully pleased you'd both be. And now you're quarrelling with me, and she's gone off crying with that Dixy fellow, and everything's about as damnable – I beg your pardon, but it really is – as it can possibly be.'

'Well,' said Lucilla, 'it's no use making it worse by being silly; of course Jane and I both wanted to go off and look for the wheelbarrow – anything to get away from *you*. You don't suppose we enjoyed standing and snivelling at you like silly, hysterical schoolgirls, do you?'

'Look here,' said Mr Rochester, 'about that man Dix, or whatever his wretched name is . . .'

'Well, what about him?'

'Don't be prickly. Do tell me about him.'

'All right. I will. We made his acquaintance at Madame Tussauds and – and we asked him to tea. Jane asked him to be our gardener. And now what about it?'

'You mean to say you just met him like that – you don't know anything about him?'

'No more than we knew about *you* when we asked *you* to tea. Now look here, Mr Rochester, we like you very much as a friend, but we aren't going to have you as a duenna. Yes, I daresay I'm vulgar, but there it is. We choose our own friends. You oughtn't to forget that we chose *you*. And you can't expect us to go through life without any friends except you. And you can't expect us not to have a gardener. And do think what a much better number four is than three for tennis.'

'That's true,' he admitted thoughtfully.

'If I knew you well enough to ask a favour . . .'

'But you do – you do.'

'Then I should ask you to be very nice to Mr Dix. There's every reason why you should. Look here, Mr Rochester. I'm beginning to understand what you said just now. If we're really to have Cedar Court, this is our day of days – the birthday of our life. And we're spoiling it with silliness. Put the black dog up the chimney. Fie, fie! Unknit that angry, threatening brow, and tell me I'm not dreaming, and that your uncle really is the angel you said he was. Are you going to be nice? Are you?'

He was smiling by this time.

'How eloquent you are!' he said. 'I've never heard you say so much at once since I've known you.'

'I'm never eloquent when Jane's there,' said Lucilla – 'she does it so much better than I do; and you *will* be nice?'

'I'll do anything you like. I'll even try to admire your far too admirable gardener. Please forgive me, and let's enjoy the day of days.'

'Mr Dix will have to be allowed to enjoy it too,' she stipulated.

'Out of working hours,' he urged. 'If he's a gardener, let him jolly well garden.'

'And now,' she said, smiling as April smiles, 'let's go and find Jane, and tell her. Monday's early-closing day – at least it ought to be. We'll lock up the shop and be free for happiness.'

They found Jane on the stone seat in the nut-walk at the far end of the garden. On the way, Mr Rochester noted with some satisfaction that the gardener was jolly well gardening. He had his wheelbarrow and was pitchforking weeds into it with due energy.

Mr Rochester thought he had never seen anything so satisfying as the light of half incredulous joy that shone in Jane's eyes when Lucilla – without any beating about the bush – broke out with:

'It's all right, Jane. It's the exact opposite of what we thought. We're to have *all* Cedar Court, my dear – and do just what we like with it.'

'You're not – not joking?' Jane asked, afraid to take this new joy in her hands.

'Joking?' said Lucilla. 'Not much. It's dream-like, but it's true. Mr Rochester's got the keys. Let's go now, this very minute, and see all over everything.'

'Oh yes!' said Jane. 'Oh, who would have thought my blundering down those stairs that day would have led to this!'

'If people only knew what results you get there wouldn't be enough stairs in the world for all the people who'd be tumbling over each other to tumble down them,' said Lucilla.

'You're wandering, dear,' said Jane. 'Oh, Mr Rochester, is it really true?'

'As true as taxes,' said Mr Rochester.

And so, led by Mr John Rochester, who by a curious coincidence had on boots as new as Mr Dix's – boots that creaked too – they explored the house. It was, they both felt, a great moment. Those trembling joys of their first furtive raid on Cedar Court, those breathless glimpses, those hurried peeps at forbidden treasures of cabinet and banner-screen – these surely would be as nothing compared with the mature joy of this absolutely lawful exploration.

They 'went over' the house. No longer now were shutters opened, a mere reluctant inch, by fumbling feminine fingers, but flung fully back by the strong hand of a benevolent authority. The treasures of furniture and hangings, of picture and ornament, which, just glimpsed in twilight, had remained less a subject for memory than the seeds of romantic imaginings, now came forth out of the shadows boldly, solidly, with all their correct curves and angles, their definite "periods", their declared colours and unconcealed textures. To the early survey the place had seemed a dream-mansion – a place with a spell on it, like the Castle of the Sleeping Beauty, or the old brewery where Miss Havisham walked in her ghostly bridal satin and dusty bridal flowers. Seen now by daylight, the May sunshine streaming unhindered through the dusty panes, with Mr Rochester's new boots creaking on its obvious carpets, it was just like a house – like any other house. Rather a big house, furnished in a rather old-fashioned style. Even the front rooms, whose boarded windows still denied the light, seemed not very mysterious, only dark and dull.

Rather a big house? It was a very big house. A neglected big house. A very charming place to dream dreams about, when all that one knew was its pleasing outside shell, and the romantic suggestion of its half-seen dusky interior. But a house to live in? A house to use and make useful? As they went through room after room the spirits of the girls sank lower and lower, and when they came to the laundry and still-room and butler's pantry the house had come to seem less a Paradise than a problem. The girls became more and more silent, and Mr Rochester, who, never voluble, had now almost the whole weight of the conversation on his shoulders, felt a growing conviction that his uncle's generosity had conferred not a benefit but a white elephant.

'Don't you,' he said, when they had been through all the rooms and stood at last on the doorstep, 'don't you *like* it?'

'Oh yes!' they both said, but quite without conviction.

'Of course we like it,' Jane said.

'Very much, thank you, of course,' said Lucilla.

Chapter XVII

'You'll like to see the stables and all that?' said Mr John Rochester. And they agreed, but without eagerness. Stables and cottages, once so gladly welcomed, now seemed only additional responsibilities. It was not till they had passed through the double gate in the wall – the gate which they had believed to open on to the road – and seen the stable-yard surrounded by stables and outbuildings, and the two cottages beyond – quite pretty cottages standing in neglected gardens – that Jane was roused to a faint enthusiasm.

'I do like this,' she said; 'look how lovely the May-bushes are, and that single rose over the door just coming out, and the vine all over the side! And the grass and the interesting little weeds coming up among the cobble-stones in the stable-yard! Do you think there's any furniture in the cottages, Mr Rochester?'

There was; and it was rather attractive furniture – plain deal and elm in the kitchen and mahogany in the best parlour – not the gimcrack plush and machine-carved walnut made-to-sell that has ousted the old strong, solid wood and horse-hair cloth.

'Made to last, you see,' Mr Rochester exerted himself to point out; 'all fitted together like Chinese puzzles – no nails, only wooden pegs and screws.'

'How is it,' Lucilla wondered, also exerting herself to converse, 'that old furniture is so nice and new furniture's so nasty.'

'I suppose because the new furniture is made to sell. Designs that can be made by the thousand, held together with glue and tacks. If the buyers don't look out when they're buying, so much the worse for them. The old furniture was made to last and it was bought to keep – to be handed down from father to son and mother to daughter.'

'How nice!' said Lucilla, detained by politeness while Jane explored shelves and chiffoniers. 'That's what I think is so jolly about Hope Cottage – my aunt having lived there when she was young and her people before her.'

'Yes,' said Mr Rochester, one eye on Jane and one on the conversation. 'In the old days young couples set up house with what could be spared from the furniture at home with a few new pieces *made for them*. In those days, you know, a man ordered his furniture to measure as he orders his coat now – chose the wood, the shape, the size, the fittings, the handles, the drawers and the shelves, and so on. Now the young people go to Tottenham Court Road and order home a houseful – or a flatful – of gimcrack rubbish, sticky with varnish, with imitation brass, imitation inlay, and machine-carving. There'll be none of it left to leave to their children – that's one comfort. It'll all break up before its owners do, even. But I go maundering on. Forgive me. It's a subject I feel rather strongly about.'

'Oh, so do I,' said Lucilla kindly. But he said no more; only, asking leave to light a cigarette, leaned out of the window among the framing vines and smoked in silence, broken after a few minutes by Lucilla's ingenuous, 'I wasn't bored about the furniture, Mr Rochester, I liked it, really!' And even then he said no more, only smiled at her, and went on smoking.

Jane meanwhile ran upstairs and down, peered into cupboards and up chimneys, with an alertness which she had *not* shown in Cedar Court. 'I believe you'd rather have this place than Cedar Court,' said Rochester at last, when he and Lucilla had followed Jane to the wash-house.

'Not at all,' said Jane cheerfully, replacing the lid on the copper. 'I was only thinking it would be the very thing for Mr Dix.'

'Oh!' said Rochester, stiffening. 'You lodge your gardener then?'

'We can now, you see,' Jane explained. 'That's the best of it. Did you notice whether there were any blankets, Lucy?'

Lucy hadn't, and Jane flitted out up the narrow stairs to settle this serious question.

Lucilla and Rochester stood outside the door under the climbing cherry-coloured rose, waiting for her. Lucilla noted that his brow was thunderous, his lips closely set.

'I am afraid,' she thought to him, 'that you are a very bad-tempered man. I don't care – I'll rub it in, then.'

'I do hope you'll like Mr Dix,' she said. 'He seems awfully nice. So kind and – and sunny.'

'Sweet fellow,' said Mr Rochester.

'And I don't think really it was so very rash of Jane to insist on having him for a gardener. Do you?'

'I've no means of judging,' he said, still black as thunder. And then Jane joined them with the information that there were plenty of blankets but they seemed to be rather damp.

'It would never do for Mr Dix to take cold,' said Rochester politely. 'Can I light a fire and fill hot-water bottles or anything?'

Jane looked at him curiously.

'No, thank you,' she said. 'Mr Dix isn't at all helpless. I think he'll manage here splendidly. Thank you so much for showing us everything. I do like this cottage – I think it's perfectly ducky.'

'I'm glad there's something you like,' he said; and again she looked curiously at him.

'Oh, but I love it all! It's splendid!' she said. 'It's so splendid that I feel knocked all of a heap – don't you, Lucy?'

'Emptied out of a sack,' said Lucilla, who had just finished reading Sandra Belloni.

'And now I think we'd better show Mr Dix his house and then get home. No, we needn't unlock the garden room again – we have everything.'

'Not everything,' said Rochester. 'Here are the keys of Cedar Court.'

Jane took the mass of jingling iron in both hands. 'What a lot of them!' she said. 'Which is the key of the Blue beard chamber? I'm sure there must be one.'

'I'm sure there isn't,' said Lucilla.

'Miss Quested's quite right. There's always a Blue beard chamber,' said Rochester; 'only you never know which it is – and you never know which is the key.'

'Do you mean really? Or are you being mystical and like Maeterlinck?'

'I don't think so. I can't believe somehow that Maeterlinck ever really enjoys a joke. Now I do – and it seems to me that my uncle has made the joke of his life in going off to a monastery in Thibet, where I'm sure they don't want him, and leaving you saddled with a large, ugly house that I'm sure *you* don't want.'

'Oh, but we do!' said both girls.

'Thank you for them kind words, lady,' said Rochester and Lucilla noted approvingly that he really did seem to be making an effort to put the black dog up the chimney. 'But it *is* a joke, isn't it? And I appreciate it so much that I should like to point out that my uncle isn't the Cham of Tartary.'

'I suppose not – no,' said Jane, who was wondering about several things.

'No; nor is he a Median or a Persian monarch. I mean that what he says doesn't necessarily have to *be* so. I thought you'd love to have Cedar Court. But if you don't want it – why, you've only to say so, and it's "as you were" for all of us.'

'For all of us? Do you mean . . .?' Jane stopped.

'She means, are you to be a sort of gentlemanly duenna to see that we do exactly what you think Uncle James would like?' Lucilla put in.

'Lucilla,' said Jane, 'I didn't mean that in the least. I meant . . . Oh, it doesn't matter,' she ended, finding it unexpectedly difficult to say what she did mean. 'But I do want to understand –'

'Forgive me,' said Rochester, 'for interrupting you, but don't you think that what you *really* want – what we all want – is tea?'

'I'm sure Mr Dix must want his,' said Jane.

'You were saying,' said Rochester, 'before we began that tiring tramp through those disheartening rooms, you were saying that this was the birthday of your life. Will you boil the kettle? – and I will nip up on my bike and get a birthday cake, and let's have a birthday party. It needn't commit you to taking over Cedar Court if you don't want to. May I?'

'Oh, please do!' said Jane, with sudden heart-warming cordiality – 'and perhaps when you come back we shall know whether we're dreaming or not'; and as he disappeared down the drive Lucilla said: 'You'd have thought he'd have had the sense to tell us about the house and go. It would have been quite different if you and I had explored it alone. Why couldn't he see that?'

'Oh, people are like that,' said Jane, fanning herself with a chestnut leaf; 'if they bring you a box of chocolates they *must* stay to see you eat them. I daresay it's natural after all,' she added, with an air of a woman of the world. 'We mustn't be too hard on him.'

'I believe,' said Mr Dix, stretching himself on the rough, newly-mown lawn, 'that heaven will be exactly like this. Green leaves and grass – sun and shade. And tea. And cake. And ices.'

For there had been ices, brought by Mr Rochester in a basin in a cloth in a basket – ices not wholly melted before they could be eaten.

'And strawberries,' said Lucilla, finishing hers.

'And agreeable conversation and delightful company,' said Jane. 'I felt someone ought to say that, and why not me?'

'Why not indeed?' said Mr Rochester.

They were all feeling the better for their tea.

'I think,' said Lucilla didactically, 'we ought to be most frightfully happy.'

'It's not a moral obligation,' said Mr Dix, 'for me, at least. It's a ravishing and irresistible compulsion. When I look at the cedars and the lawns and the fountains and think of Baker Street –'

'We ought to get that fountain playing again,' said Rochester, all the engineer in him leaping to life at the words 'but why Baker Street?'

'That is the name of the Inferno from which I was restored, no longer ago than yesterday, to the world where roses are red and leaves are green. Only those who have known Baker Street can see how green leaves are and feel the full colour of roses.'

'I suppose you don't play tennis, Mr Dix?' Mr Rochester asked abruptly.

'I didn't in Baker Street, of course,' Mr Dix answered serenely, 'but in other spheres . . . You do, of course?'

'A little,' said Rochester, who rather prided himself on his game.

'Oh, Mr Dix,' said Lucilla, 'why weren't you here a week ago? Then you'd have mown the tennis-lawn and we could have played this evening.'

'I'll do it to-morrow,' he said eagerly, 'but it won't be much good for a week or two, I'm afraid. Still, we could knock the balls about, couldn't we? Where is the court – couldn't we go and look at it now?'

The tennis-courts had a walled space to themselves where once had been a Dutch garden, but in the far-away seventies, when people began to play lawn-tennis, young James Rochester had coaxed his father to lay down these courts – the high walls still trellised with peach and plum and pear made nets needless. It was a beautiful and most unusual arena for the great game.

Mr Dix examined the turf and pronounced it not to be nearly so bad as he had feared; the standpipe at the corner excited his liveliest commendation.

'We ought to be able to amuse ourselves quite well in a day or two, and get a fairly decent game by next week,' he said. 'What a glorious place this is! I wouldn't have believed that anything so perfect could be – within a walk of Baker Street.'

Lucilla and Jane had fallen back and were talking earnestly.

'Bother Baker Street!' said Mr Rochester, but he said it to himself. Aloud he said, 'Rather a long walk, isn't it?'

'It was,' said Mr Dix – 'a very long walk indeed. I lost my way twice, which made it longer. And I couldn't be sure that I hadn't lost everything else as well, which made it longer still. You see,' he explained, before Mr Rochester had time to more than half feel that he had been snubbed, and that he rather deserved it, 'you see, I was walking down to interview Miss Quested and Miss Craye about the situation of gardener, and it would have been rather terrible to lose that chance, wouldn't it? I've been out of work for months.'

The two men were walking side by side.

'Gardening's your special work then?'

'It's my trade now. It wasn't before the war. But my people had a garden. I know all about it right enough.'

Now this pleased Mr Rochester, because it seemed to admit that he had some claim to have explanations offered to him, and he said:

'I've been at loose ends myself since the war.'

'Ah, yes,' said Mr Dix, 'but you've got something to tie your loose ends to. I've been absolutely up against it. Nothing but unemployment allowance.'

'Now why,' Mr Rochester wondered, 'does he tell me this?'

'My people are in New Zealand,' Dix went on. 'I've had rather a stiff time, in a small way, you know. However, that's all right. And I say . . .' he hesitated. 'You're probably worrying yourself, and thinking that I'm a waster, and that your friends have been very unwise in taking a gardener out of the streets like this without even asking for a recommendation, or a character, or whatever you call it. And, if you're feeling that, it's no doubt making you feel uncomfortable. You needn't be uncomfortable. That's what I want to say. I'm all right, see? I'm not a waster. These ladies haven't done a foolish thing in engaging me: they've got a gardener now, that's one thing — and you see how the garden wants one. And I shall make this garden pay. See?'

'I see,' said Rochester. 'Thank you for explaining.'

'There's another thing: I know they'd never tell you, but *I* want to tell you that these ladies have behaved to me like . . . like . . . well, it was the most perfect thing I've ever seen, and I want you to know it, and to know that I know it. And it's a thing I can never forget or think differently about. Feel more comfortable about it all now?'

'Well, yes,' said Rochester laughing. 'I think I do. Miss Quested and Miss Craye are perfectly fearless, perfectly unconventional. They are as brave and as innocent as angels. A man can't help feeling . . .'

'. . . Feeling inclined to surround them with barbed wire, but you can't do it. You could never keep them in a cage. They'd break down the bars to get at anyone who needed help, and give it.'

'I believe they would,' said Rochester, looking at Mr Dix's classic profile with less repulsion than he had yet felt.

But then Jane rattled the keys and called to Mr Dix, and as he turned back towards her Lucilla came forward and met Mr Rochester, and said softly and confidentially:

'I say, do you mind just coming round the garden with me while Jane shows Mr Dix his little house? We thought he wouldn't like it perhaps if we told him before you that he's to have it. You see, he's awfully poor, as well as being so nice, and one doesn't want to rub it in and hurt his feelings.'

'You needn't have been afraid,' said Rochester grimly. 'He's just told me that you picked him out of the gutter.'

'*Did* he say that?'

'Not exactly, but he's not ashamed of being penniless and homeless.'

'No, he isn't ashamed of anything. *He* hasn't any Bluebeard chambers. That's what's so fine about him, isn't it? And isn't he awfully good-looking?' Lucilla could not refrain from allowing herself this little malicious pleasure.

'A perfect Adonis,' said Mr Rochester. And you cannot wonder that he liked Mr Dix less than he had done five minutes before.

Chapter XVIII

Jane opened her eyes next day wrapped in the tatters of a dream in which she had been tried by a jury consisting of eleven Mr Dixes and Othello, and found guilty of black ingratitude in the first degree. The judge, who was Mr John Rochester dressed as Hamlet with plumes on his head such as hearse-horses wear, sentenced her to be stoned. So she stood up against the wall of the round tower of Cedar Court and the jury threw stones, and all the stones turned to rose-leaves – red and pink and white and yellow and bronze and coral and crimson – and made the ground all round her into the loveliest velvet carpet under which she hastened to hide herself. And when she woke she thought at first that the rose-leaf carpet was still there, but it was only the old, soft, thin velvet patchwork of her bed-quilt, touched to new living glories by the morning sunshine.

The dream was gone, but the dreamer reflected, as she dressed, that the dream-jury had been right. Was it not black ingratitude to shrink from the sudden granting of one's dearest dream? To cry for the moon, and then to grumble because the moon was bigger than the silver shilling it sometimes looks like? To covet Cedar Court, to desire it above all things, to cherish a secret resentment against the Fate which denied it and – then when Cedar Court, suddenly and without reservation, was granted, to shy at it as a nervous horse will at a sieve of oats too suddenly proffered?

Cedar Court was big? The more scope for enterprise! A whole new scheme of life would be needed? What better game could there be than inventing new schemes of life?

Inspirited by these reflections, Jane ran downstairs whistling Mendelssohn's 'I would that my love', very late for breakfast, very hungry, and very cheerful.

Lucilla, who had had no dreams, was busy at the rosewood

table in the window with account books and pencil and scribbled scraps of paper.

'It's nearly the half-hour,' she said reproachfully. 'I've fed Othello, Mrs Doveton is keeping the bacon hot – but you know how it frizzles up in the oven till there's nothing left – and look here, Jane, we've spent over a hundred pounds already, as well as what we've made out of the shop. We're on the road to ruin – and now that big house to keep up.'

'Away with melancholy,' replied Jane, 'nor doleful changes ring! I'll fetch the bacon. Pour out the coffee, sweet angel.' And so, whistling, to the kitchen.

'I don't see what you've got to be so jolly about,' said Lucilla when she came back. 'One never knows what to be up to with you. You went to bed last night as dismal as a crow, and so was I – all the responsibilities of that great house, and Mr Rochester interfering and being jealous . . .'

'That would be a great liberty on Mr Rochester's part,' said Jane, helping herself to bacon – which was not chippy after all, because Mrs Doveton had artfully kept it hot, not in the oven, but over a saucepan of boiling water – 'a perfectly unwarrantable liberty. The bacon's not half bad.'

'I wish you wouldn't always interrupt,' said Lucilla. 'I was saying that you were quite miserable last night, and well you might be. That house – and Mr Dix on our hands and Mr Rochester behaving like a bear! It's too much! And you thought so too, and now this morning you come down as jolly as a sandboy and only say, "Away with melancholy" when I tell you what a frightful lot of money we've spent.'

'Do you want me to go on being miserable? Always? That's too heartless of you, Luce. But you don't, do you?'

'I want you to be serious. You said last night that this was a crisis in our affairs and that we must seriously think whether it wouldn't be better to go on as we are.'

'We can't. I didn't see that last night – but you can never go on as you are. Things go on changing all the time, and you've got to change with them. Like chameleons. For the future I'm going to be a chameleon. Like this.'

She made a grimace intended to represent the repellent expression of that reptile.

'I do wish you'd be serious. Honey, please, and the toast. Thank you,' said Lucilla, quite crossly.

'Well, I will! Seriously, then, of course I know we were dismal last night, but why should we go on being? This isn't last night. It's this morning. We've been asleep for nine or ten hours. That's what sleep's for – to wash all the grumpiness and cowardliness and fuss away. And it does, and the little cherub wakes up as bright as a button. We lost our heads a little last night, and lost sight of our guiding principle. The great fact of life. Life is a lark – all the parts of it, I mean, that are generally treated seriously: money, and worries about money, and not being sure what's going to happen. Looked at rightly, all that's an adventure, a lark. As long as you have enough to eat and to wear and a roof to sleep under, the whole thing's a lark. Life is a lark for us, and we must treat it as such.'

'It isn't a lark to the people who haven't got enough to eat and wear and sleep under,' said Lucilla.

'Isn't that exactly what I'm saying? We have. And for us it is. As for the other people, all we can do is to help them when we come across them, and to keep going ourselves, or else we shan't be able to help anyone else. To make one blade of grass grow where two grew before.'

'That's Mr Dix's job.'

'I meant the opposite, of course,' said Jane, laughing, 'two where one grew before. That's what old Gravy used to say. Upon my word, as I get on in years I begin to see that old Gravy was not wrong nearly so often as we used to think. Grown-up people often aren't, I daresay. You remember the other thing she always used to write in our albums:

> '"Do the work that's nearest
>   Though it's dull at whiles –
> Helping, when you meet them,
>   Lame dogs over stiles."

'The work that's nearest us is making Cedar Court into a pay-ing concern. And whatever else it turns out to be, it won't be dull. Cheer up, my lovely Lucy. We have two houses – four if we count the cottages, and five if you count the summer-house. We have youth, health, strength, good looks – oh yes, we have – nearly four hundred pounds in the bank, a really excellent rabbit, and the handsomest gardener in Europe.'

'And kind Mr Rochester always at hand to help us with his advice. Jane, do you think you could ever marry a thoroughly bad-tempered man?'

Jane got up and looked at herself in the glass over the sideboard.

'We *are* good-looking,' she said, as one ending an argument. 'You're very good-looking – and I'm not half bad in my foxy, sharp-faced way. What was that you said about marrying? No, never mind. We mustn't think about marrying, or young men, or love, or any of that nonsense till we've succeeded in business.'

'We seem to be surrounding ourselves with young men,' said Lucilla. 'Even Simmons is young. We *must* think of them.'

'But not like that,' said Jane firmly. 'Mr Dix is a gardener. Mr Rochester is . . . By the way, I'm not going to call him Mr Roch-ester any more. Why should he be set up on pedestals? If Uncle James is good enough for our aged benefactor, Nephew John is good enough for our young paint-remover. Nephew John! I shall call him that for the future.'

'To his face?'

'Of course,' said Jane ironically, 'every time. Come on – we must get down to the shop. We can go on talking there.'

'You,' said Lucilla, finishing the last of the toast, 'can go on talking anywhere.'

'Cat!' said Jane calmly. 'What was it the cook called Gladys when they had that row about the rag-and-bottle man? "Cat! Fish-faced cat!"'

Thus on the morning after their accession to the crown of their dreams did the two angels of Mr Dix and Mr Rochester ingenuously converse.

Mr Rochester meanwhile was deciding with belated tact to leave Cedar Court alone for two or three days, or at least for a day or two – or for this day at any rate. Mr Dix was toiling at the tennis-lawn, having by candlelight prepared a long list of seeds and plants, which he presented to Jane when she strolled down about twelve o'clock with a full jug held carefully and the announcement that she had just come to see how he was getting on.

'It's only cold tea,' she said. 'I know gardeners generally drink beer all the time out of round earthenware bottles. Only we haven't any beer. There's lemon in the tea though. You'll have to drink out of the jug. It isn't bad.'

'I should jolly well think it wasn't!' he answered, lifting his flushed face from a long pull at the jug. 'I think you have the most beautiful ideas of anyone I ever knew. Fancy you thinking of beer!'

'We only thought of it,' she protested; 'what really happened was tea.'

'Ah, but the idea was a great one. You hitched your wagon to a star. Look here, can I have these, or some of them?' he added hastily, seeing her eye travel down about ten inches of careful handwriting.

'If it's necessary, of course. But I thought you only sowed things in the spring?'

'These are for the winter and for next year,' he said.

'But – I expect you'll get something much better quite soon. You know we can't afford to pay you anything like what you're worth. Do you think it's worth while to start a lot of things? . . . you see, we shouldn't know how to deal with them if you suddenly went to edit a poetry book, or write elegies, for the people who can afford luxuries.'

'Look here,' said he; 'sit down for a minute under this apple-tree, will you? Now look here. I've got something to propose. Don't think me impertinent – but do you mind telling me if the place is yours?'

'Oh no,' said Jane, 'I wish it was.'

'What a pity! Have you the lease then?'

'No, but we've got it for five years if we like. We had a letter telling us so yesterday. And if we want to we can go on having it.'

'You ought to have that letter stamped,' said the young man with the classic profile. 'And even then I don't know that it would be binding without a signed agreement.'

'We're to have that too. A lawyer is making it. The letter said so.'

'Well, then,' began Mr Dix eagerly, 'my idea is this . . .'

But Jane stopped him neatly.

'No, no,' she said. 'I'm dying to hear it, but it's not fair on Lucilla — and we can't both leave the shop at the same time. That's the only sickening thing about keeping a shop — someone has to be always in it, ready to sell, even if there's nobody in it who wants to buy. And it's so dull for one person alone that we both have to be there all the time, and so neither of us has any time to do anything else. And how we shall manage now we've got the whole house as well as the garden room . . . But look here, we'll bring lunch down here, shall we, and have a council of war?'

'I've got some milk and bread and butter and cheese,' said Mr Dix, 'and lettuce.'

'All right, bring them along,' said Jane, returning reluctantly to Lucilla and duty.

So, under the apple-tree, with the little green apples falling on the dishes and on the heads of the talkers, the council of war was held.

Jane opened it, of course.

'Now, Mr Dix, here we all are,' she said, 'and do smoke if you want to, and then tell us what your great idea is.'

'The idea is that we should go into a sort of partnership. No, not that exactly. You see, I don't know. Perhaps what I'm proposing is only silly. I can't help thinking that you're not rich. And yet you have this house and garden. And yet you're selling flowers, so you must want money. And yet . . .'

155

'Don't,' said Jane, 'I'll tell you. Don't go on guessing. Our relations left us enough money to do nothing on – think how dull that
would have been! Then our guardian bolted with the money. He
only left us £500 and a little house that belonged to Lucy's aunt.
Then we began to sell flowers. Then an old gentleman who used
to be a friend of Lucy's aunt gave us leave to use the garden and the
garden room here and to sell the flowers. Then we got a gardener
to do a little and put in a few seeds. Then we met you. Then the
old gentleman was pleased with us about some panelling we
cleaned, and he's lent us the house to do what we like with for five
years or longer if we like. That's our life-story in three words. You
see, it was like this . . .' She continued and elaborated her theme in
words that lasted a cigarette and a half with interjections from
Lucilla, who at last said:

'Yes, and now we haven't got quite four hundred.'

'And I haven't anything but plans and energy and some experience,' said Mr Dix. 'You said the other day that you were born
lucky, Miss Quested. Perhaps you're one of those people who succeed in everything they touch, always. I'm not. But sometimes I
succeed – and I always know when I'm going to. More than once
in France . . .' he stopped, and asked almost instantly, 'And you –
what were your plans?'

'We thought if we could get a gardener we could grow more
things to sell, but now we've suddenly got Cedar Court we
thought of having Pigs – P.G.'s, you know, Paying Guests. I should
think anyone would be glad to live in a place like this. But then if
we have Pigs – I mean P.G.'s – we can't be always in the shop, and
even as it is . . .'

'Exactly,' said Mr Dix. 'Now, you've got one thing you wanted:
you've got a gardener. And you'll get your P.G.'s all right if you
want them. The difficulty at present is money. I can run this garden properly – sell the fruit and vegetables that you don't want for
the shop to Covent Garden. But I can't do it alone. I should want
two men at once for at least a month and a boy as well. That'll be
two pounds ten a week each for the men and a pound for the boy.

I can do on a pound a week easily – having nothing to buy but my food. But I should have to have a few pounds to get my clothes out of pawn. You can't do anything serious with this garden without putting a certain amount of money into it. The garden will get worse and worse and you'll get less and less flowers. Even if you gave up the shop and devoted yourselves entirely to the P.G.'s, the garden would have to be kept tidy, and it may as well pay its way anyhow. Now that's my idea. When it pays we can discuss the question of my wages again. I've thought it all over very carefully, and this is the only way I see of making the thing pay. It's no use my taking your money and just going on trying to keep down the weeds. It's the whole hog or none.'

'Do you mean that if we don't agree to this you won't go on being our gardener?' said Lucilla sweetly.

'You know I don't. I'm not holding a pistol at your heads. Of course I'll go on, on any terms you like. Only if I'm just grubbing along, keeping the place roughly tidy and not really doing anything to help you, I shall do my best, of course, but I shall only work with half a heart. Whereas if I know that I'm really helping to pull the cart along, and making the money out of this land that ought to be made out of it, I shall work like the – like anything. Well, that's my idea; think it over. I'll get back to work.'

Chapter XIX

And, sure enough, when they went over the house again, the two girls found their enthusiasm reviving. It was, as Jane said, just the place for Pigs. If it had been designed for the accommodation of paying guests it could not have been designed better. The large sitting-rooms; the many bedrooms, most of them with their own dressing-rooms, or at least powdering-rooms, attached; the big, cool kitchen where meals could be prepared without fuss or confusion; the really excellent larders, dairies, and pantries all promised success in the new venture. Two maids would be needed or perhaps three, and a cook. Mrs Doveton was a beautiful cook, and there were such heaps of rooms that it would be quite easy to let her have her son with her, and then she could give up the *maisonette*, whose inconveniences haunted her conversation, and live as she constantly said she wanted to live — where there was a bit of green to look out on. The girls closed the shop early so as to catch Mrs Doveton before she left Hope Cottage and bring her to see the house. She said wouldn't to-morrow do, there was a bit of ironing she rather wanted to get on with, but when they said that to-morrow wouldn't do, and she must come then and there to see their beautiful new house, she said she supposed your ladies must be humoured, took the irons off, put on her hat and jacket — she always wore a jacket in the street — and came with them. They took her all over Cedar Court, asking her many times if it wasn't perfectly lovely, and she said as many times that it was very nice, she was sure.

Then they took her to the garden room and made tea for her, which she said she didn't really feel to need, thanking them all the same, and they unfolded their plan. And then after all Mrs Doveton wouldn't!

'It's very kind of you, miss, I'm sure,' she said, 'and offering to make a home for the boy and all, but I couldn't do justice to it — no, I couldn't. All them stairs, and the dining-room all that way from the kitchen, and no hot water laid on to the sink. No, there isn't, miss, for I looked; only one tap besides the rain-water, which is a convenience, of course, but no good for greasy plates and pans. Twenty years ago I don't say. But I'm too old for it now, miss, again thanking you kindly.'

She spoke with her usual gentle monotony. And when she had finished speaking she sat and stroked her smooth old wrinkled knuckly hands with the worn wedding-ring on one, and sailor's silver ring with two hands joined over a heart on the other, and looked out on the lawn where the cedars were.

'But you said you'd like to be where there was a garden,' said Jane.

'A bit of garden,' she said gently, but very firmly, 'not grounds.'

'And you'd have two maids, you know, to do all the house-work, and help in the washing-up and all that.'

'That settles it then,' said Mrs Doveton unexpectedly. 'I was just wondering whether I couldn't make a shift to do for you till winter come on, with grates and coals and that, if you could shut up most of the rooms; but with two girls to look after, and girls what they are nowadays, keeping out of work as long as they can and living on Mr Lord Joyce's bounty — no, miss, no — not for a king's hansom, I wouldn't.'

'Oh dear,' said Jane, 'and we thought it would be so nice for you! And now we shan't be living at Hope Cottage, what will you do? You said the other day it's so hard to get work. What will you do?'

'Providence will provide, miss,' said Mrs Doveton. 'It always has and it always will. What I say is, don't go to meet trouble half way, and then as like as not you won't meet it at all.'

'That's just what I think,' said Jane eagerly. 'Oh, Mrs Doveton, we're so fond of you! I hate to think of parting — and you know you like us too.'

'I've been very comfortable with you, miss, I'm sure,' said Mrs

Doveton temperately. 'Don't you worry about me. We shall meet again, no doubt, if it's for the best.'

It was then that Jane leaped up and clapped her hands, startling Mrs Doveton to something that was almost a jump.

'I've got it!' she shouted. 'Oh, hooray! Look here, Mrs Doveton. Hope Cottage is not going to be let. It's to be kept just as it is, only spick and span, with none of our untidy rubbish lying about. Of course someone will have to keep it like that. Would you like to live there, with your son, of course, and have the kitchen and the two back bedrooms and the little back parlour, and just keep the house tidy?'

But even that suggestion Mrs Doveton did not grasp at. She merely asked what the rent would be.

'Why, nothing!' said Jane. 'We lend you half the house in return for your keeping the other half tidy. And there's the bit of garden and everything.'

'It's rather a large garden – more like a pleasure-garden, miss, isn't it? But there, thank you for the offer, I'm sure. I'll talk it over with Herb to-night and let you know to-morrow, if that will do. And perhaps I'd better be moving on.'

And she did.

'Heigh-ho!' said Lucilla, stretching her arms. 'How disappointing people are! I did think she'd love it. But no! And not even half Hope Cottage, rent free, for that's what it comes to. She isn't pleased. She'll only talk it over with Herb. It's rather disheartening, isn't it?'

'It's exactly like us for not being pleased when we got Cedar Court,' said Jane. 'Hear the words of wisdom – wonderful in one so young, isn't it? But it *was* a facer! I simply didn't dare to tell her it wasn't going to be simply us. What would she have said if we'd told her we meant to have Pigs? – I say, we *must* drop calling them that or we shall do it when they're here. How many could we have? Eight at least, and Mr Dix said this morning we ought to charge three guineas a week. Three times eight is twenty-four – twenty-five with the guineas shillings. How much a year is that?'

160

'Oh, more than a thousand pounds, I should think. But then think of the maids' wages and the cook's wages and all the things to eat – and . . .'

'Well, that's all, isn't it?'

'Oh, I could think of heaps of other things – oh yes, having the piano tuned; and laundry; and gas; and there's water rates, I suppose, and things like that. And then all the rooms wouldn't always be full.'

'Mr Dix said we ought to make enough out of the house and garden to keep us comfortably.'

'It's my belief it's going to be a very tight fit. And do you see us watching the marmalade and counting the lumps of sugar and locking up the tea? Because I don't. There's one thing: Mr Dix was saying we shall have all our vegetables and fruit free – I mean we shan't have to buy them – and we must make our own jam. Look here, Jane, we've sometimes thought the shop rather a fag. It's nothing to what this is going to be. And don't you see we shall have to get a girl for the shop? Another expense.'

'Glorious!' said Jane. 'I hadn't thought of that. We shall get out of the shop, anyhow. Doing one thing all day and every day and wearing nothing but Indian pinafores – I don't know how girls stand it in factories. Selling flowers is pretty work, after all. Suppose we worked in a rubber factory. Mr Dix was saying that you eat, drink, smell, and breathe rubber and naphtha. You can't get away from it, and when you go home you take it home with you. Oh, we're very lucky, Luce. First the shop – and then the moment we're tired of that we find it's our positive duty to get someone to take it on while we go and play at something else. And I suppose if we have Pigs – I mean paying guests – we shall have to have late dinners and dress for it. I don't know why, but that's quite a blissful thought. Don't *you* think we ought to buy some new clothes?'

'No,' said Lucilla, 'we shall want all our money for food. There are heaps of lovely things of Aunt Lucy's – far lovelier than we could begin to afford to buy.'

'That grey silk,' said Jane.

'With the embroidered roses,' said Lucilla, and the conversation wandered in a pleasant maze of stuffs and silks and shapes and styles till Jane haled it back to life's highroad by the remark that an advertisement ought to be written out for a cook.

'Mr Dix said we ought to advertise at once. And we'll post it as we go home,' she said.

'You do that and I'll write to Gladys and send her the money to send us some cream. That's the worst of being at school in Devonshire. I suppose Middlesex girls would never even think of wasting their money on cream.'

'Mr Dix said it was a pity we couldn't keep a cow,' said Jane. You will observe that already Mr Dix was quoted as an authority.

That evening a youth knocked at Hope Cottage – a youth in more than tidy clothes and a necktie so evidently the Sunday one that it was difficult to look at anything else. His wrists were red and lumpy and his ears were red. His eyes were down-dropped, and his shyness was such that at first he could say nothing but:

'I thought I'd just call round.'

'Yes,' said Lucilla, with a wild wonder whether the news of Cedar Court's need of paying guests and of an under-gardener could possibly already be common talk in the neighbourhood, and, if so, whether this was come to offer itself in one of those capacities. Jane came out to the door. This gave him a fresh start.

'Good evening,' he said. 'I thought I'd just call round.'

'Come in,' said Lucilla. Gardener or guest, one could not forbid him the parlour. Once in it, he sat down obediently when he was told to, and said for the third time:

'I thought I'd just call round.'

'Yes,' said Jane helpfully, and, as a sudden inspiration came to her, 'Are you Mr Herbert Doveton?'

'Oh yes, thank you,' he answered gratefully, and still his eyes followed the intricacies of the Brussels carpet's floral garlands. 'My mother told me about what you'd offered us, and I give you my word I couldn't hardly – I mean I could hardly believe my ears. And then she told me that she hadn't accepted of your kind offer on the nail – I mean immediately – but wanted to talk it over with me. So I said, "Oh, mother! . . ." But I mean I thought I'd better come round and say at once that we accept your kind offer and thank you most kindly.'

'You thought you'd like to get the matter settled?' said Jane, rather cruelly, but not so cruelly as you might think, because she did not dream that the youth would understand the little sneer. But he did; he blushed a heavy crimson and bit his lip. Then he said:

'I don't wonder you thinking it was just me wanting to snap up a good thing.'

'Oh no,' said Jane, herself blushing miserably.

'But really it wasn't. It was only . . . I thought it looked so, mother not saying yes at once. I thought you'd think she didn't appreciate you being so kind and thoughtful. But mother is like that. It doesn't mean anything. As often as not if I buy her some trifle, or make her a fretwork bracket or what-not, or bring home a bit of relish for supper, as often as not she don't hardly seem to notice it, or says she doesn't know where it's to hang, and the fire's out, and so on. And then weeks after she'll let drop a word showing she's laid it up and pondered on it in her heart and thought much more of it than it was worth. And the same with you. And that's all, and I beg your pardon for troubling you, but –'

'But you don't like to think of anyone not understanding that Mrs Doveton is the best of mothers? – we quite understand. It was quite natural she should want to talk it over with you.'

'Always has done,' said he, 'ever since I was quite a little nipper, my dad being brought home a corpse owing to the capsizing of a crane, and she hadn't anyone else to talk things over with. And you must talk to someone.'

'Yes, indeed,' said Jane cordially. 'Well, I'm very glad you and your mother are coming to take care of our house. And we should never think anything of her that wasn't good. We know well enough that she's a dear.'

'Then that's all,' he said, and got up suddenly as a Jack-in-the-box. 'I only wanted to be sure you didn't think mother didn't care. And you don't. Good-night, miss. I mean good-night and thank you,' and with that he at last raised his eyes, and they were beautiful eyes. Clear and grey and bright, and they looked straight at you, as a man's eyes ought to look. And when the girls shook hands with him he grasped their hands as a man should grasp a hand, and he no longer seemed clumsy or awkward as he said: 'And if there's any little repairs required in the house I'm quite competent. I'll begin by oiling your gate. I'm attending evening classes at the Polytechnic. I'm a clerk at present but I'm going to be an engineer; and I mustn't waste your time, miss. I mean I mustn't waste your time. Good-night I'm sure.'

And he went out, stumbling over the red sheepskin slip-mat and stumbling again over the front-door mat that said 'Salve'.

'Well,' said Lucilla, as they heard the gate creak to behind him.

'Yes, I know,' said Jane. 'Don't rub it in. I'm going to write a book about life, and the first thing in it will be, "Far more people are nice to you than you've any right to expect".'

'And there's another young man to add to our collection,' said Lucilla.

Mr Dix gardened in a sort of fury of enthusiasm; by Saturday it was possible to knock the balls about. Mr Rochester investigated the fountain, attended to the gas-burners and the taps, and then very humbly asked whether he might try to get the paint off the library. This kept him busy and kept him near: but he was careful not to be too near or too often. It was quite pleasant. By Monday Mr Dix had an under-gardener of surly demeanour and flaming testimonials, and a boy who only opened his mouth once in the presence of Jane and Lucilla, and then he asked when the apples would be ripe. No candidate for the position of shop assistant had, however, presented herself. Nor had the cook advertisement brought a single answer.

The original beer-seeking charwoman, Mrs Veale, having been found by Mr Rochester and reinstated, Lucilla and Jane had to take it in turns to keep shop and to superintend her labours. Trade was brisk, for the time of roses was beginning, and the roses, though not of the finest shape and quite ineligible as show blooms, were yet plentiful, fresh, sweet, and eminently saleable. And the syringa was out, with its cheap, sweet mockery of bridal garlands. And there were lettuces to sell – and spring onions, but they were kept outside. And cabbage and celery and broccoli plants. And parsley for people who had cold beef. And mint for people who had lamb.

The house was gradually being cleaned and in the close inspection that the superintendence of such cleaning involved more charms were daily discovered. Jane and Lucilla, heroically reserving the best bedrooms for the paying guests, had chosen for their own two smaller rooms communicating by a door. The windows were not fifteen feet from a high, flat wall of clipped yew – at least, it ought to have been clipped, and would be next year: this year it was too late to do anything but admire the soft, vivid blue-green of its new shoots.

An animated discussion as to whether these chosen rooms must, or need not, this year at least, be re-papered led to the discovery of a secret door, or at any rate a door that had been boarded up and used as a cupboard. This opened into the first storey of the round tower. What could be more ideal: bedrooms and boudoir altogether.

'And it's to *be* a boudoir, too,' said Jane. 'A place for you and me to sulk in. No one else admitted on any pretence.'

This was a Sunday afternoon. How blessed a day Sunday to those who serve in shops, or, in any of the walks of commerce, earn their living!

'This is a most lovely room,' said Jane. 'The window looks out at the front, it's true, but when you're sitting down you only see the ilex and the horse-chestnut and the copper beech. Hullo . . . who on earth . . .'

A figure at once dowdy and resplendent, with a sported coat of a flannellettish pink and a large rust-red hat surrounded by jazz flowers, was creeping slowly up the drive. It carried a tin hat-box and several large, straggling brown-paper parcels. It walked with a sort of tired determination; it disappeared in the porch and then the bell echoed through the house.

'It can't be a cook come about the place, on a Sunday afternoon.'

'You'd think not,' said Lucilla, noncommittally.

They went down and opened the door to a very hot and rather grubby girl, who instantly threw her bundles from her on to the hall table and said:

'Phew!'

It was Gladys.

'Yes,' she said, 'I come directly I got your letter. When I read what Miss Lucy put in about the big house you'd got and no servants yet, me mind was made up in a flash. That's the service for me, I says, and I slips off by the morning train. But what a caution them Sunday trains is – stop everywhere and people in and out on yer toes for hours and hours. Now don't say you ain't glad to see me after all.'

'But we are,' said Jane, resolutely stifling a mixed litter of conflicting emotions. 'Very glad indeed.'

'Thank them as be for that!' said Gladys heartily, 'for if you hadn't a-bin, after what I've gone through, I don't think flesh and blood could have borne it. I've brought the cream.'

Chapter XX

If there had been any hesitation in the mind of Jane and Lucilla as to whether the arrival of Gladys was to be regarded as a calamity or as a godsend the question was soon settled.

Gladys exhibited all the wonder and admiration which the girls had hoped from Mrs Doveton, and even the most undiscerning of her encomiums served to endear to them both Gladys and Cedar Court.

She followed Mrs Veale in her slow progress through the rooms, and her cheery 'Ain't ye done *yet*?' did at last exasperate Mrs Veale to something almost approaching activity.

Then she was initiated into the mysteries of the shop.

'It's always bin me dream,' she said affably, 'to be a young lady in a shop. And flowers is so toney, ain't they?'

She handled the flowers lightly and carefully, and conversed with customers in a way which set Lucilla and Jane trembling for the welfare of the business. But most of the customers seemed to enjoy Gladys's conversation, and to the few who did not Gladys smiled that wonderful wide smile of hers that made you think of collie dogs, and they forgave her.

Then she went off on her afternoon out and came back full of information.

'You give too much for the money, Miss Jane,' she said. 'I bin looking at the shops and prizing the flowers. If they didn't like me asking and then not buying they can lump it. I don't know what else they expect, with them prices and the flowers not half so fresh as what yours are. Them big white lily flowers yer give away in the sixpenny mixed bunches, they're charging threepence the piece for, and putting them in funeral wreaths with made-in-hair ferns and big pinks something beautiful. Why don't you sell wreaths for funerals, miss? Now that's a thing I really *could* enjoy making up, them funeral wreaths. I could easy learn how. There was a young man at it in one of the shops. I could see by the way he looked at me with one eye he'd be only too pleased to show me how, if I was to encourage him.'

'Now, Gladys,' said Jane firmly, 'you really must *not* begin encouraging young men.'

And she explained carefully how important it is for business girls to think only of business and not of young men, and how courting and love's young dream should be left till later on. Gladys listened kindly, smoothing out the many-coloured feather-flowers of her best hat, and when Jane had quite ended the little sermon she said:

'Yes, miss; but your 'art's your 'art, ain't it? And there's so much competition too. If you let your chances go when you're young you may find yourself an old maid all of a sudden, and wish you'd acted different. Now what I say is, you should always have two or three of them anxious for you to say "Yes", and go on not saying it, and being taken to fairs and the pictures, and chocs. and cigs. and something to look forward to on your evening out. And if you find any time that you're getting old – why, then there's always someone ready for you to say "Yes" to, and you can try how you like being a married lady.'

'Well,' said Jane, 'all I insist on is that you don't bring them here.'

'Not me, you may rely,' Gladys assured her earnestly. 'Why, they'd get talking together! Keep 'em well apart's my rule.'

Jane was not sorry to get away from the subject. She felt that in her life too there were two young men who were best apart. And she perceived that Gladys might not unreasonably defend herself by a *tu quoque*. But Gladys's tact, though all her own, still was tact. She knew to a hair what you might and might not say to your mistress.

Gladys approved highly of Mr Dix.

'He's a goer. You've got a fair treasure in him, Miss Lucy,' she said, as she was taking over the shop – for now she served there every afternoon, the two girls taking charge in the mornings. Mr Dix had just brought in a sheaf of white iris and Canterbury bell and scarlet geum, and also a list of trivialities – bast, labels, wire, quassia, soft-soap – to be ordered at the Stores.

'His feet don't stick to the ground like that Mrs Veale's. Veale by name and Veale by nature. And beautiful manners. Took off his hat to me in the street, he did really; and always gets up when I come along when he's sitting down, as respectful as though I was a duchess. Ah, that 'ud be the gentleman for *me*, if *I* was a lady.'

'No doubt some lady will think so in good time,' said Lucilla.

'Let's hope she won't think so too late,' said Gladys darkly. 'A gentleman like that is just the one to get snapped up by some designing hussy: one of them vampire women you see on the films, or a woman with five other husbands like that Mrs Doria de Vere, as she calls herself, in the paper last Sunday.'

It was Gladys who secured the two maids, experienced, expensive, and so competent that they seemed scarcely human. She sniffed at Labour Exchanges, bought the *Morning Post* on the advice of Mr Dix, and made a journey to a register office in Baker Street.

'There's plenty of servants if you know how to intrap them,' she explained. 'I did it telling them what nice young innocents you two was, not knowing a thing about housekeeping, so they'd have it all their own way. But a cook I couldn't get. I see plenty, but they wants their weight in gold afore they'll come, and a tidy weight it 'ud be with some of 'em. Why not advertise for cook-housekeeper; suit widow, one child not objected to? That'll fetch someone, and the little gell'll be handy to run errands and feed the rabbit. You ought to get some more rabbits. One rabbit don't pay.'

'But suppose it's a little boy?' suggested Jane.

'It won't be a boy,' said Gladys; 'if their letters says "boy", don't you answer them. That's easy.'

It was this suggestion which led to the advent of Mrs Dadd – Adela Dadd was her full and incredible name – a thin, pale person with admirable testimonials from the superior clergy. She had been housekeeper to a rector and, before her marriage, nursery governess to a dean. Her daughter was seven – a lumpish child with an open mouth, an unconquerable stickiness of hands and face, and stockings that were always wrinkled. Mrs Dadd simpered, she bridled, and she languished. She called her employers by their names every time she spoke to them, so as to make it quite plain that she did not belong to the class which says 'Miss', or 'Ma'am'. Neither Mrs nor Miss Dadd really pleased anyone, but time was getting on. The house was ready, the servants were there, eating their heads off, and it was high time that the paying guests should begin to pay. Mrs Dadd left much to be desired, but she was better than the bouncing lady with the almost grown-up daughter who had lived in the best families in garrison towns and wore more jewellery in the morning than most ladies would care to wear at night. She was also more possible than the trembling old lady of seventy who owned to forty-eight, and had dyed her poor white hair and powdered her wrinkled old cheeks, and put on a necklace of big pearl beads, all in the effort to find work that she could not do and wages that she could not earn.

'It makes your blood run cold,' said Jane. 'Poor old thing! And she ought to be in the best arm chair, with a dozen children always running to Granny. That's what I like about the Chinese. They do look after old people. But we couldn't have taken her — now, could we, Luce?'

'Bless your heart, no, miss,' said Gladys, who was present; 'and I daresay if the truth was known she's only had a tiff with her son's wife that she lives with and started out to get a situation just to show her independence.'

'Let's hope so, anyhow,' said Jane. 'What do you think of Mrs Dadd, Gladys? Adela Dadd! What a name!'

'I think she'll be an addler, if you ask me,' said Gladys. 'Ad'la by name and addler by nature. I lay she'll try to do all her work with the tips of her fingers. But you can but try.'

So they tried. Mrs Dadd was not a good cook, but the food she prepared was not uneatable. A design of getting Mrs Doveton to give her a few lessons in cookery was negatived by both with unexpected firmness.

'I couldn't take it on me, miss,' said Mrs Doveton.

'I'm not a child to be taught things,' said Mrs Dadd. 'I've lived in the best families, where six was kept, besides a Buttons. No, thank you, Miss Quested. There's enough of the boiled mutton to do cold for to-day. It'll save cooking, Miss Quested. And the suet pudding warmed up with a nice potato, and there's your dinner.'

And there, as she said, their dinner was.

A carefully-worded advertisement setting forth the advantages of residence at Cedar Court was inserted in three papers, and in a sort of ordered hush Cedar Court awaited applicants. There was a certain restfulness. Only the shop in the morning. In the afternoon leisure, then tea tennis.

Gladys seemed to have come as a liberator. The shop no longer claimed the whole day. And tennis is a very agreeable game. 'If only we could go on like this!' said Jane. 'How nice it is to have servants and everything going by clockwork — at least, Addler Dadd certainly doesn't, but Stanley and Forbes do. I almost wish we hadn't advertised for the Pigs.'

'Perhaps you'd like to go through the accounts,' said Lucilla threateningly. But they went down to the tennis-court instead. Mr Rochester was able to play tennis almost every evening, and Mr Dix, of course, was always glad of a game after working hours.

'What a life!' said Gladys, when they came in. 'Not but what I daresay it's good for your inside, all that hopping about. And Mr Dix, he deserves a bit of fun, working as he does. But that Mr Rochester! Ain't he got nothing to do? 'As he got a ninde-penden tincome? Ain't he got no trade?'

'He's an engineer, I believe,' Jane told her.

'Then why doesn't he engineer? No, you mark my words: he's got a reason of his own for hanging about here; are you sure he ain't a detective?'

'There wouldn't be anything for him to detect here,' said Lucilla.

'I'm not so sure. There's people with pasts. Where's Addler's husband?'

'Dead,' said Lucilla.

'So she says,' said Gladys. And Jane had to say, 'That'll do,' very firmly and end the conversation.

You know how elastic time is, and how some days seem to have no time in them at all, and other days seem as though there was time in them for everything. These days were full of time – time to go from room to room, touching up the flowers, changing the position of a chair or a table, followed by little Addie Dadd, always flagrantly sticky but faithfully keeping her promise 'not to touch'. The girls tried very hard to like poor little Addie, who plainly adored them, but you cannot really love a child unless you can embrace it, and Addie was always much too sticky for that, except just after her bath, and then, of course, Mrs Dadd was always there to say, 'Thank Miss Quested and Miss Craye, Addie, for being so kind,' and then, of course, Addie said, 'Thank you,' and nothing more could be said on either side.

They had to get rid of the child before settling to their sewing, of which they did an incredible amount. Aunt Lucy's old sprigged muslins and striped barèges made the most delicious frocks and jumpers, and Jane had a sage-green, soft-satin gown for evening with little pink and white rosebuds embroidered all over it. 'By hand, too, none of your machine-made stuff'; and Lucilla had a mignonette-coloured shot silk with a short waist and wonderful gathered trimming.

'When we get enough P.G.'s together we'll have a dance,' said Jane.

'Rather,' said Lucilla, and their imagination peopled the big, silent rooms of Cedar Court with a little crowd of strangers, all young, all good-looking and good-tempered, ready to please and be pleased. It was a radiant prospect and kept them well amused.

Then the answers to the advertisement began to arrive, and the days become darkened with correspondence. There are no letters so dull as the letters in which you demand or supply what are called 'references'.

Out of the cloud of ink three human figures presently emerged, clothed with testimonials almost as glowing as Mrs Dadd's – an officer's widow and her unmarried sisters. The terms were satisfactory, the date of the arrival was fixed, the rooms were got ready.

'Towels and soap and fresh flowers and pincushions with real pins in them,' said Jane. 'The P.G. who can't be happy here doesn't deserve to be happy anywhere.'

'Perhaps they aren't,' said Lucilla.

'I only hope the dinner will be all right. The tinned mock turtle and tinned peas and tinned asparagus and tinned peaches. That only leaves the mutton for Mrs Dadd to cook, and potatoes. Oh, if only we had Mrs Doveton here!'

'Perhaps Mrs Smale won't mind what she eats. Officers' widows following the regiment all over the world must get used to having odd sorts of meals. After puppy-dog pie and birds-nest soup I daresay even Mrs Dadd's cooking would seem all right.'

'Perhaps,' said Jane, but without conviction. 'Was that the gate? Oh, what have I done?'

What she had done was to knock a vase of pinks off a table and flood the hearthrug. Lucilla flew to the bell; and they heard it clanging through the house. But they heard nothing else. No coming of footsteps. They rang again, and then Jane sped down to the kitchen.

Mrs Dadd was snatching a moment's rest with her feet on a chair. She often snatched moments' rest. Little Addie was trying to feed the cat with a jammy spoon.

'Why doesn't someone answer the bell?'

'Forbes has gone to post with a letter, Miss Quested,' said Mrs Dadd in leisurely explanation, while Jane almost danced with impatience. 'It's Stanley's day out, and Gladys is always in the shop, I understand, of an afternoon.'

'Well,' said Jane, 'I think *you* might have come.'

'I couldn't undertake to answer bells, Miss Quested,' said Mrs Dadd; 'that's the servants' place.'

'But, good gracious me! – when there's no one else? We might have been on fire or being murdered!'

'Oh no,' said Mrs Dadd, 'not that, I think, Miss Quested.'

'Well, I've upset a lot of water, and I want you to come at once and mop it up. Bring a pail, please, and a cloth, and do be quick. It's soaking into the rug and the carpet. Please make haste, Mrs Dadd.'

But Mrs Dadd was shaking her head slowly and calmly.

'Oh no, Miss Quested,' she said, 'I couldn't do that. I couldn't undertake to do anything menial.'

'But there's nothing menial about mopping up some water. I'd do it myself.'

'People feel differently about things, I know,' Mrs Dadd conceded.

'But who cleans the kitchen floor?' asked Jane.

'I don't know, Miss Quested,' was the unforgettable reply. 'Addie, come here and leave the cat alone.'

'Do you mean,' said Jane incredulously, 'that you aren't going to mop up that water?'

'You'll excuse me, Miss Quested, I'm sure. I've come down in the world, but not so low as that,' she simpered. 'Oh no!'

Jane completely and suddenly lost her temper.

'You refuse to do it?'

'I'm afraid I must say yes to that,' said Mrs Dadd, with a sort of defiant archness.

'Then you'd better go. Go now,' said Jane.

'Certainly,' said Mrs Dadd, with some alacrity. 'I should like my month's money, Miss Quested, and I'll leave at once. Come, Addie darling, and help Mummy to pack.'

'Where's the pail?' Jane asked.

'In the back kitchen, I believe. Come, Addie.'

Jane got the pail and the floor-cloth and, carrying them, reached the hall just as the front-door bell rang. She then perceived that if she did not open the door no one would. Besides, it might be Forbes.

So she opened it. The doorstep was occupied by three large ladies.

The captain's widow and her sisters had chosen this fortunate moment for their début at Cedar Court.

Chapter XXI

'There were three of them, but they looked as big as a crowd. They've got great, pale faces like potatoes, and they're all exactly alike. I've taken them up to their rooms, and one of them said hers had a north aspect; and another one said her room was like an oven with the afternoon sun — and the third one just turned up her nose without a word. Pigs!' Thus Jane to Lucilla, having shown the guests to their rooms.

'And they want hot water and their luggage carried up. The porter brought it and he's out there now, grumbling at what they paid him. You can hear him going on like a gramophone before it really begins. And they want someone to carry up the luggage; and both the maids are out; and Mrs Dadd was cheeky, and I've told her to go — and she's going. She's going *now*, this minute, while we're chattering.'

'I'm not chattering,' said Lucilla.

'No,' said Jane, 'you're always right. You're always cool and calm and collected and — and — blameless. And I'm always in the soup. And then you rub it in.' And she burst into tears.

'It's not that,' she sobbed, when Lucilla had come to her and had put her arm round her and had said, 'Don't, darling,' and 'Never mind,' and 'There, dear, there,' and all the things that girls do say to each other when one of them is weeping. 'It's not unhappiness. It's rage. I could kill Mrs Dadd. I could. I should like to. And Addie was rubbing the cat all over with a jammy spoon and it'll go all over the drawing-room cushions. And Mrs Dadd! Hateful woman! No, there's no time to tell you about her. There'll be no dinner. And those potato-faced pigs will be grunting for their swill. I don't care if I am coarse. Even now they're expecting hot water. Who's to take it up?'

175

'I will,' said Lucilla soothingly; 'and Mr Dix will take up the luggage, and then we'll see about the dinner.'

'I'll fetch him,' said Jane. 'No, it's all right. I've finished snivelling. I feel much better. Catch the cat if you can and shut her up. I *must* bathe my eyes. I'll fetch Mr Dix in a jiff. But I don't suppose there *is* any hot water. Mrs Dadd was sprawling about on the furniture with her legs up. She always is.'

'Well, she won't any more – at least, not here,' said Lucilla. 'Don't worry; we'll pull through somehow. It's all rather a lark though, isn't it?'

'Rub it in,' said Jane, plunging her face into cold water. 'I'm all right now,' she went on through the towel. 'It *is* rather exciting, as you say.' And with eyelids still very pink she went in search of Mr Dix. She did not find him, because in the hall she found Mr Rochester, just leaving his labours in the library.

'Hullo,' he said softly, 'the Pigs have come then? I heard their loud voices announcing themselves and asking for Miss Quested. I expect they thought she was forty – and an experienced letter of lodgings.'

'Yes,' said Jane, and sniffed. 'They were hateful. When I said I was Miss Quested they said they meant the elder Miss Quested, and when I said there wasn't one they snorted. They did really.' She sniffed again.

He caught her hand and pulled her quickly and gently and quite irresistibly into the room he had just left.

'Half a moment,' he said; 'they may come down. I want to ask you, but I never get a word with you – your Lucilla's always there. I want to know . . . Great heavens, what's the matter!' he ended on a complete changed note, for now he had suddenly seen Jane's face.

'Oh, nothing – silliness. Mrs Dadd was hateful and I've sacked her. And then those Pigs. I suppose I'm tired. That's what makes me so silly.'

'Sit down a minute,' he said, still holding her hand. 'It's infamous that you should be worried by these old women. It's all my uncle's fault for saddling you with this house. Do sit down and tell me all about it.'

'I can't,' said Jane. 'They are gibbering now for their hateful luggage to be carried up – it's all in the hall'; and then belatedly she pulled her hand away. But this did not improve the situation, for Mr Rochester's arm went round her, and for one moment she let her head lean against his arm, with the most extraordinary feeling of being comforted and protected. Thus they stood, almost in the position which a couple assume when the dance begins.

'Jane,' he whispered. 'Jane dear.'

But that broke the spell, and Jane shook herself free.

'Dearest,' said Mr Rochester, not at once perceiving that the spell was broken, and he reached his hands out to her. But Jane backed towards the door.

'I don't blame you,' said she, standing very upright and looking him straight in the eyes. 'I brought it on myself by going about howling like a silly kid. I don't blame you, and I'll forget it if you will. But I want you to understand that I'm not at *all* that sort of girl. No, don't say anything,' she said fiercely. 'I don't blame you – this once; but I want you to understand that I'm not going to have that sort of nonsense. Not ever. Do you understand?'

'Jane,' said he, 'don't you believe in omens – in Fate?'

'Never mind what I believe in,' said Jane, instinctively putting her hands up to her hair to ascertain whether its momentary contact with Mr Rochester's jacket had disarranged it. 'At least I'll tell you what I *do* believe in. I believe in attending to business and being good friends, and not being silly and sloppy. And you're not to call me Jane.'

Mr Rochester experienced all the emotions familiar to those who have been stroking a kitten and have suddenly found claws where a moment ago only soft fur was. This and a good deal more, he felt in the brief moment before he said:

'Very well. And now forgive me – in earnest, like a good comrade, and let's be friends again.'

'That's what I want to be to you,' said Jane, charmed by the old camouflage that love has worn so threadbare.

'Then shake hands on it.'

They did – a good, strong, manly shake.

'And now we're real friends, tell me just one thing. You do like me better than that wretched Dix, don't you? Say you do – just a little better?'

'I like you both very much,' said Jane sedately; and then with a spark of malice she added: 'Just now perhaps I like him a little the best, because *he* hasn't seen me make a fool of myself.'

A bell pealed violently.

'It's those Pigs – their luggage – Mr Dix . . .'

'Oh, I'll carry it up,' said Mr Rochester. 'Come and show me which rooms.'

They met Lucilla on the stairs.

'They want tea,' she whispered, 'and it's six. Forbes is getting it, but she says it's not her place. She's going to take it up to their rooms. And the mutton's not in yet, and the potatoes aren't peeled. And Forbes says, she'll either cook the dinner or wait at table, whichever we like, but she can't do both – and she won't.'

'Can't Gladys wait?'

'I shouldn't think so,' said Lucilla. 'And I'm sure she can't cook. It's rather unfortunate, isn't it? Because it's quite important to make a good impression on your Pigs the first day. I wish they sold roast legs of mutton in enormous tins. *Why* don't they?'

'Look here,' said Rochester, 'surely Mrs Doveton would come, just for once, to get you out of a fix? Set Gladys to peel the potatoes and I'll go after Mrs Doveton. Don't worry; we shall pull through all right. I shall be back with her in time to see to the mutton.'

But when he came back it was not with Mrs Doveton, but with Simmons.

'Mrs Doveton was out – and Simmons is a regular *cordon bleu*. The dinner will be all right.'

'Mrs Dadd has gone, that's something,' said Jane.

'Couldn't Mr Dix help?' suggested Lucilla, but Rochester said that it was not worth while to trouble Mr Dix. Then Lucilla had her brilliant idea.

'Oh, Jane,' she said, 'don't you think it would be a good thing if Mr Rochester would have dinner with us? Because who's to carve the mutton?'

'I wish you would,' said Jane, not displeased at being able to show Mr Rochester that her feelings were quite friendly. 'They can't trample on us so heavily if you're here.'

'I should love it,' he said. 'Shall I dress?'

Mr Rochester was careful not to suggest that Forbes could carve the mutton on the sideboard.

'Oh yes,' said both the girls, and Jane added: 'It would be so much more impressive.' But the next moment she changed her mind.

'Perhaps better not,' she said. 'Evening dress might look swanky – and besides . . .'

Rochester understood that 'besides' when he arrived at eight o'clock to find 'that wretched Dix' already in the drawing-room being agreeable to one of the potato-faced ladies. Jane and Lucilla in very pretty frocks were timidly submitting to be trampled on by the other two.

Mr Simmons in the kitchen, assisted by a glowing Gladys, produced a real dinner. The soup was tinned, it is true, but the fish was not, and the pineapples were made into fritters; the peaches were coated with crème caramel, there was a cheese soufflé, and perfect coffee appeared at the right moment. There were double doors between hall and what are called the domestic offices, but once, during fish (which Simmons had bought on the way to his duties), the two doors were left open and shouts of laughter were wafted across to the dining room, where four people were trying earnestly to make the best of three.

'Your servants seem very noisy,' said Mrs Smale.

'We like them to enjoy themselves,' said Jane stoutly.

'I thought I heard a man's laugh.'

'Did you?' said Lucilla, who had heard it too.

'What a terrible earthquake that was in Vitruvia,' said Mr Dix quickly.

'Yes, wasn't it?' said Mr Rochester, seconding him ably with details, which Mr Dix capped. The incident drew them together, for of course there hadn't been any earthquake in Vitruvia, wherever Vitruvia may be.

Mrs Smale and her sisters wore stuffy, black, beady dresses and had no conversation. They were like a dark blight. They did not seem to have read any books. They were fond of music. They knew nothing of politics, and they did not care for gardens. They seemed weakly curious about the two young men. And during the interval of separation and dinner Mrs Smale drew Jane aside and spoke.

'Those gentlemen? I didn't quite catch their names.'

Jane gave the names.

'Relatives?'

'Not exactly,' said Jane.

'Oh, I see,' said Mrs Smale archly. 'Your intendeds?'

'Not exactly,' said Jane again.

'I see,' said Mrs Smale, in the tone of one who didn't.

The long evening dragged itself out.

The young men went at ten, and before the three paying guests retired they made it quite plain that they wanted early tea in their rooms – at eight – hot water at half-past, and breakfast at nine. Mrs Smale liked fish and perhaps an egg. Miss Markham had been ordered meat three times a day by a Harley Street physician, and her sister could touch nothing but bacon and tomatoes. Always – every day. And they might as well mention that they each liked a glass of milk at eleven in the morning. Doctor's orders again. Yes, every day. Yes, that was all. If they thought of anything else they could always mention it.

The guests disposed of, the girls sought Gladys. They found her in the kitchen just concluding an informal banquet with Mr Simmons. Both faces were radiant.

The girls, who had never before seen Mr Simmons at his ease, looked with wondering eyes, for the fat man was transfigured. But even as they looked the mask of shyness fell on him again, and he was as they had always known him.

'We don't know how to thank you,' said Jane.

'No need, miss,' said Mr Simmons; 'it's been a pleasure to oblige you, let alone obliging my boss, and not to say nothing about pleasant company.'

'Mr Simmons does go on so,' said Gladys with a giggling toss of her head. She had found time to put on a transparent rainbow-radiant blouse and a string of green glass beads.

'I don't know how you'll manage for the rest of the day,' said Mr Simmons, 'but I'll come round and see to the dinner to-morrow, miss, and till you get another cook. The last one's no loss, from what I can see – not a pan clean nor yet a plate. Miss Gladys and me, we had to wash every mortal thing. But all's clean now,' he said, with proper pride. 'Don't keep thanking me, miss. I'll be round to-morrow.'

But to-morrow brought Mrs Doveton.

'Of course, miss, I couldn't stand aside, with you in all this upset,' she said, and fell to work.

And when Mr Simmons came all that could be done was to ask him to stay to supper. He stayed, and it is to be recorded that even Mrs Doveton was heard to laugh. Mr Simmons was, plainly, a wit, but only in his own circles; outside them he could not shine. Neither Jane nor Lucilla ever heard him say anything amusing. But Gladys, it seems, did.

And Gladys was inclined to resent Mrs Doveton. But on Gladys's day out she appeared before her mistresses, clothed, as Jane said afterwards, like Solomon in all his glory, and said almost bashfully: 'Please, miss, may I stay out till ten? I'm going to drink tea with Mr Simmons's sister as he lives with.'

Her conscious simper spoke volumes.

The presence of the paying guests was indeed hard to bear. The black blight deepened every day. It was only by constantly reminding themselves and each other that it meant nine guineas a week that they were able to bear it at all. Regular meals, in the dining-room, every day, and no picnics or breakfasts out of doors.

'I'd no idea it would be like this,' said Jane. 'It's perfectly ghastly. You're never free of them. All day long and the evenings too. To think of them out in galoshes to watch us play tennis!'

'We *must* bear it,' said Lucilla. 'Three hundred and sixteen pounds a year. I worked it out on a bit of paper.'

'I suppose they have some good qualities,' said Jane. 'All right, we'll try to bear it.'

And they did bear it – for nearly a fortnight.

Then one day Gladys abruptly asked if they had seen the colour of the visitors' money. They reproved her. But the question rankled. When it had formed the chief subject of their conversation for some days the girls decided that Lucilla should ask the guests to pay weekly.

'Certainly,' said Mrs Smale, with almost the first smile they had seen on her large, pale countenance. 'We usually pay monthly, but if you prefer it I will write a cheque in the morning.'

But she did not write a cheque in the morning, or, if she did, it was not drawn to Lucilla's order nor to Jane's. For in the morning there was no one to drink the three cups of tea or eat the three plethoric breakfasts. The potato-faced ladies had gone from Cedar Court. No one ever knew at what hour in the night they had crept hence; no one knew how they got their luggage away.

'They ain't slep' in their beds, nor yet they ain't washed in their hot water,' said Gladys, announcing the flitting to her young mistresses then at their own morning toilet. 'Them nasty old triplets has done a bunk right enough. And done you proper! I lay you never see the colour of their money, now did you, miss?'

'Oh, go along, Gladys,' said Jane, twisting up her hair very quickly. 'Go and tell Mrs Doveton we'll have breakfast on the lawn, and you bring it out if Forbes says it isn't her place.'

'That Forbes!' said Gladys. '*This* wouldn't be her place long if I was you . . . All right, Miss Jane, all right. I'm going.'

★

'We've had the most horrible fortnight of our lives,' said Lucilla. 'I'd no idea anything could be so horrid. We've fed those old cats with the loveliest meals and we've lost eighteen guineas. *I* don't feel like breakfast in the garden, I can tell you.'

'Oh yes, you do!' said Jane. 'Yes, you do, exactly like it! Why, dear me, Luce, it's worth twice the money to have got rid of them! And nothing to reproach ourselves with! Nothing! It's not our fault they've gone – and they have gone. Why, my blessed angel, it's an absolute godsend!'

Chapter XXII

With the Pigs so happily gone, and Mrs Doveton still filling with admirable contrast the gap left by Mrs Adela Dadd, with the mature maids doing their work as by well-oiled machinery, with Gladys to see to the shop and Mr Dix to see to the garden, a spell of peace settled on Cedar Court, and Jane and Lucilla tasted for a few days the habitual calm and leisure of the really well-to-do.

They advertised anew for paying guests and for a cook.

'And until we get answers,' said Jane, 'we may as well enjoy ourselves. Let's pretend we're the idle rich.'

'I should like to be rich,' said Lucilla, 'and I daresay I could manage to be idle, though I believe it's more difficult than you'd think; but I certainly shouldn't ever be rich *and* idle. Doesn't it make you want to hang people to lamp-posts when you see them with bags of money and not the faintest idea what to do with it? The only thing they seem to think of are motors . . .'

'And guzzling,' said Jane.

'I don't blame them for having nice things to eat,' said Lucilla firmly. 'I should do that myself. What I blame them for is not enjoying things. They have everything they want, every day – and, of course, a peach is just dessert to them and not the fruit of Paradise.'

'If you ever write poetry,' said Jane with conviction, 'it'll be about things to eat.'

'No,' insisted Lucilla; 'but if I were rich I'd live just nicely – like this – and every now and then I'd have something sudden and splendid – six peaches for breakfast, or roast chicken every day for a week – and then go back to plain mutton for a bit.'

'You would spend your whole income on food then?' Jane said innocently.

'Yes, cat, I would,' said Lucilla – 'or nearly all. But I shouldn't eat it all myself. I should give lots of it away. "The Responsibilities of the Really Rich." Let's write a book about them, Jane. You want to help the hard-up. How are you to know which are the respectable ones?'

'And why are we to care?'

'You can't help everybody, and you have to choose, and you may as well choose people your help is likely to *be* some help to.'

'I believe everybody knows more people that help *would* be a help to than they have money to give the help with.'

'Yes. There's our Mr Dix – wants a market garden.'

'Well, he's got it, hasn't he?' said Lucilla shortly.

'And Mr Rochester – he wants a job.'

'Not acutely, I think.'

'Well, then there's our Mr Doveton – he wants to better himself; one could help there. Mr Simmons wants to give up carpentering and grow herbs and better the world. Gladys wants –'

'Gladys wants someone to go out with – and she's got it.'

'So have we, come to think of it. Lucy, do you think a chaper-one could have any real objection – any *just* objection, I mean – to one's going on the river on Sundays with two perfectly respect-able young men?'

Two such excursions had, indeed, been part of the leisured hap-piness of that halcyon time.

'A real chaperone might have real objections,' said Lucilla. 'I don't know. But we are each other's chaperones – and we have more sense.'

'Yes,' said Jane doubtfully. 'At the same time, don't you think there's something to be said for aunts? "The Aunt in the Home: Her Use and Abuse." It would do for another little book. But I don't mean a really abusive aunt. Just a nice, comfortable aunt to admire your jewels and your singing and be a little bit shocked at your slang, and say, "I may be old-fashioned, but I don't think I *would*, my dear, if I were you." It would give a sort of solidity to the establishment, like a mahogany sideboard or a dinner-table that lets out.'

'I never,' said Lucilla, sewing placidly at a pink print gown in process of remodelling, 'I never thought you'd hanker after chaperones.'

'It isn't chaperones I want,' Jane explained, winding and unwinding the yard measure. 'But I should like to have someone who knows the rules. We may be doing quite wrong and not knowing it. There was a play once, or a book or something, called "The Girl Who Took the Wrong Turning". For anything we know, we may be taking the wrong turning a hundred times a day. We've nothing to guide us.'

'We've got our own common sense,' Lucilla pointed out.

'Yes, but it isn't common sense that makes those rules. It's something deep and mysterious that we don't understand. Why, even in little things . . . Is it common sense that decides that you mustn't eat apple-pie with a spoon or take mustard with mutton? Is it common sense that says you must always wear a hat in church except when you're being confirmed?'

'No, dear, that's religion,' said Lucilla.

'And all those other rules about what you may and mayn't do with young men? You may dance with them, you mustn't let them hold your hand or put their arms round your waist except when you're dancing.'

'Why, of course not!'

'Jamesie said you must never write letters to gentlemen; but suppose there's something important that you want to say and you won't be seeing them?'

'Common sense would settle that – for me,' said Lucilla, biting off her cotton.

'Gravy said a young lady must never invite a young gentleman to call. Well, we don't have callers, but we ask gentlemen to dinner – that's worse, I suppose?'

'Dinner is more emphatic than calling, certainly. Why are you beating about the bush like this, Jane? Out with it! What have you been doing?'

'I? Nothing but what you have too, so you can't score off me there. It's what we've both been doing.'

'We've not done anything wrong,' said Lucilla stoutly.

'Of course not – don't be silly! But have we been behaving like really nice girls?'

'You must have been talking to the servants,' said Lucilla scornfully. 'The voice is the voice of Jane, but the mind is the mind of "Sweet Pansy Faces" or the "Duke and the Dairymaid".'

'We aren't the only people in the world.'

'How true!' said Lucilla. 'And you haven't got it out yet. Can't you? In plain English?'

'Well, then, do you think Mr Dix thinks we're not behaving as ladies do behave, or do you think he looks down on us for not knowing the rules and doing just what we think we will?'

'I'm quite sure he doesn't,' said Lucilla; 'he's not such an idiot. Why don't you ask me what I think Mr Rochester thinks?'

'I wasn't thinking of him,' said Jane. (Oh, Jane!) 'I was wondering whether Mrs Dix in New Zealand would approve of the company her dear boy's keeping.'

'If you were really wondering that,' said Lucilla, 'it's time you had something to occupy your mind. Come along. Let that poor little worried yard measure alone and let's go and pick the rest of the black currants.'

They went. 'But you weren't really wondering that,' said Lucilla to herself, as they crouched under the thick-leaved, strong-scented bushes. 'You were thinking something quite different and yet exactly like it.' Aloud she said:

'Currants are jollier to pick than gooseberries, aren't they, though your hands do get so grubby? At any rate, there aren't any thorns.'

'I'd rather be wounded than be grubby,' said Jane.

'Oh, don't be symbolic and Maeterlincky,' said Lucilla.

'I wasn't,' said Jane.

There was something to occupy minds and tongues and fingers when the answers to the advertisements began to come in.

Mrs Adela Dadd – they had themselves chosen her from among a crowd of applicants; how, after this, could they rely on their own judgment?

Jane put it to Mrs Doveton. 'We don't really know anything about choosing people to work for us,' she said, sitting on the kitchen table and watching Mrs Doveton shredding black currants daintily with a silver fork. 'Of course, I mean out of the people we *can* choose from. We wanted to choose you, Mrs Doveton dear, but you wouldn't be chosen. It wasn't till we were in the depths of a dreadful scrape that you came and dug us out, like the angel you are.'

'You do talk so,' said Mrs Doveton. 'What is it you want now?'

'Well,' said Jane, 'we want two things, and they haven't anything to do with each other.'

'I don't know that I wouldn't rather you put off making cocoanut-ice again till I get these currants out of the way – if it's that,' said Mrs Doveton. 'That' was one of the sweet busy-nesses that had ruffled the surface of the perfect calm.

'It isn't cocoanut-ice,' Jane assured her; 'it's much more serious.'

'It's not to ask me to stay on permanent, I do hope and trust,' said Mrs Doveton, 'because –'

'No, no,' said Jane. 'I should never dare to ask you that again, ever. But I do wish you'd see all these people for me.' She waved a sheaf of letters. 'You've had experience; you know what sort of questions to ask and you know what you ought to expect them to do; you know what wages they ought to have and what sort of references are good and what not. Oh, Mrs Doveton, do be a duck and see them for me!'

Mrs Doveton did not refuse, but she murmured something about not being particular fond of taking things upon herself, and it was plain that she said less than the truth.

'Can't you see them yourself, miss?' she said. 'It's quite easy. I'll tell you all the sort of things you want to ask them.'

'Oh, I can't,' said Jane. 'You see, there are paying guests to see too – and you know what I am. I shall find myself telling the cook she can have breakfast in bed if she likes, and asking the young married lady with husband or brother engaged all day whether she understands plain cooking and if she's an early riser and quick and clean at her work.'

'There, now,' said Mrs Doveton, 'you see you *do* know what to ask 'em. And is there *many* more lodgers coming — if that's what you call them, miss, if I may ask?'

'Oh, *we* call them Pigs,' said Jane frankly; 'at least, we used to, but I shall begin calling them lodgers at once. It's much kinder — and besides, they *are* lodgers.'

'Boarders, if with meals,' said Mrs Doveton. 'I shouldn't have too many at a time, miss, if I was you — not all at once. Make the gells discontented — and you've got a couple that knows their work, that's one thing.'

It was evident that in Mrs Doveton's mind there were other things which knowing their work was not.

'Let me help you with the currants,' said Jane, getting another fork. ('A silver one, please, miss,' said Mrs Doveton.) There were a good many currants, but the leaves at the bottom of the basket were showing plainly — leaves streaked with currant-juice and sprinkled with strigs. Jane's hands were deeply dyed again before Mrs Doveton began to yield.

'Well, miss, if I do see these persons for you, you won't blame me if —' she was saying, and Jane was interrupting her with assurances of her complete immunity from blame whatever the creatures turned out like, when the front-door bell rang.

'Good gracious!' said Mrs Doveton. '*I* can't go, miss, with my hands this state.'

'But where's Forbes? Where's Stanley?'

'They're both out, miss. I gave 'em leave to go together for shopping. Neither of them can trust their own taste when it comes to camisoles. Perhaps Miss Lucy'll go.'

'I'll get some of this off in case she's down the garden,' said Jane, drawing water from the boiler, but she had made very little impression on the rich purple stains when the bell rang again.

'Oh, bother!' said Jane. 'Here, I must go as I am. It may be a priceless Pig — I mean lodger — and it may go away if —' She snatched down a towel from the rack, but before her hands were half dried the kitchen door cracked open with a noise like a pistol-shot and Gladys

189

burst in, very highly coloured in the face and very bright as to the eye. 'Oh, miss!' she said, and no more.

'Whatever is it now?' Jane asked, in the tone of a camel enquiring as to the exact nature of the last straw. 'Why aren't you at the shop?'

'Mr Herbert was passing, on his way to see you, Mrs Doveton, and I asked him to keep the shop while I − while I − while I answered the bell.' She giggled as one in possession of a secret joke.

'Well, who was it?' Jane asked, more relieved by Gladys's news than Mrs Doveton appeared to be.

Gladys giggled again. 'It's a lady, miss − an old lady − at least . . . And she asked to see you, miss.'

'Well, I can't see her,' said Jane, turning her purple palms upwards. 'Find Miss Lucilla and ask her to see the lady.'

'Miss Lucilla wouldn't do, the lady said. It was you, miss, as she wanted to see. Do excuse me going off like this, miss.' Gladys was still tittering tremulously. 'I don't know what's come over me, I'm sure! It must be the weather or something.'

'Did you show her into the drawing-room?'

'Of course, miss,' said Gladys virtuously.

'I wish I'd done the flowers this morning,' said Jane, at the glass by the window, dabbing at her hair with repressive fingers.

'I drew down the blinds, miss: the lady's eyes is weak − so she says. And oh, miss, I can't help laughing!' It was plain that she could not. 'You with your hands like that and all. It do seem a sort of judgment − I mean a providence. Oh, I don't know what I mean!'

'I think you're forgetting yourself, my gell,' said Mrs Doveton sharply. 'What's the lady's name?'

'Oh,' said Gladys, 'didn't I tell you? It's Mrs Rochester − our young gentleman's ma. *What* a pity about your hands, miss!'

Well, it certainly was.

Chapter XXIII

'Send in tea if I ring once,' said Jane, preparing to face Mr Roch-ester's mother in a crumpled blue print, with her hair very untidy and her hands deeply empurpled. Her dress was empurpled too, because amid the bushes she had happened to kneel on a currant or two – but of this she was mercifully unaware. The carnation tint in her cheeks, induced by agitation, was very becoming, and she looked her prettiest. But she did not know this either. 'Once for tea, Mrs Doveton. Twice if I want you to let the lady out. At least, of course, Gladys must do that.'

'I'll be handy, miss, you may be sure,' said Gladys enthusias-tically. 'I'll hang round like in the hall.'

'No, you won't, my gell,' said Mrs Doveton with some smart-ness. 'I'll find you a job to do while you're waiting.'

'Pr'aps I'd better go back to the shop,' Gladys tried. 'You hear the drawing-room bell quite plainly there, and I dessay Mr Herbert wouldn't mind staying to take over shop when I was called away.'

'Mr Herbert,' said Mr Herbert's mother, 'will stay where he is, and *you'll* stay where *you* are. Don't you be flustered, Miss Jane. I daresay the old lady's quite mild really. Them short-set men with tempers to match often have quite quiet mothers.'

'Don't make me laugh,' said Jane, beginning to feel some sympathy with the giggles of Gladys. 'You'll have tea all ready, won't you?'

She was annoyed to find, as she reached the drawing-room door, that her heart seemed to have left its normal position just above where you tuck the rose into your belt, and to have shifted itself to less suitable quarters immediately under the short string of beads that encircles your throat. And annoyance changed to fury when she found that she was trembling all over.

Had he written to his mother about her? Why should he have written? What could he have said? Why had she come? Why *could* she have come? To inspect? Why? To interfere? What with? To tell Miss Quested that young men's mothers didn't approve of unchaperoned days on rivers? To say what she thought of unchaperoned girls anyhow, and to take her boy away? Whatever she had come for, her coming would change things so that they could never be the same again, and Jane had to admit to herself that she did not want things changed. This wonder and these admissions all found time to be between her laying her hand on the knob of the door and her turning it. Then she did turn it, and went in.

The room seemed full of a dusky golden twilight; the flowers, she noted with relief, looked quite decent – only the lupins had shed their petals all over the Sheraton card-table in that aggravating way lupins have.

Then she found herself laying her violet-tinted hand in a cool, gloved hand which seemed to expect it, and saying that she was very pleased to see Mrs Rochester, because this seemed to be the right thing to say.

'Thank you so much,' said the visitor in a thin, high voice. 'That's very sweet of you. You see, I was in the neighbourhood and I couldn't resist the temptation to call. I have heard so much of you from my son. You must know,' she added, with an elegant little simper, 'you must know I'm a very devoted mother.'

'I'm afraid you're rather affected,' said Jane, but not aloud. Aloud she said:

'How nice' – again because that seemed the best thing to say.

'Ah, well, family affection involves great anxieties.'

'What are we coming to now?' Jane murmured, but the other did not pursue the theme of the affections, family or otherwise.

'What a delightful old-world spot this is,' she said – 'so quaint and picturesque. It has all the lure of the bygone, has it not?'

'I'm glad you think so,' said Jane politely, but in her heart she was saying, 'I wonder whether you always talk like the Woman's Page in the *Daily Yell*. How awful for *him* if you do.'

'I suppose you live quite an idyllic life here – surrounded by friends and relations . . . no anxieties?'

'Not at all, thank you,' said Jane.

'No, of course not. At your age life is a garden of roses, is it not? But what I really wanted to talk to you about was a little private matter between us two,' the thin voice went on with a detestable archness. 'And I needn't apologise for bringing it up, need I? For I'm sure it's a subject in which you take an interest . . . Young people, you know – so sympathetic. Now tell me candidly, and don't be afraid of offending me, dear: don't you think he's wasting his time – just the least in the world?'

'Who?' Jane felt obliged to ask.

'Why, my boy. Don't you think he's wasting his time just a wee bit?'

Jane, heavy with astonishment and impotent rage, could only say she supposed his mother knew best.

'Oh no!' A delicately-gloved but intolerably waggish forefinger was shaken in Jane's face. She would have liked to bite it. 'Oh no – you can judge far better than I can. You have so many more opportunities of seeing my dear son.'

Jane ventured to suppose that Mr Rochester knew his own business best.

'Oh no!' The voice was too thin for cooing, but it tried to coo. 'Young men never know best – never. We have to think for them, we poor, weak women. He has his way to make in the world, and –'

'Well, let him make it!' said Jane, suddenly aware that her temper was going and feeling that it was almost time it did go.

'Ah! – but the white hands on the bridle-rein. Two charming girls – quite charming, I'm sure. From a child my son John was so susceptible – almost painfully susceptible.'

'What?' cried Jane, in quite a new voice.

'Er – susceptible,' said the other, quailing a little.

'Nonsense!' said Jane loudly, and she leapt from her chair and with one purposeful jerk she pulled up a blind. Then, with the intent ferocity of a well-bred bulldog in a good way of business, she approached the visitor, who retreated with some activity. But in vain. Jane pursued her, caught her by the console table, took her by the shoulders and shook her.

'You beast,' she said vehemently, 'you absolute beast!'

It was a strange scene – a scene such as that sober drawing-room had perhaps never witnessed: the shrinking figure of an elderly lady being thoroughly and systematically shaken by a small, slim girl with flame on her cheeks and daggers in her eyes. It was almost a pity that such a scene should have had no spectators. So, evidently, it appeared to the Fates, for they remedied the oversight by permitting Gladys to escape from Mrs Doveton and enjoy the spectacle to the full through the crack of the library door.

'You beast – you little beast!' Jane repeated, and then Mrs Rochester's bonnet fell off and Mrs Rochester's hair came down, and it was Lucilla that Jane was shaking – Lucilla, half-laughing through the little wrinkles that were now so plainly only greasepaint, and begging for mercy in the voice that was her own.

'Don't, Jane, don't, you're choking me!'

'I should hope so,' said Jane, and went on shaking.

'Didn't she do it lovely!' Gladys permitted herself to say, opening the door widely enough for that purpose.

Jane stopped shaking Lucilla.

'Have you been listening at the door?' she asked, turning like a whirlwind. 'Because if you have . . .'

'Of course not, miss,' said Gladys, deeply injured. 'But when I heard the blind click – Mrs Doveton heard it too, we was both in the kitchen – I knew it was all up, and I come to help Miss Lucy off with her things. It was as good as a play when she went outside and rang the bell, and me inside, ready to open. And she says: "Miss Quested at home?" and says she'd seen the advertisement and she wished to recommend a cook. Nobody couldn't have known her.'

Jane's face cleared a little at this evidence that at least Lucilla had retained some vestiges of tact. She caught at her self-possession.

'Well, you needn't wait, Gladys,' she said. 'The fun's over now. Yes, it was very amusing.' She made herself laugh, and reflected that she would have to laugh sooner or later, and might as well begin now and laugh generously. She laughed again with more sincerity.

'I'll help Miss Lucy to undress,' she said. 'Yes, it was jolly good. It quite took me in. It was a right-down regular do. And a thorough lark.'

'Yes, wasn't it?' said Gladys. 'Miss Lucy ought to be on the halls. All right, miss – all right. I'm off . . .!'

'It was a fair score,' said Jane, folding up the silk dress that the false Mrs Rochester had worn. 'You were absolutely IT. You took me in completely. Your voice was splendid – about an octave above your natural voice, wasn't it? And that affected little laugh – like a neigh! You're a born actress, Lucilla – Gladys is quite right. There was something about the voice that seemed familiar, but I thought our Mr Rochester's voice perhaps was like his mother's.'

'It isn't a bit like *that* voice,' said Lucilla, spluttering among warm soapsuds; 'it was a nice voice, wasn't it?'

'Whatever made you think of doing it?'

'The rubbish you were talking about chaperones, I expect. I thought I'd call and offer myself as one. Then I thought I'd pretend to be a potential Pig, and when Gladys said, "What name?" – *she* acted all right too, except for giggling – I could think of nothing but Rochester. I thought you'd see through me directly. It was Gladys who thought of pulling down the blinds. I never expected to say more than, "How do you do?" before you recognised me. I couldn't have kept it up much longer. I couldn't think of anything to say.'

'You thought of a good deal.'

'Oh, *that* wash!' said Lucilla, throwing back her hair. And Jane felt somehow solaced.

'But what was it that gave me away?' Lucilla asked.

'"My son John",' Jane told her. 'He told me one day that his mother always calls him Jack. I gather that she thinks John rather – what's the word – *roturier*. So then I knew something was up, and in a flash I saw that you weren't real. Do you know, that was a horrid moment, when you began to come to pieces in my hands. I almost expected you to be nothing but clothes, like that ghastly nun in "Villette".'

'I rather expected to be torn to bits myself,' said Lucilla. 'You were violent, Jane.'

'What did you expect?'

'"Though she is little, she is very fierce." Well, it was a good rag,' said Lucilla contentedly; 'only my head doesn't feel quite safe on my shoulders yet.'

'I think I was very moderate,' said Jane.

Next day the cooks came, but none of them suited Mrs Doveton.

'I shouldn't care to trust e'er a one of them to do for you,' she said, and a wonderful tremulous hope sprang up in the breasts of the girls that perhaps Mrs Doveton herself, always so averse from responsibility, and now so delicately placed as the arbiter of their domestic destiny, might find herself unable to take upon herself the burden of decision; that she might, in fact, rather than risk the selection of an Unsuitable, continue to 'do for' them herself.

The paying guests whose letters had been approved, and who had been asked to call, did call. Lucilla interviewed them.

'It's the least you can do,' said Jane. 'I couldn't face a caller now; I should be afraid it would turn out to be you.'

'But I shall be there with you, you know.'

'So you say,' said Jane darkly. 'I'm not going to risk it. You're capable of being yourself and someone else at the same time. You're quite equivalent, as Gladys would say. I shall sit in our boudoir and boud – or read. And I shall wash my hair. So that it won't be any use your sending Forbes up to say that, "Please 'm, Miss Craye would like to speak to you a moment in the drawing-room." My hair will be wringing wet the whole time they're here.'

When it came to the point, Jane did not wash her hair, because a four at tennis had been arranged to take place directly after tea; but she sat with the hair thoroughly down over a kimono with storks on it, and, thus defended, heard three times the resonant ringing voice of the front-door bell, announcing, 'There are strangers on your doorstep, who don't know how I reverberate and clang, and how I keep it up unless you ring me very, very gently.' But only twice did she hear the tinkle of the drawing-room bell – a mincing tinkle, reminding one of the voice of the false Mrs Rochester, and saying, 'There are visitors being shown out of your high-class family mansion by your irreproachable, white-aproned, long-streamer-capped parlourmaid.'

By a simple arithmetical process she was being led to conjecture that one of the callers might have had to ring twice – though Forbes was so very irreproachable that was not likely – when she heard Lucilla's voice in the hall, the voice of one pleasantly elated in the company of congenial spirits.

'No trouble at all,' she was saying; 'of course I'll go with you to the gate.' And then, 'And wouldn't you like to go round the garden?'

A woman's pleasant voice answered her, and men's voices joined it. Jane ran through to the window of one of the unoccupied rooms that looked over the cedar lawn. Lucilla was crossing it in the company of a very elegant-looking young woman and two young men, who, if not exactly elegant, were certainly present-able. They disappeared beyond the lawn, and Jane hurried back to her room to do her hair and go down to meet the strangers.

'Why,' she told herself, 'they look quite nice – not like P.G.'s – like real people!'

And she hastened to exchange the kimono for a frock and her gold-embroidered slippers for sedate suède shoes. But before she had come to the shoes Lucilla burst in upon her.

'Oh, my dear!' she said. 'Such luck! They've taken the rooms – the three best bedrooms and a sitting-room; we can easily turn one of the bedrooms into a sitting-room, and that attic where the cistern is for a dark-room. They go in for photography. They're going to have a tap and sink put in. *They* pay for it! They're musi-cians too: they play at concerts. They're going to pay three guineas a week each, and three for the sitting-room, and two for the dark-room – that's fourteen guineas a week, my girl!'

'We'll have to be a bit more careful about their references – a bit more careful than last time, I mean.'

'They've given me three – a clergyman, and their last landlord, and their bank.'

'We must call on these references. Where have they been living?'

'In Carlisle.'

'That's convenient.'

'Ah, but their bank's in Lombard Street, and we'll go and call on that. No writing. We'll see with our own eyes whether Barclay's Bank is a real bank. Oh, Jane, what luck!'

'They're nice, then?'

'I should jolly well think so. Why, Jane, they're not a bit like P.G.'s. They're just like people you know.'

'And Mr Tombs – what about him?'

'Oh, he came; and he's taken the top tower bedroom. He's not bad either – tall, thin, middle-aged. Nice face, and a nice voice if he'd use it. Blue glasses. He's got references too. Upper Tooting. We can go *there*, you know.'

'And what's he paying?'

'Oh, three guineas, the same as the others.'

'For that horrid, poky little room!'

'Oh, well, we can't make these distinctions. He seemed quite satisfied. And if he's no other good, he'll do for a chaperone.'

'Drop it,' said Jane.

Chapter XXIV

'I feel as if we were being whirled along in a – what-do-you-call-it?' said Jane.

'Motor-car?' suggested Lucilla, her speech obstructed by pins.

'No, maëlstrom,' said Jane. 'Things do keep happening so. Don't put in so many pins, Luce. I can see how it goes all right.'

They were occupied in covering two easy-chairs with bright chintz. I am sorry to say that they had cut up a pair of curtains twelve feet long by six feet wide so as to avoid the extravagance of buying new cretonne to brighten the sitting-room which they were arranging for their new guests. The curtains were beautiful, with purple birds and pink peonies and pagodas of just the right shade of yellow to be worthy to associate with the pinks and the purples. The curtains were lined and bordered with faded rose-coloured Chinese silk, and pounds could not have bought their like. Shillings, on the other hand, and not so very many of them either, could have bought the cretonne. Pity, but do not despise these inexperienced housekeepers. They did not know – how should they? Even the most charming girls do not know every-thing. There was a girl once who cut up a fine hand-woven linen sheet to line a dress with and thought she was being economical, but that is another, and a sadder, story.

'Well, we want things to happen, don't we?' said Lucilla. 'Wasn't it rather the idea that we should live a strenuous life full of hard work, and earn our own livings with the sweat of . . . That pinky silk would look lovely under a bluey purply sort of crêpe-de-chine. There'd be plenty of it for us each to have a dress. That *would* be something happening . . .'

'Yes. Your Aunt Lucy did certainly have the loveliest things. These curtains must have come from a much bigger house than the cottage. And I don't call a new dress "things happening". Things that you do yourself aren't "things happening". It's things other people do. Those loathsome P.G.'s that didn't pay, and Mrs Dadd, and you being Mrs Rochester.'

'That doesn't count – it wasn't real.'

'Quite real enough, thank you. And now everything turned upside down to get this room ready for these horrid people.'

'They're *nice* people,' Lucilla insisted.

'I don't care how nice they are – they come upsetting things.'

'With fourteen pounds a week?'

'Guineas,' said Jane absently. 'Do you know, Luce, I think there's something to be said for the sheltered life? We had a little taste of it, just that week or two after the Pigs bolted. That's the life Emmie has, always – no anxieties; just time to be jolly and enjoy herself.'

'If that's what you feel, you'd better go and be a seraglio at once.'

'Nonsense. And I'm not saying what I mean. Did you ever notice how sometimes you don't? I think what I really mean is that I don't want strangers about – however nice they are; and I mayn't think they're nice either. Hold that corner steady and I'll stitch it now and have done with it, and we'll nail up the untidy edges underneath.'

'I wish you'd rein in your wandering mind and tell me what's happened.'

'Oh, nothing,' said Jane, and stopped short suddenly. 'Only Forbes says she didn't understand it was to be a boarding-house, and Mrs Doveton says we ought to keep accounts, and Mr Dix says we ought to keep bees, and he wants us to have pigs and a cow; and we haven't the least idea how much anything costs, or how much it ought to cost – and seventeen guineas a week looks lovely, but if you don't know how much you're spending you can't tell where you are. We may be barging along the road to ruin for anything we can tell. And I don't suppose these rooms will be ready by the time these people come. And Mrs Doveton says we ought to have in our sugar by the hundredweight, wholesale; and the drawing-room chimney wants sweeping, and we keep on saying we'll get the silver up from behind the garden-room stove, and we never do. Did you hear of people biting off more than they can chew?'

'There's nothing in all that,' said Lucilla, busy with snipping scissors. 'Everything's going on all right. But I'll tell you what, Jane. If you begin to turn coward, everything won't go on all right much longer.'

'This place is too big,' said Jane. 'It eats up all one's courage.'

'But we wanted a big place – to earn our living in. And we got it – by a miracle. I know we agreed that we wouldn't tell each other not to be silly. But really . . .'

'Every word you say is true,' said Jane – 'every single word – and I am an idiot; but there's Mr Dix going on like an intelligent steam-engine, and Mrs Doveton like – all right, I'll drop it. Let's talk of something else. Is that Thornton girl good-looking?'

'Girl!' returned Lucilla. 'She's married, to one of them – I don't know which. I must have told you that a dozen times.'

'Never,' said Jane. 'You said the tall one was her brother, but not a word about her being married to the other one. I thought they were all brothers and sisters. Hurry up – let's get these chairs done and go out and see the fountain. Mr Rochester's made it work, but I told him not to turn it on till we came out.'

She fell to work with renewed courage.

'What *was* it you were asking about the Thornton girl – just before I said she wasn't a girl; what was it?'

'Oh, I don't know,' said Jane blithely; 'it doesn't matter anyhow. Now let's fix our powerful minds on bees. Shall we have them, or shan't we?'

'Can we afford it?'

'Oh yes,' said Jane, 'if our Mr Dix says so. He knows about it all – he knows, he knows. That'll turn out all right, don't you worry.'

> '"And variable as the shade
> By the light quivering aspen made . . ."'

said Lucilla.

'Yes, I know,' said Jane. 'Yes, I was in the dumps, but you're a splendid comforter, Luce. I see that you're right, and everything's all right. And you are right. And I am right. And everything is quite correct.'

Lucilla's scissors snipped in a thoughtful silence. But to herself she said, 'Oho!' and remained thoughtful in the face of the sudden bright gaiety with which Jane now enlivened their work.

The afternoon was fine, the fountain played to admiration and Mr Rochester received the congratulations of the company. Mr Dix received permission to buy bees, Jane seemed to have received a new lease of her habitual light-hearted optimism, and Lucilla felt that she had received enlightenment.

It was Mr Rochester's day of triumph, for after the fountain had sprung and sparkled and pretended to be in turn cotton-wool and glass and fine silver, he announced that the library was done, and they trooped along to see it. The too enthu-siastic interest of Gladys had led Mr Rochester to ask leave to keep the door locked, so it was some time since anyone but Rochester had entered the room. Now they all stood in a silence of admiration that followed the first involuntary and unanimous 'Oh!'

For all the mustard-coloured paint was gone and the panels showed in the beautiful grey of their own oak. The books had been dusted and put back on the shelves, and the room had been swept and brushed to a fine bare neatness.

'Why, it's the most beautiful room in the house!' said Lucilla.

'Almost it persuades me to be a book-worm,' said Dix, and took down a book and then another book. Lucilla also began to take down books – large ones with pictures. In a moment she looked round for someone to share the delights of a book of engravings – romantic pictures of castles and monasteries and ruins, with the wonderful trees and skies of the steel-engraver and the little blurred, round, brown footprints of time.

'Oh, do look at this picture of Lindisfarne – isn't it lovely?' and Mr Dix came and looked and said it was.

'But look at this,' he said, displaying his book – 'the lovely little pictures of strange beasts.'

Jane and Rochester drifted to the window, whose big bow made almost another room. An octagonal table, leather covered, came near to filling it. They squeezed past, and leaned out of the casement among the thick-flowered jasmine and wistaria. When I say they drifted, I do not really mean what I say. To Lucilla and Dix they no doubt appeared to drift. But what really drew her to the window was the action of Mr Rochester. He too had taken a book from the shelf and had held it out for Jane's inspection. And when she looked it wasn't a rare edition or a picture of a manticore or a ruined abbey that she beheld, but a slip of paper on which was written, 'Please come to the window. I have something secret to tell you.'

Now you must know that during the last few weeks Jane by an art so consummate as almost to have deserved from an unkind critic the epithet of artfulness, had succeeded in being very nice indeed to Mr Rochester in public, and at the same time had most resolutely avoided all occasions of converse with him except public ones.

Rochester, with equal art but inferior success, had tried his hardest to get a word alone with her – in vain. Always she was with Lucilla, with Mrs Doveton, with Gladys, with one of the dismal and non-paying guests; and if he did find her alone she was always on her way to keep a most urgent appointment with one or other of her unconscious chaperones. Lucilla, who had herself no desire for *tête-à-têtes*, had seconded Jane ably, if unconsciously. And this had gone on and on. Now Jane looked at the book and said, 'Yes, very pretty,' and very, very slightly shook her head.

'Oh, but look at this!' said Rochester, turning the pages quickly. She looked. And this is what she read: 'There is a secret door. Let me show it *you* first.'

Oh, well – if it was only a secret door . . . And it was then that she moved slowly towards the window, Rochester following with an admirably simulated air of its being a moment, this, like any other moment.

'That's very good of you,' he said, in that veiled voice which sounds just like ordinary talking to anyone a couple of yards away until he tries to hear what you're saying, and finds that he can't. 'And there *is* a secret door. But first I want to ask whether I may go on using this room. I am writing a book – about my new discovery.'

'Oh,' said Jane, and her voice was not quite so veiled as his – but still, she wasn't exactly shouting, 'Have you made a new discovery? What is it?'

'Well,' he said, 'if it's what I think it is – and I don't think I'm wrong – it knocks spots off Newton. And as for Einstein – But that's all dull to you . . .'

'You mean I couldn't understand it?'

'You *could*, of course, but you'd have to understand a lot of other dull things first – mathematics, and physics, and dynamics, and things like that.'

'Can't you explain in a popular style that the beaver could well understand?'

'I suppose I could. But it would take a long time and it wouldn't amuse you. Only may I come and write here? It's so quiet, and so good. And I wouldn't be in the way. I'd go in and out through the French window.'

'And the secret door?'

'Well, I shall always be here, and when you feel you'd like to see it – well, here it is, you know.'

'But I can't have secrets from Luce – about secret doors, you know,' she added hastily.

'Forgive me for saying that *I* can. Please let me,' he pleaded. 'Let me have just this one little secret with *you*.'

'Oh, very well,' Jane mumbled, anxious to get away from any talk of secrets, especially from the memory of another secret that he had with her – the little secret of their last interview in that room, when . . . Jane looked at his coat – it was the same coat – and wondered how any fabric worn by men could be at once so coarse and so comforting. All the same . . .

'But I thought,' she said, picking jasmine flowers and laying the stalks together with earnest accuracy, 'I thought you were to take care of your uncle's house till he came back?'

'Oh, that's all off. My uncle met a chap in Paris, and he's lent him his house. He's got a lot of sixteenth and seventeenth century books, you know; and this man's got some wonderful cypher he's finding out, and his health won't let him live in London, near the British Museum, and of course, these books are a godsend. You see, this cypher is really rather a wonderful thing, so my uncle says – and . . .'

'But tell me,' said Jane, who, like most normal human beings, was deeply uninterested in cyphers, 'where are you going to live?'

'Well, that's really what I wanted to talk to you about.' Jane wondered how she could have ever thought he wanted to talk about anything else – about their last talk in that room, for instance. She could have slapped herself for that refusing shake of the head. What would he think of her? Why should she have refused to come to the window to be told about where Mr Rochester was going to live?

'You see,' he went on, 'it's much easier to say no if there's no audience. And I thought if I asked you *coram populo* you wouldn't perhaps like to say no, even if you meant it.'

'No to what?'

'To Dix's idea that I should share his cottage. Do you mind?'

'No; why on earth should I?'

'Then that's all right,' he said joyously, 'and we're friends again, aren't we?'

'We've never been anything else,' she said, sticking the jasmine in the front of her dress.

'Mayn't I have some?' he asked, and really it would have been silly and self-conscious and schoolgirlish to tell him to pick a piece for himself. So she gave him a sprig of jasmine and he put it in his coat.

'Then I'll move my traps down to-morrow,' he said. 'It's really very good of you.'

Jane reminded him that the whole place was his uncle's. 'And besides,' she said, 'isn't it better for Mr Dix? Isn't it cheaper to keep house for two than for one?' she asked.

'Not quite that, perhaps,' he said gravely, though his eyes were smiling, 'but two people together cost less than two apart I'm told. I suppose they eat up each other's crusts. And look here. Dix and I were wondering – couldn't we have another day on the river before those new people of yours come? I wish you didn't have to have them. You ought to have the place to yourself and not be obliged to –'

'And not be obliged to turn Pigs loose into it? Well, it isn't *our* place, you know. And I think how lucky we are to have a place at all to turn Pigs into.'

'I wish you hadn't to do it.'

'You'd like us to sit on a cushion and sew a silk seam?'

'I'm afraid the strawberries are over for this year,' he said, 'but – oh, well, let's make the best of it. Miss Craye says they're really nice people, these new Pigs of yours. We could get up a little dance.'

'*Oh!*' said Jane, new vistas opening before her.

'May I implore the honour of the first dance?'

'All right,' said Jane. There was certainly no reason for saying, 'No, thank you.'

And that night she and Lucilla talked long and earnestly of the lovely possibilities of rose-coloured Chinese silk and chiffon of all the shades of the fairy rainbow – the shades that you can never match in the shops.

It was the day before the one fixed for the arrival of the Thorntons and Mr Tombs. The rooms were ready, the armchairs looked beautiful, and Jane was enjoying a well-earned rest in the hammock that hung from the apple-tree on the remotest of all the lawns, when she saw through the bushes the uncompromising black-and-white livery of Forbes approaching like a large, respectable magpie.

'Whatever is it now?' Jane wondered. She was deep in 'Uncle Silas' and wished for invisibility.

Forbes very properly waited till she was quite close to her young mistress before announcing that there was 'a lady to see her'.

'Tell Miss Craye,' said Jane. 'I can't see anyone.'

Forbes said that Miss Craye was out, she believed, ma'am.

'Oh, all right.' Jane plunged angrily out of the hammock. 'I'll come. I suppose you've put her in the drawing-room? Who is it? Did she give her name?'

'Yes, ma'am; it's Mrs Rochester,' said Forbes, and something faintly resembling a smile seemed to play near her mouth.

Mrs Rochester! And Lucilla not in! And Forbes, the gravest of the grave, almost smiling! This was a little bit too much. Once was all right, and not a bad joke – but twice! And with John Rochester working in the house, too! Lucilla ought to know better. Jane quickened her pace to a run. She had shaken Lucilla last time. This time . . .

She ran on, arrived in the hall flushed and dishevelled, glanced through the crack of the drawing-room door. Yes, there she was, close to the door from the library. Jane crept quietly through the room where John Rochester was to-day fortunately *not* working, came behind the seated figure, and smote it violently on the back, crying, 'Oh no, you don't, old girl!' and her hands were raised to tear off Lucilla's disguise – not a bonnet this time, but a hat, and quite a smart one – when the smitten figure, having risen, turned, staggering, revealing to the stricken Jane the infuriated countenance of a perfect stranger.

This time it really *was* Mrs Rochester.

Chapter XXV

Many of my readers are no doubt familiar with the tremulous timidities, the doubtful diffidences, the agitation, the soul-searching with which a young woman prepares for the first meeting with *his* mother, and this even if *he* be merely an agreeable acquaintance who might possibly be suspected of harbouring sentiments a little beyond those involved in mere acquaintanceship. You will have noticed how the heart beats, how the hands tremble, how long it takes to decide on the right frock, and how impossible it is to do the hair decently. You know how desirous you are that she should like you, and how determined you are that you will like her. And how, as the moment of meeting approaches, and when it is beyond doubt too late to make any change, you wish wretchedly that you had chosen another frock and done your hair a different way.

You know how you wish that your hands were not at once warm and clammy, and how you wonder whether she can see your heart beating like a steam-hammer under your thin best jumper.

These nerve-racking experiences Jane was spared. And besides, of course, Mr Rochester was nothing to her – or, at any rate, only a friend. And she had been spared the torments of nervous anticipation. On the other hand, Mr Rochester *was* a friend, and she would have liked to be decent to his mother. Instead of which she had thumped his mother on the back and called her 'old girl', and said, 'No, you don't!'

What was Jane to do? What would you have done?

What Jane said was: 'Oh, I *am* so sorry. There's a looking-glass just behind you.'

For Mrs Rochester had put both hands up to her hat, which had been shaken from its exquisite calculated poise by the sudden and violent impact of Jane's little paw on the shoulder of the hat's wearer. Mrs Rochester mechanically turned to the looking-glass, a pretty oval Empire thing in whose frame doves and cupids fought it out amid endless loops of carved and gilded ribbon.

'I am most frightfully sorry,' Jane went on. 'You must think I'm quite mad, but I'm not, really. I thought you were my friend, dressed up.'

A silence. Mrs Rochester's fingers were busy with the hat – elegant, half-diaphanous, lacy, with floating veil of grey and perfectly-placed pink and grey velvet pansies. Jane noticed this, and noticed anew the gilded birds and boys; also she noted in the mirror the pretty, faded, furious, powdered face of her visitor.

'Do please forgive me,' said Jane again. 'I thought it was my friend. She dressed up once before and pretended to be – to be a lady.'

'Your friend is not a lady then?' was Mrs Rochester's first word. Jane resisted the old Adam and went on meekly.

'I mean she pretended to be a strange lady come to call. I thought it was her again, dressed up.'

'Do I look like a person dressed up and pretending to be a lady?' Mrs Rochester asked, flashing the front view of her perfectly dressed self on the cringing Jane.

'You look absolutely lovely,' said poor Jane quickly, 'but I saw only the back of you; and I just thought how clever of Lucilla to get up like that – so different from the last time when she dressed up. She was dowdy and old then, and she quite took me in. I'd not the least idea it wasn't Lucilla.'

'Your maid didn't tell you my name then?'

'Oh, she said something, but I didn't pay much attention, I was so sure it was Lucilla,' said Jane, perceiving new pitfalls on every hand, and wondering whether she would be forced into down-right lying. 'Do please try to forgive me – I do hope I didn't hurt you. I feel like a bull in a china-shop when I think – Oh, how could I? Do sit down and try to forgive me for being such a blundering idiot.'

Perhaps Mrs Rochester was softened by Jane's appeals. Perhaps the wisdom of the dove had not quite deserted Miss Quested in this her hour of need. Perhaps John Rochester's mother felt that in this clumsy hoyden behaving, as the hoyden herself admitted, like a bull in a china-shop, Miss Antrobus had not the serious rival she had feared. This girl at any rate was no siren — just a blowsy, blundering schoolgirl.

However it may have been, Mrs Rochester smiled — a neat, mechanical smile performed by the lips alone, wholly unassisted by the eyes — and said:

'Please don't apologise any more. I quite understand. Just a youthful frolic.'

She seated herself with a perfect grace, and Jane, standing before her, felt like a whipped puppy.

'Do sit down too, won't you?' said the lady in grey silk and violet embroideries, and Jane sat. Her frock was crumpled and crushed from the hammock and her hair in a pigtail. She looked about fourteen. No — certainly not a siren.

'You must wonder at my descending on you in this way,' Mrs Rochester went on, 'but your friend Lady Hesketh — we were neighbours in the country — wrote to me that you were — that you were desirous of entertaining paying guests. Yes?'

'Yes,' said Jane, wishing that her hands were clean, or, alternatively, that she had never been born. 'I asked Emmie to ask everyone she knew — Emmie — Lady Hesketh, you know.'

'Oh yes,' said Mrs Rochester, looking about her through the most impertinent tortoiseshell-framed lorgnettes. 'What a charming old-world place this is, is it not?'

'Yes,' said Jane, rendering heartfelt tribute to Lucilla's instinct, and found herself continuing: 'It has all the lure of the bygone, hasn't it?'

'Are you a fool or are you being clever?' Mrs Rochester mused. Aloud she said something vague about the beauties of old gardens, to which Jane alertly responded by something still vaguer about the beauties of Nature. 'So nice, isn't it?' she found herself saying. 'Old trees and lawns and things. So quaint.'

The talk stagnated in this backwater for some time. It was Mrs Rochester — Jane was determined that it should be — who moved back to the main stream.

'But I mustn't forget the object of my visit in your delightful conversation,' she said — most unfairly, Jane thought. 'We really must talk business, mustn't we?'

If Jane hadn't seen the real Mrs Rochester in the looking-glass she might have believed in that tone of gentle *camaraderie*. As it was, she answered coldly:

'Yes? About the P.G.'s — paying guests, I mean? Our terms are five guineas a week, and we haven't any rooms except on the second floor.'

'You have other guests then? Yes?'

'Yes, several,' said Jane.

'The young friend I am making these enquiries for is a Miss Antrobus — a very charming girl. She is coming to London to study something — now what is it — art — music? Oh no, I remember, it's political economy. And it wouldn't suit her health to be right *in* London. So it seemed as though this would be quite ideal. Thank you so much for the information you have given me — and for our delightful chat. And now I think I had better see your mother.'

'My mother,' said Jane steadily, 'is dead.'

'Well, your aunt then, or your cousin, or whoever it is that chaperones you.'

'Would my great aunt do?' said Jane, suddenly making up her mind.

'Certainly.'

'Well, I don't think she's at home to-day, but you can see her to-morrow if you really feel it's necessary to see her. Really, I can tell you anything you want to know. (I wish I'd said six guineas. That might have choked her off.)'

'Could I not see her if I called this evening — say at nine? I shall be dining with my son. We could come round after dinner. Yes?'

'That will do perfectly,' said Jane, rising with much the air of a duchess ending an interview with a dressmaker. She knew better, but also she heard a movement in the library which told her that Mr Rochester had returned.

'I'll see you out – this way,' she went on very quickly. 'I'll tell my aunt, and I'm sure she will be very pleased, but she's an old lady and rather deaf. Mind the step. Yes – it's a beautiful day. It's been a lovely summer. (Thank goodness I've got you out of the drawing-room!) Oh no – it's no trouble, I should *love* to see you to the gate. Aren't the evergreen oaks a nice shape? Yes, my aunt will be sure to be in this evening. *Good*-bye.'

Jane, having watched the trim, grey figure out of sight, ran like a rabbit to the library.

'You've come to hear the secret?' cried Rochester, jumping up.

'Oh, nonsense!' said Jane. 'Look here – the most awful thing's happened. No, don't look like that – nobody's dead yet – but your mother's been here.'

'My mother?'

'Yes. She came to see about a Miss Antrobus coming as a P.G.'

'Miss Antrobus?'

'*Don't*,' said Jane – and I am sorry to record that she stamped her foot – 'for goodness' sake don't keep repeating everything I say! Your mother called – and I thought she was Lucilla dressed up – and I crept up behind her and clumped her on the back, and said –'

'What did you say?'

'I said, "Oh no, you don't, old girl!" – just like that. Oh, *don't* laugh – don't!'

But Rochester had to. And when he laughed, he laughed thoroughly. Jane looked at him with suppressed fury, but suddenly something in her seemed to give way, and the next moment she too was laughing – and laughing, she felt, with far too much heartiness and abandon. Mr Rochester, she was convinced, would not like her – not *really* like her – to be laughing at a scene, however comic, in which his mother had been assaulted and battered; and how was Jane to explain to him that it had been just a toss-up whether she should laugh or cry?

'Oh, don't!' she said at last. 'You oughtn't to laugh – and I'm sure I oughtn't. I behaved like a bull in a china-shop, and your mother so sweet and gentle' – (Jane?) – 'and besides, there's no time to laugh. I want you to do something for me.'

'Anything,' he said, wiping his eyes.

'You *said* we were friends,' said Jane. 'I can't explain now, because your mother's gone down to your uncle's house looking for you, but do you mind telling her, if she asks you, that we have a great aunt living with us? Aunt – Aunt Harriet, I think; an old lady, rather deaf. I don't want you to say so unless you're asked, you know. Oh, how awful everything is! Now I'm asking you to tell lies to your own mother.'

'I don't mind,' he said truthfully. 'And look here, don't you worry. I believe one has a perfect right to tell lies if people ask questions they have no right to ask.'

'I'm sure that's wrong,' she said, 'but I can't argue. You must fly after your mother and head her off, or she'll be coming back to look for you here. But before you go you must tell me where to go to get wigs and things.'

He named Hugo's. 'But look here,' he said. 'I don't want to ask any questions, but don't do anything that – that'll be difficult to keep up.'

To wring the hands is not usual off the stage, but Jane came near it.

'I can't help myself,' she said, standing there with her straight frock and her pigtail like a forlorn child in a school scrape. 'I said there was an aunt, and there's got to *be* an aunt. I was quite mad when I said it, of course, but I can't face your mother and tell her there isn't any aunt – I really can't.'

'Let me tell her,' he said, coming nearer to her; 'let me tell her that a– and tell her something else as well . . . Jane . . .'

'No, no, no, no, no, no, no!' said Jane, edging away round the table. 'There's nothing to tell her. Don't tell her anything unless she asks. And don't come with her this evening. Because if you do I shall laugh – or else I shall scream.'

'Well, don't worry,' he said; 'everything will be all right. And Miss Antrobus, I can head her off if you don't want her.'

'Oh no, you can't,' said Jane. '*I* tried that. I said five guineas a week, and I thought your mother would say it was too much, but she never turned a hair — I mean she didn't mind a bit. And Miss Antrobus is coming to-morrow to stay. Oh, here she is back again — whatever shall we do?'

But it wasn't Mrs Rochester, it was Lucilla.

'Thank goodness!' said Jane. 'Now go. I know you'll never respect me again now you know what a liar I am, but I can't help what you think of me. It's Fate.'

'I only wish you'd let me tell you what I think of you — you *must* know . . .'

But Jane had fled.

And now behold two agitated young women with money in their purses on their way to seek the help of Mr Hugo.

'I can't *help* it, I tell you,' Jane kept saying. 'I was driven into it. I said there was an aunt, and there must be an aunt. You know you can do it, Luce. If you could take me in you could take anyone in. You must dress exactly as you did that day.'

'But I can't appear in a bonnet, in my own house, in the evening!'

'Caps, dear — there must be caps.'

'I wish you wouldn't. Couldn't the aunt be suddenly ill? Not able to see anyone?'

'Then Mrs Rochester would keep on coming till the aunt was better. And bring flowers. And grapes. And leave cards. And pump the servants. No, we've got to go through with it.'

'What shall we say to Mr Hugo?'

'Tell him the truth — say we're doing it for a lark. So we are.'

'Yes,' said Lucilla, and the third-class railway carriage rang to the music of young laughter.

'That's what it means in books when it says "hollow mirth",' said Jane.

'Or the laughter of despair,' suggested Lucilla; 'but I call it a jolt-head jest myself.'

'There aren't,' said Jane, 'any polite words for what I call it. And yet it's a sort of lark too, after all, isn't it?' she ended appealingly.

'Very sort-of,' said Lucilla.

Chapter XXVI

'You may be sure that Miss Antrobus's sheets will be well aired, Mrs Rochester. I may be old-fashioned, but I believe in airing *everything*: sheets, pillow-cases, cushion-covers, towels — all are aired here, and aired thoroughly, you may rely upon it.'

Thus spoke very gently and seriously, in a sweet, faded voice, a delicious old lady in brown satin. Her grey hair was crowned with a cap of soft lace, and her chin — rather too rounded for age, if one could have seen it properly — was buried in a lace fichu. Mr Hugo had given the invaluable hint that convex shoulders suggest a concave chest — and the old lady stooped a good deal. Her hands, where the mittens let them show, were made up with consummate art and the tiniest grey wrinkles. Her forehead was very wrinkled, and these wrinkles were not painted — they were actual corrugations, fine and deep. Even in the soft light of the drawing-room lamp, which Jane had hastily veiled with a blue chiffon scarf, the wrinkles showed plainly. The old lady sat in a big chair, her feet on a footstool, and on her satin lap knitting lay.

Mrs Rochester sat quite near her — trusting, talkative. You may wonder that she did not recall that her buffeting at the hands of Jane had been due to Jane's having mistaken her for her cousin 'dressed up', and hence made the short, irresistible deduction. But then you must remember that her own son had endorsed the fiction of Aunt Harriet's existence, and, above all, you must allow for the indiarubber forehead, complete with eyebrows and ear coverings, supplied by the genius of Mr Hugo.

Mrs Rochester was, obviously, wholly without suspicion, and Jane had to go out of the room expressly to laugh at the success of the play. Perhaps, too, she wanted to shift the whole burden of the interview on to Lucilla's shoulders for a little while. Her own felt stiff with the weight of the afternoon. At any rate, she got away and crept round and sat down behind the library door to listen unashamed. This is what rewarded her:

'Now we have a moment alone, dear Miss Lucas,' Mrs Rochester was saying, in the high, clear voice of one who wishes to be understood by the rather deaf, 'I should like to make a little confidence. These delightful nieces of yours – so light-hearted and free from care! Yes, but *you* will understand. I am sure Miss Antrobus will have a real home with you. And I have a rather special reason for having the dear girl's welfare very much at heart. I must confess to you that I look upon Miss Antrobus as a daughter already.'

'Indeed,' said Aunt Harriet, almost too calmly; 'one of your sons is engaged to the lady then?'

'My only son,' said Mrs Rochester. 'It's an old attachment – they were little lovers as children – but it's not announced yet, so, of course, not a word to either of them. You, who know my dear boy so well, will feel with me that Hilda Antrobus is a lucky girl, and when you know her you will feel that he's lucky too. Yes?'

'I cannot say that I know Mr Rochester very well,' said the spurious aunt. 'He has called two or three times, I believe. But I daresay now Miss Antrobus is to be with us we shall see more of him.'

'Well played, Lucy!' said Jane, behind the library door.

'I feel sure I may trust to your kind feeling to – to – well, to give the young people opportunities of being together – you understand? A little tact – a helpful blindness – a not *too* efficient chaperonage – a sort of *je ne sais quoi*; not exactly the making of opportunities, but the smoothing away of obstacles, if obstacles are likely to occur. But I am sure *you* understand. Yes?'

'I think so,' said Aunt Harriet. 'I am not myself an experienced match-maker, but –'

'Oh, but,' said Mrs Rochester, clasping her little grey suède-covered hands, 'the match is already *made*! I tell you this in confidence, though of course I can have no objection to your telling your nieces – so long as they understand that it *is* a confidence. No congratulations, of course – no allusions even.'

Here the front-door bell reverberated through the house.

'But I am detaining you,' said Mrs Rochester. 'You are expecting visitors?'

'Not at all,' said the wonderful aunt. 'That is probably one of the maids. My housekeeper allows them to come in by the front door on their evenings out; she tells me it obviates those undesirable lingering partings in the shrubbery leading to the back premises.'

Here the drawing-room door opened and Stanley announced, 'Mr Tombs.' Stanley was one of those admirable servants who seem made of wood and wire; she never glanced towards the ladies, but shut the door softly and retired as Mr Tombs advanced.

'Oh, poor Lucy!' said Jane, and managed to get round to the drawing-room before Mr Tombs had had time to do more than seek to excuse the lateness of his call.

'Very late, I know, for a business call, but I thought it would save correspondence if I came personally to enquire . . .'

'If Mr Tombs will wait in the library, my dear,' said the aunt to Jane, 'I shall be disengaged presently.'

'Oh, but I mustn't detain you.' Mrs Rochester spoke at once on this hint. 'Our little talk is quite over. I *have* so enjoyed it, Miss Lucas. *Good* evening. Oh no – I am not at all nervous; besides, my son is waiting for me.'

Under cover of the lady's withdrawal Mr Tombs said, 'I didn't know there was an aunt.'

'Well, there is, as you see,' said Jane, resenting what she took to be a certain cavalierness of tone.

'I beg your pardon,' he said, turning his thin face and dark glasses towards her. 'I have a detestable habit of thinking aloud. I was only wondering whether I ought to have addressed myself at first to the elder lady – as a matter of courtesy – instead of to Miss Craye.'

'Oh, not at all,' said Jane, mollified. 'Auntie, this is Mr Tombs, who is coming to stay with us to-morrow.'

Auntie greeted him with delicate, gentle cordiality.

'I hope you will be happy with us, Mr Tombs,' she said; 'we will do our best to make your visit a pleasant one. Or have you come to notify us of some alteration in your arrangements?'

'Only in so far as to ask whether I may bring my traps in the afternoon instead of the morning. Because I find –'

'Certainly,' said Jane, forgetting for a moment her part of subservient niece; 'the rooms are ready.'

'Dear Jane,' said the aunt gently, 'Mr Tombs was speaking. You were saying? . . .'

He said it again, and Jane remained tongue-tied while the untrue aunt answered with suave propriety. He replied suitably, and the interview ended by Jane's offering to show him out – an office which at all times appealed to her. 'The maids are at supper,' she said.

In the hall he said:

'I really am most awfully sorry I said I didn't know there was an aunt. I can't think how I could.'

'You won't see very much of her,' said Jane.

'Oh, the more the merrier, with such a delicious old lady . . . There I go again! Do, please, forgive me. I'm like Cheviot Hill: I'm a plain man – I speak as I think.'

Jane felt wonderfully cheered.

'Oh, do you know "Engaged"?' she asked. 'Isn't it lovely? Wouldn't it be jolly to act it?'

'Very. May I ask whether you have enough guests to make up the cast?'

'We shall be six altogether, as well as our gardener, and – but you'll see us all to-morrow. Good-night.'

Jane returned to Lucilla, who had torn off her wig, displaying her little red ears and crushed hair, and was huddling her elderly draperies together in preparation for flight.

'Your Mr Tombs *is* rather a lamb,' said Jane, 'and I do really think you're right about his having a nice face.'

'Oh, go away!' said Lucilla. 'You've got me into this, and now I shall never get out.'

'Why, it's only for once!'

'*Is* it? Miss Antrobus will ask for Miss Lucas directly she gets here, and I shall have to go on acting and acting and acting, and I can't and won't do it. You'll have to tell them Miss Lucas is dead. I can't bear it and I won't. Why didn't you be an aunt yourself, if you wanted one?'

'I can't act like you,' said Jane.

'And Mr Tombs seeing me looking like a bald-faced stag.'

'He didn't know it was you.'

'No – that's just it. You don't know what it feels like to be an old woman and have people look at you as if you weren't there.'

'Well, come and get the rags off,' said Jane, 'and we'll see if there's any way out of it. I suppose it would be a bit thick to have two aunts and have them appear on alternate evenings? Come on; Forbes will catch us if you don't look out. Suppose Aunt Harriet just receives Miss Antrobus tomorrow, and then she could have an illness.'

'And drive twenty guineas a week away for fear of infection? I'd rather go through with it than that,' said Lucilla, stumbling up the stairs in her long skirt.

'It needn't be anything catching. She might have bronchitis or asthma – something that lasts for months and doesn't kill you. Or fits . . .'

'I won't have fits,' said Lucilla decidedly. 'Whatever else I have, I won't have fits. And, whatever we do, the servants will give us away.'

'Perhaps they won't.

> '"Oh, what a tangled web we weave
> When first we practise to deceive."

'Don't look at me in that wild way, Luce. Wash your face for goodness' sake, and comb your hair out – it looks as if you hadn't any. Make yourself look pretty again whatever happens.'

'Oh, flattery's no good,' said Lucilla bitterly. 'I feel as if I were caught in a trap.'

'Look here,' said Jane, 'shall we say our Aunt Harriet is subject to fits – not kicking and screaming ones, mild aberrations – and generally keeps in her room? And lock one of the rooms and chance the servants?'

'And have people think I was a howling animal like the woman in "Jane Eyre" – yes, her name was Rochester, too – not much!'

'They wouldn't *all* think so. Mr Rochester knows. Don't kill me – I had to tell him.'

But Lucilla seemed somehow calmer. Jane pursued her advantage.

'I could tell Mr Dix too, if you liked.'

'Bother Mr Dix.'

'He likes you very much. He's always asking where's Miss Craye.'

'I'm interested in gardening, and he knows it. Don't try to hint things, Jane. You are only trying to make me angry on another side to distract my attention from *that*.' She pointed to the wig. 'But it won't do. There will Miss Quested be, all smiles and charms in her pretty frock. And Miss Craye? Oh, she's not at home this evening. And all the time she'll be here under these hot wigs and eyebrows, having no fun at all.'

This was indeed what happened. Think as they would, nothing better occurred to them than that Lucilla, as Aunt Harriet, should welcome her guests, and should be found placidly knitting when they came into the drawing-room after dinner.

The guests all arrived during the afternoon and were received by the elaborated aunt, Mr and Mrs Thornton and the brother first. They came in taxi-cabs, with a great deal of leathery new luggage – some trunks and some packing-cases. The two men were pleasant and cheerful, with dark, smiling faces. Mrs Thornton was also pleasant. They were all nice to Jane and very nice to Miss Lucas.

'I do think they'll do,' Lucilla said, when they had been shown to their rooms. 'They're new brooms, of course, but they seem jolly, and they talk as if they'd read books and seen people and done things.'

'Whereas our last P.G.'s had perhaps seen things and certainly had done people – us for one.'

'Never mind grammar,' said Lucilla. 'Are my eyebrows straight? They *feel* as crooked as a ram's horn.'

'They're as straight as – as I wish we were,' said Jane. 'The life of an adventuress is a terrible one. We are adventuresses, Lucilla – deceitful adventuresses. And here comes another cab or two. What a day! What a life!'

This time it was Miss Antrobus, with worn luggage and not very much of it. She seemed to Jane to be a very grave, reserved sort of girl; hardly smiled when she shook hands. But when Lucilla smiled on *her* the quiet smile of kindly age, and hoped in that soft voice that trembled a little, as old voices do, that Miss Antrobus would be happy here, she smiled, herself, quite nicely, and said:

'I think it is very good of you to take me in. I hardly thought you would. But Lady Hesketh and Mrs Rochester seemed quite sure.'

Jane did not quite like that, though she could not have told you why.

'You are studying domestic economy?' the untrue aunt went on.

'Not domestic – political,' said Miss Antrobus gently. 'But I have some other business to see to first. I shan't settle down to my economic studies very seriously just yet. I'm working for the Help for Heroes Society.'

'You did hospital work through the war, Mrs Rochester said,' Jane put in. 'I do think it must have been splendid. We couldn't do anything; we were at school.'

'Yes – I was in France three years,' said Miss Antrobus and immediately turned from Jane to speak again to Miss Lucas.

'I'm not going to like her,' said Jane, when Miss Antrobus had followed her luggage into retirement.

'I think I am,' said Lucilla. 'She was jolly decent to me.'

'Well, so were the others. And now there's only Mr Tombs.'

'I shan't wait for him,' said Lucilla. 'He can come when he likes. He can see the precious aunt in the evening; that's enough for *him*.

I'm going to be myself till dinner and go round the garden with the Thorntons and help you to introduce Mr Dix and Mr Rochester to them, and tell them Aunt Harriet is resting and will be in the drawing-room after dinner. It isn't four yet. I'm not going to stay like this for four or five hours, so don't you think it!'

The Thorntons were really very nice. Mrs Thornton was young and very well dressed and very gay and friendly. The male Thorntons seemed to become instantly at home with Dix and Rochester, and the party had tea by the fountain as much at ease as though they had known each other for years. The men had, of course, all been in the army, and that is a bond that makes itself felt at once. Miss Antrobus talked little, mostly to Mr Dix, and when she spoke to Lucilla it was to ask whether they were not to have the pleasure of seeing Miss Lucas at tea.

'No,' said Lucilla unblushingly. 'My aunt is not very strong. She rests a good deal. She cannot stand much society.'

'I hope we shall see her at dinner.'

'She dines in her own room, but she comes into the drawing-room after dinner.'

After this nothing seemed important to Jane except getting Mr Dix away from Miss Antrobus. She did it by suggesting that they should all go and see the sundial, and then very hastily among the currant-bushes she said to Dix:

'You'll see my aunt to-night. Don't let anyone know you haven't seen her before.'

'I understand,' he said. 'Rochester told me.'

'Oh, did he?' said Jane. 'All right, that's all I wanted to say. That's why I cut you off from Miss Antrobus. It would be kind of you to edge back to her now. You seem to be the only one of us that she's taken to.'

'She's rather wonderful, isn't she?' said Dix. 'There's a sort of radiant goodness in her face.'

Jane, a little humbled, had not seen it, but could not gainsay it.

'It's a strong face, and yet – I don't know. It looks to me as though she had been transplanted.'

223

'Transplanted?'

'You know how different plants are in different environments. Look at those tall, splendid, gipsy roses there – on the Sussex Downs in a dry season they're sometimes not an inch high. Lots of people got transplanted in the war.'

'Yes,' said Jane, adding, for the second time that day, 'Lucy and I didn't do anything. We were at school. No transplanting for us.'

'Some flowers don't need it,' said Mr Dix.

Chapter XXVII

A very curious experience this, of Lucilla's: to sit in an armchair, with the weight of old age on her bowed shoulders and on her brow the wrinkled indiarubber brand of seventy years; to be with these young people and not of them; to feel their glances meet hers – not with the hopeful give-and-take of youth and youth, but with the impersonal, distant, half-pitying tribute of youth to age. Curious, very.

Not that the young people were neglectful of Miss Lucas. Far from it. They were kind, they were attentive, they were deferent and courteous, they were everything that young people should be to old ladies. A really old lady would have found these manners charming, but to Lucilla these manners were intolerable. Her only comfort was the reflection that Dix and Rochester knew that under the wig and the wrinkles was hidden the real Lucilla, whose acting they must be secretly admiring. But the Thorntons did not know and, though they were kind, they were not interested. Yes, that was it. Lucilla was accustomed to being found interesting – and no amount of kindness or courtesy can make up in our fellow-creatures for lack of interest. Mr Tombs did not know – and he certainly *had* a nice face. Also he was the one to ask whether they were not to have the pleasure of seeing Miss Craye. It was just after Mrs Thornton had sung. She did not sing at all badly, but Lucilla sang really well. And instead of succeeding Mrs Thornton at the piano and showing the company what singing really was, as she felt quite competent to do, she had to sit on in that wretched armchair, holding that dull knitting, and talking platitudes to people who did not care twopence whether she talked or not, and only listened and spoke to her out of politeness. Miss Antrobus was the only exception: she really did seem to like the old lady and to take a pleasure in talking to her. Lucilla could have hugged her for it, but even her interest could not really charm. And when the clock struck nine, just after Mr Tombs in that pleasant, languid, Oxfordish voice had asked about Miss Craye, Lucilla could bear it no longer.

'She will be home quite soon now,' she said, and rose. The abhorred knitting fell to the ground, and at least half the party stooped, or partly stooped, to restore it. Lucilla folded it resolutely and secured it with a bright knitting-needle.

'I have to keep early hours,' she said gently. 'But you mustn't let me break up the evening. And don't be afraid of disturbing me by music. I love music, and it will soothe me to sleep. Good-night – good-night.'

She passed, stooping and slow, through the door, which five men sprang forward to open. And she felt that at least three sighs of relief were breathed when the door closed behind her. Like to like. Now they were all young together. Well, she was young too – really.

Assured that Forbes and Stanley were safely in the kitchen, she sprang up the stairs two at a time, locked her door, tore off wig and eyebrows, and dressed with feverish speed. Excitement, annoyance, and the hasty and earnest removal of paint from her face gave her a colour she usually lacked. Her hair, dressed with extreme celerity, was suddenly kind, as your hair is now and then when you have not time to do it properly and bundle it up anyhow. It went exactly as it should have gone. The mignonette silk gown took on a new charm from the carnation of her cheeks, and when, twenty minutes after the retirement of Miss Lucas, a rather breathless Lucilla entered the drawing-room, she was handsomer than she had ever been in her life. She knew this when she came face to face with herself in the cupid-and-ribbon mirror, and at once became handsomer still.

'Oh, here you are!' said Jane. 'I'm so glad. I was just saying that I can't sing much, but you sing like a bird.'

'Don't believe her,' said Lucilla gaily; 'she sings all right. But

226

I've no breath left for singing, I had to hurry. To catch a train,' she added, looking straight at Jane. And her look said, 'That lie is chalked up to *you*, not to me. It is *your* fault, not mine, that I am forced to be so untruthful.'

But presently she was not too breathless to sing, and she sang folk-songs, because Mrs Thornton had sung drawing-room ballads about rosebuds and stars. And now there was no lack of interest — even before she sang. After her song she was the centre of all things. Then she sang '*La dove prende*' with Mr Thornton, and it went very well; then there were more duets and more solos; and then songs with choruses, old favourites of Jane's and Lucilla's, which the Thorntons also delightfully knew and liked, and altogether it was half-past eleven before they knew where they were.

Only Miss Antrobus, who had not much voice, asked — after 'Outward Bound' it was — whether they were quite sure Miss Lucas would not be disturbed by such very robust vocalisation.

'Oh no, she loves it,' said Lucilla shamelessly. 'Aunt is wonderfully fond of old songs. I often sing them to her just to please her when we are alone. But I hope *you're* not bored?'

'Oh no,' Miss Antrobus assured her. 'I'm most interested, I assure you.'

This time Lucilla did not desire to hug Miss Antrobus. There was a hint of something. Patronage? Criticism? Suspicion? Antagonism? No, none of these exactly. Yet Lucilla was conscious of something inimical.

'But if she's really fond of John Rochester that accounts,' Lucilla told herself, and turned to accede to a request from Mr Tombs for 'My Lady Greensleeves'.

'Lucilla is like Sophy Traddles,' said Jane. 'She knows all the old songs that ever were invented.'

'My aunt, Miss Lucas, has a mine of them,' said Lucilla, 'and my taste is hers,' and she began the charming old melody.

It was a most successful evening, and when it was over Jane and Lucilla fell into each other's arms in a passion of mutual congratulation.

'Aren't they dears? Even Miss Antrobus isn't so bad. And don't you think Mr Tombs really *has* a nice face?'

'Nice face, nice voice, nice manners, nice straight back, nice hands.'

'But did you notice Mr Thornton's hands? Those long, delicate fingers? He's an artist every inch.'

'He's the one who plays the violin. The others are 'cello and double bass. How frightfully lucky we are! What times we shall have!'

'Yes,' said Jane pensively.

'And they're all fond of dancing.'

'Yes.' Jane had become still more pensive and was rolling and unrolling the ribbon of her girdle with a preoccupied little frown.

'And they all like acting.'

'Yes.'

'Don't keep saying "Yes",' said Lucilla, beginning to pull out hairpins. 'What do you think of Miss Antrobus?'

'I don't know. She is the one I don't feel sure about. She's the fly in the amber, or the toad in the ointment, or whatever it is. She didn't seem to fit in somehow.'

'Mr Rochester seemed to like her.'

'Yes,' said Jane, 'but not desperately, do you think?'

'No, it's not a passionate affair. Friend of childhood's hour, and so on, so Mamma Rochester said.'

'What do you mean by "affair"?'

'Didn't I tell you?' Lucilla asked, brushing vigorously. 'Mamma Rochester hinted all sorts of things . . .' Lucilla stopped. Through the double curtain of her hair she had seen, in the mirror, Jane's face.

Ought she to have gone on? To have told Jane all that Mrs Rochester had said? Anyhow, she didn't. And anyhow, it did not matter, because Jane had heard every word through the library door. Why did not Jane tell Lucilla that she had listened to Mrs Rochester's poisonous confidences? It was not that she was ashamed of listening. When she began to listen she pictured herself telling Lucilla afterwards and laughing over it with her. But she had not told her. And she did not tell her now. Instead she said: 'What sort of things?'

'Oh, the usual stuff that sort of woman would hint: that we needn't hope that my Lord Rochester would throw the handkerchief to either of us, because his mamma had other views for him.'

'What did she say exactly?'

'Oh, nothing exactly. But I gathered that Mama would be quite pleased if Mr Rochester didn't admire Jane or Lucy.'

'So Miss Antrobus is sent here to spy? I thought there was something of that sort. That must be what makes one feel uncomfortable with her.'

'Oh, but I don't think that,' said Lucilla, forgetting that she had felt something very like it, and only remembering that Miss Antrobus had been nice to the unreal aunt. 'I think she's a kind girl really, and straight.'

'She's come to spy out the land,' said Jane with conviction. 'Well, she's welcome to all she can find out. Good-night, Luce.'

But she re-opened the door expressly to put her head round it and whisper: 'I say, Luce, eight people! Enough for the Lancers. And four of them Pigs – beautiful, fat, profitable Pigs! Seventeen-guineas-a-week Pigs, Luce, my dear! Good-night!'

There is no doubt that fortune smiles on the brave; at any rate, it smiled broadly from the first on Jane and Lucilla. Even their misfortunes were mitigated. Their trustee defaulted: but he left them a house and garden and a nest-egg. The house and garden was too small to make money out of: but at once, almost, Cedar Court loomed on a not distant horizon. Jane tumbled downstairs: but she, so to speak, tumbled into possession of the garden room.

They could not afford an expert gardener and bailiff: and Destiny took them to Madame Tussauds, and behold, embodied in Mr Dix, the perfect bailiff and gardener. Old Mr Rochester threatened to become an embarrassment: and at once he retired to Thibet.

They had no servant really attached to their interests: but before they had time to feel this deeply, behold Gladys. They desired competent servants: and Forbes and Stanley were added to their staff. Mrs Adela Dadd happened: but then so, directly afterwards, did Mrs Doveton. The three greedy sisters went away without paying: but they were succeeded by the Thorntons and by Mr Tombs, who did pay.

This sort of luck does, beyond doubt, attend on some people, and it transcends all other blessings. That is why we say, 'It is better to be lucky than rich.' Cæsar had this sort of luck; Napoleon had it; Jane and Lucy had it. But this sort of luck is a bridge that sooner or later gives way. Napoleon met Blücher at Waterloo; Cæsar, even at the base of Pompey's statue, met a greater than Blücher; and Jane and Lucy felt, almost from the first, that in Miss Antrobus they had met a personality that, as gipsies would say, 'crossed their luck'.

A vague but undeniable sense of uneasiness persisted in and through and under and over the pleasant days that now followed each other at Cedar Court. It was not a strong feeling, not an overpowering discomfort; it did not destroy pleasure, but it leavened it. Quietly, persistently, unceasingly it bored its way into everything. It was like a slight toothache which the will may decide to ignore but which goes on all the same in that hinterland of the subconscious where the will has no sovereignty.

The thing could not be put into words. It was as elusive as a bird's song or a flower-scent. All you could say about it was that it was here, and that it was antagonistic. It not that Miss Antrobus withdrew herself from the gaieties of Cedar Court: on the contrary, she participated in every single one. She did not sing, but she could play accompaniments; she was a poor actress, but a good prompter and an excellent audience; her time was always at anyone's disposal, and she had all the time there was. She had too much time – she was always there. She never went to London. She never walked out, except in the garden. She was always amiable and obliging – but she was always there. And she seemed to be always looking on.

'And she looks on through a spy-glass,' said Jane: 'a tortoiseshell lorgnette or whatever it is, like Mrs Rochester had. Or perhaps she looks at us through a microscope, as if we were beetles or those things with legs that come out of pond-water.'

'She doesn't look at Miss Lucas like that,' said Lucilla.

'No,' said Jane, 'that's the worst of it. She's a great deal too nice to Miss Lucas. It's not natural. She asks after her every morning. She offers to go and sit with her – to read to her – take her out for drives.'

'That's easy for you; you've only got to say I'm not strong enough. But when she comes and sits beside me in the evenings and offers to hold my wool, and tells me she's sure I should enjoy a drive, and is so nice and kind – if it's genuine she's a dear, but if it's only that she suspects that I'm not really an aunt, then – well . . .'

'Yes, that's it,' said Jane. 'That dreadful aunt is our weak point. She's the dead secret, the skeleton in the cupboard. If it wasn't for her we could defy fifty Miss Antrobuses.'

'But as it is,' Lucilla pointed out, 'we can't.'

'What a name too! Antrobus! It makes me think of a mediaeval engine of war. Halberds and battering-rams and Antrobuses – I'm sure I've read that somewhere.'

'*I* always thought all Antrobuses had big, hooky noses. You know, noses that snort at you, and say, "Ha, ha!" like the warhorse. But really I believe she's all right. It's only our guilty consciences. And Mr Rochester says she's much jollier than she used to be.'

'And as she was the friend of his childhood he must have thought her pretty nice then. So that by now . . .!'

'I didn't take it that way. What he said was that the war had been the making of her, and he'd never thought she had so much stuff in her. That doesn't sound very – very . . .'

'No – does it? I don't think the noble lord will throw the handkerchief to a girl he never thought had so much in her, do you?'

'He's very nice to her,' said Jane.

'Yes,' said the diplomatic Lucilla, 'too nice for it to mean anything.'

'Yes,' said Jane. 'It's as if he was saying all the time, "I'll be a brother to you – I really will." If there was *anything* there'd be more ups and downs.'

'I don't know how you know,' said Lucilla.

'Perhaps I don't. But you must remember I was adored once too, like Sir Andrew Aguecheek.'

'Oh, *when?*' cried Lucilla eagerly.

'In a former state of existence,' said Jane. 'All girls must have been. That's how they know so much about love-affairs before they ever have one. Look here – let's do something new and different. Let's have a prize competition.'

'Like anagram teas?'

'Yes, but not anagrams. We'll have a prize for the best solution of the problem of how to get rid of Othello – he's always getting out of the hutch and eating Mr Dix's choicest fruits and flowers; and a prize for the best poem about Cedar Court; and for the best way of getting the silver out from behind that fireplace without taking the whole thing out, because the mantelpiece is built all round it. And another prize –'

A discreet tap at the door stopped her.

'Please, miss,' said Mrs Doveton, 'might I have a word with you? . . . No, don't go, Miss Jane. I want to have –'

'Not words with us?' said Jane.

'No, miss, far from it; but I do want to speak plainly.'

'Oh dear,' said Jane, 'whatever has gone wrong now?'

'It's that Gladys,' said Mrs Doveton; 'so now you know.'

Chapter XXVIII

'That girl,' said Mrs Doveton, 'she's an epidemic.'

'?' said Jane and Lucilla.

'An epidemic, miss – she's catching, like measles and whooping-cough. She catches every man she comes near, and the more the merrier, so she thinks.' Mrs Doveton breathed heavily.

'Sit down and tell us all about it,' Lucilla said comfortably, and a green velvet armchair creaked to Mrs Doveton's acceptance of the invitation.

'There aren't no bounds to her,' Mrs Doveton went on. 'There's Mr Simmons, *he's* hooked all right; and there's the butcher's young man – she was out with him Tuesday week; and the very boy that brings the daily papers, she stopped him in the shrubbery to ask him riddles.'

'Well, there's no harm in that,' said Jane. 'Some people think riddles amusing. I don't myself, but some people do.'

'Some riddles is all right, like "Why is Westminster Abbey like the fender?" and "Why is a hen crossing the road like Guy Fox?" But when it comes to asking him what animal falls down from the clouds – well!'

'What animal does? I didn't know any animal did,' said Lucilla.

'That's what the young boy said, miss. And then that Gladys, she says, "Don't know what animal falls from the clouds? Why, the reindeer." See, miss? – the rain – *Dear*. Just an excuse for calling the very paper boy "Dear". And chucks him under the chin, she does, and asks him whether he ain't looking for a sweetheart.'

'It's very silly of Gladys,' said Lucilla, trying not to smile. 'I'll speak to her.'

But Jane laughed and said: 'It's very funny, don't you think? But, dear Mrs Doveton, why should it upset *you*?'

'It's not respectable, miss, that's why. I never see such a gell. Asks the postman what his young lady's name is, just to find out if he's got one, because, if not, here's Gladys all ready and willing.'

'I suppose the postman can take care of himself,' said Lucilla.

'Let's hope so, I'm sure,' said Mrs Doveton gloomily, beating the palm of her hand on the arm of her chair; 'but there's them as can't. The girl's like a raging lion going to and fro seeking who she may walk out with.'

'I thought it was Simmons,' said Jane.

'So it was, and is, and ought to be,' said Mrs Doveton earnestly. 'He's a sober, solid man that won't hurt to have his head turned fora week or two, but, once married, he'll be master. But meantime here's the gell going this way and that, and bursting out here, there and everywhere like a November cracker. And there's no knowing who'll be hurt before she's pinned down for good and the sauce knocked out of her.'

'I don't suppose the postman –' Lucilla began, but Mrs Doveton went on unregarding.

'Young gells like her ought to be put in homes, or labelled "Dangerous". She doesn't stick at anything. She's been writing to my Herb. Yes, Miss Jane, well may you look! I thought it was his receipt from the Polytechnic and I opened it, little thinking. And it was to thank him ever so for the lovely chocs., and "Friday evening, same time and place", and "So long, old dear", and seventeen crosses in blue ink.' Mrs Doveton sobbed and dabbed her eyes with a blue-chequered duster.

'And I've got no hold over the girl. Herbert I can control, or could. But not Gladys. Nobody can. Show her a young man and she's off like a spider after a fly – or more like a dog after a rabbit, for there's no sitting quiet and watching about *her*.'

'But if she's fond of Herbert and he's fond of her? . . .'

'Bless you,' said Mrs Doveton, "she ain't fond of anybody. It amuses her to see 'em jigging on the end of a string. But my Herbert's a serious young man, and he looks to better himself and rise in life, and then *she* butts in and spoils everything for him and does

234

herself no good. It's for all the world like a mouse falling into a pan of cream — no benefit to any of the parties concerned.'

'All right,' said Jane, 'you speak to Herbert and I'll speak to Gladys.'

'I've spoke to Herb,' said Herbert's mother, 'and he says not to interfere, and I don't know what roseate hues of early dawn a true woman can cast over a young man's life. Lor',' said Mrs Doveton in a burst of exasperation, 'I wish all young gells could be married and put out of the way the minute they leave school. A gell ought to be married young. It's best for her — keeps her out of mischief — and she soon gets two or three little weights hanging on to her apron-strings to keep her steady. Young gells is best married.'

'And young men?' Jane asked.

'Let 'em keep single as long as they can,' said Mrs Doveton, 'for a young man married is a young man marred.'

'It would be a queer world if Mrs Doveton had the arranging of it,' said Lucilla as the door closed behind the anxious mother. 'Come on, let's go and tell Gladys not to.'

Gladys was in the shop; she was in the shop almost all the time now. Jane and Lucilla felt their hands to be full with the much more pleasant duty of entertaining their agreeable and punctually-paying guests.

'Look here, Gladys,' said Jane, sitting down between a sieve of apples and a pile of giant marrows, for it was now August, and the shop looked like a Harvest Thanksgiving, 'what have you been doing to Herbert Doveton?'

'I ain't done nothing to him.'

'Haven't you kissed him?' Jane asked severely.

'Oh, *that*!' said Gladys. 'Oh yes, I *kissed* him,' and she giggled reminiscently. 'I thought it would do him good. He was so set up. He's better now — gives you a kiss quite natural. You've no idea reely what he was like to begin with. You'll hardly believe it, miss, I know, but I'm his first. I am reely.'

'And are you fond of him?'

235

'Me, miss? Fond of him? Why, he's more like a dried haddock than a young man. I only tried to show him a bit of life and put him in the way of enjoying himself. For what's life to a young man without a girl to go out with? Why, nothing!'

'Now look here, Gladys,' said Jane, very firmly and seriously. 'This has got to stop, see? You mustn't show that young man any more life, as you call it. You don't want him, and it worries Mrs Doveton.'

'Mothers can't have it all their own way,' said Gladys mutinously.

'Do you keep a list of your sweethearts?' Lucilla asked suddenly.

Gladys actually blushed.

'Not to say sweethearts. I don't like the word anyhow,' she said. 'But I do make a note of the names of them as I've walked out with – only initials, you know – in the end of me hymn-book. Nobody would know to look at it. Why, I forget myself what the letters stand for sometimes, I do assure you, miss.'

'Well,' said Lucilla, 'you put down H.D., and then you give him up. Will you? To please me?'

'Oh, to please *you*, miss,' said Gladys gracefully. 'I'd do more than give up a little thing like that. If you'll lend me a stamp and a ongvelope I'll drop him a line this very minute to tell him cruel fate has come betwixt and it can never, never be.'

'And what about Mr Simmons?'

A curious change came over the face of Gladys: she looked like a child who in the midst of make-believe is reminded of some real and treasured possession.

'Oh, *him*!' she said slowly.

'Well, if you care anything about him you'd better be careful. Suppose he found out about the others?'

'Oh, you don't understand, miss. I *tell* him about all the others, every one of them, and what they say and all.'

'And doesn't he mind?'

A look of elfish cunning puckered the face of Gladys.

'He don't believe me, miss! He thinks I make it all up to amuse him like. So *that's* all right. Only if he did find anything out he couldn't never say I hadn't told him, see? So I'm all right whatever happens.'

'Well, spare Herbert, anyhow,' said Jane, and she and Lucilla escaped to the garden, the final words of Gladys pursuing them: 'I'll spare him by the very next post, miss, you may depend.'

Looking back afterwards, it always seemed to Lucilla and Jane that that autumn was the merriest time of their lives. Money was coming in plentifully, both from the house and from the garden, whose resources Mr Dix was exploiting in a way that seemed to them simply masterly. The balance at the bank was rising like a tide, and the relations between the right and the left hand of the bank-book grew more and more such as we all wish to see. Life was simple and satisfying. Nor was it by pleasure only that it was so entirely filled. There was work. The shop a little; accounts a little; and a good deal of cutting-out and making of clothes – their own and not their own. Miss Antrobus had interests outside Cedar Court. She never spoke of them to Jane or Lucilla, but she poured them into the ear of Miss Lucas in that after-dinner hour which was Lucilla's torture and Jane's remorse. She told of children whose fathers had fallen in France and who now, in the land that was to be a land fit for heroes, lacked food and clothes and everything that makes life comfortable. Did Miss Lucas think her nieces would help? The stuff could be found – it wouldn't cost them anything but time. Miss Lucas was sure they would, and they did.

'But how terrible that they should *need* charity,' said Miss Lucas, clicking the eternal knitting-needles.

'Yes,' said Miss Antrobus. 'But it's no use our arguing about that. What we've got to do is to see that a few of the little Toms and Sallies are just the least bit more comfortable than they would be without us. That's all we can do just now.'

And this they did.

Miss Lucas only lasted three weeks. Lucilla could not endure her any longer. Miss Antrobus's kind attentions and her amiable enquiries became more and more intolerable, and at last Lucilla flatly refused to go on with the business.

'If Miss Antrobus can't do without a chaperone,' she said, 'she must go and look for one somewhere else. Surely Mrs Thornton is chaperone enough for anything? Besides, what does a girl want with chaperones when she's been a Waac or a V.A.D., or whatever it was that Miss Antrobus was? I could stand it if she wasn't so hatefully civil to the old lady.'

'Mr Tombs is civil too.'

'So's everybody if it comes to that. But Mr Tombs is civil like Sir Walter Raleigh laying down his cloak for an aged queen to walk on. Miss Antrobus . . . well, I think there's such a thing as being too civil by half. Where is she now?'

'Gardening. Mr Dix says she's a very promising gardener.'

'It seems to me that she's a very competent person. She can cook – she told me so. I mean she told Aunt Harriet so. And she understands sick-nursing, and making clothes, and now gardening. She says the more things you can do the more interesting life is.'

'I've often said that myself,' said Jane, yawning.

'Ah,' said Lucilla, 'but *she* does them. And *you've* got to do what I say. Let Aunt Harriet vanish decently or I shall give the whole show away. I know I shall.'

The prize problem party never took place after all, for the problems were solved as soon as propounded. Gladys was 'influenced' to take back her gift, on the ground that Othello – who, Mr Dix said, ought to have been called Desdemona – must be lonely. Why not give him, or her, to Mr Simmons, who already had other rabbits? Jane and Lucilla explained how much they had enjoyed owning Othello and how they could not bear to stand in his (or her) light if a more agreeable social life seemed to open before him (or her). Othello went away, and Mr Dix and his under-gardener rejoiced.

The problem of the buried silver provided a pleasant dinner-topic. The story of the burglar was told by Lucilla – Aunt Harriet kept her room that evening – and though the story assumed a good deal that hadn't been so, it made quite a good story with Mr Dix introduced as an anonymous stranger sheltering in the summer-house from the rain.

'And that's months ago,' said Mr Thornton, 'and you've left your poor silver there ever since? Why, Dix could have got it out for you in no time.'

'He didn't know. Nobody knew. We've only just made up our minds to tell. Because really we *must* get the silver up again.'

'How much is there?' asked the other Mr Thornton – the one called Bill.

'Oh, just the teapot and milk-jug and sugar-basin. We put the spoons in our pockets.'

'We'll get it out for you. Not to-night, because we're playing at that concert. But to-morrow.'

And sure enough they did – with fish-hooks and weights coated with birdlime or something sticky. They fished behind the stove, and up came the silver – rather yellow, but not much dented – and not a chip of the panelled mantelpiece disturbed.

'Not at all,' they said to the thanks of Lucilla and Jane. 'It's a pleasure. I wish you'd let us do more things for you. Shall we clean the silver? We're rather a dab at that.'

And they did it too, amid laughter and jokes – in the summer-house, for fear of Forbes catching them at it. Certainly the Thorntons were very kind as well as very jolly. They really were ideal paying guests.

They were energetic photographers and photographed the girls and the house, reluctant Mrs Doveton and enthusiastic Gladys. They played at concerts with sufficient frequency to give their presence at home an added value. In all weather they sallied out, their evening dress closely hidden under mackintoshes, their great instruments duly encased, returning often long after everyone had gone to bed. And they were always punctual in the breakfast-room – the two men cheery and attentive and Mrs Thornton as pretty and as fresh as a pink. They never played their instruments at Cedar Court, though they sang and acted readily enough. 'We like a holiday from them when we can get it,' Mrs Thornton explained. 'They're our shop. You should never mix the shop and the home.'

'I hope your aunt is not seriously ill, you know,' said Mr Thornton that evening, when for the second time Miss Lucas failed to appear in the drawing-room.

'Oh no,' said Lucilla, and then suddenly, after a queer little pause: 'She's much better. In fact she's gone to Bath to-day with my cousin.'

'I should have liked to say good-bye to her,' said Mr Tombs. 'We shall miss her, shan't we?' It may have been her guilty conscience that made Lucilla feel almost sure that there had been a twinkle in Mr Tombs's eye.

But Miss Antrobus said outright: 'When did she go?'

'This morning, while you were at your Help for Heroes Committee meeting,' Lucilla told her, triumphing in the fact that there *had* been a space of time in which a dozen Aunt Harriets could have got away without Miss Antrobus's notice.

'I am so sorry I missed seeing her,' said Miss Antrobus calmly. 'I must write and tell her so. *What is her address?*'

Chapter XXIX

Lucilla had not thought of that. 'I will give you the address this evening,' she said. And in the evening it was, 'Oh, I'm so sorry – I'll give you the address in the morning.'

'If it wouldn't be too much trouble I should be so glad if I could have it *now*,' said Miss Antrobus. 'I usually write my letters at night.'

'Certainly,' said Lucilla, and went straight to the mahogany bureau and began to fumble in the pigeon-holes. Miss Antrobus followed her.

'It's very kind of you to look for it now,' she said; 'but surely it's not among those paper patterns?'

'I don't know where it is,' said Lucilla, shutting the secretaire lid with what was almost a bang. 'Perhaps it's upstairs – I'll go and look,' and she fled.

She returned very soon with an envelope on which she had written:

> 'Miss Lucas,
> at Mrs Scott's,
>   247, Hill Street, Bath.'

'Thank you so much,' said Miss Antrobus. 'Hill Street? Whereabouts is it?'

'I don't know, I'm sure,' said the badgered Lucilla. 'I've never been to Bath'; but she felt quite safe because she had taken the precaution to consult Miss Austen's 'Persuasion' before deciding on an address for her aunt at Bath.

'May I have the address too?' asked Mr Tombs. 'I should like to follow Miss Antrobus's excellent example and write to our dear Miss Lucas. But Mr Thornton is just going to play the Lancers.

Miss Antrobus, may I have the pleasure? Thank you. And Miss Craye, may I ask you for the next dance?'

'If there *is* a next one, I shall be very pleased.'

'Oh, there is to be a next one,' he assured her. 'Miss Quested has decided that it is to be a dancing evening.'

'"On with the dance, let joy be unrefined,"' said Lucilla.

'Thank you,' said Mr Tombs. 'That's one of my favourite quotations. Let us be tops, Miss Antrobus. But I must lend a hand with the furniture.'

'I shouldn't have thought Mr Tombs would have cared for dancing,' said Miss Antrobus, 'but he waltzes extraordinarily well, doesn't he? So unexpected.'

'Do you think that blue glasses don't go well with dancing then? Appearances are deceitful sometimes.'

'I know they are,' said Miss Antrobus. 'And there is something about blue glasses that looks a little – well – furtive, don't you think?'

'I hadn't thought it,' said Lucilla, laughing. 'It's rather hard, isn't it, if people can't wear blue glasses without being suspected of – what would the noun be? – furtivity?'

'I didn't really mean that I thought our friend deceitful,' said Miss Antrobus. 'I shouldn't like to think it. I *loathe* deceit.'

'Yes, it is horrid, isn't it?' And as Mr Thornton – the one called Bill – now came to claim her for the dance, she went on: 'I'm sure *you* hate deceit too, don't you, Mr Thornton?'

> 'The soul should be an open book;
> In which all passers-by may look;
> And nought that any would not care
> To read should ere be written there,'

replied the young man promptly.

'Whose is that?' asked Miss Antrobus. 'I seem to know it.'

'It's by "Anon", I think – that popular author,' said he, but as he led Lucilla away he whispered: 'I made it up, of course; didn't she see I was making it up?'

'One never knows what she does or doesn't see,' Lucilla permitted herself to say.

'No, but anyhow, what a lot there is that she doesn't see – that nobody sees. What a little window it is, anyhow, that you look in at anyone else by, isn't it?'

'"Yes. In this sea of life en-isled . . ."' quoted Lucilla.

'Exactly,' said he. 'And there's no Lancers like the old original. Jim always plays them. Tum-tiddy-tumpty-tumpty-tum! What a glorious game dancing is!'

'Score each point as you come to it, even if it's the last,' he said, as he led flushed and panting Lucilla to cool on the front door steps. 'That's my philosophy of life. Even if the world ends to-morrow – well, we've had to-night! If it ends to-night – well – I've had this dance with you. And I may have the next and the next and the next and the one after that?'

'Mr Tombs,' murmured Lucilla, much agitated by this sudden advance. 'I'm dancing the next one with Mr Tombs.'

He brought her a chair from the hall. 'And you?' she said.

'I can sit at your feet,' said he – 'my proper place,' and he sat down on the doorstep. 'Now give me a flower – one of those apricot-scented roses – and be kind to me. Who knows but the world may end to-night?'

'Do you always talk nonsense when you've been dancing?' said Lucilla, defending herself as best she could against this sudden swirl of an unknown sea of flattery.

'Not always. But to-night's such a night – and you're all such darlings, and it's such a long time since I've danced or talked with people who are real people, that my head's in a whirl and I see everything double. I daresay I really see you twice as charming as you are, but my fixed illusion is that you are far more than twice as charming than you appear.'

Lucilla did not know what to say, so she said nothing.

'You don't mind my talking nonsense?' he said. 'Let's pretend you're an Italian lady and this isn't the gravel path but a canal in Venice, and that isn't the garden roller, but the end of my gondola, and I'm here at the peril of my life just to tread one measure with you and tell you once more that you are the radiant star of my dreams; and though you're a noble Venetian lady and I'm only a poor outlaw, with a price on my head, yet you stoop from the throne of your maiden magnificence and lend me, in one instant of cold condescension, your hand that is like a lily.'

He glanced behind her. The hall was deserted. The others had gone out through the French windows on to the cedar lawn. He took her hand and kissed it, very lightly and softly, then laid it down on her lap as gently as though it had indeed been a flower.

'Don't say we'd better find the others. Forgive me instead. It's only a sort of play-acting, to fit the night – and in that rose-coloured dress you do so look the part. You do forgive me? Yes, I see you think I'm either very mad or very insolent, but really I'm not. Don't keep it in your mind against me, will you? Look upon it as a sort of charade. A charade that doesn't count or matter a bit. And don't look at me like that. For God's sake don't be afraid of me. I'm sorry I played the fool. Say it's all right.'

'I suppose so,' said Lucilla feebly, 'but I don't think I like that sort of charade. I don't know my part, you see,' she added, trying to speak as though it had been really a play. He turned his head away, and she thought she heard him say: 'I wish to God I could teach you,' but the next moment he laughed and said:

'Let my faults be writ in water! How I wish we could have more dance evenings! I'm sick of dragging that double bass about. Anyway, I'm going to enjoy this. No Venetian ladies for me, no gondolas – just Miss Craye and the next waltz but two – may I?'

Lucilla did not know how to say 'No' – and besides, she was not sure that 'No' was what she wanted to say. The acting of the Mr Thornton who was called Bill had been wonderfully lifelike. And that touch of warm, live velvet on her hand: she had known nothing like it. She felt as though those five minutes had upset all her ideas on all important subjects. She wanted to be alone, to think, to remember every word he had said, to make up her mind whether she ought to have been angry, to have walked away as soon as he began with: 'Now give me a flower . . .' No, it began before that. How was it it began? He, meanwhile, was talking of Schubert's songs.

The strains of a waltz sounded. 'I ought to play that,' he said, 'it's my brother's turn to dance.' And Lucilla entering the drawing-room on his arm, met herself in the mirror of the cupids, and almost felt as though the kiss on her hand were branded on her cheek.

'How different I look!' she thought. And then, as if one adventure in one evening were not enough, Mr Tombs murmured as they waltzed: 'Let us go round the garden the minute the music stops; the paths are quite dry. I have something really important to say to you.'

'All right,' said Lucilla. She could not say 'No'. To do so would be to admit to herself that she feared that Tombs also might desire to act Venetian charades and imprint velvet salutes upon hands like lilies. Also, at the very bottom of her mind something lurked that was not unlike a sort of curiosity to know how, if at all, Mr Tombs would act his charade. *L'appétit vient en mangeant*, so they say, and if Mr Tombs did act Venetian charades she would not be taken by surprise this time. Gently but firmly, with true dignity and self-possession, she would put Mr Tombs in his place, would show him that she was not to be flattered and fooled like a silly, inexperienced girl, because she was, of course, something quite different.

So as the dance ended she allowed herself to be led through the French window and round by the shrubbery and by winding walks to the sundial.

'Do sit down,' said Mr Tombs; 'there are cushions. I brought them out after the last dance.'

'What did you do with Miss Antrobus?'

'Oh, I brought her out too. That's right. I'll sit here.' He lowered himself to the brick step at her feet. Lucilla felt a little shiver of anxiety. Surely he wouldn't begin *exactly* as Mr Thornton had. (She remembered now how he *had* begun.) Did all men say precisely the same things at dances? Perhaps it was a formula, like, 'May I have the pleasure?' Was he going to say . . .? He was.

'I'll sit at your feet. It's my proper place,' he said, and instantly opened a new gambit; 'because I want to be as humble as possible, and I want you not to resent what I'm going to say and snub me. Promise.'

'But how do I know that I oughtn't to snub you?' Lucilla asked.

'Don't tempt me to say things that you might want to snub me for. Though I should never – I mean in affairs of my own I am not accustomed to being snubbed. I never advance except on sure ground.'

('Oh, what *is* he going to say?' Lucilla asked herself. 'Does he mean that I've encouraged him? Oh, I wish I hadn't come. What an awfully nice voice he has!') 'You said you wanted to say something important,' she found herself saying aloud. 'Why not say it?' ('Come, that's not so bad! Very neat and frosty.')

'I will,' said he. 'I don't know why I hesitate. I won't. Here goes. It's about Miss Antrobus.'

'Oh,' said Lucilla flatly, and began to fan herself, though the night air was cool and fresh all about her. 'And what about Miss Antrobus?'

'I'm afraid she's going to be a nuisance. She's made up her mind that you have not been at all kind to your aunt, and that the poor old lady has been sent away to some sort of home or institution.'

'Good gracious!' said Lucilla feebly.

'She says that Miss Lucas has never been allowed to be alone with any of us; that *you* have never been at home when Miss Lucas was with us; that Miss Quested has been disgracefully neglectful of your aunt – has never once spoken to her except to say goodnight; that neither of you have ever shown the faintest interest in the old lady's ailments; that the old lady has never been outside the house since the day we all came, until you sent her away. Then when Miss Antrobus has offered to read to her or take her out you and Miss Quested have always thrown cold water on her proposals. She says she's determined to sift the matter to the bottom. If there's a Society for the Prevention of Cruelty to Aunts, she'll set it on to you.'

'Oh dear!' said Lucilla. 'Oh, my goodness, how perfectly awful!'

'I thought you'd like me to tell you about it,' Mr Tombs went on, 'and at once, because I don't know what she'll do or say next.'

'Oh, rather!' said Lucilla eagerly, quite forgetting what it was that she had more than half expected him to tell her. 'I think it's most awfully decent of you. But what can I *do*? I feel all to pieces. What *can* I do?'

'Well, if I were you,' said Mr Tombs slowly, 'I should tell her all about your aunt.'

'All about my aunt?'

'Yes, tell her the truth, you know.'

'But –' said Lucilla.

'Yes, I know,' said Mr Tombs. 'She'll be awfully annoyed at having been taken in, I daresay, but anything's better than her going to societies about your affairs.'

'Taken in?' repeated Lucilla automatically, and not with any hope of continued concealment.

'Well, you know,' said Mr Tombs gently, 'you did it most awfully well, and I didn't tumble to it myself till the third evening. Your acting's been magnificent. I should tell her the first thing to-morrow. Treat it as a joke – tell her it's gone far enough. Of course I'll pretend to have been taken in all the time too; that'll make it easier for her.'

'And the others – must I tell them too?'

'No necessity at all,' said Mr Tombs.

'Oh, they're beginning to play again; we must go in,' said Lucilla, jumping up. 'Mr Tombs, you really are a lamb to have warned me. I'll tell her to-morrow.'

This, you would have thought, was enough to complete the evening's happenings. But no. After a most enjoyable fox-trot, the elder Mr Thornton asked leave to tell Lucilla that Miss Antrobus 'had the knife into her', and advised her to own that she, Lucilla, and she only, had been, in truth, Aunt Harriet.

'You acted splendidly,' he said. 'No one could have spotted you; only we're professionals, you see — and even we didn't catch on for the first day or two. It was Miss Quested's cold, cynical indifference to her aunt that opened my wife's eyes and gave the show away.'

'Do you think anyone else guesses?'

'Oh no,' said Mr Thornton eagerly. 'Rochester and Dix and Tombs are absolutely deceived. You ought to go on the stage — such acting, by an amateur; so delicate, so sustained — it was absolutely a triumph. If only Miss Quested had acted the good niece a hundredth part as well as you acted the good aunt . . . But she didn't. If you'll allow me to advise you, you'll let the cat out of the bag to Miss Antrobus at the earliest possible moment.'

Mr Rochester found an opportunity to say, 'Hilda Antrobus is on the war-path. I should own up if I were you.'

And Mr Dix crowned the evening by saying, 'You'll have to tell Miss Antrobus. She thinks your aunt has been unkindly used — and she's so generous and fine: she hates unkindness. You'll have to undeceive her. She won't be hard on you. She's the soul of goodness and gentleness. And so strong and faithful with it. She loathes deception of any kind, that's all. Have it out and get it over. Clear the sky. She'll forgive you.'

'Oh, will she?' said Lucilla. And that night she entered Jane's room expressly to say:

'Serpent, this is your work,' and to tell Jane all the events of the evening. Well — perhaps not quite all.

Chapter XXX

'Now you clear out,' said Jane next morning. 'Go right off into the garden while I tackle the Antrobus and the halberdiers and the engines of war. It was all my doing, and I'll take what's left of the bother. You've had more than your share, you poor old martyr. I'll do it directly after breakfast.'

But it appeared that Miss Antrobus had gone out before breakfast and had not returned. Lucilla wondered miserably whether the anxious reformer had gone to interview the Society for the Protection of Aged Relatives. After breakfast she withdrew to the garden with basket and scissors, and it was here that Mr Thornton – the one called Bill – came upon her among the early chrysanthemums.

'I say,' he began, 'about last night. I want you to forget it.'

Charles Reade supplied Lucilla with a sufficiently apt quotation.

'Never remind a lady of what you wish her to forget,' she said.

'Now that's most awfully good of you,' he said. 'But I do want to say that I really am not the bounding ass you must be thinking me. The fact is, my profession doesn't bring me the acquaintance of people like you and your cousin. And the war was so damnable – I beg your pardon. And the afterwards. Do you know, we three nearly starved before we got hold of a paying profession – I mean paying engagements? Oh, we're all right now, but – that sort of thing half turns your head. We've slept on the Embankment, we three – yes, really. And now we're all right again it's true. But – anyhow – say you forgive me?'

'Oh, it was only nonsense,' said Lucilla, bold in the autumn sunshine; 'don't let's fuss. You might carry these into the shop for me, will you?' She pressed a bundle of stiff twiggy, dewy-wet chrysanthemums on him and went on down the row, snipping busily here and there among the foam of flowers, creamy and pink and golden. She cut far more than were needed and carried them to the shop. Here she resolved to stay till Jane should have dealt with Miss Antrobus; though she had a sinking feeling that it would rather be Miss Antrobus who would deal with Jane.

Gladys was there, of course, and all Gladys's talk was of Mr Thornton – the one called Bill. Unerring instinct, a sort of impish clairvoyance, guided Gladys in all matters pertaining to 'walking out' and the sentiments which lead to such perambulations. Lucilla felt hotly that Gladys knew, as well as if she had been present, that there had been 'something' last night, something not quite in the usual order of things, between her and 'that Mr Thornton – the one as ain't married.'

'When he come in just now,' said Gladys, 'with them flowers, I knew that instant minute as he'd got something on his mind. Do you think his young lady's been being 'aughty to him, miss?'

'I'm sure I don't know,' said Lucilla.

'*I* should think twice afore I cast him off for ever, if I was her. He's a gentleman, he is – his hair-brushes has silver backs. Oh no, that's Mrs Thornton, to be sure, but it's all in the family. And he gives me five bob when I sewed on the bows on his evening shoes.'

Lucilla defended herself with the heaviest of the account-books.

'Don't talk,' she said. 'I'm busy. In fact you might as well go and see if you can help Mrs Doveton. I'll take the shop for an hour or two.'

'If *I* was his young lady I should throw him a kind word. I should throw him a kind word. It don't do to let 'em get too down-hearted,' said Gladys. 'If they gets too miserable they makes away with themselves sometimes.'

'Have any of your sweethearts committed suicide, Gladys?' Lucilla could not help asking.

'I wish you wouldn't use that low word, miss. No, none of the gentlemen I've walked out with ain't gone so far as that. When I said make away with themselves, I meant making away to some other young lady not worth his notice most likely. All right, miss, I'm going . . .'

She went, and almost at once Miss Antrobus darkened the door.

'Good morning,' she said, not smiling. 'Can I have ten shillings' worth of flowers for the hospital? Chrysanthemums, I think. Not any white ones, please.'

'Have you seen Jane this morning?' Lucilla asked.

'No, I have been out since seven, on business.'

Then Lucilla perceived that the gods did not intend this particular piece of work to be for Jane's doing.

'Look here,' she said, fumbling with the flowers, 'I want to talk to you.'

'Yes?' said Miss Antrobus.

'About the aunt,' said Lucilla, teasing the wet blossoms.

'Yes? Was there some mistake in the address you gave me last night?'

'No,' said Lucilla, 'there isn't any mistake; there isn't any address; there isn't any aunt. It was all a silly trick. I was the aunt, dressed up. Jane was looking for you to tell you, but —'

Here, prompt as to a cue, Jane came pattering down the very stairs by which she had first tumbled into the garden room.

'I say, Luce, I can't find her *anywhere*,' she began. 'Oh!' She ended on a different note and stopped short, face to face with Miss Antrobus.

'I was just telling Miss Antrobus — shut the door, Jane,' said Lucilla, pale and determined — 'about there not being any aunt really.'

'Yes,' said Jane, 'but *I* meant to tell you because it was really entirely my fault. My cousin didn't want to do it. She hated doing it. She only did it to please me — to get me out of a hole.'

'Your cousin dressed up to please you, and impersonated an aunt — an aunt who does not exist?'

'Yes, I did,' Lucilla affirmed. 'I used to feel such a pig when you were so nice to me, but I didn't know how to get out of going on with it. I do hope you'll forgive us for playing such a trick on you.'

'But why?' said Miss Antrobus. '*Why?*'

'Because,' said Jane — 'no, Lucy, it's no good, and I can't help it if it does offend people. This was why, Miss Antrobus. Mrs Rochester came here being superior and patronising — wanting to see our chaperone. She almost said you wouldn't come here unless there was some old lady. So I thought, "If Mrs Rochester wants old ladies I daresay we can supply them." I was in an awful rage. And I said there was an aunt – Aunt Harriet – just to shut Mrs Rochester up – and then, of course, there had to be one. And I'm very sorry if you're annoyed about it, but really I can't see that it's done anyone any harm, and if Mrs Rochester hadn't come here interfering and hinting that we weren't capable of looking after our own affairs it would never have happened.'

Miss Antrobus had sat down. Now she bent her head over the flower-table.

'Did Mrs Rochester say anything about me? Anything special? Cards on the table!' she said sharply, seeing that Lucilla hesitated.

But Jane did not hesitate. 'Yes, she did,' she answered, 'when she thought she'd got an aunt to say them to. She said that you and Mr Rochester were secretly engaged, and begged the aunt to give you opportunities of sweethearting and to warn us off. So now you know!'

Lucilla turned startled eyes on the speaker. How could Jane know?

Miss Antrobus raised a brave but scarlet face. 'Thank you,' she said. 'That *is* cards on the table. Now for mine. I used to be fond of Mrs Rochester. When I was a girl I had a passing fancy for John Rochester, and Mrs Rochester encouraged it. But the war knocked all that nonsense out of my head, and he never looked the same side of the road as I was – never!'

'But how horrible of Mrs Rochester!' said Lucilla. 'I didn't know there were people like that – out of books.'

'Oh, well, it seems there are, a few,' said Miss Antrobus drily. 'She told me that her Jack had fallen into the toils of a designing girl, a sort of low-class siren, and asked me to come here and put a spoke in the siren's wheel – be a rescue party, in fact. And for the sake of old times I agreed to come. Besides, I wanted to see a siren. But, of course, when I saw you two, and when I saw John Rochester with you, I understood – well, that Mrs Rochester was trying it on again. Only I couldn't quite make out the aunt.'

'But surely aunts do happen in most families. An aunt was quite probable.'

'Oh yes, but not an imitation aunt. I could not think why you were acting that farce.'

'Do you mean to say,' cried Lucilla, all the actress in her outraged almost beyond endurance, 'do you mean to say that you *knew* I wasn't a real aunt?'

'Of course I did – almost from the first.'

'But you went on being so nice to me!'

'That was to try to make you do what you have done – own up.'

'And when we wouldn't you tried frightening us?'

'Well, wasn't it fair? A sort of tit for tat? Pouf! how the atmosphere's cleared by a little plain speaking! I say, you two girls – let's be friends, shall we? I believe we shall get on awfully well together now there are no pretences and misrepresentations between us.' And as she smiled at them, holding out a hand to each, they saw, for the first time, that which Mr Dix had described as a sort of radiant goodness shining from her face.

'Yes, rather!' they said; and Jane added, 'It's most awfully decent of you not to be ratty with us for playing such a trick on you.'

'But,' said Lucilla, struck by a sudden thought, 'do you think the others spotted the false aunt?'

'Oh *no*,' Miss Antrobus assured her, 'not one of them! You acted splendidly. I was the only one that had the least suspicion!'

That night Lucilla woke suddenly: very wide awake she was – so wide awake that she knew it would be vain to thump the pillow and turn over. She had better read. Or, better still, write up her diary. The brown morocco volume with the shining lock and her name in gilt letters on it had been the guardian's present when she was fifteen. She had neglected it lately. True, many interesting things had happened – things that would have impelled the diarist of fifteen, sixteen, seventeen, to pages of chronicle and comment. But there had been nothing which moved nineteen to a record – under lock and key – until . . . Well, anyhow, Lucilla did now feel that she had neglected her diary too long. It was down in the bureau in the drawing-room. Well, she supposed she could fetch it.

She lit her shaded candle, slipped into the silken blue kimono with the apple-blossom embroidery on it – another of the guardian's presents – and, candle in hand, crept down the wide stairs. But as she went, the air from an open window blew out her candle. And then she saw below her a yellow streak of light from the drawing-room door. Someone else was up. At three in the morning? Jane, looking for a book? Gladys, looking for traces of secrets in her particular department of knowledge? An insomnolent P.G.? A burglar? Lucilla crept down the remaining stairs and laid an eye to the crack of the drawing-room door. And it *was* a burglar!

A strange man sat at the bureau quietly going through the papers on it. A kit-bag lay beside him on the floor, evidently full. And the silver candlesticks and inkstand and the silver Indian things off the mantelpiece – none of them there. Lucilla crept up the stairs again, fleet and noiseless as Diana in the chase, and as she went she thought.

'Call Jane? No good, any more than I am. The servants? Worse than no good. Mr and Mrs Thornton? No, a woman might scream if you wakened her suddenly. Mr Tombs? I think not. Bill Thornton? Yes, I think so.'

And she crept along the softly-carpeted corridor towards the young man's room.

'But you can't knock at his door,' said Decorum to Lucilla, 'because of warning the burglar. You'll have to go right in. That will never do. It wouldn't be proper.'

'Don't be silly,' said Lucilla to Decorum. 'I've something else to think about than things being proper.'

And she turned the handle of Bill's door, which opened noiselessly. Not locked, thank goodness! The room was quite dark, but she knew where the bed lay and felt her way to it. Fortunately she was one of those persons who do not lose their sense of direction in the dark. Presently she felt the edge of the bed against her knees and heard the quiet breathing of him who slept there. Did men scream if you waked them suddenly? Well, she must chance that. She reached out her hand to where she thought a shoulder should be, grasped an arm clad in thick silk, and whispered as she grasped it, 'Hush!'

Mr Thornton did not scream. Nor did he move. He answered her whisper with another:

'What's up?'

'It's me. It's Lucilla. There's a burglar.'

'Where?'

'In the drawing-room.'

'Righto,' he whispered. 'Cut back to your room. It'll be all right.'

'Take care he doesn't shoot yon,' she said. If you can laugh in a whisper, Bill Thornton did it.

'I've got a revolver,' he said; 'don't you worry!'

Lucilla felt her way to the door, and she did go back to her own room, but only to get the poker. And she did this without rattling the fire-irons. 'I should make a good burglar myself,' she thought.

She waited in the darkness by the stairhead and perceived the Mr Thornton who was Bill creeping down, silent as Mercury. Then she followed with her poker, feeling a heroine.

She reached the drawing-room door in time to hear:

'That's right. Any firearms?'

'No,' said a strange and husky voice.

'Any more of you?'

'No.'

'Empty that bag. And don't rattle the stuff fit to wake the dead.'

A faint rattling followed.

'Now turn out your pockets.'

Fainter rattlings. Then: 'What are you going to do with me, governor?'

'Kick you out!' said Thornton's voice. 'If you take my advice you'll chuck this lay. You don't know your own silly business. A bare light! And the door left open! You deserve the stone jug.'

'I know I do,' said the man, 'but this ain't the trade I was brought up to.'

'What's your trade?'

'Sign-writer.'

'Can't you get a job?'

'Oh yes,' said the man, 'course I can get a job. Jobs is going about waiting to be got, ain't they? Wish I was back in the trenches, I do. Or else out of it. I'd do myself in to-night if it wasn't for –'

'Don't begin about the kids and the missus,' said Thornton. 'That's what you chaps always do when you're caught. Here, take that!' His tone was so fierce that Lucilla cowered on the mat in the darkness, expecting the hard-soft sound of a blow.

But what she heard was a gasp, and then, after the gasp a pause, and then: 'Well, if ever *you* gets into a hole, I hoped someone'll be the gentleman to you as you've been to me tonight.'

'Cut all that,' said Thornton. 'You came in by the staircase window, I suppose?'

'Yes, sir, up the ivy.'

'Well, I'll let you out – this way.'

They went out by the French window. Lucilla turned to go upstairs, but someone was coming down. A light at the top of the stairs. She backed out into the open doorway of the kitchen, and Mr Tombs passed within a yard of her and into the drawing-room. She heard Mr Thornton's footstep on the gravel and Mr Tombs's voice.

'Hallo, Thornton. What's up?'

'Only a burglar,' said Thornton. 'I've just seen him out.'

'Let him off, eh?'

'Oh well,' said Thornton, 'you can't be too hard on a poor beggar like that. What's he to do? The very Church itself says you may steal rather than starve.'

'Yes,' said Tombs, 'what *is* a chap to do? Let's have a cigar and you tell me all about it. Quite an adventure for quiet Cedar Court.'

'All right,' said the Mr Thornton who was called Bill. 'I only hope we haven't roused the house. I'll get my cigar case.'

As he passed Lucilla's door he breathed, 'All right – he's gone.'

So he never knew that Lucilla had been prepared to defend him with the poker.

Chapter XXXI

The last chapter divides itself naturally, like an old-fashioned sermon, into four headings and a conclusion. And before entering on the first section I must premise that the seventh of October was a day of days – a day when Spanish castles came thundering down to dust; when new Aladdin palaces reared their stately domes and minarets, as it were, between tea and dinner; a day when truths were told and secrets revealed; when new adventures entered on old enterprises; and when, in fact, the world of Cedar Court was caught up, shaken in a bag, and tumbled out again. Or, if you prefer the image, Fate, weary of the consistent good luck of Jane and Lucilla, gave a sharp jerk to the kaleidoscope, and behold! the entire pattern was transformed.

First came the affair of the Thorntons. They had been out to a concert the night before – had said they might be late or might stay away all night, They had stayed away all night. Nor did they return next morning. Mr Tombs, on the other hand, contrary to his usual custom, did stay at home. He escorted Lucilla on her flower-gatherings, and listened kindly to her wonders as to what had become of the Thorntons.

'I hope they won't stay away two nights,' said Lucilla; 'we wanted to have another little dance.'

Mr Tombs owned that dancing was delightful and asked for the first waltz. He stayed with Lucilla while she arranged flowers in the shop. It was Gladys's 'day off'.

Miss Antrobus devoted herself wholly to Jane, who found it interesting to explore the mind of a young woman so different from herself and Lucilla. 'I wonder,' Miss Antrobus said, after a long talk about the aims of art, and about life being real, life being earnest, 'I wonder whether you'd let the other cottage to me – the one Mr Dix doesn't have?'

'Oh,' said Jane, quite hurt by this sudden defection of a new found friend and always satisfactory P.G., 'aren't you happy with us?'

'I'm sure I should be, very happy,' said Miss Antrobus, 'but one never knows what may turn up; and even if I stayed here I should like to have the cottage, and to pay rent for it, of course. Would thirty shillings a week —'

'I should think so,' said Jane forlornly; 'but your going will rather break up the happy home, won't it?'

'How nice of you to say that! But it won't really. And I want to go in for gardening, and living the simple life.'

Meeting just before luncheon, Jane and Lucilla compared notes. 'I feel as if I were being chaperoned – by Mr Tombs,' said Lucilla.

'You're right,' said Jane, with sudden conviction; 'that's what Miss Antrobus has been doing to me.'

They were all together in the drawing-room – and the Thorntons still hadn't come – when the blow fell. Forbes, looking thoroughly scandalised, announced:

'The police-inspector, please, ma'am – to see the lady of the house.'

And before she could back out of the room the inspector had squeezed himself past her into it.

'Sorry to inconvenience you, miss,' he said, breathing heavily, 'but from information received, I understand there's three parties under the name of Thornton living here.'

'Yes,' said Jane.

'Well, miss, the fact is they're wanted. I should wish to break it gently, but the fact is there've been a lot of burglaries, and – I'm very sorry it should happen to friends of yours – but I'm sure you're innocent as the lamb unborn, miss.'

'Of course we are,' said Lucilla impatiently, 'and so are the Thorntons. There was a burglar here a few days ago, but he didn't take anything, and Mr Thornton let him go.'

'That is so, Inspector.' Mr Tombs confirmed the statement, while Jane looked reproachful and Miss Antrobus sympathetic.

'That may be, sir,' said the policeman. 'Birds of a feather would naturally assist each other – even when swell cracksmen, as these Thorntons certainly are. Very sorry for unpleasantness, miss, but I've got the warrants both for arrest and search.'

'They aren't here,' said Jane.

'But their apartments are,' said the large policeman. 'Perhaps the gentleman would show us the way? One room kept locked? I daresay we shall find a way to deal with *that*. Excuse me, ladies.'

Well, there was no doubt about it. The charming Thorntons – so kind, so considerate, so well-read, so accomplished – had been just burglars. (Well, not just burglars – they had been other things as well, as Jane and Lucilla insisted on remembering.) They had used the cases of 'cello and violin and double bass to carry their booty into the house, and the locked room to conceal it in. The police had quite a rich harvest in the things the Thorntons had had to leave behind. They had not been able to take away all their plunder, but they had taken themselves away. Quite successfully – to the secret joy of Lucilla and Jane.

'But it's horrible!' said Lucilla to Mr Tombs, pacing distracted in the garden. 'I shall never believe in anyone again. And what will become of them? And what will become of them? They're sure to be caught some time, even if they get away safely this time.'

'Well,' said Mr Tombs, pulling his moustache, 'the fact is . . . Can you keep a secret?'

'Yes, if I want to,' said Lucilla making a sound distinction.

'Well, I don't think they will be caught. They've got enough money to get away – by different routes – and they're frightfully clever at disguises. They'll meet again in Rhodesia. And I've given them a letter to a chap I know. He'll put them into something. They'll be all right.'

Lucilla turned and caught him by the arms just above the elbow.

'You're an angel,' she said, shaking him gently. 'I didn't know men *could* be so sensible. Why, any girl could see they weren't the sort of people to be burglars unless they couldn't possibly help it. Why, we might any of us have been driven to it – only we have been so lucky!'

'Yes,' said Mr Tombs, 'that's what I said to myself. "There, but for the grace of God, goes little Arthur."' He took off the blue spectacles and looked at her.

'Why, you're that chauffeur!' said Lucilla, and she sat down suddenly on a stump.

'I am,' said he; 'and I am also Arthur Panton, your defaulting trustee and guilty guardian. That's a secret you really *must* keep. I made quite a lot of money in a very short time in South Africa, and I'm going back to make some more. But I had to come and see that you were all right. I had you both so horribly on my conscience. But now I see that you *are* all right I must be off – to make some more money, so as to pay all the people I owe money to and be something like an honest chap again.'

'I won't tell anyone – not even Jane,' said Lucilla earnestly.

'Mind you don't,' said he. 'And now I'm off. My bag is packed, and my bark is on the shore, and the taxi is on its way to fetch me away from Cedar Court and from you. Haven't you a kind word to say to me before I go?'

Lucilla tried vainly for a kind word.

'I think you look awfully nice without your spectacles,' was the best she could do.

'I shall look much nicer when I come back to whitewash myself – pay all my creditors, you know. You'll be glad to see me then?'

'Oh yes,' said Lucilla.

'Then good-bye. Guardians don't count,' said Mr Tombs, and the next moment Lucilla was watching his tweed back disappearing in the shrubbery and realising that she had again been kissed; and this time not on her hand.

That was thirdly.

Fourthly occurred after a breathless tea, where the Thorntons had been talked over – very gently – and Mr Tombs's sudden departure had been attributed by Miss Antrobus to an objection, natural in a shy man, to being mixed up with such a shady business as a house where burglars were harboured. Presently Miss Antrobus withdrew to inspect the cottage. Lucilla and Jane had hardly exchanged three words before John Rochester burst in upon them with fourthly. And fourthly really was a facer. He came in with a letter in his hand, and he did not say, 'Good afternoon,' or 'How do you do,' or any of the things that one does say when there is nothing the matter. He was very pale – not at all a becoming pallor, Lucilla thought – and he said straight away – like that:

'Look here – that uncle of mine –'

'Not dead?' said Jane.

'No, I wish he – no, of course I don't mean that. But he oughtn't to be at large. At least, he oughtn't to be trusted with houses – he doesn't know when they're well off.'

'He's going to turn us out,' said Jane. 'Oh, I knew it was all too good to last. I told Lucy so – didn't I, Lucy?'

'Only out of Cedar Court,' said Rochester. 'Just the house. You can still have the garden and the garden room and the stables and cottages. He's lent the house now to a Theosophist Brotherhood. It's exactly like him. And he's somewhere in Thibet himself, so I can't reason with him.'

'Oh well,' said Jane slowly, 'we've had a lovely time. We shall have to go back to Hope Cottage, that's all. I suppose it will be a lark going back to the dear little house.'

She cast one glance round the room and fled – to collapse in tears on the stairs.

Lucilla remained. 'I think it's a great deal too bad,' she said. 'Why let us have it at all?'

'Ah, why?' said Rochester. 'But all's not lost yet. I believe really you'll do better without the paying guests – they're such an awful risk, aren't they? I say – do, do be an angel and send Jane to the library for something. I must see her alone. Do, do, do!'

But when she found Jane in tears on the stairs it seemed better to Lucilla that Mr Rochester himself should persuade her to the library if he wanted her there. Lucilla herself trailed miserably after Miss Antrobus. Sympathy from someone she must have – about Cedar Court. Nobody wanted Lucilla in libraries; the two who might have wanted her had both gone over the seas, and – Heigh-ho, but it was a cold world!

But Miss Antrobus was full of plans as well as of sympathy. The three girls could all live in the cottage; it would be great fun, and not nearly so trying to the nerves as the responsibility of a big house. They sat on the edge of the sink in the bare kitchen of the large cottage and laid the foundation of sober Spanish cottages.

And Rochester had taken Jane's wet hands and pulled them from her face, and put his arm round her, and taken her into the library and shut the door. Jane instantly buried her face against a leather sofa-cushion.

'Don't cry, Jane,' he said; 'don't cry – don't. You haven't really lost anything that matters. You've got Lucilla, and you've got Gladys, and you've got Dix – the super-gardener – and Miss Antrobus, who really isn't half a bad sort; and you've got me, Jane, if you'll have me.'

'Oh, don't!' said Jane, with her face in the sofa-cushion. 'Oh, I wish you wouldn't!'

'Don't you like me to hold your poor little cold hands? But let me hold them just a minute, Jane. You know when you tried that charm, on St John's Eve, and lighted the candles, and wore the wreath of yellow flowers, and said the spell, and said, "Let me now my true love see"?'

'Yes,' said Jane, suddenly sitting up and looking at him with red-rimmed eyes. 'I suppose Lucilla's been chattering. Silly goose!'

'What did you see?'

'Never mind,' said Jane.

'No, but do – do tell me – darling Jane.'

'I saw *you*,' said Jane, at bay – 'and that's why I can't let you hold my hands or – or – hold my hands. I can't have anything to do with you. It's not right. It's uncanny. It says in the Bible, "Thou shalt not suffer a witch to live." It was witchcraft – and I saw your face – I don't know how you guessed it, but I did see you. A sort of vision of you. Your face seemed to be suspended about a yard from the ground. The rest of you wasn't there. And I've thought about it, and thought about it, and of course it *was* magic – and most awfully wrong. And if I were to – to let you call me Jane and all that, it would be going on with the wrongness.'

'There wasn't any magic at all about it,' he said slowly. 'You saw me because I was there, stooping down peering through the bushes to see what the lights were at that hour, in that lonely wood. It was just flesh-and-blood me, not a vision at all. It wasn't magic, but accident – the most blessed accident that ever –'

'Really – truly? It wasn't a vision – you were there – your real self?'

'My real self,' said Rochester.

'Oh dear!' said Jane, on a deep breath of relief. 'How perfectly splendid! I do wish I'd known before, though.'

She faced him with her own inimitable look of elfish mischief and innocent candour.

'Do you mean – Oh, Jane – I may call you Jane?'

'Yes, if you want to.'

'And I may hold your hands.'

'You've been holding them all the time,' said Jane.

'And you –'

'Don't ask any more questions,' she said, jumping up. 'Let me go and wash my face and do my hair.'

'Jane – you do love me – you'll marry me?'

'Not for ever so long,' said Jane. 'I've got to make my way in the world first.'

She got her hands away and reached the door. But he caught her there.

'Jane, darling – just one – only one.'

'Not with this dirty face,' said Jane firmly. 'Oh – I say, which is the secret door?'

'The secret door? Oh – we've got that open now . . .'

'And this door too,' said Jane, opening it, and fled.

At the stair foot she collided with Lucilla, who looked from her to Rochester, and said, 'Oh . . .'

'Yes,' said Rochester.

PENGUIN WOMEN WRITERS

BIRDS OF AMERICA BY MARY McCARTHY
With an introduction by Penelope Lively
Peter Levi, a shy and sensitive American teenager, moves to Paris to avoid being drafted into the Vietnam War, where he is determined to live a life in harmony with his own idealistic views. But the world is changing at breakneck pace, with nuclear war looming abroad and racial tensions simmering at home. Before long, Peter's naïve illusions are shattered, as he finds himself an unwilling participant in an era of extraordinary change.

Birds of America is an unforgettable and deeply moving story of personal and political turmoil; of the strange and surprising nature of growing up; and of the questions we face when we examine who we really are.

MEATLESS DAYS BY SARA SULERI
With an introduction by Kamila Shamsie
Meatless Days is a searing memoir of life in the newly-created country of Pakistan. When sudden and shocking tragedies hit the author's family two years apart, her personal crisis spirals into a wider meditation on universal questions: about being a woman when you're too busy being a mother or a sister or a wife to consider your own womanhood; about how it feels to begin life in a new language; about how our lives are changed by the people that leave them. This is a heart-breaking, hopeful and profound book that will get under your skin.

LIFTING THE VEIL BY ISMAT CHUGHTAI
With an introduction by Kamila Shamsie
Lifting the Veil is a bold and irreverent collection of writing from India's most controversial feminist writer. These stories celebrate life in all its complexities: from a woman who refuses marriage to a man she loves to preserve her freedom, to a Hindu and a Muslim teenager pulled apart by societal pressures, to eye-opening personal accounts of the charges of obscenity the author faced in court for stories found in this book.

Wickedly funny and unflinchingly honest, *Lifting the Veil* explores the power of female sexuality while slyly mocking the subtle tyrannies of middle-class life. In 1940s India, an unlikely setting for female rebellion, Ismat Chughtai was a rare and radical storyteller born years ahead of her time.